Jim Kelly lives in Ely, Cambridgeshire, with his partner, the writer Midge Gillies, and their daughter. He is the author of *The Water Clock*, *The Fire Baby*, *The Moon Tunnel*, *The Coldest Blood* and *The Skeleton Man*, all featuring journalist Philip Dryden, and also *Death Wore White* and *Death Watch*, the first two novels in this new series featuring DI Peter Shaw and DS George Valentine. The Dryden series won the 2006 CWA Dagger in the Library award for a body of work giving 'the greatest enjoyment to readers'.

DEATH TOLL

Bodies are being exhumed to higher ground at King's Lynn's cemetery to avoid flooding. But when the coffin of murdered pub landlady Nora Tilden is hauled up, the corpse of a young black man is revealed; killed by a billhook blow to the head and dumped in the grave when Nora was buried, twenty-eight years earlier. Was he the victim of a racist crime? When DI Peter Shaw and DS George Valentine investigate, they are led to The Flask, Nora's pub just along the riverbank, where her family hides more than one dark secret. It's soon clear that no one can be trusted. Can Shaw and Valentine discover the truth behind the murder before it's too late and ghosts from the past claim another victim?

Books by Jim Kelly
Published by The House of Ulverscroft:

THE WATER CLOCK
THE FIRE BABY
THE MOON TUNNEL
THE COLDEST BLOOD
THE SKELETON MAN
DEATH WORE WHITE
DEATH WATCH

JIM KELLY

DEATH TOLL

Complete and Unabridged

CHARNWOOD
Leicester

First published in Great Britain in 2011 by
Penguin Books
The Penguin Group, London

First Charnwood Edition
published 2011
by arrangement with
The Penguin Group, London

The moral right of the author has been asserted

All characters and events portrayed in this book are products of the author's imagination, and any resemblance to real places, events or people, living or dead, is coincidental.

British Library CIP Data

Kelly, Jim, *1957* –
 Death toll.
 1. Shaw, Peter (Fictitious character)- -Fiction.
 2. Valentine, George (Fictitious character)- -
 Fiction. 3. Police- -England- -Norfolk- -Fiction.
 4. Exhumation- -Fiction. 5. Family secrets- -Fiction.
 6. Detective and mystery stories.
 7. Large type books.
 I. Title
 823.9′2–dc22

 ISBN 978–1–4448–0871–1

Published by
F. A. Thorpe (Publishing)
Anstey, Leicestershire

Set by Words & Graphics Ltd.
Anstey, Leicestershire
Printed and bound in Great Britain by
T. J. International Ltd., Padstow, Cornwall

This book is printed on acid-free paper

To Dinah
For the colours

1

Sunday, 12 December 2010

DI Peter Shaw stood amongst the gravestones of Flensing Meadow Cemetery, his walking boots invisible in a ground mist that had slipped off the river with the tide and trickled over the grass, filling the reopened graves. High tide: and on that high tide an Icelandic trawler was coming up the river in the night, a house of lights and rasping chains, and bouncing across the moonlit water the voices of men speaking a savage language. Stars turned above Shaw's head like a planetarium. The mist was damp and it made the meadow smell of rotting earth. Frost was in the air. Winter was hardening by the day, and snow was forecast before New Year. But Shaw had told his daughter not to get her hopes up, because it never snowed on Christmas Day.

The clock of All Saints Church, lost amongst the ugly egg-boxes of the old council flats, chimed ten o'clock. Shaw shifted his feet, aware of what lay beneath the damp cemetery grass. Fifty yards away stood a forensic scene-of-crime lamp, a splash of grass illuminated St-Patrick's-Day green. The light left the gravestones in stark contrast, casting ink-black shadows.

'Come on, George,' he said, turning on the spot, searching the darkness for the advancing silhouette of his sergeant. Shaw's nervous system

1

was crying out for action, exercise, the release of physical energy. He wanted to run, to feel the endorphins surging through his bloodstream, and the oiled, rhythmic, beat of his heart. When he'd received the call he'd been on the beach with Lena near the house, their winter wetsuits laid out on the verandah. He'd been a moment away from the icy crush of the surf, the bitter-sweet trickle of freezing seawater into the suit. That was life. Not this: waiting amongst the dead.

What information the control room at St James's had passed to Shaw was characteristically elliptical. Several graves were being relocated as part of flood-prevention work along the riverside. During the opening of one of them that afternoon, 'irregularities' had been unearthed. The contractors had called the West Norfolk Constabulary, who had dispatched a forensic team and paged Shaw. By then it had been dark. Shaw was keen to get down to the graveside to see for himself what the fuss was about. But he couldn't take another step without a scene-of-crime suit, and that's what DS George Valentine was supposed to be fetching.

Midstream, the trawler dropped anchor. Beyond it, across the tidal river, he could see the Clockcase Cannery — a dismal landmark, a night-watchman's torch at a window, then the next, then the next. Upriver a necklace of traffic crossed the New Bridge. Shaw thought of the families within the cars, ferrying presents to family and friends, or driving home after the late-night Christmas shopping in the crowds

2

packed into the Vancouver Centre. The thought made his shoulders jerk with a shiver.

Shaw stood alone. Six feet two, his blond hair cut short; slim, neat and self-contained. His jacket, oilskin, with the Royal National Lifeboat Institution motif on the chest, was zipped up to his chin. The face was broad, with wide cheekbones, the left eye the blue of falling tap water, the other blind, a pale moon of white. It was the kind of face that sought open horizons; a face suited to scanning the steppe, perhaps, searching for wild horses, or a distant wisp of smoke from a camp fire. A young face, yet one untroubled by the uncertainties of youth.

He heard DS George Valentine before he saw him, the laboured breathing, the squelch of his shoes in the damp grass. And then he was there: picking his way through the gravestones, carrying two sets of forensic trousers, gloves and overshoes. 'Tom's down by the lights,' he said, working a cigarette along the thin line of his lips. The smoke drifted into his eyes, making them water. On the fresh night breeze Shaw smelt alcohol. He slipped the trousers on by balancing on one leg. Valentine leant against a tombstone.

'It's all a bit macabre,' said Shaw, nodding towards the serried lines of open graves — some of the stones set back against the cemetery railings down by the riverside path. Did you know this was happening?' His voice was light, and held a musical, playful, quality that he often suppressed.

Valentine shook his head. 'News to me. There's a pen-pusher from the council up at the chapel when you've a sec — he's got the details. They're getting 'em all up — reburying the bones, shifting the stones, 'cos the place floods. Spring tides go over the top — every time.' He stuck his vulture-like head forward on its narrow neck. 'Global warming.' He spat into the grass. 'Environmental health people reckon it's a risk to the public.' Another shrug, touching a gravestone. 'Last ones down were in the eighties — it's not like they're fresh. So, what *have* they found?'

Shaw shook his head. 'Something they didn't expect to find, I imagine.'

Valentine pinched out his cigarette, put the dog-end in his pocket and followed Shaw towards the lights. The DS was wrapped in a raincoat with a grease mark where his hand held the lapels together. On the left lapel was a charity sticker: WOOD GREEN ANIMAL SHELTER. Valentine loathed pets, but he couldn't resist a collecting tin. He rolled his narrow shoulders and let his head droop, his face as sharp and two-dimensional as an axe. He was fifty-three years old, sallow skin hung from tired bones. When the call had come he'd been in the Artichoke, on a settle by the coke fire, cradling a pint. He was profoundly irritated to find himself at work.

'No trouble seeing the fucker,' he said as they moved into the glare of the harsh white lights. He enjoyed swearing, chiefly because he knew it annoyed Peter Shaw.

Artificial turf had been laid round the letterbox of the open grave beneath the halogen

4

floodlight. Figures, too brightly lit to be seen clearly, worked at the edges of the hole. One of them wasn't moving and Shaw realized with a shock that it was a statue of an angel, the hands cupped for water, one heel raised so that it seemed to be caught in the act of stepping forward.

As they arrived they heard the unmistakable sound of rotten wood shearing, two linen bands taking the weight of an unseen coffin as the men tried to edge it towards the surface.

Valentine looked away, aware that all too soon his own thin bones might be describing a similar journey, but in the opposite direction. When he did bring himself to look, the splintered, mud-caked casket was already set on a pair of wooden trestles, water draining away, gushing out through the fractured wood.

But it wasn't the thought of what was inside the coffin that made his heart race — it was what the lights illuminated so perfectly lying on *top* of the coffin.

A human figure. A corpse — more like a skeleton — the narrow noseless skull turned to one side, looking at them, eyes plugged with yellow clay.

Shaw thought instantly of a stone effigy, like the one on the Crusader's tomb in St Margaret's in the town centre: a carved version in life of what lay in death beneath. The narrow legs in chain mail, the breast plate, the hands together in prayer, the ankles crossed. But this was no marble image, rather an all too human one, the bones poking out of the rich layer of wet clay that coated them, filling the ribcage, the shallow bowl of the pelvis. And this body was the personification of pain, not repose — the skull to the right side, the torso twisted to the left, one arm thrown out, the other buckled underneath, the whole image giving the sense of a body that had been spun before death — a corkscrew in bone.

'Shit,' said Valentine, unable to stop himself from taking a step backwards.

Shaw knelt to look at the skull, now at the height of a hospital patient lying in bed. Shaw's whiz-kid reputation was partly based on being a fast-track graduate, but mostly on the fact that his degree was in art — a course which had included a year out at the FBI college at Quantico, Virginia, where he'd specialized in forensic art. He was one of only three serving police officers in the country with the ability to recreate an accurate hand-drawn image of a face from a set of skull bones, or produce a fifty-year-old face from a nine-year-old's snapshot, or draw the image of a suspect from an interview with a witness.

The human face had become Shaw's obsession, his area of expertise, his touchstone as a detective. He could read *this* skull as if it was a book: he could see, in his mind, what it had been, and what it might have become. And almost instantly he knew that this was a set of bones that would be defined by its exotic DNA. Even encased in clay the skull was dominated by the broad nasal aperture, in which nestled a fat orange slug, the prominent chin and jaws, with

6

several large teeth still in situ, contrasting with the shallow sloping forehead.

'What's your story?' he said in a whisper, lowering his own face to within a few inches of the skull. Close up, the disadvantage of having sight in only one eye was at its most pronounced, so that he had to move his head constantly an inch to the left, an inch to the right, to allow his brain to construct a 3D image. He could smell death: the rich scent of decay — a human compost. Earwigs, beetles and spiders dropped from the coffin top to the turf below, their descent caught by the searing light.

Tom Hadden, head of St James's forensics unit, stood back, letting Shaw do his job, his own face aged by the horizontal light. He was a pale man, with strawberry blond hair thinning above a freckled face, his forehead marked by the lesions of skin cancer. A small scar indicated that at least one had been removed surgically.

'Peter,' he said, beckoning Shaw to his position behind the skull. He closed his eyes before he spoke, a mannerism that indicated he was deep in thought and was about to deliver a statement of fact. 'Now that,' he said, when Shaw arrived, 'is a lethal blow.'

There was a single puncture hole in the left parietal bone, close to the sagittal suture — the line that marks the division between the two halves of the skull. The impact had left a small, neat, triangular hole, but had shattered the lower cranium like crazy-paving.

'What did that?' asked Valentine, who'd joined them, his slip-ons damp in the long wet grass.

7

'Weapons aren't my territory,' said Hadden. 'As you well know, George. Justina's on her way. Till then, chummy stays put.' Dr Justina Kazimierz, St James's regular consultant pathologist, had begun her career working with Shaw's father — Detective Chief Inspector Jack Shaw — back in the 1980s. She demanded respect, and got it.

'So — a male, then?' asked Valentine, pleased he'd spotted Hadden's implicit judgement of the sex of their victim. He was standing at Hadden's shoulder now, and unless asked he'd be keeping a good distance between himself and the bones. Despite over thirty years on the force, George Valentine was never happier than when he was walking *away* from a corpse. The absence of life made his mouth dry with fear: an irresistible vacuum that seemed to tug at his raincoat.

'Who's in the box?' he asked, coughing with a sound like coal being shot from a scuttle. Valentine told himself he smoked twenty cigarettes a day, ignoring the fact that he seemed to always need to buy an extra packet before bedtime. He knew it was killing him, but he couldn't stop, and he was angry, in a listless way, with this constant reminder that he was a weak man.

Hadden checked a clipboard. 'Gravestones are either up against the railings or along the chapel wall up the hill — but the council officer's got a plan, and if it's telling the truth . . . ' he double-checked the clipboard, ' . . . then this should be the grave of Nora Elizabeth Tilden. Born eighth of February 1928. Died first of June 1982,' he said. He held up crossed fingers. 'Let's hope. It's certainly not her on top. And she's not the only occupant of the plot, according to the records. There's an earlier burial — February 1948. A child. Mary Tilden. Aged six weeks.'

Hadden nodded at the open grave. 'She'll be three feet deeper — that's the law.' They heard earth slipping into the grave, splashing into water.

'We'll need to see her, too,' said Shaw.

Hadden nodded, unhappy with the thought. 'I'll need daylight for that, and a pump.'

Three men in white suits began to construct a light-weight SOC tent out of aluminium poles and nylon. Hadden stood back from the coffin. 'Notice what's under the skeleton?' he asked.

Shaw looked, circling the bones. 'A few inches of soil?'

'Exactly. Given the downward weight and the settlement of the grave, that few inches was probably more like a foot, maybe more, when he went in. So he's been buried in the grave — but not *directly* on the coffin top.'

Hadden cast a torch beam down into the misty hole. 'There's a soil profile — soon as we've got it dry tomorrow I'll get down there and get some photos.'

Valentine shivered — a big, awkward, jolt of his thin shoulders.

'With luck I'll be able to tell you the answer to the sixty-four-thousand-dollar question,' added Hadden.

He smiled at Valentine, but the DS had no idea what he was talking about.

Shaw nodded. 'Was our man buried at the

9

same time as Nora Tilden?'

'Exactly,' said Hadden. 'Or did someone dig down, chuck him in, and then refill the grave?'

'What was the date of the original burial?' asked Shaw. Valentine noticed that Shaw often did that — asked a question, of no one in particular, but expected an answer. It really pissed him off.

'First of November 1982,' said Hadden. 'According to the cemetery records.'

Shaw looked up at the stars. 'That's odd. A five-month gap after death. Why would that be?'

Hadden started taking flash pictures of the open grave. 'Well,' he said, straightening his back, 'it's not that rare these days. Relatives have to travel — who knows, Australia, New Zealand — that takes time. Or there's a dispute over the will — that can sometimes hold it up. Or it was a job for a coroner and he didn't release the body until the court had sat. Which would make it a violent, sudden or unnatural death. Take your pick.'

'We need to find some family, George,' said Shaw. 'Get some answers.'

'I've got Paul Twine standing by,' said Valentine. Twine was a relatively new member of the squad, graduate entry, smart and keen, direct from the Met's training school at Hendon. Valentine reckoned he didn't have a social life so he'd rung him earlier as soon as he knew he might need some back-up in the office. At work Twine was professional, clean-cut, almost antiseptic, and Valentine had been astonished when a woman answered the phone.

Shaw looked around. It was one of his father's maxims — passed on during one of those rare moments when he'd talked about the job to his son — that any decent detective should have a picture of the scene of the crime imprinted on his memory bank, as tangible and to hand as the coins in his pocket.

The mist was thickening, rising slightly, so that thin strands seemed to claw listlessly at their belts. Shaw stood, partly disembodied, surrounded by the empty graves of the dead. Beside the stone angel there was a box tomb lit by the halogen lamp: it was in granite, with engraved cherubs, and had a flat top on which was etched:

Et in arcadia ego

Shaw stepped up onto it effortlessly. The lid rocked slightly, like a boulder in a stream. He let his single eye tour the horizon. The loss of his right eye two years earlier in an accident might have destroyed his ability to see in 3D at close range, but over twenty-five feet his eyesight was as good as anyone with two eyes: better, because he'd had to train himself in other ways to judge distance and perspective — such as using the way colours merge towards blue as they approach the horizon to judge distance. But that was no good at night: the view from the tomb, above the mist, was of a piebald world, just black and white. The night-watchman's light at the cannery was gone. To the north, half a mile away, he could see a light on a building — a pitched roof,

11

gables and beams; a building that seemed to crouch beyond the cemetery gates, like a mourner returning to grieve after dark.

'What's that?' he asked.

'The Flask,' said Valentine, looking at his shoes. 'Boozer — bit rough now. Used to be all right.'

Shaw's knowledge of Lynn's pubs was restricted to the Red House, the CID's haunt off St James's. Hadden unplucked the forensic glove from his right hand. 'It was named after a ship,' he said. Hadden was a Londoner who'd come north to escape an ugly divorce and find peace spotting birds on the north Norfolk sands. Like most incomers, he knew more about local history than the natives. And he spent some of his time here, on the tidal path, looking for oystercatchers. 'A whaler back in the 1880s. This was where they used to take the flesh off the carcasses — the flensing grounds. Between us and the pub is a narrow inlet — pretty much silted up now. Blubber Creek.'

Shaw looked around, trying to imagine the whaling fleet in the river after its nine-month voyage back from the Arctic, the fires on the bank heating the cauldrons in which the meat was reduced to oil. Flesh pots.

They heard footsteps through the drier grass up the bank, and for the first time the slight crunch of frost. Walking towards them, hauling a leather bag, was Justina Kazimierz. She didn't say hello to anyone, simply put the bag down and opened it up, retrieving a set of forensic gloves and a mask. When Shaw had first met her

12

he'd attributed her taciturn manner to the language barrier — she'd just arrived from Poland, via the Home Office. He'd been too kind. The pathologist didn't do pleasantries, and didn't suffer fools. Only once had Shaw seen her with her guard down in public, dancing with her diminutive husband at the Polish Club, drinking lighter-fuel vodka from a half-pint tumbler. But last summer she and her husband had moved out of town to a house on the coast near Shaw's, and she often came past now, on long walks, circled by a Labrador. Always alone, and always with an ice-cream for his daughter. A friendship had begun, if you could build a friendship on so few words. She took less than a minute to scan the body. 'I need him inside — quickly. Can we use the chapel?'

She hadn't looked at Hadden when she asked the question but he nodded.

She tapped the coffin. 'Wood's in good condition — under water most of the time? Maybe.' Even when she did talk to others she seemed to limit the conversation to a question-and-answer session with herself.

'Unscrew the coffin lid, then slide the lid and the corpse into a body-bag,' she said. 'Then we'll look inside.' She stood back, waiting for her instructions to be carried out.

'But from the general position of the body we'd conclude . . . ?' asked Shaw.

She sighed, circumnavigating the bones. 'I'd guess — and that's what it is, Shaw: a guess — that he was dead when he was thrown in the grave. The body twisted as it fell — hence the

13

posture. That'll have to do you for now, although I could say more about the wound.'

She'd called him Shaw, although in private it was Peter now. She plucked the forensic glove from her right hand as they gathered behind the head.

'The weapon was curved — you see?' she said. 'The blade is triangular in its cross-section. As it's gone through the bone it's exerted more pressure on the lower edge of the puncture wound — that's why the cracks radiate from that point. So the weapon's gone in, and then turned downwards through the brain, during the blow, so that there's virtually no pressure on the two upward sides of the triangle. Very unusual — very distinctive.'

'What are we looking for?' asked Valentine.

Dr Kazimierz straightened. 'No idea. Don't push me. A scythe would show the same pressures — but it's not triangular, and it's not this narrow. I need to get him back to the Ark. Ask me then.'

The Ark was West Norfolk's pathology and forensic laboratory, set in an abandoned nonconformist chapel on the ring road, close to police headquarters at St James's. It was Tom Hadden's kingdom, and housed the force's own mortuary. Kazimierz was a consultant, working on contract, but she used an office at the Ark too, and West Norfolk provided most of her caseload. It was a haven for the pathologist, Shaw sensed, wherein logic and reason reigned.

She pulled off the other forensic glove. 'The lid?'

Two of Hadden's team arrived with a stretcher and a body-bag and set up another wooden trestle to take the lid and the skeleton when it was lifted clear. One of the forensics officers, a woman entirely encased in a white SOC suit, worked steadily round the coffin, unscrewing screws, easing them out of the wood.

Shaw walked away, breathing in the freezing air. He thought about his father's funeral, out at Gayton, and the family in a line like a firing squad by the grave. Beyond them, uniformed officers at attention, and under a cypress tree the whole of the CID from St James's, most of them looking at their feet as the first spadefuls of earth were thrown in to thud on the coffin top. And with them, but a few yards apart, George Valentine, smoke drifting from a cigarette cupped in one hand.

'One, two, and three . . . ' said Hadden. Shaw turned as they lifted the coffin lid. Valentine looked at his shoes. As the lid was being slipped into the body-bag Shaw glimpsed the pathologist tracing a hurried sign of the cross.

Hadden pulled a spotlight over the now-open coffin. Long grey hair still clung to the skull revealed. Shaw noted the toothless jaws. 'Well — an elderly woman?' he asked.

Kazimierz pulled her gloves back on, making them tight at the base of each finger. Shaw was shocked by the realization that the movement was a feint, a cover, to allow the pathologist to gather herself, and for the first time he noticed how much she'd aged in this last year — the year in which they'd become friends. Her face had

15

always been heavy, flesh obscuring what had once perhaps been a precarious beauty. But now the skin looked wasted, hanging from the bones of her face.

She took a piece of mouldered cloth from around the neck bone and a spider crept out from the shadow beneath the jaw, then scuttled back. Most of the bones were hidden beneath a velvet drape which had been folded over the body like a pair of rotting scarlet wings. On one fold of the drape, near the neck, was a silver brooch, two simple curved lines intersecting to form a fish. One hand, each finger intact, had been laid across the heart.

The pathologist began to work at the edge of the drape with a gloved hand, trying to reveal the bones beneath.

Shaw walked away and stood by the empty grave to look down. It was dark down there, an almost magnetic black. He hoped the victim had been dead when the killers had tossed him into the grave, but knew the real crime was the knowledge, the near certainty, that they probably didn't care.

'God.' The word had come from the pathologist and as Shaw turned he saw the rapid supplication again, the hand moving swiftly in front of her face. She held her hands high, elbows down, like a surgeon. She'd parted the velvet drape and most of the bones beneath were broken, the left upper thigh, several of the ribs, the lower left arm — not just broken, but shattered, so that each was a jigsaw of fractures.

'Jesus,' said Valentine. 'She's in bits.'

16

2

Standing on the stone step of the cemetery chapel was DC Paul Twine, an iPhone glowing in his palm.

'Sir,' he said, nodding at Shaw, catching Valentine's eye, then freezing when he saw what was behind them: the impromptu funeral procession climbing the rise; appearing out of the mist, led by forensics-team pall-bearers carrying the black body-bag, then the open coffin behind. The mist closed behind them like a liquid, as if they'd risen out of a lake.

Twine had his free hand on a gravestone, propped up against the wall of the chapel. There was a line of them, perhaps thirty, each leaning on each like folded deckchairs.

'This is our one . . . ' said Twine.

MARY TILDEN

Born 3 January 1948
Died 13 February 1948

Cruelly taken, too soon, to God's abode

NORA ELIZABETH TILDEN

Born 8 February 1928
Died 1 June 1982

Loose the shoes from thy feet

Shaw noted the stonemason's single addition: the double strokes of the Christian fish symbol which had been on Nora Tilden's shroud.

'I ran the name through the system, sir,' added Twine. 'She's got a file in records with a 'V' number.'

Shaw stopped in his tracks and studied Twine's face. The DC had a ski tan and expensive skin and wore a body-warmer under a quilted jacket. Shaw had been on Paul Twine's last two failed promotion boards and he recalled the CV: a philosophy student from Bristol with a mind like a Swiss watch, but in terms of life on the streets he didn't know what time it was. But he'd already made a significant contribution to this inquiry: a 'V' number meant Nora Elizabeth Tilden was somewhere in the St James's computer system because she'd been the victim of a serious crime. Her crushed bones, thought Shaw, were perhaps a testimony to that.

'But 1982?' said Valentine, knowing that records from that time were still on paper in the basement under police HQ. The only reference on the computer would be the file number.

'I've got someone on it,' said Twine. 'An hour — maybe less. Plus, I know someone down at the *Lynn News* . . . ' He held up his iPhone. 'They're tracking back through their computer archive. Might work. And the paperwork here gives us an address, sir — the Flask, the pub along the riverbank.' He nodded to the north.

Shaw looked again at the building he'd noticed when standing on top of the box tomb

— the Gothic outline, floating over the mist, of the whalers' inn.

He led the way into the chapel through a door the shape of a church window. Within, coffins already exhumed by the council were laid out in military rows: six across, ten deep. Processed remains had been repackaged in small wooden ossuaries, stacked against one wall. On a set of three tables at the front skeletons had been laid out for examination.

Twine explained, while using his thumb to text on the iPhone. 'A team from St John's in Cambridge are here doing a study on Victorian diseases — taking their chance, I guess. They've been examining the bones, measurements, density, chemical composition — that kind of thing. When they're done the council boxes up what's left. A Professor John G. Carstairs is leading the group. I've rung his home number but it's on answerphone. I left a message, asking him to contact us.'

Nora Tilden's open coffin had been set on a table at the foot of the nave. Under the stark overhead lights it looked as if most of the woman's bones had been fed through a car-cruncher: one ankle was just a collection of small shards, although the entire lower right leg had escaped destruction, as had the skull, and the spine above the middle back.

'What are we looking at here?' Dr Kazimierz asked herself. 'A massive trauma of some kind, certainly — a car crash?' She extracted a short length of bone which had broken and dropped into the ribcage. 'Bones show some evidence of the early onset of osteoporosis — so they would have been brittle. Add a high-pressure impact and the skeleton effectively shatters, like a glass.' She looked Shaw in the eye and they seemed to share the image, a bone exploding into shards.

Shaw thought about the 'V' number — a hit-and-run victim? A passenger in a drink-driving case?

The pathologist turned to the next table where they'd set down the coffin lid. Two of the forensic officers slipped the black bag away to reveal the skeleton. These bones were darker, still damp from the soil that had clagged the ribs and joints. The pathologist removed the skull and set it on a small plastic pillow she'd taken out of her bag, using a spirit level to angle it precisely. Beside the skull she laid a tape measure, a pair of calipers and a camera tripod.

Shaw smiled, nodding.

The pathologist straightened her back. 'I presume you have made a preliminary examination yourself, Shaw?'

'Sorry.' He made a conscious effort to take any tuneful tone out of his voice, trying instead to hit a flat, matter-of-fact, note. 'I didn't think you'd welcome my thoughts before you'd taken a look.'

Shaw couldn't see Valentine, but he could feel him smiling.

'So — why don't *you* talk us through it?' she asked, producing a digital camera from the black orchid bag and screwing it into a tripod holder. Stepping back, she poured a small cup of equally black tea from a Thermos, adding a dash of something colourless from a hip flask. She

20

adjusted a wedding ring, which Shaw hadn't noticed before. The invitation was an honour in itself, a recognition that the pathologist saw in Shaw's skills as a forensic artist a professional complement to her own. It was also an invitation to fail, publicly.

Shaw took a step towards a table the Cambridge team had been using to examine the exhumed remains and picked up a skull at random: tagged with a label which read XX 88/901 — M. He held the skull on the palm of his hand and lowered it until it was set beside the victim's.

'The shallow forehead in our victim is the most obvious point of difference. And here, around the jaws, the bones project forward, and there's the eye sockets — that's the real giveaway. In this labelled skull — in all these skulls, I suspect — the sockets are roughly triangular. But with our friend here, they're essentially square, and set more broadly leaving this gap for the nose, which is set flat and wide. See?'

Valentine did see, and he couldn't stop himself nodding, fascinated.

'He was almost certainly of African descent,' said Shaw. 'It's not absolutely clear cut — the genetic pool's complex. The teeth — for example, are large, but smaller than the stereotype would suggest. There's some Caucasian influence . . . ' He stopped talking as one of the civilian staff from the St James's mobile canteen came in with a tray of teas. Mugs were taken, then cradled.

Kazimierz's face simply registered her pleasure at the contents of her own cup. Shaw, forcing himself to be cautious, added a rider. 'Picking race from bones is dodgy territory, but the signs are difficult to ignore.'

She screwed the top back on the Thermos. 'Bravo. African, indeed. Bone lengths are very pronounced as well — long arms relative to the skeleton. And the skull shape's classic as you said — alveolar prognathism,' she said, indicating the protruding lower jaw. 'A big man, maybe six feet two.' She ran the retractable tape measure along the femur. 'Less — but not much. As you also observed — there's some conflicting evidence. The teeth — yes. And the forehead is actually higher than you'd expect, given the prognathism.'

'Should make him easy to find,' said Valentine, stretching until one of the vertebra in his back gave way with a plastic thud. 'If he was buried at the same time as the coffin in 1982 he'd have stood out like a spot on a domino round here. Peterborough, the East Midlands, loads of 'em — but Lynn . . . nah.'

Valentine shifted feet, knowing he'd combined insensitivity with a dollop of non-PC language. He thought of Shaw's daughter, playing on the beach at the CID summer picnic, her skin a subtle shade of butterscotch. In the awkward silence he edged a finger round the collar of his shirt, and pulled at the knot in his tie. One of the other things that really annoyed him about Shaw was that he *never* wore a tie: just a crisp white creaseless shirt, open at the neck.

Dr Kazimierz began talking into a digital voice recorder that hung round her neck. 'According to Mr Hadden and his team, the clothes on our coffin-lid victim here are right for the 1980s or late 1970s. Quality is good — possibly very good.' She held up a shred of material, the original mercury red still visible. 'In fact this shred — removed from the left side of the chest — is silk. I am entering it into the evidence.' Rummaging in the black bag she found a batch of forensic envelopes and bagged the item.

'And three further items,' said the pathologist. 'Which are from the area alongside the right hip, where a jacket pocket would have been.' She lifted a wallet and a multibladed pocket knife, encrusted with mud, and a few coins, describing them as she did so.

She placed the wallet on an evidence bag and briefly teased at the leather with her gloved fingers. She switched off the recorder and spoke to Shaw. 'We have a wallet, leather, once black, pretty much rotten. Anything left inside? I doubt it. The leather will fall apart if I try to empty it here, so unless it's a matter of life and death — literally — I'll get this to the lab. Inspector?'

Shaw nodded reluctantly. But he couldn't argue with the judgement. This man had probably died more than two decades ago. Getting inside his wallet now rather than in six hours' time was hardly a priority.

'The coins all dated before 1982. Several from the 1970s. One 1969 shilling,' she added, setting them out.

She shone a pencil light on what looked like a

shard of green glass embedded in clay next to the victim's right leg. Using a bowl of water and a paint brush she gradually softened the clay, then let it dissolve. Gradually a broken glass began to appear. Below it was another — this time apparently unbroken. It took her a minute to work it clear, and when she held it to the light they could all see it was a Victorian-style tumbler, etched with an illustration of a whale at sea being pursued by an open boat. The whale was exquisitely drawn, each flute engraved, as was the single staring eye of the whale, and there was a tense energy in the harpooner's arm, ready to unleash his weapon from the small boat in which crowded a dozen hunters. In the background, on a still horizon, stood the distant mother ship, a frail-outline of masts and rigging.

The pathologist set the glass aside, and beside it the broken shards of its sister.

Shaw and Valentine tried to see what might have happened: the victim offered a final drink? Or the killers, administering Dutch courage before the fatal attack — or a stiff drink to calm their nerves after it was over? But why bring glasses — why not drink from the bottle? It added, thought Shaw, an almost ceremonial detail.

'What's missing?' asked Shaw, looking at the bagged items.

Valentine bit his lip, trying to think. He'd been up in front of a promotion panel a week earlier and they'd turned him down. Senior officers needed more evidence that he was committed to the CID after a decade out in the sticks. So far tonight he hadn't done his chances a lot of good. He took a breath, his shoulders aching with fatigue.

Clarity under pressure was essential if progress was to be made in the first few hours of a murder inquiry, even one that had taken place nearly thirty years ago. 'Keys,' he said, with a flood of relief. 'You've got a wallet, coins. You'd expect keys.' He massaged his neck. 'Either he didn't need keys, or whoever dumped him took the keys first.'

'Tom's boys and girls will sieve the earth — every last ounce,' said Shaw. 'They might be in there. They're heavier; perhaps they fell out of the pocket on the way down.'

Kazimierz raised a gloved hand. 'Or . . . '

She was down on one knee, working away at the clay under the knee joint. Poking from the soil was a curve of metal, gleaming dully. It took her a minute, perhaps two, to work enough clear space to edge it out.

It was a billhook, the metal rusted, the handle rotted to a stump.

'Perfect,' she said. 'Your murder weapon — almost certainly. Fits the wound like a glove.'

It was an odd metaphor, and it made Shaw shiver.

'Like this,' she said, taking Valentine by the shoulder and turning him away, so that he faced the serried rows of coffins. She bagged the billhook, held it lightly in her hand, and then brought her arm over like a fast bowler until the tip touched the DS's skull where the hair had thinned. 'Maybe just to one side . . . an inch, maybe less. This kind of blow — he'd have been dead before he hit the ground. The hook would have cut through the brain. It's like throwing a light switch.'

She clicked her fingers and Valentine felt his legs give way, just for a second, as if he too were falling into his grave.

3

Greyfriars Tower stood floodlit opposite police HQ, the frost picking out the medieval stonework. The old monastic bell tower leant at a heart-stopping angle, its fall to earth arrested by a million-pound restoration scheme. It stood on the Lynn skyline like a grounded ship's mast, tilted seawards. Valentine stood at an open window of the CID suite, smoking into the night. The tower had cast a shadow over his life since he'd gone to school a few hundred yards from the crumbling walls of the old monastery. He didn't see it any more, like so many things.

Shaw sat at a computer screen scrolling through missing persons for 1982 — the year Nora Tilden had died and been buried. There were eight, six of them young girls. Of the two males, one was a sixteen-year-old from the North End, white, with a tattooed Union Flag under his left eye. More to the point, he was only four feet eight inches tall. He was still missing. The other was a sixty-three-year-old man from Gayton, diagnosed with Alzheimer's, who'd put the rubbish out in the side alley by his house one night in August and not been seen again until 1993, when his remains were discovered on a railway embankment 200 yards from his front door by a courting couple. He was identified from dental records.

'Nothing,' said Shaw, pushing himself back

from the desk and massaging his neck, then his injured eye.

He examined Valentine's back. Shaw, too tired to prevent his mind wandering, analysed what he felt about George Valentine: irritation — always that — because he was a living relic of the kind of old-fashioned copper Shaw despised. A man who thought the rule book was useful only if you needed to wedge a door open. But beyond irritation there was envy, and guilt.

George Valentine had been a DI once, and his DCI had been Shaw's father, Jack. Both of them had been on a skyward career path until one fatal misjudgement had brought them to earth. Accused of planting evidence in a murder trial, they had been suspended: Shaw's father had died after taking early retirement, Valentine had lost a rank and been exiled to the wilderness of the north Norfolk coast, and a decade of policing beach yobs, small-time burglars and the odd credit-card fraudster. So, envy because Valentine had known his father so well, while his own relationship had been distant, cool, a reflection, perhaps, of his father's determination to shield his family from the realities of police work. And guilt because Shaw had failed to fulfil a promise: that one day he would clear his father's name, remove from the record that withering epithet 'bent copper'. George Valentine was a living reminder of that failure.

The internal phone rang. It was DC Twine, down in records. 'Sir? Just got the 'V' files on our victim. She was murdered by her husband. He got life. Eight case files — a dozen on the trial.'

28

Shaw thought of one of his father's maxims: delegate, don't try to process all the information yourself. 'Read what you can in twenty minutes, Paul, then come up and give us a summary. Relevant details only. We're just waiting for Tom — he's got some preliminaries from the scene.'

Shaw cut the line and checked his watch, which not only showed the time and the phase of the moon but was set to give the state of the tide at Hunstanton — just up the coast from his house.

The display read 11.48 p.m. High tide.

This is what he really hated about CID. The joyless time wasted waiting for other people to do their jobs. He thought about Lena, wrapped up, watching the beach through the double-glazed windows of the Beach Café, the icy rollers pounding on the sand. They'd bought the then derelict Old Beach Café three years ago. No access road — just the hard sand of the beach at low tide — no mains electricity, and accounts that showed an annual trading loss of £2,000 per annum. The stone cottage to the rear, in the dunes, and the old boathouse to the side, were all part of the £80,000 deal: both listed, both dilapidated. But the purchase had fulfilled two dreams in one go — Shaw got to live on his beloved beach where he'd played as a child; Lena got the independence she wanted and a business that filled nearly every waking hour. The cottage was now watertight, the café made-over in stripped pine, with an Italian coffee-making machine glinting behind the counter like a vintage motorbike. The boathouse was now Surf

— a beach shop selling everything from £1,000 diver's watches to 50p plastic windmills.

The urge to go home, park by the lifeboat house and run the mile to the cottage, was so strong that one of the muscles in his leg flexed involuntarily. Just the thought of it made his heartbeat skip, adrenaline seeping into his system at the prospect of exercise.

Despite the open window the CID room was hot and airless, the stale smell of sweat engrained in papers spilt across desktops. Valentine ditched a cigarette and closed the window as they heard the lift doors clash in the corridor and Tom Hadden's unhurried steps echoing off the bare walls. He came through the doors backwards, because he held in his hands two glass trays. Wordlessly he set them on the desk in front of Shaw, tapping one with a ballpoint pen: a jumble of clods of clay mixed with a few pebbles and some darker humus.

'This is some of the spoil from this woman's grave — the soil the council workmen dug out today. They used a digger, then spades. It was in a pile by the graveside. It's from the top of the pile — so that's the earth just above the point where they stopped because they saw the bones on top of Nora Tilden's coffin.'

He tapped the other glass. 'This is a sample from underneath the skeleton — the strata sandwiched, as it were, between him and the coffin below. The science here is dull . . . ' He paused, and Shaw knew that was a lie, because Hadden lived for the science. 'But the principles involved are very helpful. Soil, undisturbed,

30

evolves . . . it becomes stratified, some minerals are drawn up, nutrients washed down, clay forms distinct layers — like those bottled sands you see in souvenirs from the Isle of Wight, a kind of natural layer cake. There's one other useful process — the cemetery uses a chemical weedkiller. That washes down through the soil at a steady rate. Broadly, all this means that I can put an age on soil — in the sense that I can tell you how long it has remained undisturbed.'

He closed his eyes, considering exactly what he was about to say.

'In this case the major finding — taking into account the way the skeleton itself has affected the soil — is that these two samples are the *same* age. In soil terms, 'same' means give or take a year, probably less. The actual age will take a lot more science than I can bring to bear in an hour. But in many ways that doesn't matter — the fact is, the earth thrown on top of the coffin has lain undisturbed for the same amount of time as the earth above the bones. So we have a clear picture. Imagine you're there. If you looked in the grave you'd see Nora Tilden's coffin at the bottom. Then a few feet of earth goes in. Then the corpse of the second victim. Then the rest of the earth. The only question is when. Did this happen on the day Nora Tilden was buried — before, in effect, the burial was complete, or did it happen at a later date — within a year of the burial?'

'What's your instinct?' asked Shaw.

'Well, I'd rule out the possibility this happened on the day of the funeral,' said Hadden. 'Given that this woman was undoubtedly buried in front of her family and friends. In broad daylight. In fact, given that I'm told she was murdered, and the killer convicted, there were almost certainly members of the CID present as well. So it's pretty unlikely someone was able to slip a second corpse into the grave by sleight of hand.'

'Why go dig up an old grave to hide a body — if you're going to dig a hole, dig it somewhere hidden. Right?' asked Valentine, adjusting his tie.

'It makes more sense than you think,' said Shaw. 'Dig a hole anywhere and it can be found — OK, you can pick a bit of woodland, sand dunes, whatever. But someone *might* find it, because the ground's disturbed. A dog, maybe. But if you think about it, the best place to hide a hole is in a cemetery. And for six months — longer — there's nothing on the grave — no stone, usually nothing except rotting flowers. They let the soil settle first. So if you can do it without being seen it's nearly perfect. And that's the best opportunity — the first year.'

Shaw picked up one of the glass trays. 'And that would remove any necessity for there to be a link between the two victims — because the grave might well have been chosen simply because it was fresh.'

Twine came through the door, a pile of files only just wedged under one arm. He ditched them on a desk, took a marker pen and wrote the name Nora Tilden on one of the perspex display boards. He looked at Shaw, Hadden and Valentine, confident enough to wait until they were ready for him to speak.

Shaw nodded.

'Our victim was Nora Elizabeth Tilden. Her husband was Albert Ellis Tilden,' said Twine, adding the name next to hers. 'He pushed her down a flight of stairs, and as we've seen, broke nearly every bone in her body.'

'OK — just a summary, Paul, please,' said Shaw. 'Relevant details. Tom's in a hurry.'

Hadden sat, his shoulders slumping. Shaw guessed he wouldn't sleep for days now — not in a bed, just snatching naps in the lab. Valentine took a seat and crossed his arms, thinking that they were about to find out how smart Paul Twine really was, because at this stage of a murder inquiry almost all the details were relevant.

Twine wrote Nora Tilden's dates on the board: 1928–1982.

'She inherited the Flask — the pub down on the riverside — from her father — Arthur Melville, in 1947. She was just nineteen.'

First mistake, thought Valentine. We can all add up.

Twine put her father's name on the board above Nora's, in the style of a family tree. 'Nora married Albert — a sailor — after the war — he was merchant navy. Always known as Alby, by the way. Became a bit of a hero, apparently, sailing with the Arctic convoys. He was twenty when they married. They had a daughter, but the kid died within a few weeks of being born. Cot death, it looks like. That's Mary — buried in the same plot.'

Hadden raised a hand from the desktop. 'We'll

have her up in the morning — but the team down in the meadow say there's definitely another coffin there. And it's pint-sized.'

Twine added the child's name under her father and mother's.

'Alby Tilden left home — went back to sea in 1955,' he looked down at his notes. 'Didn't come back for six years. This all came out at the trial. When he did turn up he was on his uppers. Looks like he spent most of his time in Gibraltar and North Africa. Bit of a colourful time there, apparently — not so much hero any more as villain. Court was told he'd contracted various venereal diseases on his travels. There were also signs of mental illness. Anxiety attacks — agoraphobia. He was an engineer at sea, stayed below decks. On deck he freaked out. Nora took him back — but plenty of witnesses said the marriage was always rocky, although they had another child — Elizabeth, known as Lizzie. She was born in 1962.

'During the year Nora was killed, the rows with Alby had been getting worse — physical, not just verbal sniping from prepared positions. She stopped Alby working behind the bar of the Flask because he kept giving the booze away — so he got a day job in one of the canneries to put beer money in his pocket. Locals said they could often hear the china breaking upstairs. Witnesses were happy to talk about that, but the reason for the rows — the specific reason — never came out. The daughter, Lizzie, said they'd always fought.'

Twine added Lizzie to the family tree.

'The night Nora Tilden died, the first of June 1982, Alby had been drinking heavily in the bar. He had mates on the ships in the new docks and they all used to drink in the pub. Lizzie was working behind the bar. Nora was upstairs. Apparently she kept out of the way when he was on a bender. Alby went up himself about nine o'clock for food and several witnesses said they heard the familiar sounds of an argument, then stuff being thrown, then a scream.

'Lizzie told the court she ran from the bar to the bottom of the stairs. She found her mother in a heap — dad standing at the top. The pub's stairs are as steep as a ladder, so the fall could easily have killed her, but the pathologist said there were pressure marks around the dead woman's neck — as though she'd been throttled. Alby said they'd argued because he wanted to go downstairs, back to his mates. She followed him, caught him at the top step, and they started pushing and shoving. According to Alby, she lost her footing and fell. According to the jury, he either pushed her or throttled her or both. The judge gave him life.'

'So he's probably out by now, then,' said Valentine.

'Home Office link is down,' said Twine. 'I'll check first thing, but yes, he's very likely free — if he's still alive. With good behaviour he could have been out in fifteen. He'd be in his early eighties now. If we do find him there should be no problem recognizing him.' He waved a

35

piece of paper. 'This is the original warrant. It lists any identifying marks. Tilden was covered in them. It wasn't just VD he brought back from the East — nearly thirty tattoos are listed, over most of his body. He's the illustrated man.'

4

Monday, 13 December

Shaw and Valentine sat on identical straight-backed chairs in Detective Chief Superintendent Max Warren's office. A single picture window gave a view over the rooftops to the church of St James — stark Victorian neo-Gothic, with a neon cross on the roof in lurid green, lit now, but only just visible in a light snow shower that looked like the fallout from a pillow fight. Out in the adjoining office DCS Warren was dictating a letter to his secretary: he'd be with them in a minute, he'd said, offering coffee, which they'd turned down. So they sat, each alone, despite being together. One wall of the office held a bookcase, Christmas cards crowded on the shelves. Shaw thought, not for the first time, what a depressing word 'festive' could be.

Shaw had his right leg crossed over his left to support a sketch pad. He'd spent an hour in the Ark the night before, after leaving the CID suite at St James's. Dr Kazimierz had been finishing her preliminary report: she was happy for him to photograph the skull, as long as she was present. His forensic art kit was always on hand — stashed in the boot of his car. It included a tripod camera and a perspex stand on which the skull could be supported, then angled precisely to meet the Frankfurt horizontal plane — the internationally agreed angle of tilt which allowed for the uniform comparison of all skulls.

Even then, with just the bones set at the correct angle, he could see the face. He'd noted, for example, the asymmetry of the eye sockets, the left a few millimetres above the right, the narrow mastoid process on both the left and right sides of the skull, a formation that would have made the ears almost impossible to see fully from the frontal view. And the slight gap in the front teeth: a defect that would have been notable as part of the victim's essential 'lifelong look' — the subtle alignment of features by which he would have always been recognizable to family and friends. The kind of facial feature everyone uses, often without thinking, to spot a loved one in an old snapshot.

Shaw had left St James's at 2.00 a.m. with a complete set of digital images of the skull. He'd driven to the lifeboat house at Hunstanton, parked the car, then ran the mile along the sands to home in four minutes and forty-two seconds: six seconds slower than his average. The Beach Café's security light had thudded on as he'd stepped up on to the wooden verandah. The cottage, to the rear in the dunes, had been in darkness, the shop boarded up out of season to protect it from the winter gales.

Letting himself into the cottage, he'd stopped for a second inside the closed door to smell the scents of home: pasta, paint, washing powder and — best of all — wood. He'd checked on his daughter Francesca, the terrier at the foot of her bed only raising its old head as Shaw looked in.

He'd left Lena to sleep and taken a shower. In the bathroom, on the window ledge, had been a line of pillboxes he hadn't seen before: he'd counted them — eight, each marked with the logo of the local allergy clinic. He'd let the water run down his skin, washing away the day, until he'd felt clean.

Dry, in shorts and a T-shirt, he'd unlocked the door that led to the café down the short connecting corridor they'd built between the two buildings. Reflections from the café's neon lights would have concealed the view outside, so he'd used the small light above the counter, then fired up the Italian coffee machine. Through the windows he'd just been able to see the ghostly white lines of the waves breaking out on the far sands, snow clouds beginning to blot out the moon.

Booting up the laptop, he'd scanned in the pictures from the camera, then printed them out at precisely life-size. He'd taped up two of the pictures on an easel retrieved from the deckchair store, and illuminated them using an anglepoise lamp from the office, then stood back with his coffee to study them.

He'd covered the two images on the easel with sheets of tracing paper and opened his copy of Rhines Tables: the standard set of multiples which would allow him to put flesh on bones. Then he'd worked on each set of features using Krogman's Rule of Thumb to add fleshy details not dictated by skull structure — the mouth set at six teeth wide, the angle of the nose extrapolated from the nasal spine. He'd modified the rules, using some educated guesses based on the mixed ethnicity — for example he'd set the nose at 16mm wide compared to the standard 10mm for Caucasians. He'd made the eyes dark in the black-and-white image, but left the hair indistinct, reduced to just a few pencil lines. The pathologist had considered the clothing to be of good quality, so Shaw presumed a healthy weight, and he'd taken her guesstimate of the age at between twenty and twenty-five.

He'd been brushing in the tonal shadows, adding art to the science, when Lena had wandered down the connecting corridor and stood at the door in a short silk nightdress the colour of antique silver. They'd kissed and stood back from the easel, Shaw holding her waist close, so that he could feel their hips touching.

'A brother,' she'd said, and they'd laughed. Lena's own skin was darker than the tone he'd chosen for the victim: Jamaican brown, though not so lustrous as it would be in the summer months, when it picked up a distinct bronze tint.

'The pills — in the bathroom?' he'd asked, looking her in the eyes, one of which had a slight cast.

'Oh, yeah — for Fran. We've got to try each one — see what she's allergic to. One a week.'

Their daughter had been allergic to milk at birth — but the reactions, once violent, had dimmed over time. Then, suddenly, the previous September, she'd had a full-blown anaphylactic reaction to a pot of yoghurt.

'It's the milk — right?' asked Shaw, aware that there was too much aggression in his voice, which betrayed the guilt he felt for being absent that day, out on a case. No — that was self-delusion, out on *the* case, his father's last, unsolved, murder inquiry, the case that seemed to run through his life like letters through seaside rock.

'No, Peter, it isn't the milk,' said Lena, failing to hide her anxiety. 'She still has a slight sensitivity to it but now there's something else, probably something benign, and when you put the two together you get the reaction we got. So it's milk plus X. We just don't know what X is. It could be anything in the yoghurt I gave her. Flavourings, colourings — the usual stuff. So we're trying them out. Till we find out, she has to keep off real milk. It's back to soya and rice substitutes.'

Her shoulders had sagged and Shaw had guessed she was thinking about the first few months of Fran's life — the endless vigilance required to make sure a small child didn't ingest anything containing milk.

He hugged her too hard. 'OK.'

'Handsome,' she'd said then, nodding back at the picture. 'Innocent.'

'Interesting word,' said Shaw, adding shadow beneath the broad chin. 'Why innocent?'

'It's a presumption — the dead are innocent, aren't they?'

They'd chatted for a while over fresh coffees before going to bed. An hour together before the day began. When Shaw had walked back into the café to retrieve the sketches at dawn he'd stopped six feet from them, aware that he'd recreated someone who had once been alive. The face of this man who had died so violently looked at him over the twenty-eight years separating that last terrifying moment from this one.

'All you need is a name,' said Shaw out loud. Then he'd held out his hands, as if pleading before a jury, laughing at himself. 'And justice.'

And now, sitting in Max Warren's office, he looked again at the sketch. The adrenaline of the murder inquiry had dispelled all tiredness, despite the lack of sleep, but he did feel that nauseous buzz, his blood rushing with the effects of several doses of strong coffee.

He handed the frontal view to Valentine, who took it, then held it out at arm's length.

'Get it out for me, George. Usual suspects — TV, radio, *Lynn News*. We'll give it twenty-four hours and if nothing bites, let's go for posters — five hundred will do.'

Valentine pushed his bottom lip forward. 'Reckon the Old Man will pay up? Posters cost a fortune.'

In the outer office Max Warren was finishing his dictation.

'He won't know until it's too late,' said Shaw, flicking over the sketch pad to work on the side view.

Valentine rubbed his eyes, feeling a gritty resistance. He hadn't slept after leaving St James's either. It wasn't that he hadn't wanted to — he'd walked into South Lynn by the towpath until he'd reached the ruins of Whitefriars

Abbey, then turned into the network of streets in which he'd been born, married and widowed, and where he still lived. The cemetery in which they'd found their victims that night was less than half a mile away. He'd considered returning there, but thought better of it. Instead, he'd walked to the church of All Saints and stood before his wife's headstone:

JULIE ANNE VALENTINE

1955–1993

Asleep

The stone was mottled with moss and the inscription partly obscured by the charity lapel stickers he'd stuck on it. He added WOOD GREEN ANIMAL SHELTER, thinking how, like him, she'd hated dogs. It always annoyed him, that cloying euphemism — *Asleep*. He wondered who'd chosen it, because it hadn't been him. But then he'd walked through her death, and the funeral, as if it had all been happening to someone else.

On the corner of Greenland Street he'd stopped outside an old shop. His house was in sight, but he often lost the will to go home at this precise point. The old shop's double doors were glass and curved gracefully. Within was a second door, with a fanlight, from which shone a green light. And a sign hung from a hook up against the glass. Chinese characters, but ones that Valentine could pronounce.

Yat ye hoi p'i
The game is on, the game is open

He'd looked up and down the street, then knocked twice and waited; then twice again. A man had quickly opened the door, and Valentine had slipped in like a cat. Inside, enveloped in the scented warmth, the man they called the sentinel had taken his raincoat. Valentine had held on to his wallet, keys and mobile. The den was on three floors, but he always went down to the basement for fan-tan. He'd taken a glass of tea from the pot set on a table in the hall — there was no alcohol at the house on Greenland Street — and that suited him well, because he'd always liked to enjoy his vices serially.

In the basement room were a dozen men sitting on high stools around the gambling table. There was a room to one side for smoking, but Valentine never went over the threshold.

On the table he'd bought £60 worth of chips and put £5 on the number 2. The dealer had swirled a pile of golden coins and covered them with an ornamental lid. Then the sharing out began — in little collections of three — until only three or fewer were left. On the table sat two coins. Valentine had picked up his winnings and bet again — this time on 1. An hour later he'd won £30. He'd taken a break, going upstairs to drink more tea, then returning to stand on the edge of the circle of light which blazed down on the fan-tan table. His bladder had been aching so he'd slipped out of the basement door into the yard. There had been ice

44

in the toilet pan, and as he'd stood there he'd felt that his life was raw, and that he'd never wanted it to be like that — he'd sought warmth, but it had been denied him.

He'd cashed his winnings and walked out into the street, the snow falling steadily now, muffling the noises of the town at night. Sleep had become a distant dream. He'd walked briskly past his house. In the next street there had been a single light in the bedroom of number 89 — his sister Jean's. He didn't see her much. He told himself he didn't like her husband, but the real reason was that she was an echo of his past, because she'd been a good friend to Julie, and so a reminder of what might have been. But he found the light comforting because he liked to know she was still here, in the streets where they'd all grown up.

He'd walked on down to the quayside. Greyfriars Tower provided the only light in the sky, a lighthouse in a gentle snowstorm. He'd checked his watch: 2.30 a.m. The St James's canteen opened at 5.30 a.m. and the thought of a cooked breakfast made him feel better about the day to come. He'd zigzagged towards the tower through the Old Town, past the Jewish Cemetery where the fine blown snow lay in the chiselled Hebrew inscriptions. When he'd reached St James's he'd taken the curved steps two at a time and breezed past the front desk, where the duty sergeant had nodded once before returning his attention to the previous day's *Daily Mail*.

He'd gone back to his desk in the open-plan

CID room and swung open the window to smoke. Then he'd flicked through a shelf of reference books until he'd found what he was looking for . . . *Old Lynn — A Social History.* The Flask appeared once in the index.

Of South Lynn's whaling past, little is left except in the street names. The dockside for the whaling fleet was on Blubber Creek, now just a grassy, reedy, inlet off the Nar, opposite the end of Explorer Street. The only physical reminder of this once lucrative trade is the Flask — the pub named for one of the fleet's most famous ships. The building is much altered but the main structure is still the timber-framed inn set up on the edge of the flensing grounds in 1776, possibly on an older site. It very soon fell into the hands of the Melville family — wealthy merchants who had moved south from Boston, Lincolnshire. Originally called the Jetty, the pub was renamed to mark the £6,000 profit made by the Flask when she returned to port at the end of the whaling season in 1848. Court records show that an action was brought against the Melville family because of the stench of blubber boiling in the vats on open ground for more than six weeks as the eleven 'fish' aboard were rendered. In 1885 the building was renovated after one wall collapsed in a storm. In the 1950s the pub became famous as one of the last outposts of the sea shanty. Local choirs were recorded — preserving for

46

posterity Lynn's unique tradition of whaling songs. Ralph Vaughan Williams came to the pub on several occasions in the summer of 1947. Several of the songs Vaughan Williams recorded in his notebook were to reappear in his later works: particularly A Sea Symphony and Norfolk Rhapsody No. 1. In 1976 the neighbouring houses were demolished, leaving the building to stand alone with the help of steel buttresses. In the 1980s the Arts Council funded further recordings of the Whitefriars Choir. A documentary film was produced in 1993 and shown on Anglia TV — called The Song of the Sea.

Valentine had checked the date of publication: 1995.

He'd stood, stretching, wishing it was dawn. Shaw's office was to one side, behind a glass partition. On the desk Valentine had spotted a set of forensics reports. He'd let himself in, sat in Shaw's seat and flicked through them. There was no new relevant information from Hadden's team — just a set of pictures of the evidence removed from the victim's clothing, including a single shot of the pocket knife, opened out to reveal all the blades and tools. There was a handwritten note from one of Hadden's assistants to say that the wallet was in a precarious condition and would have to be dried in a vacuum before any attempt was made to prise it open.

Valentine had seen Twine using a Swiss Army

knife to cut open a package in the CID room a week earlier so he'd gone to the young DC's desk and slipped open the top drawer. The knife, glinting, had caught the light. But it wasn't a match to the one in the grave, although that was clearly a forerunner of the modern iconic model.

Back at his own desk he'd gone online and found the home page for Victorinox, the makers of the Swiss Army knife. He clicked the 'History' link. The knife was first produced for the Swiss military in the late nineteenth century after it was discovered that its men were being supplied with German-made models. In an ironic twist, by the time of the Second World War German soldiers were carrying them because they were so much better than the ones with which they were issued. American infantrymen — obsessed with collecting souvenirs on the long march from the D-Day landings to Berlin — would often pick the pockets of their dead enemies. The knives they collected were taken back to the US and fired up the market for what became known as the Swiss Army knife. There was a picture of one of the wartime knives, and it was a direct match for the one retrieved from the cemetery.

Valentine had smiled, thrown open the window and enjoyed another Silk Cut. Lynn had plenty of GI connections — there were two US air bases within twenty miles, and during the war one of Lynn's cinemas — the Pilot — had been a popular haunt for GIs and local girls. He'd retrieved the social-history book and found a picture of the Pilot: couples in a queue along the pavement, the GIs in smart uniforms, all smoking, the girls — some of them — daringly cheek-to-cheek with black partners.

The only problem was the age of the victim: between twenty and twenty-five in 1982. But then he looked again at those couples cheek-to-cheek, and thought about the children to come.

5

Max Warren sat behind his desk, fists bunched on his blotting pad like a pound of butcher's sausages. Shaw recalled what his father had said about Warren when the ex-Met high-flier had arrived at St James's from London in the early 1990s: that he'd end his days in a bungalow at Cromer, chasing kids away from his garden gnomes. And it was true that the passing years had obscured the tough streetwise copper who'd been posted to north Norfolk to revitalize a sleepy seaside constabulary. He'd gone to fat, his neck slowly expanding to fill the gap between shoulder and jaw, and the once-vital sense of anger which had driven him to patrol the night streets with his men during the gang wars of the mid-1990s had turned in on itself, leaving him tetchy and impatient for the haven of retirement which was now just a few years away.

'Right. First things first, Peter. This cemetery stiff — what's the story and is it worth a DI's valuable time?' Valentine stiffened, noting that he, a lowly DS, apparently had no valuable time to waste.

Shaw touched his tanned throat where his tie should have been. 'It's probably a twenty-eight-year-old murder. If we get a few breaks we might get close to the killer — but that's a long shot. There are some interesting forensics — including a wallet which Tom's drying out so we can look inside. I'd planned to give it forty-eight hours. Then we'll scale down if we're nowhere.'

Valentine leant forward, relieving the stress on his back, trying not to think he wanted to cough. He couldn't help but admire Shaw's manipulation of his superior officer. Valentine guessed Warren was planning to give them a week — Shaw had under-cut him, which would mean Warren would back off, and they could manufacture a 'breakthrough' if they wanted to keep the investigation going. Not for the first time he recognized in Peter Shaw something that he lacked himself — the ability to discern the petty politics that dominated life for the top brass and to use it to his own ends.

Shaw slipped the forensic sketch he'd made on to Warren's blotter. 'That's our victim.'

'Bloody hell,' said Warren. He looked up at the neon strip above his desk, the wooden chair creaking beneath him, and spoke to the ceiling. 'I don't have to tell either of you that if the words 'race crime' appear in the local rag then our lives will be a continuous sodding nightmare; so can we try and avoid that?'

Shaw nodded. 'George thinks there may be a GI link, sir. So we may have to get the military involved too. It'll hit the press tomorrow — TV as well.'

Warren smiled, a gesture that did not signal good humour but had developed as a kind of facial grammar, indicating a change of subject.

'Whatever,' he said. 'Just get it cleared up, or move on. Now. We know why we're here — the Tessier case. Three months ago I gave you

51

clearance to take it forward. Since then I've heard nothing from either of you. Now you want to see me. Why?' He tipped forward, then looked at his watch. 'The short version, please — I've got the chief constable's finance committee at ten. I'd love to be late, but then I'd like a pension, too. So just get me up to speed.'

Shaw stretched out his legs, crossed them at the ankles and took a breath.

'You know the basics of the case, sir. But for the record . . . '

The case. The one crime that bound Shaw's life to that of George Valentine, like a sailor lashed to a raft. The case of nine-year-old Jonathan Tessier. His father's *last* case.

The bare facts were undisputed. Jonathan Tessier, aged nine, had been found dead at three minutes past midnight on the night of 26 July 1997. He was still dressed in the sports kit he'd put on the previous morning to play football on the grass triangle by the flats in which he lived on the Westmead Estate in Lynn's North End. He'd been strangled with a ligature of some sort, the condition of the body pointing to a time of death between one and seven hours earlier, between 6.00 and 11.00 p.m. on the 25th. DCI Jack Shaw had attended the scene, with the then Detective Inspector George Valentine. They were St James's senior investigative team, with a record going back nearly a decade including a string of high-profile convictions — notably a clutch of four gang murders on the docks in the summer of 1989 and a double child murder in 1994.

On that night in 1997 they quickly ascertained the facts of the case so far: the boy's body had been found in the underground car park beneath Vancouver House — a twenty-one-storey block at the heart of the Westmead Estate — by a nurse, parking after her late shift at the local hospital. She said she'd seen a car drive off quickly — a Volkswagen Polo, she thought — when she'd got out of her Mini. The fleeing driver had failed to negotiate the narrow ramp to ground level and clipped one of the concrete pillars, spilling broken glass from a headlamp on to the ground.

DI Valentine had radioed an alert on the damaged car to all units. A uniformed PC on foot patrol in the North End found a Polo abandoned on the edge of allotments at just after two that morning, its offside headlamp shattered, the engine warm. A police computer check identified the owner as Robert James Mosse, a law student aged twenty-one who, like the victim, was a resident of Vancouver House. He was studying at Sheffield, but home for the summer vacation. Back at the scene the body had been removed, revealing a single glove below the corpse: black leather with a fake fur lining. Jack Shaw and George Valentine had gone to the first-floor flat Mosse shared with his mother to interview him.

Here the accounts of the night diverge. Jack Shaw and George Valentine's statements dovetailed: they maintained that they showed Mosse the glove in a cellophane evidence bag before obtaining permission to search the flat. They

53

conducted the search and failed to find the matching glove. Mosse, in contrast, agreed in evidence they had shown him the glove, but only *after* the search. He also maintained that the glove had not been contained in a bag of any nature, but simply handed to him. His mother corroborated her son's version of events, adding that at one point DI Valentine had reversed the fingers of the glove, turning it inside out to display the fur lining inside. Both she and her son denied ownership of the glove. The other glove was never found.

Mosse said his car had been stolen that evening, a crime he himself had reported earlier, as verified by the duty desk at St James's. He had been at the cinema alone. His mother had accompanied him to the same complex but they had opted for different films: she went to see *LA Confidential* on the small screen while her son had watched *The Full Monty* on the main screen. Mosse had produced a half-torn cinema ticket as evidence. His film had finished first and so he had walked back to the flats. His car had been parked outside on the street because there'd been a spate of vandalism in the underground car park and he'd been worried about the Polo, which was second hand but in good condition. He'd found the car gone and phoned the police from the flat.

Overnight the smashed glass at the scene was matched to pieces found still clinging to the rim of the headlamp of the abandoned car — Mosse's car. Three pieces were later found to be exact matches — as good as fingerprints in terms of material evidence. Staff at the cinema were unable to recall Mosse in the audience that evening, despite the fact that the auditorium had been only a quarter full. The cinema ticket did not specify the screen, and Mosse's mother said she had thrown away her own ticket stub. Mosse was charged with the murder of Jonathan Tessier at three thirty on the afternoon of the 26th. Bail was denied at a hearing the following day. Analysis of skin residue found in the glove was ordered through the Forensic Science Service, an agency of the Home Office. The report estimated that there was a chance of only one in three billion that the residue came from anyone other than Mosse.

The trial began in October. The case was thrown out of Cambridge Crown Court at the first recess on the first day. The judge agreed with the defence's claim that Jack Shaw and George Valentine had made a basic error in taking forensic evidence from the scene to the suspect's flat, and then compounded that error by exposing the forensic evidence to potential contamination. In dismissing the charges he went further, suggesting that, given the apparently flagrant disregard for police procedure shown by the detectives involved, he was unable to ignore the possibility that they had deliberately falsified the evidence. While the defence accepted that the glove had been found at the scene — a forensic officer confirmed the item was under the body — it was possible they'd taken it to Mosse's flat to expose it to dust and skin residue. The shadow was cast, and would always be there.

'And that's where this case should have rested,' said Warren, cracking his fingers and wincing as the force helicopter swung over the building towards the St James's rooftop helipad. But the case hadn't rested there, and Warren knew that as well as they did.

Following a decade of exile in north Norfolk, the demoted George Valentine had been reassigned to the serious crime unit at St James's two years ago. It was his last chance to regain the rank he'd lost. His superior officer was DI Peter Shaw — the son of his former disgraced partner. Between them, sometimes acting in concert, sometimes alone, they had tried to build again the case against Robert 'Bobby' Mosse. Three months ago they'd made a major breakthrough in the case and Warren had reluctantly given them clearance to push on — to try one last time to get Robert Mosse back in the dock. It was a decision that still rankled, because he was as aware as they were that he'd had little choice.

Shaw stood and walked to Max Warren's window, then he turned to face his superior officer, effortlessly in control.

'As you know, we made some progress last year. Since then we have been waiting for one last development to fall into place before coming back to you. We now believe we understand the motive behind this crime. I'd like to get you up to speed now, sir, briefly.'

Warren glared at them. 'Just get on with it.' A

bead of sweat appeared on his forehead, catching the light.

'The key, sir, to what really happened on the night Jonathan Tessier died lies in a road-traffic accident a few days earlier, just after midnight, on the edge of Castle Rising. The spot is a lonely T-junction. A speeding Mini shot out across the intersection and hit a Ford Mondeo. There is CCTV footage of the accident, although it's very poor quality. There were kids in the Mini. They got out and examined the wreck of the other car, then they drove off. A motorist came upon the scene thirty-five minutes later and called an ambulance. Both passengers, two OAPs, were dead. The driver was seriously injured. There is evidence on the CCTV that at least one of the passengers was alive when the joyriders left the scene.'

'Bastards,' said Warren, interlocking his fingers. 'So?'

'Well, we now believe that Robert Mosse was at the wheel of that car. His passengers were the other three members of a group who had — over a period of several years — meted out rough justice on the Westmead Estate. A gang, if you like. Mosse had left the Westmead the year before to go up to Sheffield to study — but he was back for the summer holidays and we believe he'd linked up with his old mates for a night out on the town. One member of that gang — probably Alex Cosyns — looked inside the wrecked Mondeo that night and retrieved a puppy from the back seat. We'll never know why: maybe it was the one thing he thought he could do to make things right — other than doing the decent thing, which would have been to ring 999.'

'So he was a dog lover — big deal.'

Shaw held up both hands. 'The key to this is that one of the victims in the Mondeo was Jonathan Tessier's grandmother. The dog was hers. Jonathan was fond of his grandmother — but fonder of the dog. After the accident he pestered his parents to have the dog — a request they couldn't meet. They told him the dog had died in the accident. The investigating team had kept the truth under wraps — a detail they'd use to weed out false witnesses and crackpot confessions. And I think they were troubled by the detail too — because it didn't, and doesn't — seem to fit the picture.' Shaw got up and walked to the window.

'Go on,' Warren said, forced to push his chair back and swivel it to see Shaw clearly.

'OK,' said Shaw, turning to face them. 'So, the gang drove off in the car that night from Castle Rising. Every uniformed officer on the force was out looking for a two-tone damaged Mini. The CCTV didn't give us a plate number, so that's all they had to go on. We now know that Cosyns's family owned two of the lock-up garages on the Westmead — numbers 51 and 52. Last September, as you know, inside those lock-ups, George and I discovered the rusted body of a two-tone Mini — partly resprayed an industrial yellow. It's undoubtedly the car from the accident. The paint they used for the respray came from a factory where three of the gang worked — Askit's Engineering. Flecks of yellow paint were found on Jonathan Tessier's clothes and there are traces of the same paint still on the rusted Mini in the lock-up. There was also a single paint fragment from the Mondeo on Jonathan's football shirt. Two pieces of unique forensic evidence, sir, which link the crash to the murder.'

Shaw perched on the window ledge.

'This is what we think happened on the day Jonathan died. It was three days after the crash at Castle Rising. He was playing football on the grass below the flats, sent out for the day because his grandfather was with his parents — in the middle of a breakdown in the aftermath of his wife's death in the hit-and-run. Someone boots the ball off the pitch and it bounces off down past some shops, out of sight. Jonathan wanders after it and never comes back. He was bored, anyway, because he didn't like football and he'd only been told to go out for the day so that his grandfather could grieve with his daughter.

'We think Jonathan ended up down by the lock-up garages on the edge of the Westmead. We think that somehow he stumbled on the missing puppy. Maybe one of the gang was taking it for a walk — after all, our press statements hadn't mentioned the dog, so the gang probably thought we weren't going to be bothered about a missing terrier when two people had died in the crash. Or maybe it just got out of the lock-up, I don't know. But what I do know is, as soon as that boy saw the dog, sir, he was dead.'

Shaw let the silence stretch so that all they

could hear was the tap, tap of Warren's secretary typing on her keyboard.

'No one could have stopped that child going home and telling his parents he'd found the dog. We can be pretty sure Jonathan never left the lock-up alive. It would have been impossible for the gang to let him leave: the only thing he wanted in life was the puppy. If they gave it to him the police would be at the lock-up within hours. So they couldn't give it to him, and they couldn't let him tell anyone he'd seen it. They could have told him it wasn't his grandma's dog, but he wouldn't have believed them. They could have tried a bribe, but it wouldn't have worked, and they knew it.'

The door opened and Warren's secretary put three cups and a cafetière of coffee on the desk. Shaw poured, added sugar for Valentine, milk for Warren, taking his own black and unsweetened.

Shaw let the silence re-establish itself. There was absolutely no doubt now that he had Warren's full attention.

Shaw sat down. 'For nearly fifteen years Robert Mosse, and the rest of them, thought they'd got away with it,' said Shaw. 'Two members of the gang left Lynn: James Voyce emigrated to New Zealand and Chris Robins moved to the Midlands and a life of petty crime that deteriorated into mental illness. Alex Cosyns stayed. And we know now why, in part, he did stay. Subtly but persistently he milked Mosse for cash. Mosse is clearly in a vulnerable position. He has a thriving career in the law, a position that makes him a prime target for blackmail. The

60

gang were all fans of stock-car racing — speed and cars is what brought them together — and Mosse set up a team under the name 'Team Mosse' about ten years ago. Cosyns was his only driver. In effect, he bankrolled Cosyns's hobby. And we think that, over the years, he'd been giving him money as well.'

Warren slapped his fist down on the desk. 'Hold on. This is nonsense. How could Cosyns have blackmailed Mosse? He could have come to us, told us the truth, but then he'd have been in the dock too. Doesn't add up, Peter.'

'Well . . . no. Not completely. But consider this: Mosse's career is over if there is any hint of scandal. He's up for the Bar this year. He's got a lot to lose. Plus, we don't know which of the gang killed the child. What if it was Mosse, and only Mosse? That changes things.' Shaw thought about that. 'No — it *transforms* things. And remember, this is a gentle, persistent, form of blackmail, not the usual one-off demand. A grand here, a grand there. Worth it, surely, from Mosse's point of view, for a quiet life? But I agree — Cosyns would still have been facing some very serious charges if he'd informed on Mosse. No, there's something else at the heart of this relationship. We just don't know what it is yet.'

Shaw sipped the coffee, holding it just below his mouth so that the steam played on his lips.

'What we do know is that, as soon as George and I started to come close to the truth, Mosse decided he needed to improve his security. By this time Robins was in a secure psychiatric unit not far from here — near Sutton Bridge. As you know, Robins took his own life last May by cutting his wrists with a pocket knife — a brand-new one. He had a visitor shortly before he died. One of the orderlies recalls the face — and says it could have been Mosse.'

' 'Could have been' isn't good enough,' said Warren. 'We've already been through this — '

'So that was Robins out of the way,' said Shaw, pressing on. 'As you also know, I found Cosyns dead in the lock-up garage last September when we found the Mini.'

Warren slopped coffee into his cup and struggled with a tube of sweeteners. Shaw couldn't stop an image from that day surfacing — Cosyns lying under the exhaust of his stock car, its engine running. He'd tried to revive him but had been attacked by an unseen assailant. He'd have died right there if George Valentine hadn't turned up at the scene, having trailed Mosse's BMW to the lock-ups. It was an unpalatable fact, but he owed Valentine his life.

'Mosse had ample time to stage Cosyns's suicide,' he continued. 'There is no evidence that Cosyns had any reason to kill himself. There is, however, evidence that Cosyns was force-fed narcotics prior to the 'attempt' to take his own life.'

Warren leant back in his chair, the legs creaking. 'But we can't stick it on Mosse, can we? Otherwise we wouldn't be here.'

'Doesn't mean the fucker didn't do it. Sir,' said Valentine, shifting his weight on his thigh bone to ease the pressure on his bladder.

Warren gave Valentine a look which consti-tuted a written warning.

'I beg your pardon?'

Shaw raised a hand. 'You'll recall that Mosse says he went to the lock-up that evening after the stock-car racing at the Norfolk Arena to talk about the performance of the car Cosyns had driven that day. He'd won. Mosse says he wanted to enter the car at a meeting in Peterborough the following weekend. All explicable as part of 'Team Mosse'. Then he left. He said Cosyns was depressed about the failure of his marriage and the continuing financial burden of the regular maintenance payments he was being forced to make. He admits giving £1,000 to Cosyns shortly before his death as a favour. He admits he'd done it before. He says they were friends. More than that — family.'

Shaw finished the coffee. 'So: a gang of four. Guilty of murder. Two dead.'

'So where's the third man?' asked Warren, hooked now by the narrative, despite himself.

'Voyce arrived back in the UK from New Zealand three months ago,' said Valentine. His bladder ached like a bad tooth now and his craving for nicotine was making the saliva drain from his mouth.

'Since then we'd lost him,' added Shaw. 'Until two days ago, when he checked into the Novotel on the bypass here in Lynn.'

He'd deliberately left this new information until last and he could see that Warren was furious that he was being manipulated.

'Why wasn't I informed about this?'

'It's taken us that long to be sure it's our man. We had an alert out with all the hotels, B&Bs, the lot.'

Warren looked from Shaw's face to Valentine's and back again.

'The Auckland police tell us that Voyce is married, with one child,' said Shaw. 'He's a garage attendant — pump man, cashier, low-end mechanics. Earns a pittance. His wife works at the local supermarket. It's pretty clear he could do with a bit more money. My guess . . . ' Shaw looked at his hands, then at Valentine. 'Our guess is that's why he's back here — to tap Mosse, just like Cosyns did. We think he knew Cosyns was getting cash out of Mosse, and we're pretty sure he now knows he's dead — which might explain the three months lying low before making his move and coming back to Lynn.

'I don't think he can afford to go home empty handed. We reckon he's been biding his time, coming up with a plan, and now he's ready. As far as we know he hasn't made contact with Mosse yet. We propose round-the-clock surveillance. If he makes a move on Mosse then his life will undoubtedly be in danger. We can bug Voyce's hotel room, maybe his car, and hope that Mosse incriminates himself on tape.'

Warren reached for the cafetière, then shook it, annoyed that only the dregs remained. 'So. You think that's smart . . . Police entrapment with a corpse as a possible first prize?'

Shaw looked through Warren, focusing on a point just behind his head, a technique his father had used to effect on his only son. 'With respect, sir. If we're right — and we are — Mosse is responsible, either solely or collectively, for the deaths of at least four people: Jonathan Tessier, the elderly passengers left to die at Castle Rising and Alex Cosyns. He also very probably assisted the suicide of Chris Robins. And there are . . . ' he searched for the words, 'other consequences of this man's perjury.'

Shaw thought of the last time he'd seen his father, lying propped up in a hospital bed after a third, massive, stroke, his face already undergoing the process which would transform it into a death mask.

Valentine shifted in his seat. It was a measure of the degree to which he'd buried his emotions for the last thirteen years that the simple fact that they might at last bring Robert Mosse to justice had made his eyes flood.

Warren looked at his watch, frustrated to find that so much of his life seemed to be about stopping one thing he didn't like doing in order to start something he didn't like doing even more. He went to a mirror on the wall and set his peaked cap straight, but Shaw calculated that his superior officer was carefully considering what he said next.

'All right. I'll give you ten days. You can peel off the manpower from the murder unit. Then that's it. Case closed. If it's not wrapped up by then, I'll burn the sodding file myself.'

He stood and looked at Shaw, some of the belligerence which had once made him such an effective police officer returning. 'I am making you, Peter, personally responsible for Voyce's safety. Screw up and you will look upon George's career as a sparkling success. The highlight of your working week for the next twenty years will be lecturing on speed awareness courses to spotty boy-racers. And I'm still expecting a result on the body in the cemetery. Now, get out, both of you.'

6

A freezing fog the colour of pickled eggs had fallen on the waterfront as Shaw drove alone down to South Lynn: under the black bones of the quayside cranes, a Meccano set lost in the gloom, then round at the Millfleet into the gridiron of streets around All Saints. He was aware that the Porsche — black, polished and sleek — turned heads in this poor neighbourhood. He'd chosen it because it had a narrow 'A' bar — the stanchion which separates the windscreen from the side windows. In most modern cars the 'A' bar was at least a couple of inches thick — a considerable handicap for someone with only one eye. He'd taken advice from websites set up to help the partially sighted and found the cash to pick the car up third-hand. The bodywork was dented here and there, the engine well past its sell-by date, but even so, parked overnight on these streets it would be gone by daybreak, or up on bricks minus its spoked alloy wheels.

He slowed to take a corner by Whitefriars primary school and noted a man standing back on the pavement, most of his body hidden in an overhanging hedge of copper beech laced with snow. He wasn't standing still: one arm jerked without rhythm, his head ticking like a metronome, and he was greeting the freezing fog in a T-shirt emblazoned with red letters that spelt

67

ESPAÑA. He watched the Porsche balefully as it crept past.

Shaw rang the control room at St James's on his hands-free mobile, reporting the dealer's presence. Most of Lynn's drugs came in off the ships, peddled in pubs and a handful of town-centre clubs. Street-selling was rare, and Shaw guessed this man was desperate to fund his own habit; desperate and disorientated, because trying to peddle outside a primary school was not the recommended first step in a career as a drug baron. The lack of topcoat suggested he hadn't come far to his pitch, so he was probably a resident of the brutal block of low-rise flats which clustered around All Saints — a cordon of concrete that effectively encircled the medieval splendour of the old church.

The Porsche cut through the street-mist until the lines of terraced houses petered out. Shaw trundled the car forward along the narrow quay — the river to one side, the tide low enough to reveal the thin grey outline of a wrecked wooden barge on the near sandbank, the cemetery on his left showing glimpses of hawthorn and cedar crated with snow. Early-morning dog walkers had hung plastic bags on the railings, like offerings for the dead. He could just see the outline of the Flask, no lights showing in the three floors of its timbered façade.

At the cemetery gates he found DC Jacky Lau by her parked Mégane. Lau's car was adapted for rallying, with a complete set of spoilers, multiple spotlights and a trio of go-faster stripes. She was leaning on the car, staring into her mobile phone. Outside the office she always wore reflective sunglasses. She was ethnic Chinese, and possessed a kind of unpredictable energy which matched her driving. She was respected in the squad, but not especially liked. Her ambition, to make DI within five years, was naked. When she wasn't pursuing that ambition she was wrapped up in her hobby: cars, and the men who drove them.

'Sir,' she pushed herself off the car's bonnet with her thighs. 'Paul said to meet you here. Cemetery's still sealed off. Forensics are down by the open graves. I'm leading house-to-house, starting at nine — St James's are sending a dozen uniforms down for the day. What are we looking for here?'

It was a good question. Shaw took in a lungful of fog. 'For now, stick to the houses overlooking the cemetery. Anything over the years, I suppose . . . ' He suddenly felt the weight of the task before them — solving a crime at a distance of nearly three decades. 'See if any group is known to hang around the place regularly after dark — druggies, lovers etc. We don't know when chummy got dumped, but it's probably way back. Throw in Nora Tilden's name — if anyone remembers the funeral, get a full account. Names, anything unusual . . . you know the routine.'

He wondered what was going on behind the reflective glasses. 'We should have more from Tom and Justina to go on later.'

He left her making a note and walked on through the open gates of Flensing Meadow

Cemetery, the visibility down to twenty yards so that his world was reduced to a circular arena of tombstones and the path cutting through them, the only movement coming from the crows that flitted in and out of view over his head as they swapped branches in the trees, prompting showers of damp snowflakes. He wondered whether the silence of graveyards was an illusion. He strained his ears to catch the swish of traffic on the new bridge and — just once — the distant crackle of a police radio.

He'd left Valentine back at St James's organizing the bugging and surveillance of Jimmy Voyce. Max Warren had given them ten days and it would take twenty-four hours to put a unit fully in place. The priority was to get listening devices into Voyce's hotel room and, if they could, into the car he'd hired. Twine had been scouring the airline passenger lists and had just discovered that Voyce was booked on a flight to Auckland via Hong Kong leaving in six days' time.

That was a break: if Voyce was going to try to blackmail Robert Mosse his timetable was actually narrower than theirs. Today they needed to get a rough idea of Voyce's movements so that they could time the bugging operation — and obtain a court order allowing them to carry it out. Once Valentine had got the ball rolling he was due to meet Shaw at eleven to interview Lizzie Tilden, now Lizzie Murray — Nora Tilden's daughter and, in her own turn, owner and landlady of the Flask.

The cemetery chapel came into view. When

Shaw pushed open the Gothic-arched door he was surprised by the efficient hum of activity, and the mechanical gasps of a coffee maker. Twine had put in place a standard incident room in record time: desks, phone lines, internet link and a screened area for interviews. Outside, the St James's mobile canteen was still on site; beside it was a 4×4 Ford with CAMBRIDGE ARCHAEOLOGICAL TRUST tastefully signwritten in gold on the passenger door. Despite the early hour Twine had found two civilian switchboard operators to answer the phones. A perspex display board in front of the altar was covered in photographs taken at the graveside and one that Shaw hadn't expected — an enlarged black-and-white shot of a woman in her mid-fifties, greying hair pulled back off her face. It was a hard face, and no doubt she'd had a hard life to go with it, but Shaw doubted it had been *that* hard. A Victorian face, shipwrecked in the twenty-first century: a round head, puffy, with no discernible bone structure; a cannonball, the small black eyes lost in the flesh.

Twine brought him a coffee.

'Paul,' said Shaw, looking round. 'Well done. This her?'

'Nora Elizabeth Tilden. *Lynn News* archive, 1981 — just a year before she died. Taken at a charity presentation at the Flask — raised three hundred pounds for Barnardo's. Looks like a tough bit of work,' he added.

Shaw took a closer look, thinking for the first

time what a mismatched couple they seemed: Nora Tilden and her fun-loving errant husband, Alby.

DC Fiona Campbell unfolded herself from the nearest desk. She stood six feet two but tried to look shorter, shoulders slightly rounded, always in sensible flat shoes. Campbell was a copper from a family of coppers — her father a DCI at Norwich. She'd come out of school with the kind of A-levels that could have got her into university — any university. But this was her life. And she wasn't just smart. She'd earned her street stripes the hard way. The scar on her throat — an eight-inch knife wound from ear to collarbone — was a livid blue. She'd received a Police Bravery Award for trying to disarm a man with a knife who had been determined to take his own life. She'd put the medal in a box, but she'd wear the scar for ever.

'Sir. You wanted to talk to the gravediggers?' she asked, shuffling a handful of papers. 'All gravedigging was done by the council's Direct Labour Unit until five years ago. Now it's contracted out to a private outfit, but it's the same people doing the digging. There's a hut . . . '

Shaw let her lead the way. Shrugging on a full-length overcoat, she pushed open the door of the old chapel and walked out into the mist. She hunched her shoulders a bit more once they were out in the cold. The damp was extraordinary this close to the river. Droplets covered Campbell's coat like sequins. They walked together away from the chapel on a slowly curving path edged with savagely pruned rose bushes. In the folded silence of the mist they could hear the forensic team still working down by Nora Tilden's grave, the sharp metallic tap of a tool striking a pebble preternaturally clear.

'Anything from Tom?' asked Shaw. This was the third major inquiry Shaw had led with this team and they'd learned the value of sharing information within a tight-knit circle. He was confident DC Campbell would be up to speed.

'No — nothing. Paul says everything the Cambridge team has found so far has been *inside* the coffins, with documentation to match.'

Soon a stand of pine trees came into view, shielding a set of ramshackle outbuildings lit by a security light that struggled to penetrate the fog. A Portakabin door opened, letting a cat slip out, its black fur bristling. They caught a thin blast of a radio tuned to Classic FM. A man appeared on the threshold in a Day-Glo yellow workman's jacket, tipping out a coffee mug.

'Hey up,' he said over his shoulder. He stood aside to let Shaw and Campbell into the single room. It had no windows, only air vents that did little to disperse the fug of heat and burning paraffin from the enclosed space. A single neon tube provided scant illumination.

Shaw closed the door and leant against it while Campbell took the one vacant seat. The room was chaotic. Against one wall stood a row of metal lockers. There was a table around which three men sat, a bench holding a kettle and mugs, and a gas ring attached to a fuel bottle. Waves of heat rolled out of an industrial paraffin heater. The floor was crowded with tools, coats, stuffed black bin-liners, here and there split to reveal the rubbish inside them. The space the men occupied was reduced to where they sat.

The metal walls were damp with condensation, their only adornment a calendar, curled so much that Shaw could see only the girl's face, a fake smile failing to mask her boredom.

'This won't take long,' said Shaw, addressing them all. 'You'll know what we've found — a body on top of a coffin, sharing a grave it had no right to be in. So I need to know the usual procedure before and after a funeral.'

The three men looked at each other and the youngest, who drank from a tin of Red Bull, began to fiddle with a roll-up machine and a tin of Golden Virginia. 'Yeah, procedure,' he said. 'Got to follow the rules.'

The man in the Day-Glo jacket, who appeared to be in charge, introduced himself simply as 'Michael' and said he'd been working in the town's cemeteries for thirty years — first at Gayton and now Flensing Meadow — and the routine for a burial was unchanged. The council had set down procedures, as had their union — and everyone was a member.

They all nodded at that, the youngster licking his roll-up.

'Mind you,' said Michael, 'the crew they've got in to move the bones off the riverside, they're not union — just cheap labour. No rules for them.'

'Scabs,' said the kid with the Red Bull.

'Right,' said Shaw. 'I see. But the normal procedure for burial . . . '

Michael composed himself. First thing on the day of the funeral the grave was dug by two men. Nine feet by four feet, he said. If the grave was for one coffin then it was five feet deep — allowing the statutory three feet of clearance above. One of the men operated the mechanical digger, the other set down duckboards for access to the graveside. In the days before the digger it took two men two hours to dig by hand. The union had managed to keep it a two-man job — but only on safety grounds. With one man on the digger, there had to be a stand-by in case of accidents.

In poor weather a shelter could be set over the open grave to stop flooding.

They all laughed, but it was the third man, who hadn't spoken until then, who said, 'Useless — they're all wet here. Every one. Down with a splash.' He was in his mid-twenties, with hair prematurely slate grey; handsome, but when he told Shaw his name was Dan he revealed broken teeth.

'Then we cover the grave with a board,' said Michael, nodding back down the shadowy room to the far end where they could see a set of reinforced wooden panels. 'These days we put artificial turf at the edges and lay some over the spoil. The pall-bearers arrange the floral tributes on the turf. Some mourners scatter earth in

— or throw a flower, that kind of thing. Since Diana, all sorts goes on.'

The three of them nodded at this truth.

'We fill the grave in at the end of the service. We don't rush people, but some days it's busy. So we keep an eye out; then, when the mourners leave, we fill in the grave — usually with the digger again. Takes ten minutes.'

'But you always wait?' asked Campbell.

'Absolutely — don't want to upset no one.'

Campbell nodded, knowing that wasn't true. She'd been to an aunt's funeral at Gayton the month before and she'd had to walk her mother away from the graveside, away from the sound of the earth and pebbles falling on her sister's coffin.

'Then what?' asked Shaw, rolling his shoulders. Michael looked at him and Shaw guessed that for the first time he'd noticed the detective's moon-eye.

He stabbed a finger at a piece of A3 paper Sellotaped to the wall. 'There's a schedule. We go back to check on subsidence — after twenty-four hours, then a week, then every fortnight. When there's no more movement we let the masons know and they put the stone in — that's usually a good six months, maybe more. Then we hand over to the gardeners. If the family's paid, they keep it tidy, maybe even plant flowers. If not, they just gang mow the grass.'

He laughed, and there was something in his eyes that Shaw thought was more than graveyard humour. 'Then they rot.'

Dan lit the gas ring and set the kettle on it, the

hissing sound loud in the enclosed space. As he waited for it to boil he stood, running a hand through the slate-grey hair.

'So this grave — the one we're interested in. This was 1982 — anyone we could talk to who might have been there?' asked Shaw.

Michael rubbed the heel of his palm into his chin, across a week's worth of stubble. 'Freddie Fletcher's your only chance. He packed his job in a few years ago — before I came in from Gayton. He took the redundancy money when we all got switched to the private sector. He's kept himself busy.'

All three workmen smiled in precisely the same way, inwardly sharing a secret.

'Where can I find him?' asked Shaw.

'Not far. He's got an office — but you'll never find it. I'll take you. I need to get breakfast for these boys, anyway.'

He stood, putting a donkey jacket over his Day-Glo tunic.

But Shaw hadn't finished. 'Sorry — this grave — the one we're interested in down by the river. The burial was the second in the plot — there'd been a child in 1948. Then the mother in 1982. So, how does that change things?'

'The kid's coffin would have been sunk lower,' said Michael. 'Parents often want to go with their kids, so they'd have dug it deeper to start with, leaving room for another one on top.'

Shaw went to open the door but DC Campbell had one last question. 'The gravedigging procedure — you're saying it wouldn't have been any different in 1982?'

Michael shook his head. 'Apart from they'd have dug it by hand — and filled it by hand, too. Takes longer. But otherwise, no — just the same.'

'Unless there's a piss-up,' said the kid with the roll-up machine, who'd made two cigarettes already, lining them up on the Formica table top, and was now constructing a third.

The two older men exchanged a quick glance but Shaw caught it — and a hint of what was in it: a flash of anger, something quick-witted and cynical.

Shaw let Campbell run with the questions, knowing that she'd realize she'd hit gold. 'How d'you mean?' she said, making her voice as light as possible, standing and buttoning up her coat to go, as if the answer didn't matter.

The kid had picked up none of the vibes and was still looking at his rolling machine, smiling to himself. Dan and Michael — Shaw could see — were desperate to intervene, desperate to stop him talking, but unwilling to speak.

'If there's a wake close by — they might use the old chapel on Whitefriars, or the school hall at the primary, something like that — then we sometimes tag along, pall-bearers too. Put the board over and fill it in later. Like — you aren't gonna get a complaint from whoever's down there, are you? And you might get a glass, out the back. One of the perks. If it's in the Flask, we always go — 'cos they serve out the yard window to the riverbank, and if there's a free bar they just pass us a few bevvies. Does no harm.'

Shaw zipped up his jacket, the RNLI motif on

the left breast pocket. 'Nora Tilden — the woman in the grave we're concerned with — she was the landlady at the Flask.'

The kid whistled. 'Then that, my friend, was a piss-up to be at.' He laughed, and it didn't seem to worry him that he laughed alone.

7

'Jason's pretty much a tosser,' said Michael, leading Shaw away through the tombstones, across the soaking grass. 'But he's right — you know, we're all human. But it's rare — really rare. It's just in this job the perks are few and far between. So, chance of a free bevvy, course we go. But we'd be back in, what, an hour? Less. And we'd see, we'd look — if there was anything there, we'd see it.'

Shaw didn't answer as he followed the track Michael was making through the grass. He doubted very much that they would notice if the level of the grave was higher than they'd left it. And after a skinful of free beer he didn't think they'd be at their most observant. A winter's afternoon, the light fading, keen to get by a fire, or back to the wake. It might have happened like that. It could well have happened like that. He'd left Campbell to take a statement from Jason, just for the record.

He rang Valentine on the mobile for an update. The surveillance squad on Voyce had struck lucky — he'd gone out first thing for breakfast in town so they'd slipped in and wired the single room — two mics, one in the light fitting, one in the bedside phone. They'd set up in a room on the same floor and were monitoring round the clock. Shaw decided not to ask if the warrant had arrived in time. They

80

arranged to meet at the Flask in an hour.

The mist in the cemetery seemed to be closing in, and all Shaw could see was gravestones and the figure ahead, making a track through the snow.

'I'm sorry,' said Shaw. 'It's Michael . . . '

'Brindle,' he said, stopping suddenly and looking around at the tombstones in the mist. 'There,' he said, pointing to the outline of a stone wall which had come into sight. 'The east gate.' He led the way to an ironwork door set in the wall and selected a key from the bunch hanging from his belt.

'It's a short cut,' he said, motioning Shaw through. They emerged onto one of South Lynn's dead-end streets, one of many in a dead-end town. To the left Shaw could hear the traffic on the distant London Road, lorries churning gears in the mist, but to the right the street ran into a wall of white, where he knew the edge of the Nar would lie in its deep channel. Opposite was a small café Shaw had never seen before: a converted front room, the condensation obscuring the interior.

A handwritten sign above the door read TINOS.

Inside, eight tables were crammed full, largely with council workmen in road-digger gear. Full English breakfasts congealed on off-white plates, while behind the metal-topped counter a man in a vest was squirting steam into a pot, the sound obliterating the nasal whine of KL.FM — the town's local radio station.

Brindle nodded to the man, ordered three

breakfast baps and led Shaw through a door marked TOILET into a hallway, then doubled back up a narrow staircase. The door at the top was preceded by a metal security frame on which had been fastened a hand-painted sign.

P.E.N.
THE PARTY OF ENGLISH NATIONALISM
LYNN FOR OUR OWN FOLK

'Keeps Freddie busy,' said Brindle, grinning at Shaw but giving up on the conspiracy when he saw the expression on the DI's face. As they waited outside the locked door he looked down at his feet.

Their footsteps had announced their arrival, and Shaw could hear someone turning a key. By the time the office door was open he had his warrant card out, straight-armed, in the occupant's face.

'DI Shaw, King's Lynn CID. Just a few questions, sir.'

Freddie Fletcher was bald, a sculpted head, bony, like a clenched fist, the skin shiny as if it had been polished. In contrast, the visible skin that wasn't on his head was covered in black hair — his chest where the shirt was open, his wrists, and the backs of his hands. He was in his fifties, perhaps younger, and remarkably alive — grey eyes, dove-grey, which locked onto Shaw's without flinching.

Shaw looked around the room. In the centre was an oak desk. One wall was dominated by a map of Lynn, the various council wards marked out. He knew that in the last district elections the BNP had done well in Gaywood, one of the wards on the outskirts of town. The town was on the edge of the new BNP heartland — rural East Anglia — where the party could tap into anxieties about migrant farm workers. And there had been a charm offensive, too; an attempt to play down the party's violent and racist past — lots of community work, helping the elderly, fundraising for the local working-men's club. Not a word about repatriation for blacks and Asians — but then in Lynn, as in much of the surrounding area, that wasn't an issue. But he'd never heard of the PEN. A splinter group, perhaps.

'Give me a sec,' said Fletcher, walking away to the window with a mobile to his ear. Shaw judged his height at five-eight, five-ten at most.

On the desk was a pile of leaflets, fliers for a forth-coming concert:

THE OLD SONGS ARE THE BEST
Hear some of Lynn's famous sea shanties
performed by the Whitefriars Choir
Nar Bank Social Club

Monday, 3 January 2011

All proceeds to local charities

The PEN motif was in the bottom right-hand corner, the size of a thumbprint.

Fletcher killed his call and took the captain's chair behind the desk. Shaw and Brindle sat on a short bench against one wall.

'Can I help?' He picked up a pen and leant back, like a bank manager considering a loan. But his fingers were a working-man's fingers — fat and inflexible. On the desk was a framed picture, turned to face visitors, showing Fletcher at a back-garden barbecue, his arms round two children.

'Maybe,' said Shaw. 'It's about a burial on Flensing Meadow — 1982. The graves are being exhumed because of the flooding, and something has been found — something that shouldn't have been there. A body.'

'It's a graveyard — what did you expect to find?'

'An *unidentified* body,' Shaw continued, 'on top of the coffin in one of the graves.'

Fletcher's fleshy eyelids slid down, fluttered, as if he'd been asked a tricky maths question. 'Oh, right. Where, exactly?'

'Down towards the riverbank, a few feet from a big Victorian stone tomb.'

'Yeah, I know where you mean. Well, in that case there's a good chance it's one of mine.'

Brindle shifted on the pew. 'It's Nora Tilden's — Lizzie's mum.'

Fletcher's eyes widened. 'Christ. Of course — yeah. I was on that.' He laughed, bringing both hands together to cover his mouth. 'The husband killed her, you know that. Alby, they called him. Scum. Nobody ever understood why she took him back. He'd been off on the ships, sleeping with blacks. Came back with what he deserved as well — riddled with it. Christ! And

84

she took him back into her bed.'

He leant forward, as if to share a secret. 'He even had a picture of one of the women — a tattoo, on his back. A black.'

Fletcher tried a smile of incredulity on Shaw, a glint of gold dental work catching the light.

Shaw tried hard to make sure Fletcher didn't see him swallow, his mouth dry with anger. 'So you went back for a drink that day — to the wake at the pub? The grave would have been left open?'

Fletcher worked his palm over the black stubble on his face.

'Yeah. Course. We all knew Nora. And he'd been banged up for it — so that was a celebration. We'd have covered the grave — but if you're asking if someone could have chucked a body in and we'd miss it, then I guess the answer to that is yes, it's possible.'

Brindle shifted in his seat.

'So you would have filled it in by nightfall? It was November — so before five?'

'Problem was,' said Fletcher, 'it wasn't really a wake — like I said, more of a party. Nora ran a strict house, Inspector. No swearing, no dancing, no singing. If she caught you enjoying yourself, you were barred for life.' The glint of dental work again. 'Fact is, while she was a pillar of the community, the pub was like a morgue — had been since the war. Alby used to drink down the Albatross on his night off, that's how bad it was. So when she died the great and good turned out, but they fucked off as soon as the cucumber sandwiches were gone. Then the party kicked off. Lizzie's not her mother's daughter . . . Lizzie likes a party. Still does. So we had one. A corker.'

Shaw had decent radar when it came to listening to a witness. So far he felt Fletcher had worked with the truth. But he sensed something else, a guardedness.

'None of which answers my question, Mr Fletcher. The time that you filled in the grave.'

'We didn't. At least, not that night. I went back up next morning — me and the hangover. Filled it in by spade with Will Stokes.' He held up a hand. 'He's dead — has been for years, so he's not getting any better. You'll have to take my word for it. That would have been ten, maybe half ten, the morning after.'

Shaw looked at a poster over Fletcher's shoulder; it was of Fletcher's face, jaw set, a Churchillian squint. 'The corpse that we found — there's every chance the man in question was black. That would have been rare then, in Lynn?' asked Shaw.

Fletcher leant back, hands behind his head, revealing grey patches of sweat at his armpits.

'You'd be surprised. We had 'em all right. Still do. The bus company took on some from Peterborough, the Queen Vic's got 'em on the nursing staff — few of the doctors. But not many — you're right. Spot on a domino.' Cruelly, Shaw wished Valentine had been there to hear that coming from Fletcher's mouth. 'But there's a touch of the tarbrush in a few of the schools — even round 'ere.'

Fletcher placed his hands flat on the desk, a visible effort to maintain his self-control. 'But

86

they're not a concern to us.' Fletcher's tone of voice had lightened, and Shaw sensed he'd slipped into a stock stump speech. 'It's the Poles, the Portuguese, the Serbs — all kinds of Eastern rubbish. And we sympathize with you, Inspector. All the policemen who have to deal with 'em — 'cos your hands are tied, right? The law — that's one of the things we need to change. 'Cos you have to admit — '

'Actually, I don't,' said Shaw. It was one of the many things he found distasteful about people like Freddie Fletcher, the need to find converts. 'I've never heard of the PEN,' he added.

'You will. BNP's gone soft round 'ere. Someone needed to keep the flame alive. So I left — set up in South Lynn. They'll want me back one day.'

Shaw wondered if Fletcher had been booted out. That was a grubby badge of honour. 'And for future reference, Mr Fletcher, Portugal is in western Europe. So that would make them Western rubbish, if any kind. But for the record — that night at the Flask, or at the funeral, were there any black faces?'

Fletcher pinched his fat chin. 'Yeah — two of them, from the Free.'

Shaw could see that his witness had become hostile.

'Which is?' asked Shaw, standing, going over behind Fletcher to look out of the window. In the street a council Scarab was parked in the gutter. And behind Fletcher's desk he noted a box in the corner, cardboard, full of second-hand toddlers' toys.

'Church,' he said, throwing a thumb over his right shoulder. 'The Free Church, on Tope Street. Nonconformists. Reformed Baptists. Nora was one of 'em . . . one of the *Elect*.' He lingered on the word, as if it was of value in itself. 'That's what they call 'em — 'the Elect'. Anyway, blacks go — always have done. They were against slavery, see? So they had to let 'em in when they were free. Bit fucked-up like that.' He faked a belly laugh.

'Could you give me some names?' said Shaw.

Fletcher swung round in the seat, looking at Shaw, the hint of a smile in the eyes. 'Didn't know they had names. What next, eh?'

Brindle shifted in his seat again, and Shaw noticed the blood had drained from his face.

But Fletcher couldn't stop himself now. 'I got six hundred votes last time, less than fifty the time before that. The BNP got thirteen per cent of the vote in one ward. Twice what the Greens got. It's coming, Inspector. Doesn't matter what the party's called. It's the message that counts. It's a message that's getting through.'

Shaw didn't respond, but stood, studying a notice-board crowded with posters, business cards, a few snapshots of what looked like BNP outings: one on the beach at Hunstanton by the funfair, everyone pale white, trying to get a tan.

'How about a ticket for the annual Christmas fundraiser, Inspector?' Fletcher waggled a bunch of multicoloured raffle tickets. 'Nice bit of grub at the Shipwrights' Hall. I've taken a whole table on behalf of the Flask — shows we support our local community.'

He came round the desk and tapped a finger on a printed menu he'd pinned to the wall. 'Good British fare,' said Fletcher. 'Better than that, even ... ' He stabbed a finger on the starter. '*Local* fare.'

Shaw let his eye run down the menu — each item accompanied by a brief account of its sourcing.

Norfolk Turkey

Supplied by C. J. Tilte & Sons of West Norfolk

'Food this community has been catching and eating for centuries. None of your foreign muck,' added Fletcher, standing at his shoulder, as Shaw noted the starter.

Olde Lynn Fish Soup

Supplied by Fisher Fleet Shellfish, and the Clockcase Cannery, West Lynn

Shaw thought about the turkey they'd had last year — Jamaican-style jerk turkey, marinated in scallion and garlic.

'I'll stick to Christmas dinner with the family,' he said. 'One's enough for me.' He was astonished to see that of all the things he'd said to Fletcher, this was the one that made him break eye contact.

'We'll need to take a statement, Mr Fletcher,' he added, avoiding a handshake. 'You'll be here later?'

Fletcher spread his hands as if he never left the

room. 'If not, there's always a note on the door.'

They left him and clattered down the bare wooden steps into the steamy fug of the café. Brindle collected three greasy bags from the counter, their contents now cool and congealing. Shaw thanked Brindle and walked up the street, opting to take the long way round to the cemetery gates where he had left the Porsche. It was a bit early to be assessing suspects, he thought, but there was every reason to keep a close eye on Freddie Fletcher. But despite the fact the man had had opportunity, and his own twisted motive, he felt there was something profoundly ineffectual about Fletcher, something fundamentally weak. He couldn't imagine him delivering that fatal blow — although, he reminded himself, buttoning up his coat against the chill wind, it *had* been from behind.

8

The church stood on the corner of Whitefriars Street and Tope Street — a simple chapel of stark geometrical lines with long narrow windows in green glass. On the brickwork was a sign — a silver fish, two sinuous lines, crossing once to leave an open tail, just like the brooch on Nora Tilden's shroud but this one set above the door on which was a wooden panel, painted green, carrying the name.

THE FREE CHURCH OF CHRIST THE FISHERMAN

Shaw stopped, checked his tide watch and the mobile. He still had time before they were due to interview Nora Tilden's daughter Lizzie at the Flask. He was haunted by an image of the graveside on that day in 1982 when the family would have come together: the small crowd of local mourners and the two black faces amongst them, members — according to Freddie Fletcher — of 'the Free'.

Had one of them come to regret the decision to show respect, to claim a rightful place in that community? Times had changed in Lynn, the appearance of the east European migrant workers shifting popular prejudice away from the few black families in the town. But back then they would have been marked men: outsiders in a seafaring community renowned for its insularity. He wondered what Nora Tilden had felt about those black faces; she was a member of the 'Elect', in a church once dedicated to the emancipation of slaves.

But she also had a husband who'd left her to travel the world, finding comfort in the whorehouses of North Africa.

He heard footsteps and a figure walked out of the mist, as narrow as one of the chapel windows, the head held forward like a vulture's. Valentine was wrapped in his raincoat, holding the lapels at his throat, a cigarette lit. Shaw noted he'd picked up a new charity sticker: BARNAR-DO's, an orange sticky disc stuck over his heart.

'Pub's not open,' he said.

'George,' said Shaw, nodding at the chapel. 'Nora's church. Some of them turned up at the graveside that day — and two of them were black.' Low in the sky to the south the sun found a thin patch of mist and appeared as a disc, so that the two lines of the silver fish caught the light, like knives.

Valentine nodded, thinking of the wispy grey hair on Nora Tilden's skull.

Shaw filled him in on the rest of his interview with Freddie Fletcher.

'Suspect, then?' asked Valentine.

'Get Paul to organize a statement,' said Shaw, avoiding a direct answer, surveying the chapel's façcade.

'He's not just a racist, is he?' said Valentine. 'He knows the grave's open. And he knows whose job it is to fill it in. That's opportunity, that is.'

'I know,' said Shaw, pushing open the door so that they could step into the porch, lined with bibles stacked on shelves. He thought that despite his apparently casual indifference Valentine had a rare gift for seeing the bigger picture, for rising above the detail. He was right in one key respect. In this crime, opportunity was everything. The killer had to have known that the grave was still open.

Shaw picked up one of the bibles, seeing the words without seeing the meaning. They'd been read, all of them, almost to destruction. Several had lost their spines while others were spilling pages that had come free. He thought of the hands that had held them over the years, either open to read or closed and pressed to the chest in prayer. The thought made him feel like a visitor in a foreign land.

A further door led into the chapel itself. It was a simple room with whitewashed walls. Shaw was immediately aware that, once inside, it seemed to be both lighter and colder than outside. He thought he could smell the sea in here, too, and the illusion suggested the walls might be made of salt. In the silence the air rang, and held within it the sound of the sea, as if they were in a giant shell.

They walked down the aisle, some of the wooden parquet blocks in the floor rattling under their feet.

'Christ, it's cold in here,' said Valentine, rolling his shoulders. 'What are they? Methodists? A sect?' The last time Valentine had been in a church had been for his wife's funeral at All

Saints. It was whitewashed too, he recalled, and perhaps that was common in seagoing communities. The memory made him feel the guilt of the survivor.

Shaw turned to look back at a modest set of organ pipes set over the door by which they'd entered. 'Music, at least,' he said. 'Rest of it's a bit joyless.'

Set on either side of the pipes were two portraits in plain gold frames. To the right a man in a severe white wig, the face pinched, the cheeks slightly flushed. It was one of those rare images — Shaw guessed from the late eighteenth century — which actually looked like a human being, even if it was not a particularly attractive human being. The other portrait was of a black man: Caribbean black, with a fine red silk scarf at his throat. Shaw guessed he'd be in his twenties, perhaps thirty, the strong white teeth still intact, the skin tension taut, the eyes searching and intelligent. He couldn't fail to see again the skull they'd found on Nora Tilden's coffin. It too had once been clothed in a face like this.

'Who the hell are you?' asked Valentine, studying the picture, juggling a cigarette into his mouth.

'*He* is Olaudah Equiano,' said a voice behind them. Shaw jumped, despite himself, and Valentine coughed back an apology for the blasphemy, but the man was already laughing. 'While *you* . . . ?'

Shaw stepped forward, holding the warrant card at eye level. 'DI Peter Shaw — DS

Valentine. Just some routine inquiries.' Shaw wondered if anyone, anywhere, believed that cliché any more.

'It *is* a bit of a surprise — isn't it?' said the man, holding out a hand. 'I'm Pastor Abney, John Abney. Just 'John'.'

Shaw shook it, thinking the pastor was dressed like a travelling salesman, in a cheap suit with shiny black shoes. He looked like the kind of man who'd own a trouser press.

Abney studied the pictures. 'This man,' he said, opening a hand out to the portrait of the white man, as if offering a sugar lump to a horse. 'This man is our founder — Webster Barents. Barents was a follower of Wesley until he decided to set up the church here. That was in 1778. He was a patron of the arts — especially poetry and narratives written by slaves and ex-slaves. It was all part of the movement — the great movement against the slave trade.' As he said the word 'great' he raised his hands for emphasis. 'Equiano wrote an auto-biography in which he told the story of the *Zong* massacre — do you know this story?'

Valentine, tiring of the lecture, walked off, examining a list of the church's previous pastors written in white on black wood. Shaw leant against a pew end, folding his arms across his chest.

Abney ploughed on. 'The *Zong* was a ship, carrying slaves to the Americas from West Africa. Halfway through her passage it was clear that virtually none of the slaves would survive long ashore due to disease on board. The captain faced a dilemma. Under the insurance contract for the cargo — that's the slaves, of course — he would get nothing if he landed them alive and they died before sale. But if they died en route he would get his money — so he threw them overboard.'

Abney stopped for emphasis, and in the silence they heard a ship's foghorn out on the Cut.

'It was called the 'jettison clause' — and was perfectly legal. He threw a hundred and ten live slaves overboard, and ten more threw themselves over — as an act of empathy, I would guess, or possibly just despair. Anyway, Equiano's telling of this incident caused a sensation.'

Valentine coughed. He was pointing at the list of pastors.

'George Gayton Melville,' he said, '1807 to 1843.'

Shaw tried to work the generations out. It could be Nora's grandfather. 'The Melvilles,' he said. 'That's why we're here, Pastor. A woman called Nora Tilden, née Melville, was buried in the cemetery at Flensing Meadow in 1982 — we've just recovered her remains. There are some issues we need to clear up. She was buried wearing a silver fish — a brooch.'

'She was one of the Elect, then — those chosen to be saved by God.' Abney released a fold in his tie from beneath the waistcoat. On it was a small silver fish. 'George Gayton Melville was a wealthy merchant. A Cambridge man — Sidney Sussex. He bought and sold fish oil from the whaling trade. He paid for this building to be renovated and modernized out of his own pocket. And he bought the Flask.'

'The pastor bought a pub?' asked Valentine, smiling, 'That's my kind of religion.'

Abney studied his feet, but when he looked up the smile hadn't slipped. 'Well, all the pastors were — and are — part-timers like me. In civvy street I'm an insurance agent.' He looked at them as if this should be a great surprise. 'George was a merchant, as I said. When he bought the pub it was actually a kind of seaman's mission. There was always a bar, but also rooms, a small library, a soup kitchen — you know, hearty food for a few pennies. Beer was just what people drank then — you wouldn't have touched the water. But the bar was popular and it made him another fortune. Which provided the money to keep our church beautiful.'

Abney picked up an overcoat and started to shrug himself into it.

Behind him, in the east wall, a door Shaw hadn't noticed opened and a man stepped through carrying a coal scuttle.

'Ah,' said Abney. 'Just the man. I must go — but this is Sam Venn. Sam runs the London Road Shelter — you know, for the homeless. Great work. And, more importantly, he's our boiler man. It's all a bit antique, Victorian coal-fired. Only Sam knows how, like his father before him ... ' Abney stopped, suddenly inarticulate, as if he'd said something shocking.

He fumbled with the buttons on his raincoat. 'He'll know about this woman if anyone does.'

He turned to Venn. 'Nora Tilden, Sam? These gentlemen are from the police and they're making inquiries about her burial.' He looked at them all briefly, then said, 'Goodbye. A mystery — you can let me know what it's all about later.' He broadcast a smile.

Venn stood awkwardly still, watching the pastor leave. He was slight, with very narrow shoulders and an unsettling face: it slumped on one side, as if it had been made in wax and left in front of a fire, the effects of what Shaw guessed to be cerebral palsy. The right eye was much lower than the left, lazy and, Shaw guessed, blind. And the mouth on that side turned down as well. He was middle aged, dressed well in a thermal jacket and moleskin trousers, and he said nothing, instead waiting confidently for a question.

Shaw showed him his warrant card.

'Mr Venn,' he said. 'Nora Tilden. Does the name mean anything to you?'

Venn put the scuttle down and Shaw noticed for the first time that he held his right arm awkwardly, as if it was in an invisible sling.

'Yes. Yes, I remember Nora. But what is it — nearly thirty years? It's a very hazy memory, I'm afraid.' He looked around, as if speaking to a delegation. Venn's voice was strong, educated, with only a slight inflection of the Norfolk accent, and his manner was smooth. Shaw was ashamed to think he'd presumed his character would reflect in some way his damaged body.

'Nora was a devout woman, so most of our church members would have been at the

98

graveside. I was there — but, as I say, it's a long time ago. All those who could have attended would have. Her grandfather had been pastor . . . ' Shaw nodded. 'I'm sure her soul's with the Elect. Her faith was her life in all things.'

'What does that mean?' asked Shaw, failing to keep a note of animosity out of his voice. There was nothing like the hint of dogma to spark a flash of the Shaw family temper.

'Calvin taught us, teaches us, that we should live according to the principles of our church in everything we do. And that we should be regulated in our worship. And we are. To step outside the Word invites his retribution.'

On the word 'retribution', Venn's left hand crossed to touch the damaged right.

'Does that include music and dancing?' asked Shaw.

'Yes, we allow both. Some of the churches which were once our sisters and brothers ban certain forms of music and dance. But they are not proscribed by the Scripture. And we follow the Word in all things. Without exception.'

'Alcohol?' asked Valentine, happy to indulge in his favourite subject.

'Calvin made sure there was a copy of the Bible in every tavern in Geneva. Moderation was his teaching, not abstinence.'

Venn was struggling, under cross-examination, to keep the smile going. 'What is this about, may I ask?'

'I can't be specific,' said Shaw. He could have told Venn the facts, as he'd told Fletcher, but something made him want to keep the man guessing. 'Nora Tilden's body has been disinterred as part of the ongoing work at the cemetery. There are some irregularities — we need to clear them up. She was murdered by her husband, I believe — is that right?'

Venn seemed to start at the sudden question. 'Yes. Of course — terrible.'

'We're told that two black men attended her funeral. Do you know who they might have been?'

Venn shook his head. 'Not by name, though I might be able to find out. There was a father and son, I know that much. The father worked for the corporation; at the bus depot, I think. They were with us a year — no more. After that I think they went to Peterborough. I'm sorry — the name really is gone. Shall I try to find it for you?'

'Please,' said Shaw. 'It's important. So you knew the Tildens well?'

Venn looked at his wristwatch. 'A bit. Nora was an unhappy woman in many ways. I think the only joy in her life was experienced in this place. She didn't really want to run the pub — any pub. But her father left it to her, so she didn't have much choice. It was the family business, the family inheritance. Her father — Arthur Melville — made it pretty clear that's what he expected of her. And there'd been a child at first, I think. Died in infancy. I seem to recall we always put her in our prayers . . . yes, a daughter. I always got the impression Nora spent the rest of her life grieving.'

Shaw checked his watch, frustrated by a sense

100

that Venn was deliberately skirting direct answers to his questions.

'But you'd have known Alby, when he came back from his travels?'

'Yes. Some of his stuff used to clutter up the pub, I remember.' Venn closed his eyes, as if trying to see into the past. 'I recall a gong which stood in the billiard room. Vast thing. And some prints. And a gold Buddha he had up on a shelf — that always scandalized our church councillors. It's still there.'

'You used the pub?' asked Valentine, surprised.

'Yes. Still do. Two or three times a week for lunch. I was born here, Sergeant; went to the school. I see old friends. The Flask's a special place, you see — it's pretty much all that's left of the community, except for our little church.'

He didn't volunteer any more information, although Shaw felt certain he knew more than he'd said.

'Thank you for your time, sir. Those names — the two black men who attended the Tilden funeral. We really do need to check them out. So, if you can . . . '

Venn looked at the coal scuttle he'd set at his feet. 'I need to ring our archivist — she keeps the records. Every church member makes a tithe, so we should have something written down. Today, with luck?'

'Please — soon as you can,' said Shaw, turning towards the door. Under the twin portraits he stopped and turned. 'Did Alby Tilden attend church?'

Venn laughed. 'Er, no. Alby was one of those

101

men who thinks that it doesn't matter what they do, what rules they break, they should always be welcome in their own homes. I have no idea what he was like *before* he left . . . but we all knew the stories, the war hero. What's that terrible euphemism: a man's man?' Venn looked up at the ceiling, the lightest of blues. 'Some nights, if he'd had enough beer, he'd show you. Show anyone.' He arched the brow over his good eye.

'Show you what?' prompted Valentine.

Venn glanced past them at the portrait of Equiano.

'He had this tattoo, on his back, of a woman. A black woman. She was naked — a loose woman, I suppose. He could make her move with his muscles. Locals loved it. As party tricks went it was a winner every time. He'd do it in front of Nora . . . ' He shook his head, looking at the parquet floor. 'I was there to witness this and I think it is one of the cruellest things I have ever seen. She was a hard woman, and she set her face against the world. But she didn't deserve that. I thought it was . . . ' As he searched for the word he cradled his damaged arm. Then he looked with his good eye into Shaw's. 'Evil. Which is a rare thing, thanks be to God.'

9

The Flask stood on a slight rise by the river, a small clay cliff holding it clear of the tidal reach of the sea, four miles distant along the Cut. It was impossible to hide the building's architectural heritage: the second floor jutting out above the first, the third above the second, the original beams exposed between the intricate brick-work. It stood at the end of Greenland Street, a stub of terraced houses petering out a hundred yards short of the river, leaving the pub to stand alone — the one property left behind when a line of slum tenements had been cleared. The demolition had left the Flask without vital support, hence the two steel buttresses which held up the end wall. Beyond the pub lay Flensing Meadow, and through the cemetery a riverside walk the council had cleared in the 1980s. Vandals had ripped up the wooden benches, and a plinth which told the story of Lynn's whaling fleet was drenched in graffiti. Dog bins gave off a pungent scent, even in winter.

The pub sign hung from the first tier of the building and depicted a whaling ship. Over the beamed doorway a small plaque read ELIZABETH AND JOHN JOE MURRAY; LICENSED TO SELL BEERS, WINES AND SPIRITS.

In front of the door stood DC Fiona Campbell.

'Sir — Tom wanted you to see something.'

Valentine put a hand on the pub door, pushing it open. 'I'll suss the place out.'

Shaw led Campbell round the building to a wooden deck which held six picnic tables, all dripping, snow melting from the slated tops. They stood looking out at the grey water. Just below them was an old stone wharf, a small clinker-built sailing boat moored by a frayed rope, the deck enclosed within a stretched tarpaulin. On the far side of the river they could hear the mechanical grinding of a conveyor belt in the cannery. Shaw thought about Freddie Fletcher's 'good British fare' — local shellfish, cooked and canned. In midstream the trawler stood silently, while mist lingered on the water like steam drifting from a hot spa.

'Fiona?' He looked her in the eyes, which were brown and liquid and unflinching. Shaw had noticed that several people he knew well had developed a strategy when looking into his eyes. They focused only on the undamaged left, never the moon-like right. It gave him the impression she was looking over his shoulder.

Campbell flipped open her notebook to show Shaw a picture she'd drawn: a child's image of a gibbet, a stick-man hanging by the neck, but unfinished, with no legs and just one arm.

'Tom found this drawing — well, one just like it — in the victim's wallet. It's my copy. The wallet had given it some protection from the water, but the paper's virtually dust after the drying out. Tom could see some ink marks — used a box of tricks to get the image. There were other pieces of paper, all in a bundle, all the same size, but he couldn't lift an image except for this one, which was halfway down. But there are ink traces on all the pages.'

Shaw tried to think straight, aware this might be important but irritated by the playfulness of the little drawing.

'It's from a game of hangman, isn't it?' asked Campbell.

'It looks like it,' said Shaw. He'd always found hangman macabre, a vicious echo of Victorian childhood, with its humourless grinning clowns and nightmare automata. 'But it isn't — is it? In the game you have to try to guess a word, and that's usually spelt out on the same piece of paper. So it probably isn't a game.'

Campbell looked at the sketch she'd drawn, baffled.

'And our victim's how old — twenty, twenty-five? A bit old for games, anyway.'

'Keeping them in your wallet's a bit weird, too,' she said.

'The paper?'

'Tom says standard notebook — each sheet a torn-out page. The ink could have come from any high-street biro.'

Shaw looked up at the riverside façade of the pub. It hadn't been a thought that had even crossed his mind, the idea that the pub had been home to children — first the infant Mary, then Lizzie. He'd always thought of pubs as being aggressively adult, having spent many hours in his childhood sitting outside them.

'Circulate a copy of this to the team, Fiona. For now I can't think of anything else we can do with it.' He put a finger to his left temple. 'Just keep it here.'

He led the way back to the front of the pub, letting Campbell go in first. It had just turned twenty past eleven but the only customer was George Valentine. He pushed a half-empty pint glass away from himself as if it wasn't his. Music played, filling up the empty room with something melodious from The Jam: 'That's Entertainment'.

The quarry-tiled floor had been mopped, though the disinfectant hadn't quite erased the fug of the cellar, or the odours of a fried breakfast. But there was another smell — a scent — which drifted from a vase of white orchids on the bar. The room was panelled, wooden settles running round the walls, the windows glazed with coloured Victorian glass. Old prints crowded the walls — whaling ships, dockside scenes. Christmas decorations gilded the wood-work and ceiling beams. There was a large brass gong at the foot of the stairs, mounted on a dark wood frame, and Shaw recalled Sam Venn's words: that when Alby Tilden had returned from his exotic travels he brought back a cargo of equally exotic memorabilia.

Two bay windows looked out on the wide river, the clear glass engraved with the name of Lynn's Victorian brewers — Cutlack & Sons — now long defunct.

The barman did a little routine out of central casting: rearranging the beer cloths on the bar, touching one of the pumps, trying out a smile. He was in his late forties, early fifties, but clearly clung to the years of his youth — a vain shock of greying black hair swept back to flop over both ears, and he wore a T-shirt emblazoned with a bleached-out portrait of Ian Dury. The bones of his skull had once supported a handsome face: a narrow pointed chin, high cheekbones and a thin, fine nose. On his neck was a tattoo of an electric guitar in a vivid moss green. His eyes were green too, bright and youthful, but his skin had all the surface tension of a week-old party balloon.

The little ceremony of welcome didn't include saying anything, while his right hand picked out a complicated beat to match the track playing through the speakers.

'Coffee?' asked Shaw, nodding at a well-used Italian coffee machine. He ordered an espresso. Campbell went for fizzy water. Valentine got a second pint on Shaw's round. As the barman pulled it Shaw noted a wedding ring and a bronze bracelet.

'Landlady around?' asked Shaw, laying his warrant card on the bar.

The smile on the barman's face fell like a calving iceberg. Behind the bar was a small wooden door, as narrow as a coffin. The barman inched it open. 'Lizzie,' he shouted. They heard footsteps on the wooden floor above.

'What?' asked a disembodied voice.

'Police, Lizzie. They want a word.'

'I'll be five.'

Everyone pretended to relax. Another customer came in — a pensioner in a threadbare jacket, shirt and tie. The barman pulled a pint without asking what he wanted, holding the finished article up against the light to check its clarity.

He turned to set up the coffee machine for Shaw's espresso. 'So, what's up?' he asked over his shoulder. 'Postman said you'd found something in one of the graves — something you shouldn't have. That right?' Shaw noted that as the barman set aside the crockery he held it with both hands, one on the rim of the small cup, one on the saucer.

'I'm sorry — you are . . . ?' asked Shaw.

'John Joe Murray,' he said. 'It's over the door. I'm the landlord.'

'Ali, at the shop,' said the man in the threadbare jacket, butting in, 'he says it's one of those Polish immigrants. Ali says they cut him up, in bits.' He extended a purple bottom lip to the edge of his pint glass.

'Ali's talking out of his arse,' said Valentine, reaching for his pint, then stopping himself. He was nearly at the bottom. Then his mobile rang and he got up and went into the back bar, which had once — he guessed — accommodated a full-sized billiards table, because a raised platform that had run around it for chairs and tables was still there, but it had all been cleared away to make a dining room. Each table was neatly laid for a meal. In one corner on a plinth was a gold Buddha, glowing against the polished dark wood.

Shaw and Campbell took a seat in one of the bay windows in the bar, the river at their backs. Valentine came back in, still rolling his shoulders

108

to get rid of the morning's damp. He waved the mobile at Shaw. 'Voyce took the hired car out to the Bellevue Psychiatric Hospital to visit Chris Robins. Bit late — even for his funeral. He left flowers and fruit juice with the ward sister — so clearly Robins's death was all news to him. Makes you wonder why, though. What did he think Robins could tell him? Anyway — it shook him up. He drove back, dumped the car, then bought a bottle of vodka from an offy on the London Road and drank it in the park. Then he walked back to the hotel and phoned Mosse.'

Campbell looked bemused as they beamed at each other.

Shaw thought about Chris Robins. An original member of Bobby Mosse's little teenage gang, who'd lived a life of petty crime and diminishing mental powers until he'd been sectioned under the Mental Health Act.

'What did he say?' asked Shaw.

'Didn't use the phone in the room — he's got a mobile. We're trying to trace it. But we heard his end of the conversation: he said he was in town seeing family, thought they should catch up on old times.'

'Where?'

'Pier at Hunstanton — six tomorrow night.'

'It's all shut up.'

'I guess. They'll go somewhere — a pub? Car?'

'OK. We need to be there. Sort it, George.'

Shaw watched Valentine's narrow back as he retreated to the bar, downed the rest of his pint, then left, holding the lapels of his raincoat tight to his throat, braced for the cold outside.

Campbell shifted uneasily in her seat, aware she'd been shut out of something but equally aware she shouldn't try to muscle her way into another inquiry.

They heard a door hinge scream and turned to see a woman appear behind the bar, through the coffin-top door, coolly assessing the clientele while trying to get an earring in place: a diamond stud just catching the light. She was about John Joe Murray's age, but her hair was still a lustrous black, like a patent-leather shoe. Her face looked hard, but not effortlessly so. Shaw thought she betrayed not the slightest remnant of the DNA which had built the face of her mother, Nora Tilden. This face was a fine one, sculptural, like a ship's figurehead. Keeping her eyes on Shaw and Campbell she let her hand rise to find a switch she knew was there, and a one-armed bandit in the corner flickered into life.

'Someone wants to see me?' she asked, resting a hand on the bar, demanding an answer, radiating the kind of self-assurance that women rarely feel in a pub bar unless they own it. Her voice helped: it was furred by nicotine and had an edge, like corrugated paper. She rearranged one of the bar towels, again without looking at it, and Shaw reminded himself that she'd probably spent her entire life in this building, and that she must know every nail and latch, like a ship's cabin.

John Joe nodded at Shaw. 'Coffee, love?'

She didn't answer but glanced up at the optics behind the bar, which seemed to be a signal. A crew of four men came in, all in overalls. John Joe turned away to serve them.

Lizzie Murray flipped up the bar top and walked to Shaw's table. She had a good figure still, a narrow waist, and something of a catwalk step. She wore black trousers and a fitted top with a V-neck, in butterscotch, and practical plain court shoes. As she walked she smoothed down the material, and Shaw noted the absence of a visible panty line, imagining something in Lycra beneath, comfortable and snug. When she sat he saw a necklace in gold, again with a single diamond.

'Is there somewhere private?' asked Shaw.

'Not really,' she said, sitting. She licked at the pearly lipstick at the corner of her mouth. 'This'll do. Sorry — it's just that Mondays are hell. Brewery delivers at noon — then comes the frozen food for the week. So . . . ' She briefly held Shaw's good eye. Hers were green, like her husband's, but flecked with brown and blue, catching the Victorian colours of the bar's windows. 'What's this about?'

Shaw wondered if she was like this with everyone she met. Despite her manners, which were coolly professional, she radiated an almost tangible sense that she didn't have time to waste.

John Joe brought her a drink, a gin with ice, lots of ice, so that you couldn't see how much spirit was in the glass. Shaw watched her raise it to her lips and sip. The glass was green, with an etched drawing on it of a whaling scene. DC Campbell went to speak but Shaw, almost imperceptibly, shook his head.

111

'It's about your mother . . . ' said Shaw.

'The cemetery?'

'You'll know the graves are being emptied and the bones reinterred because of the flooding. You'd have had a letter about it, from the council?'

She shrugged. 'Maybe. So what?'

'I wanted to talk to you about her death — specifically, the funeral. I realize that might be painful . . . '

'Not particularly,' she said. 'We weren't close.'

'OK,' said Shaw, taking her answer in his stride. 'I just need to know what happened that night of the wake. She was murdered, your mother — by your father. There must have been tensions. Did anything boil over? Anyone have too much to drink, perhaps? We understand there were two black men at the graveside — from your mother's church. Did they come back to the pub? Were they welcome?'

She looked out at the Russian trawler which was venting water, taking a swig from the glass, letting one of the ice cubes click against her teeth. 'I don't know about tensions. Dad was in Lincoln — they'd held on to Mother's body until after the trial.'

Shaw noted the clash of idioms: 'Dad' — but 'Mother'.

'She'd been dead for months. The family all came — her side — the Melvilles, but nobody from the Tildens. There'd have been a riot, so they kept away. It was a party. Sorry, but that's the truth. I don't remember anyone from the church staying late, black or white. We don't run

112

a colour bar — now or then. There'd have been no trouble. They might have been here earlier, I suppose. I was upstairs with Mother's friends from the church. We gave them tea, sandwiches. I left Bea in charge behind the bar.'

'Bea?'

'Mother's sister. She came back to look after me when they took Dad away. Well . . . ' She looked at her empty drink. 'I was nineteen, so I didn't really need looking after. She came back because she was a widow, and she was lonely. But it was a big help — having her around. Dad phoned her, from Bedford when he was on remand, asked her to help. That's what family's for.' She caught Shaw's eye but couldn't hold his gaze, looking away instantly. 'After that, she stayed. She runs a B&B up on the coast at Wells.' Shaw thought she was lying, or only telling them a facet of the truth, and that in some people that became a practised skill — concealing reality behind a screen of small, partial, truths.

She drained melted ice from the glass, rattling what was left, and glanced at the bar. The drink had brought colour to her face to go with the hint of blusher she'd applied. John Joe was looking at her directly and nodded once, coming over with another identical drink in an identical etched green glass.

Campbell had slipped out her notebook and they could hear her pen scratching over the paper.

'Look — what is this about? I've got a pub to run.'

'Just a few questions,' said Shaw, sipping the

113

espresso, which was excellent: potent and bitter. He retrieved his sketch pad from the leather satchel he'd brought with him and set it on the table top, closed.

'I wanted to show you something,' he said. 'Something we found in your mother's grave. On top of your mother's coffin . . . '

She ran the top of her tongue along her upper lip, and Shaw noticed how hurriedly she'd applied the lipstick, so that it spilt beyond the vermilion border, the dividing line between the skin and the fleshy tissue around the mouth. He briefly tried to imagine what it was like to look at that face in a mirror each morning, thinking about going downstairs to face the customers, most of whom she'd probably known all her life. This was a woman, he thought, who lived her life in public.

'We found another body in your mother's grave,' he said. 'Bones.' He watched her fingers tighten around the glass. 'He — it's the remains of a man — would have been thrown into the grave, we think, possibly shortly after your mother was buried. Perhaps that very day, or the next, before the gravediggers filled it in.'

She looked over Shaw's shoulder and he half turned to see her husband standing behind them. 'Ian can run the bar,' he said, sliding onto the settle beside his wife, but their bodies didn't touch.

Shaw flipped the pages of the sketch book until he got to the facial reconstruction he'd finished that morning in DCS Warren's office.

She fished out a pair of reading glasses and

took the piece of cartridge paper, snapping it once so that it stood upright in her hand.

'This is a very rough idea of what he might have looked like,' said Shaw. 'You probably won't recognize the face — but try to see if it reminds you of someone. Anyone.'

She nodded several times. Blood drained from her skin, as if she'd been turned into a monochrome snapshot. 'God,' she said. But it wasn't an exclamation, just a statement. Her husband took one corner of the piece of paper. Her eyes flooded and her body slumped, so that she seemed to shrink. 'Oh, God,' she said, again, still staring at the image. John Joe put an arm round her, drawing her upright. She half-turned to look at the bar. It was such an extraordinary look in her eyes — a kind of bitter pity, that Shaw turned to follow her gaze. The barman was in his late twenties, close-shaven hair, a symmetrical handsome face, a cook's white smock, and skin the colour of Caramac chocolate: like golden syrup, as exotic in the Flask as the vase of pale orchids.

10

Lizzie Murray led them behind the bar, and she managed to close the coffin-lid door behind her before she fainted, kneeling then keeling, so that her head came to rest quite gently on the bottom step of the stairs. Her husband sat with her while DC Campbell fetched a glass of water. Shaw sat halfway up the flight of wooden steps, the steps down which this woman's mother had fallen, bones breaking with each twist of her brittle body. They made her drink, then John Joe carried her up. Ian, the barman, watching from below, was told to mind the bar until noon, then take over in the kitchen, and he should call Aunt Bea, tell her to come, tell her she needed to be with the family.

'It's all right, Ian,' said John Joe. 'Just get Bea — then we'll explain.'

They sat Lizzie on a tattered floral sofa in the sitting room of the Flask, looking out through two identical bay windows at the river, now filling with the tide, the mudbanks shrinking. From below they could hear the sounds of the bar: a tape playing Elvis Costello, the clunk of pool balls, and from the kitchen the crackle of a deep fat fryer.

The room they were in was a collection of anachronisms: an Artexed ceiling, a Victorian chandelier and peeling fake Regency wallpaper: Shaw guessed it had been used for functions over the years, an endless unbroken series of wedding receptions, parties and christenings — and, no doubt, the wake for the members of the Free Church after the funeral of Nora Tilden, while downstairs the real party was waiting to begin.

The furniture was out of scale: the modern sofa and two armchairs lost in the space, the disconnect between the room and its furniture driven home by the fireplace, which was big enough for an ox-roasting. A flat-screen TV sat on a flat-pack unit. Next to it was a small table upon which stood an electric kettle, cups, sachets — Shaw was reminded of a B&B's tea-making kit. A birdcage hung from a gilded wrought-iron stand; the bird within was white and hit the same note rhythmically, like an alarm clock.

Lizzie drank coffee and more water, and seemed not to notice that they were all watching her. The touch of mascara on her upper lashes had run. She set Shaw's sketch on the coffee table and every few seconds adjusted it slightly, as if it had three dimensions and she might see more if she altered the angle.

'I've got to tell Ian,' she said eventually to John Joe, and the thought seemed to release the tears, bringing her eyes alight.

'Christ, Lizzie — just take a moment,' said John Joe, shaking his head. 'Bea can tell him — she's on her way.'

'Who is this?' asked Shaw, impatient, tapping the sketch.

She wiped her lips, smudging the lipstick.

'It's Patrice — Pat — Aunt Bea's son. My

cousin. Bea married a GI — a black GI. She brought Pat back when she came home from the States to look after me. Pat was twenty.' She looked at her hands, the fingers working in knots. She looked at Shaw's picture with a kind of fond fear.

'And Ian?' asked Campbell. 'The barman?'

'Yes — Ian's his son.'

Shaw let the silence stretch out until she answered the question they hadn't asked.

'And I'm his mother.' Her chin came up then, rekindling the figurehead defiance, daring them to tell her it had been wrong. Shaw worked it out: she'd have been nineteen, maybe twenty. They were cousins — first cousins. In some areas of the States the relationship would have been illegal on three counts: age, race and consanguinity. And here in Lynn, in 1982, it would have raised a few eyebrows too, not least in the God-fearing Melville family. Shaw thought about Alby Tilden and his lost years at sea, and the tattooed image he'd brought back home. Lizzie had grown up in a house where the issue of race was a toxic one: a running sore on the family's collective skin.

They heard a car engine ticking outside the pub's front door and a minute later Aunt Bea was with them. Shaw knew she had to be in her late sixties, but she looked and moved like a fifty-year-old; a bustling, sinewy woman, with grey hair cut short but expertly. She wore knee-high brown leather boots and woollen tights under a knitted skirt, and she had a vivid blue pashmina wrapped round her neck. No

118

necklace or earrings, but Shaw noticed that both hands bristled with silver rings.

Of Nora, her sister, there was hardly an echo. Shaw worked out a rough age difference — the two sisters would have been born more than a decade apart. But the resemblance to Lizzie was striking: two figureheads. Bea's face was set against the world too, but it was open, challenging perhaps, and devoid of the bitter irritation that seemed to disfigure her niece.

She came into the centre of the room, dusting snow from the shoulders of a heavy Barbour which she had already taken off. She wasn't alone. The woman with her was Lizzie's age, late forties, but blonde, with the kind of skin that reveals the veins beneath, especially on the high forehead, which was only partly hidden by a fringe. Unlike Lizzie she wasn't dressed for customers, but in a pair of faded jeans and a T-shirt. Shaw sensed immediately that she was a rare woman — unaware, to some extent, of her own beauty, as if her own self-image didn't match the reality. She hung back, one arm held awkwardly just beneath her breast. She radiated a strange anxiety, as if she perpetually thought she didn't belong. Shaw was reminded of the embarrassed hesitancy of a teenage child.

Aunt Bea walked forward and picked up the sketch on the table. Shaw noted that she hadn't even looked at Lizzie. 'John Joe told me,' she said. 'It's true?' she asked, looking at Shaw and then, finally, at her niece. Shaw noted she wore no make-up except a dash of concealer, and a smudge of foundation on her cheek, perhaps to cover a liver spot.

Shaw showed his warrant card.

'I'm Bea Garrison — Lizzie's aunt.' Her voice still held the unmistakable twang of the American Midwest. 'This is my son,' she added, gripping the sheet of paper so tightly it buckled. She flattened the vowel in 'son' — making it rhyme with run. The other woman, whom nobody had bothered to introduce, had slipped round behind the sofa and put a hand on each of Lizzie's shoulders.

'This is Kath — Kath Robinson,' said Bea. 'She drove me down. She knows us — she's always known us.' They watched Robinson kiss Lizzie's hair, but all the emotion of the moment seemed to be lop-sided, as if only Kath actually felt it.

'That's true,' said Lizzie as her aunt sat beside her and took her hand.

Bea studied the image, her brown eyes softening, but free of any hint of a tear. 'I knew he must be dead. Even if I never said,' she looked at Lizzie and Kath. 'It's been too long, hasn't it? Nearly thirty years. He's just faded away for me, like an old photo.' She shook her head, putting the sketch back on the table, letting Lizzie's hand fall free.

Bea looked at Shaw. 'I'll tell the story. It's my story in a way, as much as Lizzie's, as much as anyone's.'

John Joe came into the room. Bea looked at him. 'Stay with Ian, John Joe. He's young, the words won't mean anything.' Shaw noted her

120

easy authority in this house, the almost casual power of the true matriarch.

He nodded, leaving, as if he recognized the wisdom of her words. But Shaw couldn't entirely disregard the idea that he'd been dismissed, as if he was outside some privileged female circle.

Bea went to the bay window.

'So what *is* the story?' said Shaw, his tone softer, because he knew now that these women held the truth, and that if he was going to get to it quickly, it would be only with their help.

'I married here in Lynn in 1959,' she said. 'Latrell Garrison — a US GI. I was just a teenager. He was older — twenty years older. He'd been in Lynn ahead of D-Day. After the war he went home, but stayed in the army, then got a posting back here — up at the airfield at Bircham. He was lonely — so he worked his way through his old girlfriends, and then he got to me.' It was said as a joke, but even she didn't laugh. 'We went to the Free together, too — that was his kind of church.'

Bea looked Shaw straight in his blind eye. 'I didn't love him. But I hated . . . ' She looked around the room. 'This, Nora got the pub after Dad died, and whatever he'd said about this always being our home I knew Nora better than that. No — this was hers. I knew she'd never wanted it, so that helped.' She shook her head. 'There's nothing quite like the hatred between sisters.'

She turned, taking a deep breath, rearranging the pashmina. 'Alby was on the scene by the end of the war. *He* loved the place. I liked Alby — we all did. But we knew why he'd married Nora, and love didn't come into that, either. He'd take her money, take all this, then live his life the way he wanted to. But then the child came — Mary — and they lost her, and he never really got over it — did he, Lizzie?'

Lizzie's head was down, but she shook it.

'So he went back to sea. And that left the two of us, sisters, here, together. Latrell was good-looking — you can see that in Ian. So we got married at the register office one afternoon. It's crazy — you think your life gets changed by the big events, the big decisions. Then you do something like that — on a whim, just because it feels right.'

Bea was quite calm — at ease, even — and Shaw thought she had a rare gift of being truthful to strangers about her own life. She touched her bottom lip and Shaw saw he'd been wrong, that there was lipstick, but just the subtlest of touches.

'When Nora found out she said she'd never talk to me again, and that was one virtue she had, Inspector: she kept her promises. And you know — this is difficult to believe — I don't think then it was about the colour of Latrell's skin. I think it was the fact that he was going to take me away. And she wanted me here — in my place.'

Bea turned her back on them. Kath picked up the coffee pot, swilled what was left around. 'I'll get a fresh one,' she said, and went to the kitchen.

'Latrell applied for a posting back home. We

flew to the States on a military transport,' continued Bea. 'I wasn't going to be able to live here anyway, was I? Not with a black man. During the war it might have been OK — people like Latrell were considered exotic, exciting. But when the local men came back, things changed. What had happened was forgotten. So we had to go.'

She held out her hands so that they could see her silver rings more clearly.

'Latrell took me home — to Hartsville, North Dakota. Small-town America's smallest town.' She laughed, but caught sight of the sketch on the coffee table and turned away again.

'Latrell's father ran the town drugstore. Latrell trained up as a pharmacist — there was a programme for GIs — and I just helped out in the shop. We tried for kids, but it didn't work. I'd pretty much given up, and then Pat was born — in 1962.' She stopped for a few seconds, and Shaw knew what she was doing — working out how old he would have been now, if he'd lived.

'Latrell died in 1980 — cancer of the liver. He was fifty-nine. He drank. Everyone drank in Hartsville because of the winters. You've never seen snow like it — and nobody moves, especially if they're snowed in at the town bar. The thing that really got me in the end was the quietness of winter. It just sucks the life right out of the day, that blanket of suffocating snow.'

She walked to the window again. Outside, big wet flakes were falling. 'I tried to stay, I thought I wanted to stay, after he died. I kept the business going. There was someone new, someone I'd known but who'd kept their distance in those last years. Pat was at high school in Bushell — he was a bright kid. Journalism — that was the big thing. But suddenly, the second winter after Latrell died, I just couldn't stand it any more. It's such a mundane emotion, homesickness. I'd lived in Hartsville all those years and then woken up to find it was a foreign place — just like that. One moment home, the next minute somewhere I couldn't stand to be.'

She looked around the room. 'Then I got a call from Alby. He was at Bedford, before the trial. He told me what had happened. He said he wanted to tell me the truth before someone else poured poison in my ear — that's what he said — *poured poison*. He asked me to come home — just for a while — and look after Lizzie. She was only nineteen, she couldn't run the pub on her own. A year, maybe three, she'd be OK. He couldn't live with it, he said — the thought that she was on her own. I couldn't say no — not to Alby.'

Kath had been standing on the threshold unseen, holding a fresh pot of coffee.

When Bea saw her she seemed to change tack. 'She wasn't on her own, of course — she had friends, people like Kath. But I came back and brought Pat with me. I told him it would be like a holiday, just a couple of years. An adventure. He was Lizzie's age. But the tickets were one way. Pat resented the move — he didn't really like Lynn. I got him a place at the college — on the media studies course. I got him his own flat — well, a bedsit. I sold up the drugstore in

124

Hartsville, so I wasn't short of money — Pat always had cash in his pocket.'

She stopped at that, thinking about what to say next. 'He was popular with the girls. I knew that.'

Shaw looked at Lizzie but she, oddly, was looking at Kath Robinson, who'd sat down with the coffee pot. Lizzie pressed her hand and the other woman's pale skin suddenly flushed.

There was an awkward silence, then Bea went on. 'He was growing up, he had a family around him, so it wasn't such a bad life. Then, when he went missing, Lizzie told me what I hadn't seen — what had been so obvious, but unnoticed.'

Kath stood quickly, started moving things about on the table to set down the coffee. She didn't seem able to create a space. Bea gently took over, taking the pot. Kath retreated, looking at her shoes, to stand at the window.

'Pat and I fell in love,' said Lizzie, then covered her mouth as if she wanted to claw back the words. 'It was a secret.' She touched the sketch. 'We thought it was a secret.'

'No one knew — absolutely no one?' asked Campbell. She tried to keep a note of incredulity out of her voice but even she'd admit she'd failed.

'I made a mistake,' said Lizzie. 'I told Dad — when we went to see him at Lincoln after the trial. He still had lots of visitors then, so I suppose it got back.'

'I didn't know,' said Bea, and she even managed to keep a sour note out of her voice.

Shaw was trying to imagine what life had been

125

like for this family back in 1982 — conflicting, heated emotions crowded beneath this single roof.

'Dad was happy for us,' said Lizzie, and Shaw couldn't help but think the remark was directed at her aunt. A flash of anger brought Lizzie's eyes alive, the flashing green dominating the grey and brown. 'Dad liked black girls. The girls he'd met in the ports. He'd tell his cronies about them in the bar.' She looked at Shaw. 'It wasn't all about sex. He liked the life in them, black people, the joy. He met Pat in jail, on visiting days. He was fond of him. Pat liked a good time too — and he was always out to get it. Pat made him smile, even in jail.' She looked down at her hands, suddenly ashamed.

'When did you last see Pat?' asked Shaw, but he'd guessed the answer.

'The wake,' said Lizzie. A whisper again. 'He went to the funeral too, and stood at the graveside. Nora was his aunt, after all.' She bit her lip, wrapping both her hands around Bea's. 'It was that evening, at the party, that I told him *my* news.'

She looked at Shaw, the kind of look that made him ask himself again if this was a career he really wanted: a lifetime spent watching other people's lives unwind.

'I was pregnant — with Ian. He was really happy. We talked about what to do. We'd talked about getting married before, though never seriously. But now we had the business — the pub. And the funeral was over — finally over, after all those months. And the trial. I could sell

126

up. Start a life somewhere else.' Her voice had changed, become lighter, almost joyful, as if she was reading a line from a fairy tale.

'The States?' asked DC Campbell.

'No. We couldn't go back to Hartsville — North Dakota's one of the states where . . . ' she tried to find the right word, 'where it's illegal. Still. Leviticus — that's what they always say, isn't it? Leviticus, chapter eighteen. They should read it sometime.' Her thin mouth set murderously straight.

'So . . . ' prompted Campbell. 'What did you do?'

'That night? I didn't tell anyone else. Just Kath.'

'I didn't tell anyone,' said Kath quickly. 'You made me promise, didn't you, Lizzie? I keep my promises.' Again, thought Shaw, the childlike cadence of speech.

'There were people who already hated Pat — for his colour,' explained Lizzie. 'But if they'd guessed . . . So we couldn't touch each other, nothing, not in public.' She looked at her hands, trying to focus. 'The idea of a child — it was frightening. Wonderful, but frightening.'

She looked squarely at Shaw. 'When I told Pat that night, he was happy — like I said. But the wake was in full swing by then, so we couldn't talk, not properly. We arranged to meet the next day. Then he left. He said we had so much to discuss, so much that was exciting, and if he couldn't talk to me then he'd rather go home.' She set her jaw again. 'He said he hoped it was a boy, said we'd talk more tomorrow, then he

127

walked out. I never saw him again.' She looked at the sketch.

'What time?' asked Shaw. 'When he left the bar.'

'Ten — maybe later.'

'The time's important,' said Shaw.

She looked up at him, struggling to keep focused on the question. 'We had a party licence and we had the choir in — the sea-shanty choir. It's sort of their home, really — they've always sung here and Mum liked to hear them. Some of them sang at the Free too, so they'd all been close. We all listened to the first half of that, so . . . I don't know. Ten fifteen, bit earlier. Ten thirty they'd start up again — so, before that.'

'And he just walked out — didn't speak to anyone else?'

'No — he went and got his coat. That was behind the bar, upstairs. Then we talked a bit more. He held my hand.' She brightened at the memory. 'Just for a second, over the bar. In public. We'd never done that before. And then he did go.'

She picked up Shaw's sketch. 'Can I keep this?'

'What happened then — the following morning?' asked Shaw, nodding.

'When Pat didn't show up, I just thought the worst of him . . . '

Campbell held up a hand. 'Sorry — just a detail, where did you arrange to meet?'

Lizzie's eyes glazed. 'The Walks — we had a place, a bench, by the Red Tower, where we'd sit.'

128

Lizzie folded the sketch, looking at Bea. 'We thought he couldn't face it. That now there'd be this child, it wasn't a game any more. That we *should* marry. That it was up to us. He was very young, we both were, and I've always clung to that. That he couldn't handle it — so he ran away.'

She said it in a flat voice, without emotion. But Bea, who'd been looking through the window, suddenly buckled. Kath went to her, holding her up, bringing her back to the sofa.

'And you didn't report the fact that Pat was missing?' asked Shaw. 'Either of you?'

'That was my fault,' said Bea quickly, wiping tears from her eyes, talking over Lizzie, the Midwestern accent suddenly sharper. 'Lizzie — she wanted to go to the police, didn't you?'

'I couldn't believe he'd gone — that he'd deserted us,' said Lizzie. 'I went to the park. I waited, and he didn't come, so I went to the flat. But I never had a key. And there was no answer. So I came back here. I thought we should report it. If he wasn't at home — where was he? Where was he?' she repeated, almost shouting now, almost out of control.

'He'd only been gone a few hours,' said Bea. 'You'd have laughed at us if we'd panicked. Lizzie told me then — what she'd told him, about the baby. I said he'd be confused. I knew Pat better than he knew himself. He was like his father. Neither of them ever grew up. I thought he'd be frightened too. That he might want me with him — to talk about it. This was what? Noon, Lizzie? So I went home — I had a flat on

Explorer Street, where we'd both lodged when we came over. There was a note on the mat, addressed to Lizzie. I took it back to her.'

'He said he was sorry,' said Lizzie. 'That's what it said. A lot more words, but that's what it boiled down to. *I'm sorry.* Poor Ian — when he was growing up he'd say that, too. *I'm sorry, Mommy.* And I'd scream at him all the more. Because it's such an empty thing to say.'

'No explanation?' prompted Campbell.

'Just that he couldn't stay — that this wasn't his home, and he didn't belong here. That he wouldn't be back. I burnt it . . . '

'But you recognized the handwriting?' asked Shaw.

She didn't seem to understand the question, looking from Campbell to Shaw and back again. 'Handwriting? No. Pat typed everything — didn't he, Bea? But the signature was his — it looked like his? Next day I went round to the flat again — there was a woman who cleaned the place and she let me in. Everything was gone — including the typewriter.'

She seemed to weigh the folded sketch. 'I've always thought he didn't want our child, that he had that in him — to just walk away from me.' She smiled. 'And now I know none of that's true, is it? For nearly thirty years I've thought about his other life — the life he had without us. I thought he was out there, loving other people. I used to think, in those first few years, that he might be thinking of me, and that if I did the same, at exactly the same moment, we'd connect.' She smiled at the picture, and Shaw

130

noted that her fingers had tightened on the paper. 'I know now he loved us.' She looked at Shaw. 'But someone hated him — hated him enough to kill him.'

'Someone like Freddie Fletcher?' asked Shaw.

Lizzie's eyes widened and Shaw sensed she was seeing something again, an image from the past.

Then she shook her head. 'Freddie's harmless. Nasty. Bigoted. Ignorant. But harmless. They chucked him out of the BNP because he wouldn't shut up about the blacks. Loose cannon. But it was all talk — always has been.'

'People like Freddie? Back then — Freddie wasn't alone, was he? Who did he used to hang around with? Can you give us the names?' Shaw glanced at Bea. 'Can *you*?'

Both women nodded, apparently eager to help, but perhaps just eager to be left alone.

'My DC here will organize statements — I want you both to try to put a list together for us. We need to piece together what happened that night: minute by minute.'

Fiona Campbell had been thinking about the choir, the packed back room, the music.

'Didn't the Whitefriars Choir record itself? I thought I'd heard them on a CD or something — at the folk festival?'

Bea was nodding, suddenly animated, but Lizzie examined a tissue she'd been shredding in her hands.

'That's right. In fact, that night there was a camera. A cine camera, on a tripod — remember?' Bea asked.

Lizzie shook her head, neither yes or no.

'That must be right because we asked people not to move around between the songs,' said Bea. 'It was special that night, because Nora had been good to them. They always sang in that room, and I don't think she charged them, did she, Lizzie?'

Lizzie shrugged.

'A film? There's a film of the night of Nora's wake?' pressed Shaw.

'Somewhere,' said Bea.

They left them then, the three women huddled on the sofa, and let themselves out, down the narrow wooden stairs and through the coffin-like door into the bar. Outside, Shaw buttoned up his overcoat and considered the eccentric façade of the Flask — the crazy angle of the tortured beams, the 1970s steel buttresses holding up the gable end. He'd left Campbell inside, trying to fix a time to take statements from John Joe and Ian, and picking up a contact for the Whitefriars Choir. If that recording had survived, they needed to see it. But Shaw doubted their luck would stretch that far.

He walked out to the edge of the cemetery and looked back at the Flask. Bea Garrison's face was at the mullioned glass of the room above, and then it was gone.

11

Shaw parked the Porsche on the slipway beside the old lifeboat house at Hunstanton and walked down to the new building. Through the small observation portholes in the metal doors he could see the hovercraft within, the diffuse glow of the security lighting picking out the polished yellow and blue of the housing in the nest of the deflated skirt. He checked his RNLI pager, anxious that it was now more than a fortnight since the last 'shout', when they'd taken *Flyer* out over Holkham Sands to lift a two-man crew off a yacht foundering near the entrance to Wells at low tide. He thought about letting himself in, then thought about the rigmarole of resetting the security system, the safety gear, and how he should be home because he might just catch Fran before bed-time. And that was why he was here — why he'd made himself walk out of the incident room after the late-night briefing. But he sensed the silence within the boathouse, like a magnet, promising a space to think inside. It was irresistible.

He used an electronic key to open the data pad and punched in the code, rolling up the door. He didn't bother to roll it down. After dark, in winter, the beach was deserted, the white line of surf shifting, insubstantial in the gloom. He swung a leg over the side of the skirt and slipped into the pilot's chair — his chair. He flicked on the power so that the sonar and radar screens filled the cockpit with a luminous green light. The radio automatically scanned the emergency bands. He heard a snatch of Dutch, then something else — possibly Russian. But nothing tense, nothing laced with the unmistakable edge of fear. He could recognize panic in any language.

The summer had been busy for *Flyer* — nearly sixty callouts. They'd added twenty-six names to the list of the rescued which hung in the boathouse. The winter, in contrast, had been long and damp but until now free of storms. The last thing he wanted was a shout in the middle of a murder inquiry, but he missed the adrenaline rush, the sudden incontrovertible *priority* a rescue imposed on his other, more complex, responsibilities. It was like a release: permission to live for a few hours a simple, focused, life, uncomplicated by motive or concealment.

Relaxing into the seat he tried to think straight. Not about the sea, but about the Flask that night in 1982. He didn't want to think about suspects. There'd be enough of those. He didn't want to think about murder. What he wanted to do was *see* — fix in his head the dramatis personae of the wake, the stage, the complex relationships between the principal characters, dominated by the two sisters who'd been brought up in the Flask — Nora Tilden and Bea Garrison. Nora — buried that day, murdered by her husband Alby. Bea — back from the US, a widow, to help Nora's daughter Lizzie run the family business. But Bea hadn't

134

returned home alone. To Shaw, that fact underpinned the central image of the night: Pat, Bea's son, at the bar, sliding his hand across to cover his cousin Lizzie's — the first public betrayal of their secret. And the last. Had someone seen? Bea said she hadn't known about the relationship between her son and her niece, but was that really credible? And Kath Robinson certainly knew — Lizzie said she'd told her that night. Kath: a childlike figure on the edge of this family tragedy, a woman they needed to know more about. That was one of the tasks he'd allotted the team during the briefing.

He opened his eyes, aware he had achieved a sense of clarity. He swung himself out of the cockpit, rolled down the doors and reset the security code, turning to break into an easy loping run along the sands towards home.

Ahead, a mile distant, he could see the Old Beach Café, the cottage behind, and lit sideways by the floodlight on the verandah the boathouse shop — the apex of the roof marked by a string of white festive lights. Within 500 yards he felt his bloodstream pumping, promising a narcotic flood of endorphins, so that he was tempted to run past the house, along to the distant point at Holme, and then back. But in the white light spilling from the verandah of the café he saw two figures. A couple, arm-in-arm, one leaning on the other. If they'd been walking he'd have felt no anxiety. But they were stock still, waiting, in the middle of a winter beach. He slowed and heard a dog, out of sight, chasing a shadow in the dunes. He had a powerful sense that these people were waiting for him.

'Peter,' said one of the figures, as he approached. The light was behind, so he couldn't see the face. A woman's voice, and one he knew, but her identity was elusive. Squinting, he came level, allowing the light to shine over his shoulder. With a start he recognized Justina Kazimierz. He'd so rarely seen the pathologist touching anyone living that her familiar voice had gone unrecognized. She'd always appeared so self-contained, solitary.

'Justina?' said Shaw. 'What's wrong?' He'd often seen her on the beach, but always in daylight, and always alone.

She laughed, and he realized how rare that was. She tugged at the arm of the man beside her. 'Nothing's wrong. This is Dawid,' she said.

Shaw smiled and extended his hand. They'd met once, a few years ago, at the Polish Club, the night he'd watched them dance — hands touching, nothing else. Justina had changed a little since then, but her husband had aged, and he leant into her, one shoulder held low, a coat collar turned up to cover his neck to the chin. Even then he'd seemed small beside her sturdy middle-European frame. Now he just seemed frail. Despite the soft background soundtrack of the sea Shaw could hear him wheezing, each breath a miniature labour.

The couple's Labrador joined them, sniffing Shaw's boots.

'This is wonderful . . . ' Justina turned to the sea, making a little drama out of filling her lungs. 'I'm sorry — you'll want to get home. This is for

Fran, I was going to leave it on the stoop . . . '
She retrieved a brown paper parcel sticking out
of her overcoat pocket and held it out for Shaw.

'You can give it to her yourself,' Shaw said.
'You know you're welcome anytime.' He
gathered them up and the three of them
ascended the pine verandah steps into the café.
Lena was working at the table by the windows,
the account books spread out, a tape playing the
Penguin Café Orchestra. The smile when she saw
Justina was genuine, reminding Shaw how few
friends his wife had. Shaw made coffee while
Lena talked about the summer season — how
the café had been packed some days, then
deserted, but that the beach shop had kept their
heads above water. Then they talked about Fran.
On her last walk past the house Justina had
brought her an old pair of binoculars because
she'd started watching the horizon from the
beach, just like her father, and she only had a
plastic telescope.

'We might as well get her a job with the
Coastguard,' said Lena. She refilled Shaw's cup.
'She's as nosy as you are. And now she's nosy at
high magnification.'

'Intellectual curiosity,' said Shaw.

'Actually,' said Lena, considering whether she
knew Justina well enough to embark on an
argument with her own husband in public, 'it's a
kind of arrogance, isn't it? The idea that you've
got a *right* to know, to find out how everything
works.'

Shaw laughed. 'She's eight — curiosity can't
be bad.'

'I wasn't talking about her.'

'Justina's the same,' said Dawid. He leant forward. 'Always delving.' His voice was low and rich, and very gentle. For a small man his head was big, rounded, benign, but Shaw sensed that he found other people a trial. He sipped his coffee, satisfied perhaps that he'd defused the subject. Shaw tried to recall his profession: something medical, he knew, but specialized. Cytology, or urology. Lena had switched tack, and was telling them how she'd sold three winter dry suits to three teenagers who planned to swim every day until March the following year as a charity stunt. When Dawid smiled Shaw saw a vivid splash of blood on his upper gum. He looked away, and tried not to look again.

Shaw heard a footfall in the corridor that led up to the cottage and, catching Lena's eye, he saw that she'd heard it too: his daughter, edging nearer, trying to hear. This close to Christmas they'd become used to late-night appearances as the excitement began to build.

The footsteps grew louder and faster as the little girl ran down the corridor. Then Fran was at the table, laughing, happy to see Justina. The old terrier padded in after her and barked once at the Labrador before laying down on the spot where the hot-water pipes ran beneath the floorboards.

'I have something for you,' Justina said, handing Fran the package.

Fran tore open Justina's present, suddenly an eight-year-old on Christmas morning. Shaw was always fascinated by the way her behaviour

138

seemed to ricochet between adult and child — never a constant medium. Inside the package was a short illustrated guide to clouds — one of the many things she tracked from the beach. She said thank you, several times, but was still packed off to bed, Shaw leading her away down the shadowy corridor to the cottage.

When Shaw got back they were talking about the village — how the little shop and post office might close, and whether the tourist pubs would be open during the Christmas break. Then the conversation began to lag, running out of steam, because they could all sense that Shaw wanted to talk about the case, but that he couldn't break the house rule: that work and home shouldn't mix.

'So, it's all very Gothic,' said Lena, lifting the invisible barrier, cradling the coffee, letting the steam — Shaw noticed — wet her upper lip. 'Bones on coffins, open graves . . . ' She glanced at Shaw, letting him know that she didn't want the exclusion of work to become an obsession. She'd heard a report on the radio, so she knew the details. And anyway, they were stronger than that as a family — resilient to the reality of Shaw's other world.

'Anything new to report?' asked Shaw. Justina hadn't been present at the briefing.

The pathologist was already ordering information in her head, focused intently on turning her coffee cup in its saucer.

'I tracked down the original autopsy on the child — the one buried in the grave under the mother,' she said. Lena winced, glad Fran wasn't listening.

'Looks like sudden infant death syndrome. Cot death,' said Justina. 'The mother was the principal witness. She said she'd put the child to sleep upstairs in the pub at about six on the evening she died. The husband was running the bar but she went down to help. She checked the child regularly — she said — although when questioned by the coroner she admitted the last time she'd seen her daughter alive was at seven o'clock — she knew that was the time because she'd taken the chance to make herself a cup of tea and listen to the news on the radio. She next checked at eight fifteen. The child wasn't breathing. She started screaming, the husband went up, they called an ambulance which arrived at eight thirty-two p.m. The child was DOA at the Queen Victoria.'

Lena covered her mouth at the appalling euphemism. DOA.

'Awful,' said Dawid. Shaw presumed they didn't have children — certainly none were ever mentioned. He wondered if that had been their choice.

'The child's coffin contained something else,' she said. The pathologist produced an iPhone and touched the pad to bring up a picture, then slid it across the table. A model ship, exquisite, made of wood and lovingly painted. It was clear this was a specific vessel, hand crafted. A cargo ship. The superstructure was oddly out of balance with the dimensions of the hull, a small double crane set on the deck and a single gun on

140

the fo'c's'le. Shaw recalled that Alby Tilden had been a war hero, Arctic convoys with the merchant navy. Perhaps this had been his ship. A touching last gift for his daughter.

'How did it survive?'

'Child's coffin was lead lined — watertight, airtight. Most of the paint's fallen off since we took the picture.'

Lena stood abruptly and brought them more coffee, bringing the discussion to a close.

Later they all stood on the verandah, despite the raw breeze. Justina and Shaw had broken open a bottle of malt, Lena had a glass of wine. The Labrador, anxious about smells it couldn't locate, tried to force itself under the café into the space where the sand had blown. The heavy snow clouds had drifted on so that the sky was clear and moonless, and across it fell a meteor storm. They watched the sudden lines of light, gone almost before they could be seen. Shaw turned to see Justina's face turned upwards, at the exact angle of Lena's. But Dawid's eyes looked out to sea.

12

Tuesday, 14 December

The car park at St James's was full so Shaw parked the Porsche behind the Ark on a narrow side-street behind the Vancouver Shopping Centre. When Shaw cut the engine he and Valentine could hear the tinny soundtrack of piped-in Christmas carols leaking from the back of Wilkinson's. An inflatable Santa flew over the multistorey car park. In the road two cats pulled at a piece of Kentucky Fried Chicken in the snow. The clock on St Margaret's chimed the quarter hour. Mid-afternoon, but the December light would soon be dwindling fast. They had fifteen minutes before the autopsy on Pat Garrison. It was the third day of the inquiry, and they were little nearer finding his killer. They knew so much about him, so much about his family and his life, but the truth about that night twenty-eight years earlier remained elusive. It was like having a family photo album from which the vital picture had been torn out.

Shaw felt thwarted, frustrated, and worried that despite setting in train a textbook murder inquiry he was missing something obvious. For now all he could do was stick to his basic rules: keep it simple, check everything and share everything. He'd spent the morning getting everyone up to speed on the tangled history of the Melville family — including Tom Hadden and Max Warren. Then he'd organized a trawl through the list of guests Lizzie Murray had given them of all those she could recall being at her mother's wake. They needed witnesses, and after twenty-eight years that was going to be their biggest hurdle. Every name had to be tracked down, even if some of the trails led only to the cemetery. So far DC Lau's door-to-door operation had yielded little: a couple of people had been at the wake but memories were shaky, detail scant.

Valentine had contacted the secretary of the Whitefriars Choir and they had a volunteer trawling through old cine-film tins to see if they still had the one filmed on the night of Nora's wake. A few members of the choir remembered the evening and they'd be giving statements — but so far they'd uncovered nothing substantial, nothing new.

Overnight, Twine had made contact with the FBI and the state police department in North Dakota, based in the capital, Bismarck. He'd requested the paperwork on Pat Garrison — including his birth certificate and medical records. Shaw obtained clearance from Warren for DNA tests to be undertaken by the Forensic Science Service on the bones they'd found in the grave on top of the coffin and on a saliva sample provided by Bea Garrison. That was one relationship they needed to nail. Formal statements had been made by Bea, Lizzie Murray and Kath Robinson. Valentine had taken all three and reported that Robinson appeared to have learning difficulties — she seemed often confused and was unable to read her own statement. She was nervous and disorientated before being reunited with Bea, who had driven her home.

Shaw had talked to the coroner, who'd agreed to open an inquest, using Bea Garrison's identification of Shaw's forensic reconstruction as the basis for a preliminary identification of the victim. The brief hearing, scheduled for the following day, would be used as an appeal for witnesses to come forward, then adjourned until the police inquiry was over. To maximize publicity the opening hearing would be held at the Flask — which would also allow the coroner to visit the scene of the crime. It was a rare example of the coroner using an ancient power — to call an inquest close to the place of death, rather than in the characterless surroundings of the courts. The rarer the better, thought Shaw, because it would guarantee coverage in the local media and possibly even make the national newspapers. It was a long shot, but it was just possible, in a tight-knit community like South Lynn, that it would encourage witnesses to step forward whom they'd otherwise have missed.

Shaw checked his watch: 2.30 p.m. Low tide.

Valentine worked a finger into the hole on the dash-board that had once held a cigarette lighter. His mind constantly drifted from the case in hand to the Tessier case. He briefed Shaw on the surveillance units he'd set up for the scheduled evening meeting between Robert Mosse and Jimmy Voyce: a textbook operation — three mobile units, a back-up on standby and the police helicopter on call.

'Anyone farts, we'll have it in triplicate,' said Valentine.

Shaw left the heater running. He was aware that through the chassis of the car he could feel the gentle rumble of cars queuing on the ramps of the multi-storey car park, busy with less than nine full shopping days to Christmas. He made an effort to focus on Pat Garrison's death, trying to file away any anxieties he had about that coming night's operation at Hunstanton. There was nothing more he could do until the two men met. Meanwhile, any real progress in the hunt for Pat Garrison's killer remained elusive. As cold cases went it was beginning to feel icy. They needed to breathe life into the dead.

'So what do you *see*, George — that night, in the Flask? In here,' said Shaw, tapping a finger to his temple. 'Was the killer there?'

Valentine's stomach rumbled. Breakfast had been a single round of toast and a mug of tea in the canteen at six that morning, the brew laden with enough tannin to keep a shoe factory supplied for a month. He didn't really do lunch in terms of solids. His main meal of the day was usually administered after the pubs closed — a tray of chips and curry sauce, or a Chinese takeaway, noodles crammed into a silver-foil container. He played with his packet of Silk Cut, setting it at 90 degrees on the dashboard, then 180, then back to 90. He wanted to get a smoke in before the autopsy, but he forced himself to concentrate on Shaw's question. He knew the DI didn't ask questions unless he wanted answers. This was teamwork, and as much as neither of them wanted to be in a team, they had to make it work.

'Yeah,' he said. 'I think the killer was at the party. I don't think anyone in the family is telling us the whole truth — but that's because there are family secrets, and they're not sure what's coming out in the wash and what isn't. But the heart of it's clear . . . ' He heaved in a lungful of air, but it wasn't enough, so he flicked a switch to drop the passenger side window to cover up a second breath. 'It's dynamite, isn't it? Black kid . . . ' He held up both hands. 'Black *American* kid starts pawing white barmaid,' he said. 'We know Fletcher was there — maybe some of his chums share his political beliefs. Pat Garrison was just the perfect target — black and foreign. How excited can a bunch of bigots get? It's racial — I know Max don't want to hear that, but you know, it's pretty much screaming at us.'

'Go on,' said Shaw, knowing he was right, knowing this is what he could learn from Valentine, the ability to hold on to the obvious in the middle of a complex murder inquiry.

'Pat leaves the pub,' said Valentine. 'A couple of people who think like Fletcher are beered-up; they follow him out along the riverbank through the cemetery. Maybe Fletcher goes too. They confront him — they'd do that, right? That's how they think — they need to tell him why they want him out, to his face, like it's a form of courage or something, even though they've

146

turned up mob-handed. So they tell him that he's trash. Spit in his face. Then — from behind — one blow. Lights out. Then they chuck the body in the grave and shovel in some topsoil off the pile.' He pointed forward through the windscreen, suddenly animated. 'In fact, Fletcher *was* there — had to be, because he knows the grave is still open, and knows he'll have to fill it in.'

Shaw found he could imagine it happening. 'We need to see if that works — on the ground. Let's get an address for Garrison's flat. See if it makes sense that he'd walk home that way.'

Shaw closed his eyes, his nerves were making him fidget. One of the reasons he was finding it an effort to concentrate was that he hadn't had his early morning swim, and he hadn't run to the Porsche, because the tide had been too high and he'd had to pick his way through the dunes, so there was a lot of bottled energy in his system that needed to be dissipated. He'd spent the morning doing what he hated most: admin. Running a murder inquiry from behind a desk. His foot jiggled uselessly on the accelerator.

'What about the cousins thing?' said Shaw. 'Nora was a regular at the church. It's only a guess, but I reckon the Free Church of Christ the Fisherman doesn't take too kindly to that sort of relationship. Sleeping with your relatives. It's all part of the *don't do* list. So, don't marry your cousin. And Lizzie told her dad, who probably told everyone else, which was helpful.'

Valentine thrust his head forward, his narrow shoulders squaring off. 'So the Elect, or whatever, they get to know about it and they get uptight. Perhaps one of them decides to stop it — dead.' He hit the dashboard with the heel of his palm. But it was a half-hearted blow. He didn't believe it himself.

'Doesn't add up, does it?' said Shaw. 'It's been legal to marry your cousin in this country since the reign of Henry the Eighth. Back then, big issue. Now — no issue. OK, this isn't now — it's 1982 — but it's still thirteen years after we put a man on the moon. I'm not saying it wasn't a principle that was important to the believers. But killing someone? I don't think so. If this lot think Leviticus bans marriage between cousins then they sure as hell know their ten commandments. I don't think murder's an option.'

Valentine set the cigarette packet on its head. 'What about money? You've got a nineteen-year-old girl like Lizzie — she's not bad looking now, back then she must have been turning heads since she was fourteen. All of a sudden her mum dies and she's left the pub. That ain't gonna make her look any uglier, is it? I bet the likely lads were all over her like a horse blanket. This black kid was lining himself up for the money too, right? If he marries Lizzie, he gets the lot. And don't give me any of that 'it's all a secret' tosh, either. I don't think anyone had to tell anyone else what was going on — including the mother — Bea Garrison. She knew, betcha. Which means she's lying. If they fancied each other then everyone knew — it didn't need Alby to let his mates know from jail. I bet they all knew — just no one said. That's what they say, right — you suspect it, then it's happening. That's a powerful motive.'

'Maybe.'

Valentine put a cigarette in his mouth but didn't light it.

Shaw took pity on him, kicking open his door. 'Let's get some air,' he said.

They stood together in the street, their feet on the circumference of an imaginary circle six feet wide, their bodies angled in different directions. Flecks of snow began to fall.

Shaw took a fridgeful of cold air into his lungs. Valentine inhaled half of his Silk Cut.

'Couple of things,' said Shaw, holding up a handful of fingers. 'Press Twine to track me down Alby Tilden, will you — it's a loose end, and I don't like loose ends. In her statement, Lizzie says her dad stopped seeing visitors in the late eighties. She said his mental condition was poor, and he was ashamed of what he'd done. He wanted her to remember him as he was. According to Paul, the Prison Service says he got out in the late nineties. Since then, nothing. Lizzie gets letters — his are postmarked Peterborough. She keeps them — it's all pretty innocuous stuff, and no hint as to where he is. Return post goes via Bea Garrison to an address up north — then they're passed on. Nothing for a year now, by the way. We've got the address off Bea Garrison and Paul's been on to the local nick; they'll go round, see if we can get the forwarding details. But he clearly doesn't want to be found. And he's got the perfect alibi as he was banged up in Lincoln jail on the night of his wife's wake — but I want words, if he's alive. Paul said he was going after the pension records — see how far he got.'

He thrust his hands down deep into the pockets of his RNLI jacket.

'But the key is that night: the wake. The problem is, we can round up witnesses — and we will — but they're all family and friends; that's why they were there. Who do we trust? What we need is a reliable witness with nothing to gain from lying. Still no luck with the choir?'

'It'll take time,' said Valentine. 'One thought. My sister, Jean? She knew your dad. I think she did some kitchen work at the Flask, right through the eighties. Functions, parties, that kind of thing.'

Shaw remembered her: when Shaw's father was alive his DI had been a regular visitor at the house, usually late at night, so that Shaw would hear them downstairs, talking over a whisky bottle, worrying away at a case. Jean had come to family celebrations because she'd married a copper: a DS from Peterborough. Shaw recalled a stoical woman, always in the background, helping in the kitchen, the kind of woman who only spoke to annotate her husband's stories: a series of well-rehearsed asides.

'She about?' asked Shaw. A pair of seagulls dive-bombed the squabbling cats.

'Yeah. Don Walker — the copper — he died years ago. But she's about. Lives in the next street. I'll ask her. Even if she wasn't there, she might know someone who was. South Lynn's a tight community — there'll be someone.'

Shaw's mobile buzzed. It was a text from Twine. Sam Venn at the Free Church had given them the names of two black men who'd been members of the Elect in 1982 and might have been at Nora Tilden's funeral. St James's had tracked them down through the old electoral roll and found a relative at the same address. Jesse and Emmanuel Rogers, father and son, were both alive and well in Northampton; Jesse retired, a widower, Emmanuel working as a hospital porter.

He handed the phone to Valentine to read.

'They both lied,' said Shaw.

'Who?'

'Venn and Fletcher. Venn was happy to track down the two black men — but he didn't mention, when he could have, that there were three. Pat was at the graveside. So was Venn. An oversight — maybe? But what about Fletcher? He said there were two faces — and only two. He led us away from Pat Garrison.'

Valentine shrugged, judging whether he had time for another smoke. 'It's twenty-eight years. People forget.'

'Maybe — like I said, maybe Venn forgot. But Fletcher? There's a lot of things wrong with Freddie Fletcher, but being colour blind isn't one of them.'

13

Inside the Ark the lights were neon; a bank of them hung from the old roof beams. The old chapel was partitioned across the middle. On the far side of a set of plastic swing doors was the force's mortuary and autopsy suite. This side was Tom Hadden's forensics lab complete with a ballistics chute, mass spectrometer, fume cupboard and a bank of computers. The team 'hot-desked', so that the nest of tables was paperless and clinical. Stores and files were kept in the old organ loft, reached via a metal spiral staircase.

Hadden was at one of the desks as they came in, his monitor showing a flock of Arctic tern in flight as a screen-saver.

'Peter — for you,' he said, closing his eyes to concentrate on what he was going to say. 'Something you really need to see, I'm afraid.' The way he said it stopped them in their tracks.

'Soil profile from the grave,' said Hadden. 'I've got some graphics here. Take a seat — you'll need it. Both of you.'

The lab had a large whiteboard for showing computer images. Shaw and Valentine dragged up some chairs and Hadden tapped a button on his keyboard to project a single picture of Nora Tilden's empty grave. In order to get a flat shot of the long side of the grave it had been dug out so that the hole was nine feet by nine feet — a square, with three of the original sides preserved.

'We do this so that we can get back far enough to see the wood for the trees and get a good shot of the soil profile.' He tapped the button again and the next shot came up: a flat-on picture of the grave profile. Shaw could see the various layers of the soil — the black decaying humus at the top, a dark layer of soil, a thin yellow line where the clay began and then the grey, almost silvery, waterlogged strata below.

Valentine yawned so wide that a bone in his jaw cracked.

Hadden looked at the DS's exposed teeth. 'A soil profile can tell you as much as a fingerprint. It's evidence, very compelling evidence, if you read it properly, and interpret what it's telling us.'

Valentine looked at the screen.

'Now,' said Hadden, his eyelids closing, then fluttering slightly as he concentrated. 'You need to recognize that you've had a big slice of luck here, because the archaeologists who found our victim's bones dug out the grave using a mechanical digger, so it's really precise — engineered, if you like. What this picture shows, I believe, is that *before* they dug their hole someone else had dug down into the same grave, by hand, with a spade, about four feet, then stopped, then filled it in. This earlier hand-dug hole was not as true as the one made with the digger. It's slightly to one side, slightly slewed, so you can still see the ghost of it, if you like, in the profile that's left, cutting through the nice neat strata of the profile. You see?'

153

Shaw stood, staring into the bright image. Hadden was right, because the neat wedding-cake layers had been disrupted, the shadow of the hole breaking the thin yellow clay line.

Which left them with one key question. 'When?' asked Shaw.

'Well, I know someone at Cambridge's soil-science lab who can give us a better call, but I'd guess — and it's a good guess — that we're talking between six and eight months.'

'This year?' said Shaw, his voice sharp and energized. Suddenly he felt ten years younger. 'We're saying someone dug down towards those bones this year — then filled it in, then along came the digger?'

'The disturbed soil,' said Hadden, pointing at what he'd called the 'ghost' of the hole revealed in the soil profile, 'has been settling for one winter, and almost certainly only one. That's when a lot of the soil processes work through the strata — forming layers, rotting the leaves to form the mulch at the top, creating the soil.'

He interlaced his hands, turning them upside down to form a basket, to show that science could do miracles too. 'This part of the profile, where's there's been disruption, is just a jumble of soil — there's hardly any stratification.'

Valentine tried to concentrate, distracted by the gurgle of a coffee machine on the next desk. 'We're saying someone dug down into this grave sometime this year and then gave up?'

'Yes. That's right. Or they found what they were looking for and stopped,' said Hadden. 'Four feet brings you pretty close to the bones

154

we found. They could have got close, then just dug at a precise spot — further down. We'll never know because the archaeologists just ejected the spoil, as you would expect. They weren't interested in the graves, just what was supposed to be at the bottom of them.'

'Animals? Natural subsidence?' asked Shaw, aware that the basis of his inquiry had just been shifted twenty-eight years closer. He felt his bloodstream coursing, as if he'd just finished his morning mile.

Hadden held up a hand, closed his eyes, thinking through Shaw's multiple question. 'No. Animal damage would be much more localized. Subsidence is out — you can see the underlying clay base is solid.'

Shaw tried to imagine the scene. At night, perhaps? One or more men, working by a small light, digging down towards the three buried bodies.

He clicked his fingers. Valentine winced. 'Hold on. What about the archaeologists? Perhaps they did it, filled it in, then came back, like a trial dig to see what the soil conditions were like.'

Hadden shook his head. ''Fraid not, Peter. Nice try. I've checked.'

Shaw was still thinking. 'George — when did the council announce the programme of reinterment? Can you find out for me . . . ' He held Valentine's eyes, so that he saw the DS's eyebrows rising slightly at the insistent tone. Valentine stood, walked towards the partition with the mortuary and flicked open his mobile.

'They were after something,' said Shaw,

tapping the whiteboard. 'And if they gave up at four feet, and what they wanted was at six feet, then what they wanted was still in the grave when we opened it. Or — they got close, knew exactly what they were after, and just dug down to get it — like a miniature well. To do that they'd need to know precisely its location — but then that's not difficult if you know a few basics: like which end of the grave the head lies, that kind of thing?'

Hadden nodded and took Shaw to one of the lab tables which had been cleared and covered with a white plastic sheet. On it were the items they'd extracted from Nora Tilden's coffin and from amongst the bones found on the coffin lid.

Each one had been labelled, numbered, dated. The green glasses with the engraved whaling scene first, the penknife, the wallet, the few coins. And from between the coffin lid and the bones, the billhook. And finally, from inside Nora's coffin, the silver brooch.

'No wedding ring on Nora's hand?' asked Shaw.

Hadden shook his head. 'Then we go inside the wallet,' he said. He'd set the contents out separately, under a single sheet of glass: the rotted pieces of paper, one with the faint pen strokes of the gibbet and hanging man just visible. There was one rectangular piece of paper, white, as if it had been leached of colour. 'I'm working on that — maybe a receipt?' said Hadden. 'The paper's shiny, like . . . I don't know — a football match ticket? A concert? I can't raise any images at the moment but it's early days. Just a three-letter grouping — MOT, just that — with a space before and a space after. That's all I can get — MOT. It could be an MOT certificate, I suppose — I've asked someone to track down a copy of the standard form from 1982, see if it matches.' He let Shaw think about that, rearranging the remains of a ten-pound note and three fives.

'Big question is — if they were after one of these items, which one was it?' asked Hadden, smiling broadly, enjoying himself.

'The penknife,' said Shaw. 'George says it's a collector's item — and a link to the GIs. So maybe that?'

'Maybe.'

'The billhook?'

Hadden picked up the bagged item and turned it so that Shaw could read the word stamped into the metal haft, where it sank into the wooden handle.

STANLEY

'Toolmaker's name,' said Hadden. 'No other marks.'

Valentine came back, his mobile extended with a straight arm. There was a text on screen from Paul Twine: 18 JUNE 2010.

'Bang on six months,' said Valentine.

'So, last June the council announces the coffins are coming up, someone panics, thinks we'll find the bones and some evidence which points to the identity of the killer. They go to the cemetery after dark, dig down. Someone, clearly, with a lot to lose,' said Shaw, turning to Hadden.

Hadden nodded. 'Maybe. I just do the science,

Peter. The clever stuff's all yours.'

'There was something else in the grave,' said Valentine. 'Garrison's bones. Perhaps they wanted to get him out. Then there'd be no inquiry at all. Fuck all. But they gave up.'

Dr Kazimierz pushed her way through the swing doors and helped herself to coffee. She caught Shaw's eye, smiled, then retreated back through the doors. The greeting had been warmer than usual, and Shaw wondered if the meeting with Dawid on the beach had been a rite of passage, an entry into a different circle of friendship.

'George,' said Shaw. 'After we're done, ring Paul. I want everyone to know that we need to focus on this attempt to reopen the grave. The timeline is pretty conclusive. Night time? Almost certainly. How'd they do that? Let's crawl all over this — local uniformed squad cars, beat, council security, any local low life that hangs out in the cemetery after dark — you know the score, brief everyone. This may well be a cold case, George — but it just got a whole lot hotter. And tell Jacky to rerun the door-to-door in the immediate vicinity — someone must have seen or heard something.'

Shaw took a deep breath. Beside the swing doors there was a tray of boiled sweets. He took one, passed another to Valentine.

'Ready?' he asked, with the surfer's smile. 'Or are you going to fit in a quick bacon sandwich?'

Valentine didn't smile back. 'On the subject of food . . . ' He took out his wallet and slipped out a ticket, handing it to Shaw. It was for the

158

Shipwrights' Hall Christmas dinner they'd seen advertised on Freddie Fletcher's wall at the PEN office.

'Traffic division have taken a table — that's how it works. You buy a table, then flog your tickets. I thought I'd go along, Thursday lunchtime, so we can see who Fletcher's mates are. The Flask's got a table, too.'

'Enjoy,' said Shaw, pushing his way through the doors into the autopsy suite, unhappy that the thought of the Shipwrights' Hall lunch conjured up an image of turkey and gravy on Christmas morning, his father attacking the bird's carcass with a carving knife.

There were three metal tables in the autopsy suite, all occupied. The rest of the room was metallic and cold, except for the stone walls and the single statue, left from the original chapel, of an angel high on the apex of the wall, its hands covering sightless eyes.

They moved to the first table. Shaw's blood had begun to migrate to his heart, leaving his fingers cold, because on the brushed aluminium slab lay a tiny coffin, and beside it a shroud, wrapped — he guessed — around an infant's body. He hadn't been expecting this, and the tattered intimacy of the small bundle made him feel like a grave robber.

The pathologist carefully unwrapped the shroud to reveal the skeleton of a child wrapped in a second, rotten cloth.

'We know the story — there's nothing new to tell. I'll do some toxicology but cot deaths were just as inexplicable then as they are now.'

'It happens,' said Valentine, unable to prevent his words sounding harsh and cynical.

Hardly any of the child-sized bones remained intact. That didn't stop Shaw trying to clothe them in flesh, seeing the baby flexing its limbs in a cot. For the first time he thought that his gift, to see the flesh on bones, might be a curse as well as a blessing.

Kazimierz moved to the second mortuary table and uncovered the body of Nora Tilden: the skeletal frame stripped of the remnants of clothes and funeral wear, the bones held together by wire. Kazimierz put her hand on a brown blotched file at the head of the table. 'These are the original records used at Albert Tilden's trial,' she said. 'Everything is consistent: the leg bones are shattered, as is one arm, the collarbones, the lower spine.' Shaw thought about the narrow steep staircase at the Flask. He thought of tumbling down, his limbs cracking against the wall, the wooden banisters. Sympathetic pains ran through his nervous system.

'She's not been disturbed in any way since burial?' he asked.

'Tom's your man on that,' she said. 'But there are no breaks or fractures other than those listed.' She looked at the bones, shaking her head. 'No. I think she's lain like this for twenty-eight years. There's no soft tissue, so I can't tell you anything else. But I've analysed the bones, and I can tell you one thing — she was suffering from osteoporosis.'

She picked a photograph out of the file of a woman, late middle age, greying hair tied back, a

160

broad match for the one they'd got up in the incident room, but younger. 'This is her,' she said. In this photograph the lighting was better, so that it was possible to see the eyes, which were humourless, and the lips, too thin to support any kind of smile. But there was a hint of something else — an earlier beauty, perhaps; a delicate, rounded, childlike grace.

'What age was she when the child was born?' asked Shaw.

Kazimierz worked it out from the file. 'Twenty — just.'

Shaw looked again at the face, trying to run it backwards in time, trying to retrieve the young mother who'd lost her first child after just a few weeks.

They moved to the corpse provisionally identified as Patrice Garrison.

'I've extracted a sample of marrow for DNA analysis. Tom's got the ID in hand. My initial summary of the cause of death stands. In fact, I can show you . . . '

She leant forward and lifted the top of the trepanned skull so that they could see into the brain cavity. Shaw couldn't help noticing how at ease Kazimierz was dealing with the dead, and recalled how awkward she'd been the night before at the café, clutching her husband by the arm.

Shaw got close, but Valentine looked at the clock on the wall, concentrating on the shuddering second hand, thinking only of the clean metallic mechanism within.

'You can see here,' said the pathologist, 'where

the tip of the billhook curved right round through the brain and actually indented the inside of the right parietal bone.'

'This would take force?' asked Shaw. 'A man — a powerful man?'

'No. I don't think you can make any such surmise. The physics of this are complex, Shaw. You've got a swinging blow with a curved weapon meeting a round object. It's all luck. Catch it just right and you'd slice through the bone like butter. An inch to one side, a few seconds later, it would sheer off, leaving only a flesh wound.'

Shaw filed that detail in his memory, noting only that it clashed with the two etched green glasses, which had suggested a ritual: something planned and meticulous.

Kazimierz turned her back to fill in some paperwork on a lab bench, dismissing them without a word.

Hadden's suite on the far side of the partition was empty, so Shaw pulled out from the wall a blackboard on hinges. Taking a piece of chalk from the runnel he wrote 'Arthur Melville' at the top, followed by Nora, then 'Albert Tilden' and their dates.

'What's this?' asked Valentine. 'Hi-tech policing?'

'Just keeping it simple.' Shaw drew the rest of the family tree. The result was starkly instructive, because it didn't look like a family tree. 'It's like the old Norfolk joke,' said Shaw. 'Everyone in the village has got a family tree — it's just that they don't have any branches.'

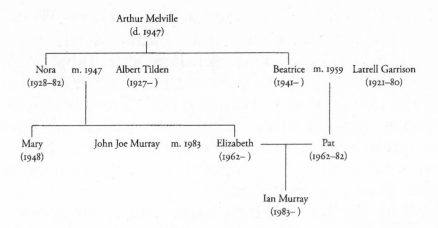

Arthur Melville
(d. 1947)

Nora   m. 1947   Albert Tilden   Beatrice m. 1959 Latrell Garrison
(1928–82)   (1927–)   (1941–)   (1921–80)

Mary   John Joe Murray m. 1983 Elizabeth ——— Pat
(1948)   (1962–)   (1962–82)

Ian Murray
(1983–)

Valentine put a Silk Cut between his lips.

Shaw underlined Nora Tilden's name.

Valentine stood and drew circles around three others. 'Three of them are black,' he said. 'Latrell — Bea's husband, their son Patrice, who becomes our victim in Nora's grave, and then his son Ian. Three generations.'

Shaw stubbed the chalk on Ian's name, breaking it. 'What do we know about him? This isn't all about the past, is it, George? Because we know that someone was out there in Flensing Meadow digging up that grave just six months ago. Which transforms the inquiry — even Max Warren would have to admit that. Someone alive, someone with enough youth left to dig a four-foot hole after dark, someone who feared what we'd find in that grave.'

He stood back. 'So perhaps it's a family secret, and Ian knows what it is.'

Valentine checked his notebook. 'Ian Murray. He's twenty-seven. School at Whitefriars primary, just round the corner. Then Springwood

High. Trained as a chef at the college. Works in the kitchens at the Flask lunch-times — then evenings and Sundays at Kirkpatrick's — the posh wine bar on the quay. Holidays, days off — that's Monday and Tuesday — he cooks up at Bea Garrison's B&B. Single — girlfriend works at Kirkpatrick's too. Name of Sharon Hare; she's local as well. He lives at the Flask, in the attic.'

'OK. We'll catch him later. I fancy an oyster.'

Valentine pulled a face. He didn't do wine bars.

Shaw checked his watch and chucked the chalk back in the runnel. Outside the green glass windows of the Ark the dusk was gathering, so that they could see a scattering of Christmas lights in the gloom decorating a crane. They'd got a second interview set with Sam Venn at the London Road Shelter in an hour. Freddie Fletcher had eluded them: he was either out or ignoring the hammering on his door. The owner of Tinos, the greasy spoon downstairs, said he often went out canvassing for hours. He could be anywhere on the street. Shaw had asked for a uniformed PC to stay on his doorstep. Twine had overnight orders to put most of the manpower on the door-to-doors in the morning, in and around the cemetery, because they needed to throw everything they had at trying to find out who had dug up Nora's grave in the last few months.

Shaw felt good. The inquiry was humming now: efficient, logical and professional. They'd got their break — thanks to Tom Hadden's brilliant forensic work. Now, Shaw sensed, Pat Garrison's killer was no longer an insubstantial ghost from the past. Whoever it was, Shaw felt that soon he'd be able to reach out and touch them.

14

The stumpy remains of Hunstanton's pier shook with the impact of a storm wave, the white water erupting around the metal legs, spilling across the promenade. It was dark and starless, but the town's streetlights caught the seawater in the air, a cloud like smoke, drifting in from a sea the colour of mulligatawny soup, and turned to orange the patches of snow in the ornamental gardens. Winter had turned violent. A single string of coloured Christmas lights swung and snapped in the wind between lamp posts.

Shaw had agreed to sit out the surveillance as a passenger in Valentine's Mazda, and he was unhappy with the heating system, fiddling constantly with the switches. Valentine smoked with the unhurried focus of the true addict. Shaw's mobile phone buzzed and he brought up a text message and picture from Lena — a shot of Fran out on the snow-covered beach at dusk, standing by a snowman with a snorkel.

Shaw checked his watch. It was five forty. Twenty minutes until Robert Mosse's appointment with Jimmy Voyce. They'd agreed to meet at the pier head — but all that was left of the pier was a café and a bowling alley, both closed for the winter. The main pier had largely burnt down in 1939, and what was left had been similarly damaged during the 1950s, leaving the superstructure to be washed away in a storm in

1978. An attempted partial rebuild in 2002 burnt down, too. The people of Hunstanton — who included Shaw after his parents had moved out of town when he was a kid — could be forgiven for thinking someone was trying to tell them something: that perhaps they could do without a pier. But no. Shaw noted a developers' billboard advertising the project for a new one, the finance provided by the EU.

In a peculiar way Shaw was proud of the place. Because of its position on the coast of The Wash, looking west, it had a unique claim to fame. 'It's the only pier on the east coast that faces the setting sun,' he said.

Valentine stirred in his seat. 'Far as I'm concerned, if it's facing the sea, it's facing the wrong way.' Valentine had always hated the beach — any beach. There was the grittiness of it, and the sunburn on the tops of his feet, and the cloying scent of cooking flesh. As a child he'd come here from South Lynn on school trips and with his parents. The best part of the day was the ride home. He'd never admitted, even to himself, that it was the sea that really made him anxious: the way it seemed to draw you away from the promenade towards its dangerous, shifting edge. He always thought it was a bit like a net, being cast and recast on to the shore, as if the ocean was fishing for him.

They heard the town clock at the top of the green strike a quarter to the hour. Snow began to fall in the gusts of wind off the sea. All they had to do was wait. One unit had tracked Voyce north in his hired car to the edge of town, then backed off before they'd seen him park. Mosse had left home an hour ago, driven north, but the unit had lost him on the road. Mosse was here, they were sure of that, they just didn't know where. But they knew where he'd agreed to be at 6.00 p.m. precisely. By the pier head Shaw watched a flock of seagulls land, fighting over scraps, then tumbling on to the green, standing — each one — identically angled into the onshore wind.

Shaw reviewed the interview they'd just completed with Sam Venn, warden of the London Road Shelter and a member of the Elect of the Free Church of Christ the Fisherman. DC Twine had provided them with a brief CV culled from Venn's employers, the Vancouver Trust. Born in Lynn in 1959, both parents members of the church, attended the grammar school and took a degree in sociology at Lampeter College, University of Wales. He'd worked in the voluntary sector since graduating — Age Concern, Shelter in Leicester, then back to Lynn to take over as warden at London Road. He also worked two days a week for the council's housing department, with a remit to oversee social housing in the town. Unmarried, he lived alone, in a flat at the shelter, which provided food and a warm place for the homeless from 6.30 a.m. to 8.00 p.m.

Venn had been in an office behind the kitchen, working through the order book for foodstuffs. Shaw had been struck again by his first mistake — that he'd underestimated this man's intelligence because of that face, one side sloping

168

down, as if gravity was stronger on the left than the right, and the hand, held awkwardly on the lap or set on the desktop like a paperweight.

Shaw wasted no time: Why had Venn failed to mention the presence of Patrice Garrison at Nora Tilden's wake?

Venn's answer was smooth and plausible. He knew Pat Garrison, he'd talked to him in the pub that summer, seen him about the town. Bea Garrison had even come to the church one Sunday with her son. They'd joined in the prayers for Nora, although Venn said he suspected they'd come to pray for Alby. He hadn't mentioned Pat Garrison because he didn't think of him in terms of his colour, but in terms of his character, which was typically American — brash, confident, focused. But, Venn admitted, vanity was his principle vice. Shaw guessed it was a characteristic to which Venn was acutely tuned.

'That happens, doesn't it?' he'd asked Shaw. 'That you just forget the colour of someone's skin.'

Yes, thought Shaw, it happens. It should happen. The question was, had it happened to Sam Venn?

Venn denied that he, or anyone else in the church, knew about Lizzie's affair with her cousin. But he was happy to expatiate on the Free Church's attitude to the marriage of cousins.

'That's forbidden — yes, absolutely. We believe that Leviticus is clear on that point, and as I've said to you, Inspector, we live only by the Word.'

169

Shaw, faced with dogma, failed to mask an aggressive tension in the next question. 'I see. And what does that mean? If cousins did marry — and they were members of the church — what would happen?'

'Cast out,' he'd said. And that's when the mask — the lop-sided, damaged mask — slipped. There was a flash of real anger, and he'd had to swallow hard, and Shaw got the sense he was fighting to keep his breathing shallow.

'And that's happened, has it?' Shaw asked.

Venn's eyes were blank, windows obscured by reflections. 'Yes. But Pastor Abney would have the details. It was some years ago, certainly. Years ago.' He rearranged papers on his desktop, appearing to resist the temptation to read a bank statement.

'And the children of the Elect are bound by the same rules, Mr Venn? But if they're outside the church, presumably they are beyond the church's punishment?' asked Shaw, pleased with the question.

Venn had smiled then, a smile quite devoid of humour, or even the semblance of humour. 'The world is full of evil. We seek only to keep it outside our church. We are a beacon. An example of the way the world should be, not of the world that is.'

Valentine had ascertained Venn's movements on the night of the wake. He'd gone straight from the graveside to the pub, stayed for food, then taken his place in the choir. He thought he'd left about eleven, but he couldn't be sure. He hadn't noticed Pat Garrison in the bar, though he thought he'd probably been there. Venn had asked then — outright — if he was a suspect. Valentine had noted down the question, because in his experience anyone who asked it was rarely guilty. Shaw had given him the answer: No — he wasn't a suspect, but that didn't mean he couldn't be. The inquiry was ongoing. Shaw felt Venn was an unlikely killer, but he was as sure as he could be that he was lying to them about something. When asked, he denied all knowledge of an attempt to reopen Nora Tilden's grave in the last year. He seemed genuinely astonished at the idea.

Once they'd left Venn's office Shaw had called Twine: he wanted more on Venn, anything they could find from his university days, perhaps. Or one of his earlier employers. Family history, too: his parents, siblings. People like Sam Venn worried him; an incomplete character, as if presenting only two dimensions to the world, an image without depth. It was too easy to see in his religious fervour a reaction to his disability. Shaw sensed something else, something less passive.

'Here's someone,' said Valentine, leaning his head forward until it touched the windscreen of the Mazda. A figure walked the snowy promenade of Hunstanton, slanted seaward into the wind, in a thin and cheap thigh-length cagoule. Valentine flicked a pen torch into life, illuminating a black-and-white picture the Auckland police had faxed them. Voyce was a member of the British Legion in Hamilton, the small town in which he lived, on the strength of his father's wartime service in the Royal

Artillery, and they'd lifted his son's mug shot from his application form. He was fifty yards away but they could see the distinctive bald dome of the head, and the heavy bone structure of the face.

And then, eerily, there were two of them.

'Where did he come from?' said Shaw, sitting forward, his voice shredded with anxiety.

His radio buzzed and he heard DC Birley's voice. 'Must have been under the pier, on the prom, waiting. We've got him now.' Mark Birley was ex-uniform branch, a heavily built rugby player who'd originally only joined the force for the weekend matches with the St James's XV. But it hadn't taken long to discover that he could transfer the ruthless focus of his game to a major inquiry. Birley was 'point' for the operation — the kingpin, ensconced in a surveillance van up at the end of the green with a live feed into the town's half-dozen CCTV cameras. He alerted the other two units on the open channel and asked them to stand by.

'Wonder where the BMW is,' said Shaw. The promenade was deserted and the car park held only a VW Camper and two Vauxhall Corsas parked next to each other with their lights on. He considered calling the whole thing off right there, right then. Mosse's movements so far had been perfectly judged to throw them off the trail. Shaw had to admit he had less than full confidence that they could guarantee Jimmy Voyce's safety. And less than full confidence was not good enough.

They watched the two men shake hands,

embrace in a brief, awkward, clinch.

Had Mosse guessed he was being followed? If he had, would he have made his appointment at all? Or was he simply taking precautions? If either man had any idea the police were watching then Shaw's surveillance operation was dead in the water: Mosse would lie low, Voyce would go home — probably encouraged by a vague promise from Mosse of a cheque by air mail. But crucially they'd watch what they said, weigh every word, aware of the dangers of entrapment.

Shaw hesitated, then decided they could let the op run, as long as they kept both men in sight. Their only real hope of building a case against either man depended on picking up a recording from one of the bugs in Voyce's car, on his phone, or in the hotel room. He had to give them more time, more rope. If he'd coolly analysed his options at that point, as he did six hours later, his decision would have been different. But he was fired up by the idea, the mere possibility, that after all these years he'd be able to wipe that satisfied half-smile off Bobby Mosse's ski-tanned face.

The two walked towards Valentine's Mazda, then across a pelican crossing and into a pub called the Wash & Tope. It was one of the half-dozen likely places the two might go, so a plan was in place: DCs Lau and Campbell were round the corner, already walking towards the side door which led into the pub's pool room. Voyce and Mosse went into the front bar. The windows of the pub were frosted glass, the light within too bright, reflecting off the wet pavement. After a minute they could just see two heads in shadow at the window, drinking.

Shaw checked his tide watch: 6.14 p.m.

Campbell and Lau had orders to observe, nothing more. If they could get close enough to hear any of the conversation, well and good: if not, they should play pool, chat up the barman. They were the odd couple: one six feet two in jeans and a bomber jacket, the other five feet four in a leather jacket and wraparound reflective glasses. No one would guess they were undercover CID. They stood out too much.

At 6.31 p.m. a low, oiled rumble made the pennies on the dashboard of Valentine's Mazda vibrate. Thirty seconds later a BMW slid down the narrow alley at the side of the pub, pausing a half-beat, then pulling out into the street. The car was doing 80 mph before Shaw had alerted all units, its distant brake lights reflecting on the road as it headed south, then signalled to turn down a side-street. They followed in the Mazda, taking the same turning down towards the sea, but seeing nothing moving ahead.

After forty-five seconds of silence Birley's voice crackled on the open channel. 'Got 'em. Just through the roundabout by the water tower, heading south. He's got his foot down.'

DC Campbell cut in. 'We're on the road. They went out the back to smoke. Left their drinks on the table.'

Valentine slid out on to the coast road, forcing the ageing Mazda to hit 75 mph. Shaw sat forward in the passenger seat trying to see tail lights ahead, but knowing they were losing ground with every mile. He'd been a fool to leave the Porsche at St James's. He chewed over DC Campbell's report: he didn't like the sound of the half-finished drinks. What was suddenly so urgent they had to leave their drinks? Had they cut straight to business over the cigarette — and decided to go somewhere less public? It was a chilling thought, because going somewhere private with Bobby Mosse was literally the last thing Jimmy Voyce should do. And Shaw cursed his luck: his two prime targets were travelling in the car they hadn't managed to bug.

Birley again. 'Unmarked car's picked 'em up at the Sandringham T-junction. Still doing eighty-five, sir. They'd like advice.'

'Tell 'em to do ninety,' muttered Valentine.

Shaw thought about it. If the unmarked CID car tried to stay with them at that speed they'd know they were being followed. But if the car backed off they'd almost certainly lose them. He had another car stationed at the ring-road roundabout at Lynn. If Mosse was going anywhere in the town they'd have to pass it before turning off the dual carriageway.

'Tell them to follow — but at a distance. Don't try to stay with them. Get through to the forward squad car, Mark. If they see the BMW they can follow from there.'

They drove in silence. It was an odd silence. Shaw remembered as a child listening live to the TV broadcast from Mission Control in Houston as the damaged capsule of *Apollo 13* had fallen through the earth's atmosphere: eight minutes of

175

enforced radio silence, with the world waiting for a sound of life. Every ticking second added to the expectation of bad news. It was a silence like that.

Shaw checked the radio to see if the frequency was still open. South of Snettisham they got caught behind a line of caravans, forcing their speed down to 50 mph. Finally, they saw ahead the ringlet of high floodlights over the round-about on the ring road. Traffic was light, a single HGV thundering around the curve. The convoy of caravans swung round and continued on the main road. With a sinking heart Shaw spotted the unmarked CID car in the lay-by — a Volkswagen Polo with spoilers and a 'ball-of-fire' paint job. Valentine parked behind it. No one moved.

After ten minutes Shaw got out and stood on the verge, thinking that a ring-road roundabout was one of the bleakest spots on earth. The air was laced with fumes, and there was some snow in the air, as apparently aimless as the circulating traffic. In the central reservation, on the grass, a teenager sat with his shirt off, drinking from a gold can.

Question: Where were Mosse and Voyce? Between the last sighting south of Hunstanton and the Lynn roundabout there were half a dozen turn-offs — all minor roads, leading either down to the tidal marshes or inland to the villages on the edge of the Norfolk hills.

He tried to imagine the conversation in the speeding BMW. Voyce trying to avoid the semblance of blackmail, Mosse playing dumb, both of them attempting to negotiate a number without actually talking money. And Voyce's promise — that would be the key bargaining point, that he had a flight home booked, that he'd be gone in five days. So this was a one-off. But Mosse, thinking it through, judging, perhaps, that there was absolutely no reason that Voyce should turn out to be different from most blackmailers, who always, *always*, come back for more.

And that worrying unknown: with exactly *what* was he blackmailing Mosse? Just a stark threat to go to the police? Or something else — something more substantial, something that would put Mosse behind bars while Voyce would walk free or face a nominal sentence? Is that why Cosyns and Robins had died? Did they harbour the same lethal secret? If Voyce was trying the same game, he was risking his life.

Stress made Shaw's vision blur, so that he had to blink until the image cleared.

The driver's side window of the Mazda came down. Smoke drifted out.

'I'll buy you a drink,' said Valentine.

15

Kirkpatrick's Bar stood on the quay, just beyond the Grade I listed Custom House, close to the Purfleet, the black gullet of water that cuts into the heart of the Old Town. Outside the snow had thickened and was driving in with the tide. A chalk board offered oysters, mussels or crab. The bar was empty so Shaw and Valentine took a table by the window and ordered two pints of Guinness and a dozen oysters, from a waitress who appeared from the kitchen: mid-twenties, spider-thin, with blonde hair, tied up to one side and so thick it threatened to bend her narrow neck with the weight. Shaw had his radio and mobile on the table top, keeping track of the units he'd sent back up the road to Hunstanton to try to find the missing BMW and Voyce's hire car. He had a traffic unit stationed near Mosse's house with orders to alert everyone if he came home. Shaw's stress level had hit a plateau: but it was a high one. Twice he'd actually imagined he'd heard his mobile ring tone, grabbing the phone only to find no incoming call.

'Cheers,' said Valentine, trying not to wince as he took the top three inches off the pint. He'd asked for a pint of bitter but they only had bottles, and he never drank wine if he was paying, so he'd gone for the black stuff. He looked at the glass now, knowing he'd made the wrong decision. 'Christ,' he said, wiping his hand across his lips. 'How can you drink that?'

The events of the night so far suggested that both their careers were in danger of imminent collapse — a prospect Valentine found oddly appealing. He realized, perhaps for the first time, that since his demotion he'd been living a kind of half-life, waiting, scheming, and dreaming only of his return to St James's and the reattainment of his lost rank. He could see now that this was not so much a healthy goal as his *only* goal. An obsession. Now that the prospect of success was so slim he sensed a new freedom, a chance to accept failure and the lonely retirement that would follow, and then do something else with his life, even if it was just to walk away. He cracked his fingers at the joints and took a second swig at the Guinness. Not lonely perhaps; just alone. He could live with that.

Shaw was less sanguine. He had no intention of passively watching his career implode. But the first step to recovering the situation was to recognize that they'd made a mistake: losing Mosse was a critical error. They had to find him, and quickly.

'We should have put a wire in the BMW, or tagged it,' he said, setting his glass carefully down on a slate coaster. He took one of the oysters, slid it into his mouth, bit down twice and let it slip down his throat. The effect was always the same, a rush of well-being, because the taste was of the sea.

'Bit late for that bright idea,' said Valentine. He looked Shaw in the eye. 'My fault.

179

Surveillance was down to me. My op. I underestimated Mosse — I've spent a lifetime doing it.' He drained the remaining Guinness in one draught. 'I never learn.' The waitress was sitting on a bar stool, reading a paper. He caught her eye, asking for a re-fill, keen to have more of what he didn't like. When she brought the drink they asked to see Ian Murray — adding that they'd phoned ahead.

She retreated to the kitchen and they could hear a conversation in low tones. Then Murray appeared, wearing chef's whites and carrying a glass of fizzy water, ice and lemon. The waitress joined him, standing.

'Manager says I can have ten minutes,' said Murray. He didn't meet their eyes and his tone was hostile, hovering between exasperation and irritation, an almost exact mirror of his mother's emotional temperament. Shaw couldn't help but wonder why. They were there to try to find out who had killed his father. What was his problem with that?

'Ten minutes,' he repeated, taking a seat.

Valentine looked around at the empty tables. 'Wouldn't want to miss the rush.'

'He's the boss. You can argue the point with him if you like.'

Ian Murray was a confident young man. When Shaw had seen him in the Flask he'd seemed more vulnerable. Here he sat with one leg hooked over the arm of his chair, holding his glass with both hands in a cradle of fingers. He would have judged him handsome, the skin tone almost exactly matching his polished leather boots. His hair was fashionably shaved to reveal a fine skull. When he blinked, which he did slowly, one lid — the right — seemed to stick, opening more slowly than the left. He moved in a way that seemed calculated to accentuate the flexibility of his limbs, as if his joints were oiled.

'I don't know how I can help,' he said, shrugging again, managing to make even that small movement silky and fluid. 'I was like, you know, not born.'

The door swung inward and a couple almost fell in, shaking snow from their coats. They watched as the waitress reappeared to take a drinks order and hand out menus. Shaw wondered if the blonde was Murray's girlfriend, and struggled to recall the name he'd given them.

He reminded himself why they were there. Family secrets. Yes, he hadn't yet been born on the night his father died, but he'd grown up in a family defined by that moment. Not death — because that wasn't the truth he'd had to live with. Something worse: desertion.

'What did your mother tell you about your father?' Shaw asked.

'Very little. She was ashamed of him, ashamed of herself — for making a mistake like that. We always thought he was low life after what he did — running out on her. Now, of course, things are different. Now we know he wasn't a good-for-nothing womanizer. It doesn't say a great deal for my mother's judgement of character, does it? Or perhaps it does. There's just a lack of consistency.' He sipped the water. 'Trust.'

He brushed an imaginary speck of dust off his boots.

'She chose John Joe,' said Shaw. 'He's stuck around. You've always had John Joe. Was that a mistake?'

Ian set the glass of water down and turned it, examining the ice. 'Look. This isn't Walt Disney. John Joe isn't my wicked stepfather. But he isn't my dad either. We're OK, but there's nothing . . . ' He looked around, suddenly angry. 'Nothing else.'

'Really? He seemed very concerned about you.'

'He's concerned about Mum. She's concerned about me. That's the way it works.' He leant forward. 'Look at my face. You think John Joe understands what it's like to be inside this skin?'

'Does your mum understand?' asked Shaw, annoyed that Murray had played the race card so shamelessly.

'She tries,' he said, watching the waitress, his eyes lingering on the tight black cocktail dress.

Shaw thought about what this young man's childhood had been like. A black kid in South Lynn. It hadn't been easy, he was sure. But it hadn't been Montgomery, Alabama, either. He got out his wallet and flipped it open to his latest family snapshot of the three of them: Lena and Francesca in swimsuits on the sand, his daughter hugging his neck, a white wave breaking in the background. He took it out and flipped it across the table.

'I don't know your stepfather, Ian. But he married your mum when she had a black kid to bring up. You ever thought about that . . . ?'

Murray looked at the picture, then at Shaw's good eye. 'No. What d'you reckon — he deserves a medal for it, does he? The Big Man. Look: two things matter to John Joe — Mum, and music. He lost the music, his little dream, back in the eighties. He's still got Mum.' He watched a car creeping past on the quayside, the tyres crunching in the snow. 'For now.'

'Why d'you say that?' asked Valentine, trying hard to keep his voice neutral, because Shaw had failed to.

'She's confused. It's a different story now. We always thought Dad had run out on us. Now we know someone put that hook through his brain, we get these lives instead — not the ones we had. The past makes us, right? Change the past, you change what we are.' He looked around the restaurant, one hand gently smoothing the polished table top. 'It's made her think about him, us, about the future. It's unsettled everything. I don't know what she'll do.'

'What does John Joe think?' asked Shaw.

He smiled, the genuine article this time. 'John Joe's a dreamer who got lucky and married the woman of his dreams. But luck is all it was. He didn't make it happen — he's never made anything happen. So what he thinks doesn't matter. But . . . ' He thought about what he was going to say. 'It isn't good news, is it, for him? He's always been the knight in shining armour who did us all a favour. Not quite so shiny now. But you never know, perhaps it'll do them both good. He may even do something with his life.'

Shaw sensed he despised his stepfather. 'What are you going to do with your life, Ian?'

The young man squared his shoulders. 'I'm gonna run a restaurant — a good one. Michelin stars. You watch. Bea and I have got a plan. I need experience, but I've got the ideas. I'm doing lunches at the Flask, experience here, certificate at the college. I've got the talent. We've started plugging the food at Bea's guest house — you know, local seafood, samphire, Norfolk veg, game. It's a winner. You'd be amazed what people will pay for that stuff.'

Shaw noticed Aunt Bea's B&B had been upgraded to a guest house. He always admired ambition in young people, but he didn't admire ambition driven by money. He looked at his watch, then checked his mobile. 'Six months ago someone tried to dig up Nora Tilden's grave. At night, we guess. Why would anyone want to do that?'

'No idea.' He hadn't even heard the question, let alone thought about an answer.

'Who d'you think killed your father?' asked Valentine quickly.

'Someone who didn't like his face for two reasons.'

'Two?' asked Shaw.

'Wrong colour — and it was too close to Mum's.'

'Right,' said Shaw, smiling. 'So someone knew? About them? Is that what your mum really thinks, because she told us it was all a secret.'

Valentine noticed that the young man gripped the glass now, his knuckles white. He drank the water, showing a glimpse of pale throat through the bottom of the glass.

'First thing I said stands: I wasn't born. So what do I know?'

'But growing up — at the pub — you must have asked questions.'

'Know what I wanted for most of my childhood? I wanted to be white. I've got over that now. But back then the last thing I needed was to remind anyone in the Flask that I wasn't like them. So no — I didn't 'ask questions'. It's what we do well, isn't it, the Brits? Avoid taboo subjects. Until this last week I haven't spoken half a dozen words about my father to another human being — OK? Nothing.'

He put a lot of emphasis on the last word, and as he said it he leant forward so that a small silver chain slipped out of his open shirt — and on the chain a silver emblem: two lines, curved to make a fish.

'You go to church?' asked Shaw, nodding at the necklace.

'It was a present, from Bea.' He sunk his chin so that he could see the fish as he took it in his fingers. 'She used to go to the Free when I was little. I went on the outings, that kind of thing.' He looked at Valentine. 'Then we stopped. I wear it for her — 'cos it makes her happy.'

'You're close?' asked Shaw.

'She's my grandma. Of course we are. She's had time for me, always.' Shaw sensed it was the first thing he'd said that hadn't been framed, designed to produce an effect.

'Why'd you stop going?'

Ian nodded, rhythmically, as if he'd finally decided to tell a truth.

'I used to feel — perhaps Bea did too; I don't know, I've never asked her — feel that we were welcome, but like it was a different kind of welcome to everyone else. They were big on slaves, right? The Free. They fought the good fight. But even back then the only black faces you saw were passing through. They were made welcome — but it was a kind of a temporary welcome. They overdid it, like it was a favour. Ask 'em how many blacks they've got in the congregation now. I'll tell you the answer — the only black face on a Sunday's hanging in that gold frame over the door.

'Nothing was ever said,' Murray continued, 'but we knew we'd always be outsiders. Then one Sunday we went, Bea and me, for the service, and I sang in the choir — 'cos that's something John Joe did teach me, I can hold a tune. Afterwards we had tea in the yard, like we always did, and I played with the other kids. There was a swing and stuff because the pastor had his own family — all girls. There was plenty of noise, as usual, and then it all kind of stopped. I could hear these two adult voices, raised in anger. And one of them was Bea's. The pastor said one word — really clear. He said: 'Please,' like you'd say to shush someone up. And Bea just said, 'It's ten years, for God's sake. Ten years.'

'She came and got me and we left. She never went back. She gave me this instead.' He let the silver fish fall so that it swung on its chain. 'We never said a word to each other, just walked

186

home. I pestered Mum to tell me what was wrong — kept pestering, until she told me. There was this concert coming up at the Free and she'd wanted to come and listen 'cos I was going to sing. Bea had mentioned it to the pastor and he'd said Mum couldn't set foot inside the church. Leviticus, see? They're still the same today. Unbelievable. It's the twenty-first century, not the seventeenth. But it's a sin they don't forgive. And do you know what that made me think? It made me think, what kind of people can keep that kind of hatred alive?' He looked from Shaw to Valentine. 'How *damaged* do you have to be — to hate like that?'

16

Wednesday, 15 December

They found Freddie Fletcher in bed in the one-roomed flat above the PEN office, two floors above Tinos. He'd ignored the knocks on the door, the grit against the window. But they'd finally obtained a spare key from the Greek owner of the café, telling him they were worried Fletcher was ill — or worse. And when they found him in bed, he did look ill: his skin held a green tinge in the half light, and as he smoked his hand trembled, his fingers resting on the bedside table. The edge of the wood was marked with a line of small burns where, Shaw guessed, he'd fallen asleep over the years, a cigarette laid ready at his side. The façade of brisk good humour he'd managed to maintain in their first interview was threadbare here in this sad damp room. The original wallpaper had been for a child's room — red and blue balloons — but now they were covered in posters, one showing Churchill's face with the slogan DESERVE VICTORY.

Fletcher lay on top of the covers, propped up against chair cushions in a white vest and jogging pants, his skin swirled with black hair at the shoulders. 'Don't get your hopes up,' he said. 'I'm not dying. Big Christmas bash tomorrow — so I'm just making sure I'm up for it. Can't beat a plate of good British turkey.'

Valentine stood with his back to the wall, promising himself that he'd never lie in a bed in a room like this. Shaw took the only seat, removing a pile of newspapers to the floor: all of them the BNP's *Voice of Freedom*.

'Seen a doctor?' asked Valentine in a tone of voice which implied that he didn't care either way.

'Yeah.' He thought about what he was going to say next, then went ahead. 'Fucking Paki. Said it was something I ate. Well done, mate. Course it's something I ate.' He put his hand under his vest and massaged his stomach.

'You were less than truthful, Mr Fletcher, when we first spoke,' said Shaw. 'You said there were only two black faces at Nora Tilden's funeral — from the Free Church?'

Fletcher avoided their eyes by shutting his. They heard something give in his guts, a deep-seated rumble of intestine buckling.

'Fuck,' was all he said, rubbing his fingers into his flesh.

'What about Pat Garrison — Nora's nephew? He was there. He'd been on the scene a few months. Why didn't you mention him?'

'It's twenty-eight years ago,' he said, keeping his eyes shut. 'Not yesterday.'

'Were you active then, in 1982, in the BNP?'

'National Front. I'll be on one of your files down at the nick, too. Couple of fights. I've spilt blood for the cause. Mine and theirs.'

'Right. And you didn't notice the black kid in your local pub?'

He opened his eyes, then swung a foot off the bed, forcing himself to sit on the edge. 'I didn't say I didn't notice him — did I? I said I didn't see him at the funeral. It was a big do — you know, coupla hundred at the cemetery. I knew the kid — we all did.'

'But back at the pub — you were at the wake? Not two hundred there, were there? What did you do — drink, eat, sing? And still no sign of Pat Garrison?'

'Nora liked us playing games: dominoes, crib, darts, stuff like that. So when the hangers-on had gone we got stuck into that — bit of a competition, with the choir on too. Folk stuff, sea shanties — British music. I suppose he was there. Yeah, maybe. I don't know. He used to hang around the bar with Lizzie, or his mum.'

'What did you think?'

Fletcher licked his lips and Shaw guessed he was thinking carefully about what to say.

'I thought — we all thought — that he must be ashamed of his mother and what she'd done, you know, while the men were out there, fighting for King and Country. Men like my dad. Whatcha think they'd have thought if they could've seen *her*, Bea, walking out with a black in a uniform like she did, while the white lads were out there dying in the trenches?'

Shaw found it almost impossible not to respond: to point out that the war had been over for years when Bea met Latrell, that trench warfare was a century old, and that the beaches of Normandy saw thousands of black GIs dead on the sands. But this wasn't the place for that argument, however much he'd like to have it.

Valentine coughed on to the back of his hand. 'Trenches are the First World War, Mr Fletcher.'

Fletcher froze, staring at Valentine, even as Shaw quickly asked the next question. 'So Patrice wasn't welcome. Or is that an understatement?'

'He had a home — some place he was welcome,' said Fletcher, tearing his eyes off Valentine. 'He should have gone back to it. Then he wouldn't have had a chance to do what he did — leaving Lizzie that child. The two-tone one. We didn't know then what was going on. But he knew we wanted him to leave — walk away. It's our country, not his.'

'Anybody suggest that to him — that he should leave?' asked Shaw, walking to the window.

Opposite was the wall of the cemetery, beyond a single cypress tree in the mist.

'Not me. Maybe one of the lads — you'd be surprised, even then we had plenty of members, and plenty of 'em went in the Flask.'

'So he knew what you all felt? It was clear — no ambiguity?'

Fletcher laughed, rubbing his stomach with energy. 'It was fucking clear all right. If he missed the signals, he was blind. You think one of us put him in the ground?' asked Fletcher. 'Me?'

'Well, someone murdered him, and almost certainly on the night of the wake. Dumped him in the open grave with a couple of feet of topsoil over him. Then you came along and filled it in. You've admitted *that*.'

Valentine pushed himself away from the wall because the damp in it was making his shoulders ache.

'So did you decide to give him a lesson, Mr Fletcher?' asked Shaw. 'Not just you — that's a bit dodgy, bit risky: but what, one or two of you — three, even. 'Cos you wouldn't want to give a black man an even chance. Things get out of hand?'

Fletcher took a pill bottle from the side cabinet and downed two, with a glass of off-white milk. 'That's bollocks. You know it's bollocks.'

Shaw stood, zipping up his jacket. 'How would you describe the relationship between Pat and Lizzie?'

Fletcher shrugged. 'They were fucking each other.' He shook his head. 'But like I said, we didn't know, not then. There might have been rumours — I can't remember. She certainly didn't seem to mind the fact he was a black. Some of the girls are like that. Like father, like daughter, right?'

Valentine saw his chance, the sudden vulner-ability in his voice when Fletcher had said the word 'daughter', the contrast between that and the anger which seemed to permeate every other word he used. 'You got kids, Mr Fletcher? Family?'

'No,' he said, almost in a whisper.

'Never been married?' asked Valentine.

'No.' He rolled his shoulders. 'But I don't go short. Never have done.'

'But you like children — your nephews,

nieces?' Valentine walked to the mantelpiece over the blocked-off fireplace. There was a picture there of Fletcher and a woman. He had his arm round her shoulders but her hands hung limp. She was in her fifties, poorly dressed in a tracksuit top and joggers, her hair permed to destruction.

Fletcher glared at Valentine. 'What the fuck does that mean?'

Shaw looked at a spot right between Fletcher's eyes.

'Did you kill Pat Garrison, Mr Fletcher?'

Fletcher removed something imaginary from his lip. 'No. I didn't kill him. If I had I'd deserve a medal — but I didn't.'

'You ever dig graves at night?'

Fletcher's eyes narrowed with what Shaw thought was genuine surprise. 'What? Why would I do that?'

'Six months ago someone opened up Nora Tilden's grave. Was it you?'

'No. That's crazy.'

'And you didn't notice — no one noticed, that a grave had been opened, then refilled?'

'Summer you get that — bare earth. Relatives plant flowers, tidy up. Seriously, you wouldn't notice. No one would.' Fletcher closed his eyes and stretched back on the bed, the springs creaking.

'The night of the wake, Mr Fletcher. Can you tell us your movements?'

'I went to the Flask from the graveside — we all did. Church mob went upstairs to the function room for cucumber sandwiches. We

193

stayed in the back room. Choir got there about eight. That's it. I left when they kicked us out . . . ' He shook his head on the pillow. 'No. No — I left about eleven. I hadn't done her grave so I knew I had to get up and do it next morning before anyone was about. I was pretty much pissed. It was a decent job — I didn't want to lose it. So I made sure I got to sleep. Set the alarm.'

'Anyone verify that — anyone who's alive?'

Fletcher blew air out between his lips in a steady stream, like a balloon deflating.

Shaw stood. 'We may need you to answer these questions formally, under caution at St James's. I'd like you to stay in Lynn — and inform my sergeant here if you have any plans to leave the town. Do you understand?'

Valentine put his card on the bedside table.

'I'm not giving you any names,' said Fletcher. 'But there's plenty of people who wanted that piece of shit wiped off the floor. Dead — maybe not. But gone? Oh yeah — plenty.'

As they went to leave Fletcher stood for the first time, grabbed a copy of *Voice of Freedom* and thrust it at Shaw.

Shaw looked at the front-page headline:

MIGRANT WORKERS BLAMED
FOR CRIME WAVE

'No thanks, Mr Fletcher. There's only one crime I'm interested in at the moment.'

Fletcher shrugged. 'What about the wife? We get a lot of women now, in the party, on the

194

streets for us. And there's the lunch tomorrow — still a few tickets on our table. Fifty quid — three courses. Local fare.'

Shaw nodded, looking at the paper. 'It's only a guess, Mr Fletcher. But you know, I don't think it's really her kind of thing.'

17

The incident room at the Flensing Meadow chapel was dark within, each of the Gothic windows shuttered, the only illumination coming from the bulb inside a digital projector. The room was damp, despite the antiquated heating system, which they could hear pumping steaming water around creaking radiators. Outside the early morning mist had coalesced into a solid wall of earth-bound fog, the pale disc of the sun which had briefly shone now lost, Shaw guessed, for the day. The fog muffled the whisper of traffic on the ring road, leaving the cackle of the cemetery crows to provide the only clear soundtrack.

DC Twine flipped open a laptop on the desk beside the projector and the cool blue glow showed a tidy desktop.

Shaw sat on one of the pews cradling a double espresso, trying hard to relax, picking at a sandwich. He checked his mobile, as if the mere action would spark it into life. He hadn't heard from George Valentine for three hours. After their interview with Fletcher the DS had taken personal charge of the hunt for Jimmy Voyce, who had failed to return to his hotel overnight. Mosse's BMW had got back to his street at eleven the previous evening. It was impossible to tell if he had a passenger. He'd left for work at six. His wife at eight. But there was a light on in the house. Shaw was worried, more than worried, and he'd stay that way until he had a positive sighting of Voyce — alive. In a few hours' time he'd have no choice but to confront Mosse and report Voyce's disappearance to Warren: a double hit which could indeed signal the end of his career.

DC Twine tapped the keys on the laptop. 'Our luck was in, sir,' he said. 'The choir's archive is in a mess — hundreds of recordings, mixed up with cine tins. Most of them are unmarked. This one just said 'Tilden'. One of the conductors was a film buff — but it's not Zeffirelli or anything. Strictly a one-tripod shot, although they do move it. We've had it transferred to DVD.' Twine spoke for the audience he couldn't see: Shaw's squad — eight DCs, two PCs from uniform branch and the three civilian admin/phone bank operators. 'Here we go . . . '

The screen was set perfectly to catch the rectangle of projected light. They saw a room, beamed, people crowded round tables, and the choir on the higher step, about forty men in three lines. Shaw recognized the dining room in the Flask. In the corner, on a plinth, sat Alby Tilden's gold Buddha.

Twine let the first sea shanty get under way — 'The Captain's Chair', a Lynn favourite. A few faces in the audience on film turned inquisitively to the camera.

'I'll run the whole thing for you if anyone wants, but there were just three things I've spotted I wanted to flag up.' He'd bookmarked the relevant frames so that the film jumped to a new image, then froze. Twine stepped forward and used his finger's shadow to point out one of the singers in the back row. 'I got one of the old guys at the choir to name this lot. That's Sam Venn, from the church.'

He magnified the image so that Venn's distinctively lop-sided face almost filled the screen. Shaw thought he'd grown into his disability, accommodated it, because as a younger man the disfigurement was more obvious.

'Now,' said Twine, 'that image was taken at eight thirty. Venn stays in the back row the whole of the first session until nine thirty-five. This next image is the first song of the second session — there's no digital time on the film but the clock in the room says it was ten thirty. There . . . ' he used his finger again to trace the whole of the back line. 'He's gone. He doesn't appear again.'

Shaw stared at the image. He'd had Sam Venn down in his book as many things, but outright liar hadn't been one of them.

'Anyone else step out?' asked DC Lau, coming in with a Starbucks coffee in her hand, unzipping her leather jacket.

'No. Absolutely not,' said Twine. 'The rest of the choir are all still there.'

Another image flashed up. The camera had moved slightly so that they could now see the doorway into the main bar — a Moorish arch, a kitsch 1950s addition. But there was another door visible, a side door, marked STAFF. As Twine let the image roll forward in slow motion

198

the door opened and a man came out: early twenties, black, in a yellow silk shirt and jeans. He stood in the half-open doorway, as if protecting his escape route.

'This is earlier. I think that's Patrice Garrison — our victim,' said Twine. 'I've got a grab of the image, so we can get it to his mother for a formal ID. But that's him, got to be.'

Shaw stood and walked to the screen, keeping the cone of light from the projector to his left. He should be proud of his forensic reconstruction, because the likeness was near perfect. The figure didn't smile, but his lips were parted, and Shaw could see the tell-tale gap between the front teeth. The structure of the face was very close to that of his son Ian's — less fine, the skin tone darker. In the background the clock read 9.10 p.m.

'This is the only time he comes into shot,' said Twine.

'Right,' said Shaw. 'And Lizzie said they talked at about ten. So at this point he doesn't know he's about to become a father.'

They watched him drink from a small shot glass he held easily in his hand. Shaw noted that no one in the room had greeted him, and that he made no eye contact with anyone.

But he'd been noticed, even if he appeared not to notice anyone else. There was a table to the right crowded with five or six men, their hair uniformly and aggressively short. As Pat Garrison opened the door one of them watched him, nudged his neighbour, and they all looked, their heads edging closer, as if conspiring. One, in a T-shirt, had bare arms covered in tattoos: a Union Flag conspicuous. 'Him,' said Shaw, touching the screen on the face of a man at the back of the group. 'Can you blow that image up?'

Twine worked at the laptop, the screen went blank and one of the DCs in the dark whistled. Then the screen lit up again. The face — slightly distorted by magnification — was wide and belligerent, caught in the middle of a snarl. It was Freddie Fletcher.

'Let's see if we can get names for the rest of the men at that table, Paul,' said Shaw. 'Can we see the shot without Venn again?'

Twine had it up instantly. The crowded group of skinheads at the table was still there, but the camera angle was different, three men nearest the camera blocking the view, playing cards, concealing the spot where Fletcher had sat.

'Run it forward,' said Shaw.

For a minute the table was in shot but they couldn't see whether Fletcher was still at his seat. Then the camera moved, taking up a wider angle to one side, so that the skinheads were no longer in shot at all.

'Damn,' said Shaw, taking his seat. 'And the third thing you want to show us?'

'Lizzie Murray, sir. Well, Lizzie Tilden then, it would have been. They gave her a framed photo — of Nora with the choir. Here.'

The image froze, then broke into pixels before reforming and flowing on. Lizzie stood on the little stage, most of the men in the room on their feet, clapping.

Again, a whistle from the dark. 'She's

amazing,' said Shaw. Her figure was sinuous, in a simple black dress, the black hair loose. Of the starched stiffness of the woman she'd become there was no hint. She rubbed the palm of her hand down the line of her waist and hip. The noise of the applause seemed to unsettle her, the smile a nervous one. Shaw thought she was an exotic figure, the only female in the shot, her young face an almost painful contrast to those around her. At one point she looked to the door marked STAFF, but it was closed.

Twine ran the film back, but too far, so that Lizzie Tilden was gone. 'Sorry — I'll run up to that image if you like.'

The image of the choir returned, the choirmaster speaking . . .

'Thank you. Thank you. It's been wonderful for us to sing here tonight for Nora. She was a real friend to the choir and we've always felt this is our home.' There was a perfunctory round of applause and someone said something on Fletcher's table that caused a scandalized hushing. The choirmaster looked around, searching faces at the back of the room. 'We have something for Lizzie — but I understand she's gone to ground.' There was a shout from the back of the room. 'Is she there?'

Applause filled the room, genuine this time, the volume sustained.

Lizzie stepped up on the stage and accepted the framed photo. 'Thanks. I know Nora loved the choir, and their singing. I'm sure you know you'll always be welcome here.' The choir applauded that — and Shaw realized that was the point. That the choir had turned out to perform in order to stake their claim. This had been their home while Nora was in charge. They wanted the same commitment from Lizzie, and they'd got it.

Lizzie's voice rang out again. 'She used to say that when the choir was here it was the one time the Flask really came alive.' She turned to the choir. 'You made her very happy.'

The room was silent, waiting to see what she'd say about her mother, and whether she'd say anything about her father. Cigarette smoke drifted from hands, swirled round spotlights. Shaw had to remind himself that this was a wake, that the woman they'd gathered to honour had died just a few feet away, through that door marked STAFF, murdered by her husband.

'Some of you sang with her, didn't you? Years ago. She had a good voice. It was a shame we didn't hear it more often.' There was a scattering of applause. 'Well, we won't hear her again now.'

Shaw thought she was struggling to bring emotion, any emotion, into the little speech.

She looked at the picture they'd given her. 'But this is how she'd have wanted us to remember her.' Applause again, a voice crying out, 'A song!'

But she held up her hands. 'Not me. I inherited a lot from Mother, but not her voice.'

There was laughter again, dutiful, confused. 'A toast . . . ' She held up a small green glass. 'To Nora.'

Relief flooded the room, feet stamped and they all stood, drinking and clapping. Lizzie left

202

the stage through the Moorish arch to the bar. Matches flared as fresh cigarettes were lit.

Twine tapped away at the laptop. 'Do you want to see the whole thing?' he asked Shaw.

'Please, Paul. First — coffee. Updates?'

The neon flickered back on as they refilled mugs.

'One thing,' said Mark Birley. 'I had a look back through the log book at St James's to see if there were any incidents in the last year in or near the cemetery. In June, the eighteenth, there was a report from one of the houses overlooking the graveyard — on Gladstone Street: lights at night. The incident sheet has the time down as three fifteen a.m. Woman up with a sick teenage daughter. Said she looked out the balcony window and saw a cluster of lights — two, maybe three, over down by the river. Her brother-in-law's on traffic. She rang him, he rang the incident room. They got a car out, and the cemetery warden who had the keys for the gates. The archaeologists had started by then, so there were open graves, some digging gear. Best guess was it was someone trying to lift some of the plant. Anyway, no trace by the time they got there. But they went back — it was on the squad-car schedule for a month. They'd check twice, three times, a night. Nothing.'

'OK,' said Shaw. 'Let's get the notes on that call. And we need to talk to the cemetery warden. How'd these characters get into the cemetery — given they're probably carrying spades and lanterns? Or did they borrow the tools — or take them? Let's check that out with

the Direct Labour boys and the Cambridge unit
. . . Anything else?'

Lizzie Murray and Bea Garrison had already
put together a list of all those they thought had
been at Nora Tilden's graveside — and later at
the wake. DC Twine said he'd try to match the
lists with the film, see whether there was anyone
they'd missed. The rest of the team would
continue interviewing those people still alive
who'd been at either the wake or the funeral or
both. Two key questions for them all: had they
seen Patrice Garrison leaving the pub that night,
and had they seen anyone leaving at around the
same time. Shaw reckoned they could clear the
list in twenty-four hours: then they could liaise,
get a 3D picture of the night.

'While all that's in train let's get Sam Venn off
the street and down to St James's,' said Shaw.
'We need to get him on the record telling us he
was in the pub till closing time. Then we show
him this. He wanted to know if he was a suspect.
Well, he is now.'

For an hour they watched the Flask coming
alive again on film. The colour was poor, the film
quality patchy, but the atmosphere was perfectly
rendered: a close-knit community coming
together to celebrate a life lived amongst them.
Nora Tilden had been born in the Flask, and she
died on its wooden stairs. She'd given birth to
two children in a bedroom with a view over the
cemetery in which she and her lost child would
lie. These people may have despised her, ignored
her, or even hated her — but they'd lived their
lives with her. By the time the choir sang the last

song the whole room was on its feet, the sound thunderous, making the soundtrack crackle.

From his viewing of the film Shaw had made two mental notes. First, in the break between the two choral sessions, sandwiches and food had been served by five people: Lizzie, two men Shaw didn't recognize and two women he did. The first was Kath Robinson, the second was George Valentine's sister, Jean. He must prompt his DS to track her down.

Second, and more importantly, when Patrice Garrison had come into the room, or at least stood on its threshold, he had at first indeed been ignored by everyone except those at Fletcher's table. But then someone else had noticed him, a man standing by the stage, cradling a pint. He had long black hair, swept back, a fine pointed face and a thin poised body, which he held stylishly, one leg angled behind him so that the sole of his shoe rested against the wall. With his free hand he kept the beat; over his shoulder was draped a white dishcloth. In a room of hard faces it was an outsider's face: watching, not taking part. He wore a T-shirt, the front of which carried a slightly faded picture of Elvis Costello. When this young man did notice Garrison he didn't take his eyes off him, not once, until he turned and left. And despite the intervening twenty-eight years Shaw had little trouble putting a name to the troubling face: it was John Joe Murray, later to be Lizzie's husband, a surrogate father to Ian and landlord of the Flask.

18

The cellar of the Flask was a barrelled vault, with a shuttered watergate at one end leading out to the river. The brickwork had been plastered and whitewashed, the barrels raised on stone stoops on either side. A central gutter ran to the river, a sluggish trickle of stale beer foaming slightly. Shaw noted a plastic rat trap. He watched as John Joe Murray drank a pint of bitter drawn directly from the barrel he'd just tapped.

'Perks,' he said, sitting on the stoop, his legs straight out to reach the other stoop. Shaw wondered how many hours he'd spent there, perfecting this exact position for maximum comfort. He tried not to judge John Joe as Ian, his stepson, had done. He didn't bring judgement, he brought questions. Had John Joe married Lizzie for love or fortune? Had he become a father to the infant Ian out of love for his mother, or expediency? Had he taken the chance that fate had given him to become Lizzie's husband — or had he tried to force Patrice Garrison to leave? Could he have murdered him that night in 1982 to get her? Now, nearly thirty years later, it seemed impossible that this greying, diminished man had followed his rival out into the night and driven a billhook into his skull. But Shaw recalled the image on the cine film they'd all watched — the murderous look in the young John Joe's eyes as he contemplated Pat Garrison, cradling his glass, surveying the back room at the Flask like an estate agent assessing a property ripe for development.

'What's this about?' asked John Joe. He ran a hand along his hair to the black pigtail band and pulled it clear, letting the lifeless tresses flop over either ear. It reminded Shaw of one of Lena's many fashion edicts: that no man over twenty looks good in a ponytail. John Joe rubbed the green guitar tattoo on his throat and the friction brought a flush to his pallid skin. His face had not aged well — narrow, fleshless faces seldom do. The bone structure, the feline cheekbones, were pushing out beneath the dry skin.

Shaw studied John Joe while DC Birley asked a list of routine questions about the night of Nora Tilden's wake. Shaw tried to concentrate on the answers but kept thinking about the still-missing Jimmy Voyce. George Valentine had radioed the incident room shortly after the screening of the DVD. They'd found Voyce's hire car, burnt out, in a lane near Holkham, up on the coast. No sign of Voyce. Valentine would set up a couple of search units to check the area, then come back to Lynn. Tom Hadden's team were on their way to the scene. Shaw didn't know what that abandoned car signified, but he was pretty sure it didn't improve the likelihood of Jimmy Voyce being alive.

While the questions continued Shaw also checked a text from DC Twine. Sam Venn had been taken down to St James's and cautioned before repeating his statement that he'd been singing with the choir at the Flask all evening on the night of Nora Tilden's wake. He'd left at closing time and walked home. They were now showing him the film of that night they'd watched on DVD in the incident room. He'd text again with Venn's reaction to the proof that he was lying.

Above their heads they could hear footfalls, furniture being hauled over the quarry-tile floor as preparations were made for the opening of the inquest into the death of Pat Garrison.

Birley finished questioning Murray. They had a brief outline of his movements that night: he hadn't gone to the funeral because he didn't like Nora Tilden and she didn't like him. The year before her death he'd tried to get a spot at the Flask for his band but she'd stuck with the choirs, folk music, nothing electric. He'd come along to the wake because he knew the crack would be good and because Lizzie said they needed people to collect glasses, wash up, if things got really busy, and he needed the cash. There'd been food, and at the end a free drink or two. He'd lingered, talking to friends, and wandered home about midnight to his parents' house in Gayton, a leafy suburb. He'd been born and raised in South Lynn, but his father had got a better job and they'd moved up in the world. Up and out. He had his own key so hadn't woken them up that night when he got home.

He'd been there all evening, in the back room? No — he hadn't seen the choir's second session because he'd found the atmosphere stifling, fevered; so he'd gone out on the riverside stoop to smoke in the crisp November air. That's all he could remember — except that he had talked to Pat Garrison, information he volunteered before he'd been asked. There was a gig coming up at the Lattice House and he'd asked Pat if he'd come along because the tickets weren't selling. Pat said he would — he liked John Joe's music and he'd heard the band at the festival on The Walks that summer.

'The kid knew his music,' said John Joe. 'Graham Parker, Ian Dury — that's the kind of thing we were into. And he got it, which is more than the losers here did. No, Pat was OK. I liked the kid.'

Which was odd, thought Shaw, because no one else seemed to have liked him. He'd been variously described to them as arrogant and selfish. It was illustrative that John Joe had felt the need to point out that he was perhaps alone in valuing the young man's company.

John Joe stood, walked the central gutter between the barrels, his boots in the bubbling spilt beer, to a door at the opposite end to the watergate, and pushing it open stood back to let them see. Beyond was another vaulted cellar, but the brickwork here was lost behind stippled soundproofing board.

'Wedding present from Lizzie — sound studio. We cut a disc, tried the labels, but they all passed. Everyone's got a dream, right? This was mine.'

Shaw could almost hear it, as if the brick walls were a solid-state tape, replaying those years again, the countless demos, the draining repetitive sessions, the dream slowly fading, until one day they'd all convinced themselves they'd never shared one, that it was just a hobby, a way of staying sane. That it had all been for fun.

'Did you know Mrs Murray well then — in 1982?' asked Birley. The narrow vaulted space of the cellar seemed to accentuate the DC's muscled bulk. He stood, his backbone curved to match the wall, taking up too much space.

'Lizzie? Went to school with her. Fancied her then, along with most of my mates and half the town. She stopped the traffic, that girl. Still stops mine.'

John Joe flipped open a wallet to reveal a black-and-white snapshot — Lizzie, in a bikini on a sandy beach, her legs folded underneath her. 'That's Lizzie — twenty-first birthday. Talk about turning heads.' He let his eyes linger on the picture, but Shaw noticed instead the ticket tucked into the other side of the wallet — the charity Christmas lunch at the Shipwrights' Hall.

John Joe let the door to the old studio close.

'And you were married when?' asked Shaw.

'In 1983 — the summer. Ninth of June. Just after she'd had Ian.'

'That's quick work,' said Birley.

John Joe gave him an old-fashioned look. 'Yeah. Well, I tried my luck with Lizzie — a few times. When Nora died we were going out, but that kind of faded away. No hard feelings. It happens. When she fell pregnant, when the baby arrived, I understood why she'd been different that summer. I went back — told her I didn't care what had happened. That I could live with that if she could. Ian's my son. Has been pretty much from the day he was born. So that's our story. You got it now. Satisfied?'

Birley didn't flinch. 'Did you try your luck that night — the night of the wake?'

Shaw admired Birley's direct approach, and he couldn't help thinking John Joe's indignation at the question was manufactured.

He shook his head and walked to the watergate, unbolting the two quarter-circle doors. The light flooded in with the cold, straight off the water, which lapped at the stone edge. They all stepped out on the stone wharf. The tide was full. On the water bobbed a small sailing boat, clinker-built, covered in with a tarpaulin, the one that Shaw had seen the day before, moored to a single bollard.

'The beer came in this way back in the eighties — always had done, I guess. Now the cellar floods once a year, sometimes more. We'll have to do something about it — God knows what.'

He dipped the toe of his boot in the grey water. Across the river was the brick river frontage of the cannery. Shaw thought again of the Shipwrights' Hall Christmas dinner, the promise of 'local fare'.

'The boat?' asked Shaw.

'Mine. I fish — up along the coast, days off. It's an escape. Used to take Ian when he was a kid.'

Shaw wondered what he'd had to escape from.

'One last question, Mr Murray,' said Shaw. 'Did you suspect that Lizzie and Pat were an item before the wake?'

John Joe spat in the water. 'Others did — coupla my mates said later they knew. But me — no.'

The sailing boat nudged the quay, unsettled by the wake of a passing tug.

'I tell you what I did know, mind . . . ' He smiled, tapping a finger to his temple. 'Still laugh about it. I *knew* about the baby. She looked incredible that night — Lizzie. Like I said, she was a stunner anyway, but that night, Nora's wake, she just kind of radiated something.' He shook his head, eyes closed, as if to see her more clearly. 'Everyone was watching her that night. It was her mother's wake, for Christ's sake. But everyone knew where her sympathies lay. She loved her father. I'm not sure she felt anything about Nora. I never saw them swap a word that wasn't . . . ' he hesitated, looking for the right word, 'businesslike. So she kind of bottled up her real emotions. But there was something in her eyes. Just amazing. I've got sisters — I've seen it before. It's like her whole face was plugged into some kind of power supply. I thought — there's a baby. I didn't say it — but I knew. And you know what? I bet I wasn't the only one.'

19

The inquest into the death of Patrice Garrison was not the first to be held in the Flask. Stan Glover, the coroner's officer, a former DS from Cromer, was an old friend of Shaw's father. He'd been back through the records and found one in 1958. A child, a two-year-old girl, found strangled on waste ground down by Blubber Creek. They'd opened the inquest in the pub for the same reason they'd chosen to do it for Pat Garrison — to get the community involved, appeal for witnesses, and to give the coroner a chance to view the scene of the crime. A place like South Lynn had few secrets from its own people. In the nineteenth century they'd have had the body there on the first day as well, laid out on a couple of floorboards. Putting Pat Garrison's bones on show would have achieved little, but Glover had arranged for a large-scale picture of the victim from a snapshot of 1982 to be mounted over a desk set aside for the coroner. On the desk was a glass water pitcher, an upturned tumbler and a bible. To one side was a seat for witnesses.

Glover's close-shaved hair was greying, but the stubble on his face was still black. He came through the door marked STAFF carrying a bundle of documents.

'Please rise for Her Majesty's Coroner,' said Glover.

The coroner, Dr Leslie Shute, followed him into the room. He wore a tweed jacket with leather patches, shirt and tie. Shaw always thought he looked like he'd been scrubbed with wire wool — his cheeks so flushed they might bleed, his ruddiness accentuated by a shaving regime which seemed to involve a machete. Shute ran a medical practice in Burnham Market. He was known widely as a breeder of greyhounds, which he ran at Mildenhall Stadium. Shaw sometimes saw him on the beach in the winter, the dogs circling him at speed as if on invisible gyres.

The dining room was packed, the round tables removed and replaced with rows of single chairs. Alby Tilden's gold Buddha looked down on proceedings with an enigmatic smile.

Glover took a chair beside the coroner. 'Mobiles off, please — all of them.'

Shute smiled inappropriately.

'Thank you all for coming.' He had a light clear voice that Shaw had heard him use to call the dogs. 'I'm going to formally open the inquest into the death of Patrice Eugene Garrison and will presently adjourn those proceedings to enable the police to complete their inquiries and for any criminal prosecution to take its proper course.' Shute began to search inside his jacket pockets for something he'd mislaid, and Shaw noted that he could do so without breaking the thread of his preamble. 'What I need to do today,' he continued, 'is to confirm the identity of the deceased, the cause of death, and then my officer here will give us a brief summary of the

214

details, the circumstances, so far as we can ascertain them, of the death in question. I've visited the spot where this young man's bones were found, and I hope that opening the inquest here will encourage as many people as possible to come forward and help this court — and the police — to find the person or persons responsible for his death.'

Shaw was standing at the back and he noticed that Lizzie Murray had joined him, together with a young woman with blonde hair cut savagely short whom he recognized as a reporter with the local paper. She leant close to Shaw. 'This isn't worth my time, is it?' she asked. She looked skywards, didn't wait for an answer and slipped between rows to a desk set at one side for the press, already occupied by an elderly man who Shaw knew worked for Hospital Radio. Shaw thought the reporter's doubts over the news value of the proceedings were probably justified. The powers of the coroner were a pale imitation of the office's traditional authority — he could no longer name suspects or accuse the guilty. And while Shaw had agreed it was worth calling for witnesses to come forward, he wondered how many of the locals would have the courage to tell the court anything it didn't know already.

'We already have a list of six witnesses who have indicated they wish to speak — but anyone may do so, even at this stage. In fact, especially at this stage,' said Dr Shute. He flicked open the single file he had before him. 'First of all, I am able to confirm that a DNA analysis to be undertaken by the Forensic Science Service is

215

expected to provide conclusive evidence of the identity of the victim. However, I am able to accept a preliminary identification based on a facial reconstruction of the remains together with forensic evidence from the scene and corroborating dental records. The deceased was an American citizen and the US Embassy has been notified of these proceedings. I can also report that a post-mortem examination was completed here in Lynn and that the cause of death is understood to have been a single traumatic blow to the back of the skull with a pointed weapon — probably the billhook that was found with the remains. I have examined the medical notes in this case and discussed it with the pathologist — Dr Justina Kazimierz.' He surveyed the 'court'. 'I am entirely confident this finding is the correct one. Given that the deceased had been dead for many years there is no likelihood of any forensic evidence being recovered from tissue. But the bones tell us enough.'

He readied a fountain pen over a blank notepad. 'Anyone giving testimony will be speaking under oath and may subsequently be required to make a formal statement to the police. Mr Glover?'

Glover then gave an outline of the bare facts of the case: Garrison's family background, the death of his aunt Nora Tilden, his journey to the UK, her burial, his disappearance. He then described the uncovering of the bones. He sat while he read in a dull monotone, but the room remained silent, watchful. Shaw indulged in a

216

childhood fantasy — the idea that he could read people's thoughts in bubbles which hung over their heads. He wondered what he would have read now. It was particularly difficult in Lizzie Murray's case because she gave so few hints of an interior life behind her brittle exterior.

'Before we get to the events of 1982,' said Shute when Glover had finished, 'I'd like to ask briefly whether anyone has information regarding an attempt, in June this year the police believe, to reopen the grave in which the remains of this young man were discovered. This was on the night of the eighteenth. We have already a statement from a resident of Gladstone Street who says she saw lights in the cemetery that evening and called the police. They attended but found the cemetery empty.'

Four of the six witnesses who had already contacted the coroner's office then gave evidence. They all reported that the cemetery was used by young people, late at night, for the purchase of drugs. One witness was a council workman from South Lynn who said that syringes and other detritus were often found, especially in the area down by the riverside, close to two breaks in the iron fencing and the part of the cemetery most distant from local housing. While that corner of the graveyard was also closest to the riverside path, all the witnesses pointed out that the walkway was rarely used after dark, and that the council lighting was often vandalized. Shaw noted the timings of the witness accounts of sightings in the cemetery — all before midnight — whereas the woman who had seen lights from her window that night in June had reported them to the police at 3.15 a.m.

Shute moved on to the night of Nora Tilden's wake. He said that anyone who had already given evidence to the police did not need to repeat it here. They had two further witnesses listed: the first, a woman who lived less than fifty yards from the pub, said that noise from the wake had continued until well into the small hours. She said it was a regular problem, and had been since she'd moved to the area in 1975. She said she had reported the nuisance to both the police and the local council and they had failed to take action. Dr Shute thanked her for her time.

The second witness was a man who said he had seen Pat Garrison on the night of the wake walking away from the Flask towards the cemetery. The man, now in his sixties, was a night-shift worker at the old jam-processing factory in West Lynn and always went to the pub in the evening during his break — which was supposed to be between 10.30 p.m. and 11.30 p.m. but which he always 'stretched' by a quarter of an hour each side. The man said he knew Pat Garrison, though only by sight. The only things he noticed, or could remember, were that the time was 10.15 or just before, because he usually heard All Saints chime the quarter-past before he went into the pub, and that Garrison was carrying two glasses in one hand, the rims held together between thumb and forefinger.

Shaw nodded to DC Birley to intercept the

witness as he left the stand and fix an interview at St James's.

Dr Shute then asked for new witnesses to come forward. Seven merely added detail to the picture Shaw and his team had so far constructed of the evening of the wake. Three had been at the graveside for the funeral and recalled Pat Garrison standing with the family. Prompted, they also confirmed the presence of the two black men from the Free, Jesse and Emmanuel Rogers, standing with a group of the Elect, including the pastor. Shaw caught the young reporter's eye and she pulled a face, then gave in to the urge to yawn.

The eighth and last witness to come forward was a woman in her mid-fifties, Shaw judged, wearing cleaner's overalls. She gave her name as Jayne Flowers of West Lynn, her age as fifty-nine and her occupation as hospital cleaner. She said that at the time of Patrice Garrison's disappearance she had a part-time job as a caretaker at a block of private flats in Snettisham Road. Mrs Bea Garrison, the victim's mother, paid a weekly rent, she recalled, of £25 for a bedsit in the block for her son — the deceased.

'What can you tell us?' asked Shute, leaning back, and Shaw noted — not for the first time — the coroner's skill at setting an informal tone in the court.

'I went to the funeral because I knew Nora, and I wanted to pay my respects.' Shaw realized that giving evidence for this woman was an ordeal, because her voice buzzed, vibrating with a stress she didn't show in her face. 'But I couldn't go back to the wake. I had to work that afternoon, at the hospital, then get back to the flats to cook tea. We had the bottom flat, you see — that was part of the deal. And when I'd done — the tea, I mean — I had to start cleaning. All the stairs, and do the rubbish.'

She looked at her hands. 'I heard Pat come home — but late, about one o'clock.'

Shute stopped her there, trying to make sure of the time. Did she wait up for tenants to come home? No, never. But she was a light sleeper and she heard the door open, and Pat's flat was above theirs. So she heard his door open and close. And because she was a light sleeper she always had a clock — right there — that she could see without moving her head. And she knew for certain that it was one o'clock.

But how did she know it was Garrison? Shute asked.

'Well I didn't, not then. But I was sure, because I heard him typing. It's showing my age, isn't it? These days it'd be a computer and you wouldn't hear it, but back then everyone used a typewriter. It was portable, but you still needed a sledge hammer to hit the keys. We often heard him typing — he was at the college, doing journalism, and he did bits for the paper even then. Sport and stuff. But this — he'd never done this, not at that time. I couldn't sleep. I just lay there. Then — after about an hour, he stopped. I knew something was up because I heard his door open again. I thought he was off out so I got up to get my dressing gown because I was going to have words. 'Cos it wasn't right.'

Out of the corner of his eye Shaw saw Lizzie sidling across the room to the far wall, to stand beside one of the red velvet curtains. Her hand played with the gold buttons on her black formal jacket, then touched the single diamond pin in her ear lobe.

'And I'd had problems before,' she said, hesitating. 'With girls — Pat brought girls back, and that was a problem. Not that I'd mind, but the landlords said if people wanted a flat for two the rent was higher. So no double occupancy. I should have said something earlier, but I let it drag. He was just a kid, and I didn't hear the girls complain. Quite the opposite.'

There was nervous laughter. Shute was nodding and Shaw guessed he was trying to work out what he should ask next. As coroner he had certain duties — to fix the time and place of death, for example. But he also had a duty to probe the cause and circumstances of that death.

'Girls?' he said. He checked the file. 'The deceased was only in Lynn for a few months before his disappearance — but in that time he had several girlfriends?'

'Yes,' she said.

'I see. I expect the police will want to ask you more questions about that, Mrs Flowers.'

Shaw watched as Lizzie took a seat.

'But back to that night — so you went to the door?'

'Yes. But I couldn't put the light on because that wakes Frank up, so it took me a minute to get my things. I heard him come down the stairs and go out the door. I followed — right out in the street. It was a cold night, but there was a moon, and so I could see that he'd gone. He must have cut down Jenkyns Street to the river. But I tell you what I heard — one of those suitcase things on wheels, like a trolley. That's what I heard. So I thought, he's done a moonlight flit, even though that didn't make any sense because his mother paid the rent and it was paid a month in advance. So I didn't call out or anything. I just let him go.'

'But you didn't see anyone — how can you be sure it was Pat Garrison?'

'He left me a note — typed. I saw it when I went back in our flat by the hall light, under our door. Just saying he was leaving, and thanking us for being kind. And that's what really made me remember it — Frank laughed when he saw it — because we hadn't been kind. Frank doesn't like 'em . . . ' She shrugged, looked around. 'You know, the blacks.'

There was a brittle silence.

Shute thanked her for her evidence, asked for any more witnesses to step forward and, when none did so, adjourned the inquest.

DC Birley waylaid Jayne Flowers, taking her to a table to fix a time for a formal statement. The room emptied quickly, many people staying out in the bar. Ian Murray appeared, helping two waitresses quickly set out the tables for lunch.

Shaw took a chair and walked over to Lizzie. 'A quick word,' he said, and sat beside her. She shook out her hair, then ran a hand through it. Over their heads was a loudspeaker and they heard the opening piano chords of 'Oliver's

Army' from the juke box. There was a wire hanging loose from the speaker, within reach, and she took it and with one abrupt tug pulled it out, cutting the music dead.

Shaw waited for her to speak but the figurehead face remained immobile, the piercing green eyes locked on Shaw's.

'Pat saw other girls, then?' he said.

'I need a smoke — so can we keep this short?' she asked. She knocked out a cigarette and held it in her lips, and Shaw thought that was one of the reasons her beauty had diminished over the years, that she'd taken on the manners of men, living and working in a man's world.

'Kath Robinson?' Shaw suggested. 'Was she one of the others?'

Lizzie smiled. 'Yup — she was the first. Nothing happened. Kath's always been a bit slow, a bit trusting. These days they'd have a word for it. But we just looked out for her. She fell for Pat. Pat should have walked away, but he didn't. She tried to play him along a bit. Not clever. She was just looking forward to a first kiss, I think — but Pat had other ideas. Like I said, nothing happened. But Kath was upset. Confused.'

'She told you this?'

'She's always told me everything — we were best friends at school. She spent more time here as a kid than she did at home. Mind you, her old man was in the bar most of his life.' She took the cigarette out of her mouth. 'Yes, she told me. This wasn't long after Pat had arrived. We hadn't started seeing each other then. I had words. Pat

223

was sorry — he said he hadn't understood.'

'She's a quiet girl,' said Shaw, offering her the chance to paint a fuller picture.

'Cursed with beauty,' she said bitterly, and Shaw thought Lizzie's abrupt and tetchy manner might hide a fine mind. 'She wants someone to love her — always has. But men can't see past the boobs and the Barbie-doll looks. Married a couple of times but she's not interested any more — she's taken refuge as Bea's housekeeper up at the B&B, does most of the cleaning, cooking and stuff. She wears a wedding ring — it's like mosquito repellent. Works, too.'

'So, despite Pat's reputation — I presume there were others if Mrs Flowers's statement is true — you became lovers?'

'He didn't cheat on me, if that's what you're after,' she said. 'Once we were together, that was it. When he went, disappeared, I thought he had found someone else. I admit that. But it turns out we were all wrong. He didn't run away, did he? He would have stayed if someone hadn't killed him. So perhaps I was right to trust him.' She took in a ragged breath, her fingers working at the skin of her neck.

Through the door marked STAFF her son Ian appeared in his chef's whites, using his back to push through, with three plates effortlessly held. 'Three daily specials,' he announced before heading across the room in response to a waved arm.

The place had filled up quickly with lunch tables and diners. At one of the tables Shaw recognized Pastor Abney from the Free Church,

224

and at another Michael Brindle, the chargehand from the cemetery labour gang who'd walked him to Freddie Fletcher's office that first morning of the investigation. Shaw was struck again by the claustrophobic intimacy of this small community, even now, in the first years of the twenty-first century, as incestuous as it had been, perhaps, when the whaling fleet was still coming home.

Lizzie's eyes followed her son across the room.

'Presumably Pat carried keys, Mrs Murray? A key ring?'

'Yes. Flashy — like fake gold, in the shape of that mountain with the presidents' heads on it . . .'

'No spare?'

'No. But he had one for here — Bea gave it him.'

Shaw's mobile rang so he stood and apologized, walking to the window that looked out onto the cemetery. It was DC Twine: Sam Venn had changed his story. He remembered now. He'd been ill that night — and it wasn't the first time. His illness, the cerebral palsy, made standing for long periods of time difficult, and he'd often had to leave midway through public performances, because the effort of keeping his bones still, and the stress, made him feel sick. So, yes — he'd gone early that night, after the break, and walked alone to his uncle's house. But his uncle was dead now, so they'd have to take his word for it.

Shaw agreed with Twine's recommendation that they release Venn for now; they had no evidence he'd followed Pat Garrison to the cemetery that night, none that would get them past a magistrate's court hearing, let alone to a trial. Shaw cut the line, troubled that they were uncovering so many lies, and troubled also by that strange detail — that Venn had gone to his uncle's house rather than his own home. But Pastor Abney had said his parents lived locally, that his father had been a member of the Elect.

When he turned back to Lizzie Murray she was gone.

20

Bellevue Psychiatric Hospital stood on a wooded hill overlooking the estuary of the River Welland — a culvert of glistening black mud with boats beached in pools of water left by the outflowing tide. It was the bleakest spot in a bleak landscape. A stand of cedar trees on its southwest side had been bent over the building by the wind like thinning hair over a skull. Snow and ice lay in the ditches — a mathematical grid traced over a landscape rolled flat by steel-grey snow clouds blowing in from the sea. As Shaw approached in the Porsche he thought how the hospital's position, eight miles from the nearest town at Sutton Bridge, encapsulated the planners' attitudes to mental health. Bellevue was as far away from anything as anything could be. And, despite its name, the view was a study in melancholia.

He swung the Porsche over to the opposite side of the road to avoid a patch of ice. The days of the warm snow had gone. Shaw had the window down and the wind smelt of iced ozone and carried a Polar chill. He'd just been out to Holkham woods to see how the search for Jimmy Voyce was going. Beneath the canopy of pines the dry needles on the forest floor had been frozen too. And so far, no trace of Voyce, but he'd left Valentine in charge, organizing a systematic trawl though the Holkham estate, around the great eighteenth-century hall. In winter, a few estate workers were the only people to wander the acres of parkland. If Voyce was in there it could take them months before he was discovered. The problem was that, if he *was* in there, he was almost certainly dead.

Then Shaw got the call. A firm of solicitors called Masters & Masters. Apologies for the short notice, but could he make a meeting with a client? The client was Mrs Peggy Robins — the mother of Chris Robins, one of the four young hoodlums who'd made up Bobby Mosse's juvenile gang on the Westmead Estate. Chris Robins had died in Bellevue. His mother had a part-time job in the kitchens at the hospital. Shaw didn't really have time for the diversion, but the idea of escaping the twisted maze of Lizzie Murray's family history, even for an hour, was irresistible. And getting closer to Robins — and, through him, Mosse — was too good an opportunity to pass up. What did Peggy Robins have to tell him? And why was she telling him now?

The Porsche slipped between the twin pillars of the hospital gates and Shaw pulled up at a brick kiosk, flashing his warrant card to a man behind glass. The gravel drive snaked up to the main building: a residential facility for patients with chronic mental health problems. A hundred years earlier it had been Bellevue Lunatic Asylum, and the word Bellevue had since become a Fenland euphemism for madhouse. Shaw had checked the hospital's website before setting out: there were rooms for 132 patients, and a training unit for nurses wishing to gain accreditation in the care of the mentally ill. Half of the original building was mothballed, the windows covered in metal shutters. The only press cutting he'd found was of a coroner's court hearing on a patient who'd been found in the mud down by the river. There had been the usual ritual calls from relatives for tighter security and surveillance.

He went to reception in the main block, an echoing marble hall with a black-and-white chequered floor. A child's mural of a townscape covered one wall in primary colours. Mrs Robins was in the grounds, he was told. She had left a note for him with a sketch map attached showing where Shaw could find her. He followed a sinuous path through snow-laden cedars. With the sudden Arctic cold had come a preternatural calm, so that when a crow flapped its way from a branch the dislodged snow fell straight to earth.

Shaw saw her before she heard his snow-quietened footsteps. A small woman, neat, self-contained, reading a book which had been covered in brown paper. But as soon as she moved, something about the way her shoulders slumped reminded him of the Westmead: as if — like the community of women who'd fought to bring up children in its warren of concrete — she was braced for something, always waiting to absorb the next blow. Old age hadn't made her movements any less brisk or workmanlike, as if she didn't have the luxury of a retirement ahead. She had a slight cast in one eye, which Shaw noticed because she looked directly at him as she took his hand. It reminded him of Lena, so that he couldn't restrain the smile he gave her.

She thanked him for coming, asked about his journey, apologized for the icy cold and for dragging him out of town.

'It's a dreadful place,' she said, but somehow she seemed to hint at some kind of affection for it, as if it was an errant child.

She'd taken a job in the kitchens, she said, both because she'd needed the money and so that she could see Chris every day. Although his death — she avoided the word suicide — had removed one incentive, she couldn't afford not to work, so now spent her days eternally reminded of her loss in this place where her son's life had ended.

Shaw thought of the grainy CCTV footage of the car crash at Castle Rising, wondering which of the peak-capped figures had been Chris Robins. He was fighting to keep hold of that scene, and what it said about this woman's son: that however blameless she might be, he had been guilty of a particularly ruthless crime, even if it had been a crime of omission. He'd driven away from that buckled car and left three people to die. Only fate had limited the death toll to two.

'I can't stand it inside once I'm done working,' she said, looking back over her shoulder at the red-brick mass of the old hospital. 'When Chris was alive it seemed worth the effort. Is it all right if we stay out here?'

Shaw said he was happiest outside.

Fumbling inside a heavy coat she produced a

white envelope with Shaw's name on the front — in full and typed: Peter Summerville Shaw — his middle name being his mother's maiden one.

Shaw tore it open. It was a one-line letter asking him to attend the reading of the last will and testament of Christopher Alan Robins at the offices of Masters & Masters on 24 December at 10.00 a.m.

'I don't understand,' he said.

'Chris appointed me as executor. There'll be some money. It can't be much. Bloody bank and the lawyers have had most of it already. It's been a nightmare. There was the coroner's court too, that held things up. Then I couldn't find the will.

'But, like I said, there'll be a little cash. Chris always said we might have the chance to make amends. He always said 'we'. Now I know why — because he wasn't planning on being here.'

Her jaw line set firmly. 'I think he wanted me to confess on his behalf. Which isn't easy — because he never really confessed to me.'

She turned slightly and looked at Shaw's face, momentarily distracted by the moon-eye. 'It was your father, wasn't it, who arrested Bobby Mosse? Yes. The link's important. Chris was like that, good with people.'

She smiled. Somewhere in the building behind them an electronic bell rang. Shaw thought of the two-tone Mini driving away from the lonely T-junction.

'I think you know the truth, anyway. I guessed it long ago, I think, by instalments over the years. I didn't ask Chris about it — but towards the

231

end he couldn't stop himself talking, spilling it out. That was part of his illness.'

She thrust her hands deep into the overcoat pockets and took a deep breath. Shaw remained silent, allowing her to order her thoughts.

'The police said they were a gang. One of the community coppers came to the flat a few times, asking us to keep Chris in at night, to stop him playing with the rotten apples. He'd be thirteen, something like that. But I'd always thought of them as friends, because that's how it started. They'd meet in our kitchen and I'd make them egg and chips. I knew Bobby was the smart one from the start, and in a secret way I hated him back then, because I knew he'd escape one day, get away from the Westmead, make the most of life. Alex — Alex Cosyns — was a tyke, and a crook in the making. He'd be, what, ten, eleven, when he and Chris fetched up at the school together. I knew the first time he came into the flat he was going to be bad news for Chris, because Chris wanted friends — needed them, really — and he let Alex be his hero. It was Alex who'd cheek the police who were sent in when there was trouble; it was Alex who took him shoplifting. By the time they were teenagers they were like that . . .'

She took out her hand, held it in a fist, and Shaw noticed the slim band of a wedding ring.

'Chris was a timid kid. Quiet. Drove his dad to distraction because we had ambitions for him.' She turned on the seat to look Shaw in the face. 'People seem to think that if you live on the Westmead, you don't want better for your kids.

But you do. We did. But Chris was scared of anything that was big.' She laughed, looking up into the trees. 'Like life. Like getting a job. Marriage — commitments. Anyway, life was easier for him when he was with the others, so that's where he stayed. The four of them. Like the police said, I suppose — a gang.'

Shaw nodded in agreement.

'When your dad arrested Bobby Mosse for killing that little boy, everything changed. Chris never said anything, but I could see the fear in him — feel it. Those months before the trial, he never got over that. He'd sit in the front room watching the TV — anything, sound down. I didn't see Alex at all, or Bobby, or Jimmy Voyce, and that was what made me think the worst. One day I took Chris's dad out along the riverbank — he was in a wheelchair after a stroke, the year he died — so we went out along the towpath by the Boal Quay and I saw the three of them on the scrub there, sat in the wreck of a boat. I didn't get close but I know my son — he was crying, and Alex had an arm round him, and Jimmy was drinking cider from a big bottle.'

She stopped. Shaw let the silence stretch. Snow thudded down off one of the trees.

'When he got off — Bobby — things changed again. He went back to university, of course — escaped, like I knew he would. Jimmy Voyce was the next to get out — running off to New Zealand. Then one night there was a uniformed PC on my doorstep. They had Chris down at St James's — they needed me to come down. He'd been caught climbing out of a back window of a house in the North End with a video recorder under his arm. I'm pretty sure Alex was with him — but he'd got away, of course. Chris got a suspended for that, but he got caught again within weeks so they sent him down. Durham. When he got out he didn't come home. He never came home. I tried to keep in touch but he was in and out for years until one of the judges ordered a mental-health review — that was in 2003. They sent him here. He'd tried suicide before, inside, and he tried again and again here, but he just couldn't make the cuts deep enough.'

Shaw wondered how many times a mother had to repeat that before she could say the words without tears.

'I used to look at his wrists when I came, to see if he'd tried again. They kept knives away from him in the end, so he'd try to make one out of bits of metal, or sharpened nails. Alex Cosyns came to see him a few times. I don't know why. They had a secret — not just the past — but something else they wouldn't share. About three months after Alex's last visit I got a cheque — drawn on Alex's personal account — for £1,000. There was a note. He said he'd keep in touch with Chris, but that he didn't think there was much point giving him any money, so I might as well have it, because it was his due. He said there'd be more. A few weeks later Chris was dead. He finally had another visitor just before he did it. Whoever it was didn't sign in, so they never got a name — they've upped the security since; anyone visiting a patient has to fill in a form now. But I think it was Bobby Mosse who came to see him, and I think he gave Chris the knife.' Shaw went to speak but she carried on. 'And now he's had another visitor.' She laughed, shaking her head. 'The woman on the ward who looked after Chris — kept an eye on him for me. She said Jimmy Voyce had been looking for him, all the way from New Zealand. He left a card, some grapes. She said Jimmy cried, which is nice, but I wonder who he was crying for?'

She flattened and folded a sheet of greaseproof paper that had been on the bench beside her — the remains of a packed lunch.

'I said I understood things, Inspector, and I do. But some things are frightening still. I had Chris cremated. There was just me and my sister at the service. When we got home someone had been through the flat — torn it apart. I had a tea chest from the ward, with Chris's stuff, and they'd literally taken it apart — the wood, smashed it up. I don't understand that.'

She stood and offered her hand. She seemed light on her feet, suddenly weightless. 'That's odd,' she said. 'I somehow feel better for talking about it. I thought I didn't care any more.'

'Is your shift finished? I can run you back to town,' said Shaw.

Peggy Robins shook her head. 'There's a mini-bus, on the hour.' She rearranged her scarf. 'The Westmead's changed over the years, Inspector, but it's still not very clever to let anyone see you being dropped off by a DI from St James's. It's still my world, and it's a world away from yours.'

21

Thursday, 16 December

Lynn's medieval Shipwrights' Hall stood on Cross Bank, its red-brick decorated façade looking out across the sea wall, a narrow band of reeds and the black river. Built in the thirteenth century, it was a monument to the fortunes made by the merchants of Lynn. Today a freezing mist clawed at its mullioned windows, while a rusting German coaster in mid-stream vented water. The wind had died by noon, so that the damp air just lay in the Fisher Fleet like a ghostly spring tide.

Shaw and Valentine sat in the Porsche. The atmosphere was one of mutual anxiety. A search of the woods and estate at Holkham had been suspended overnight, resumed that morning, but had still failed to find any trace of Voyce. Tom Hadden's team had crawled over the hire car and found nothing. Shaw had not yet reported to DCS Warren that their surveillance operation on Mosse and Voyce had been a fifty per cent failure, but he had an urgent message from Warren's secretary on his mobile requesting an update — a request he couldn't ignore for much longer. He'd sent DC Twine to the magistrates court to obtain search warrants for both Mosse's house and the BMW.

Shaw had a large-scale map of west Norfolk

on his lap, showing the coast road down from Hunstanton that Mosse had taken once he'd left the town at speed. How had Voyce's hired car ended up further back up the coast at Holkham? He thought carefully about the night they'd lost Mosse and Voyce on the road. The BMW had turned down a side-street before accelerating away from Hunstanton. What if Mosse had dropped Voyce off by his own car? They hadn't been close enough to see whether Mosse had a passenger, and the glass was tinted anyway. What if they'd made their deal at the Wash & Tope. Voyce gets dropped back at his car and agrees to disappear. Did they know they were being followed? Is that why he'd ditched the hire car?

'You ain't gonna find him on there,' said Valentine, looking down the street, waiting for a familiar figure to walk out of the mist. The main doors of the Shipwrights' Hall were open now, and a steady line of people were filing in, mostly elderly, all smartly dressed. As he watched, a Daimler glided into the kerb and the mayor got out, rearranging a chain of silver links around his neck. A photographer stood by the main doors but didn't bother to take any pictures.

Shaw snapped the map wider. 'What do you suggest, George — a seance?'

Valentine held his raincoat lapels closer together. 'We could take Mosse down town, shake him up.'

Shaw shook his head. 'Yeah. Once we've got the warrant, that's our next move. But forgive my reluctance, because it's also our last move. He is a solicitor, George. I think he'll have a response ready. What d'you reckon — a complaint to the chief constable? Police harassment? Two bitter coppers trying to prove a judge was wrong? Warren will have us off the streets in half an hour.'

'Hey up,' said Valentine, pushing open the door, hauling himself up out of the Porsche's bucket seat. A woman had appeared out of the mist, middle-aged but with a jaunty walk, a raincoat failing to conceal a black waitress's uniform.

'Georgie,' she said when she saw Valentine, stepping closer and taking his head in her hands. Shaw looked away, embarrassed by the sudden intimacy.

'This is my sister Jean,' said Valentine, looking at Shaw. 'Jean, DI Shaw.'

He shook her hand. 'Peter, please, Mrs Walker.'

She looked at him with frank blue eyes. 'You look just like your dad,' she said. 'Uncanny.' Then she looked at her brother. 'I told you on the phone . . . ' She looked at her watch. 'I've only got a moment.'

'It's OK — I'm here for lunch. So, nothing lost,' said Valentine. He wasn't really looking forward to the meal; he didn't usually do food in daylight. But he thought there'd be booze — one of those shiny buckets with ice in the middle of the table, stuffed with wine bottles, maybe a good malt. The ticket was a stiff enough price to warrant something decent — Glenfiddich, perhaps.

They followed Jean Walker through a narrow

side entrance, down an alley and into a service yard. The medieval elegance of the Shipwrights' Hall's façade extended to medieval squalor at the back: food bins overflowing, an outdoor staff toilet giving off a powerful stench of stale urine despite the cold air, and a pile of empty catering-size cans of vegetables, all empty, all rusting.

'Nice,' said Shaw.

Jean laughed. 'I wouldn't eat here.' She patted her raincoat. 'I've brought sandwiches. If I was you, Georgie, I'd give it a miss.'

Valentine shrugged. 'I'll stick to fluids.' As he said it, though, he felt the stirrings of real hunger. He hadn't had a proper Christmas dinner in years. Perhaps he'd look at the turkey after all. Or the soup he'd ordered when he'd bought the ticket — he fancied something hot, nourishing. What had it said on Freddie Fletcher's menu — Olde Lynn Fish Soup?

She led the way through a fire exit and down a narrow set of stairs to the kitchens. Preparations for lunch, they could see, had been under way for hours. Two cauldrons in brushed aluminium bubbled: sprouts bobbing in one, sliced carrots in the other. A man in stained cook's whites hauled up an industrial oven door to reveal a line of half a dozen roasting turkeys, the sudden wave of heat reaching them from twenty feet. At a long metal table three women were arranging bread rolls and moulded pats of butter, each bearing the Shipwrights' crest.

On a set of open gas burners soup simmered

239

in three pots, the scent on the air something fishy, with a bite.

'I'm serving,' said Jean, shrugging off the raincoat to reveal the uniform underneath, black with white cuffs, a white ruff. 'Latest fashion,' she said, pulling the skirt straight. 'Like I said — I've just got five minutes.' She took them to a small room set off the kitchen where there was a machine to dispense drinks.

'I wouldn't touch that, either,' she said, sitting, smiling again at Valentine.

'Just tell Peter what you know, Jean.'

They heard a plate crash to the stone floor outside, the curse that followed greeted with a chorus of cheering.

'George asked if I remembered Nora Melville's wake. Sorry — Nora Tilden. It's just that I grew up with the Melvilles, so it's difficult to let the name go. I didn't know anyone who wasn't glad to see the back of her, frankly. And of course, with the murder, everyone gossiped, everyone wanted to be there, at the wake. Place was heaving. I'd done catering for the Flask at weekends when I was at school — washing up, mainly. So I knew they'd ask. I was in the kitchen most of the night, although we came through a couple of times for a fag and to listen to the choir sing, and once to set up the buffet.

'Anyway, I was standing there listening when Freddie Fletcher came up. This was by the arch — between the bar and the dining room where the choir was singing. I was at school with Freddie. He knew I worked in the kitchens — I think he thought I knew the family, although to

240

be honest Nora treated everyone like a stranger so I didn't know anything that wasn't common knowledge. Freddie had been drinking. He tried a bit of conversation but I could see straight off he wanted something. I let him burble on till he got to it.'

In the kitchen something sizzled in fat.

'He wanted to know if I could tell him where the black kid lived.'

'Pat Garrison?'

'Yes. I had no idea, but I didn't tell him that. I asked him why he wanted to know. He smirked a bit, said there was something they wanted to give him. A present.'

'What did you think he meant?' asked Shaw.

'Freddie was a cruel kid — the girls always thought he picked on other kids to make sure no one had time to pick on him. When he got older he picked on blacks, him and his mates.'

Shaw just let her go on, because he knew she wanted to tell him. He had a sudden insight into life in South Lynn. A life accompanied by the commentary of neighbours, an endless litany of whispers, just on the edge of hearing.

'Freddie's mum left home when he was a kid, she found herself a new man down at the bus station where she worked. Freddie's dad never got over it — let the house go to ruin. And the kids — Freddie had a sister — they just ran wild. This was when we was at school, so Freddie would only have been a teenager — just. His sister . . . ' she searched her memory for the name, 'Milly — that was it — she was still in junior school. Those days people just stepped in and helped in situations like that — before the council stuck their oar in. An uncle, I think it was, over at West Lynn took them in, but it didn't last. So the worst happened — they both went into care, and the council split them up. Milly went miles away — can't remember where; Freddie was fostered in Lynn, but he moved about, nothing permanent. It's not an excuse, is it, for what he turned out like, but it's an explanation.'

Perhaps, though not a good enough one, thought Shaw.

'And for all the talk, d'you know what? Freddie was pretty much all mouth. I don't know what I thought that night, when he asked about the Garrison kid, but I imagined, I s'pose — that they'd break his windows. Piss through the letterbox. They weren't the Ku Klux Klan. And the kid was right up himself. I don't care what colour he was, it wasn't like he didn't deserve a thump.'

A woman in a suit appeared at the door. 'Jean, you're needed, please. Soup's going up.'

Jean mouthed a silent 'cow' and hauled herself to her feet. She said she'd be serving for twenty minutes, then there'd be a gap before the main course — but she didn't know anything else that might help. Shaw said he'd wait, because he had a few more questions. Valentine stood, buttoned up his jacket. 'Right. Lunchtime for me, then. I'll see what I see.'

Alone, Shaw listened to the staff in the kitchen plating up the soup. He tried to rationalize what they knew about Pat Garrison, and what Jean's evidence, and that which had come to light at the inquest, told them about his death. Superficially, Shaw thought, the picture was clearer. They had three suspects — Fletcher, Venn and John Joe Murray — all with motives. They could have struck individually or collectively. The person who'd been heard typing at the victim's flat that night could easily have been one of them. Whoever it was could have taken the key from Pat Garrison's body, which would account for none being found in the grave, then gone back to his flat to type the notes designed to allay suspicion when he went missing. But Shaw was increasingly unhappy with the emerging picture. Garrison's own character was as difficult to grasp as the winter fog lying in the streets — twisting, insinuating itself into the alleys and yards of the Old Town. Was he a devoted lover, determined to stay with his new child, the victim of prejudice for his colour, his nationality, his youth, his looks; or was he a cynical womanizer, arrogant and calculating? It was as if all the hatred which seemed to obscure Pat Garrison was obscuring something else as well.

His mobile rang. It was Jacky Lau. In the background he could hear a wind, surf and an engine running.

'Sir. I'm on Holkham Sands. There's a club — strictly illegal — they run hot-rod cars on the sands after the tide's gone out. I know someone who knows someone. They had a meet down here night before last. They ran a few cars, then called it all off because they saw lights in the

243

woods, thought it might be traffic division. They've been busted before and they didn't want a repeat. But I've checked with both Burnham and Hunstanton; they had nothing up here after dark.'

'Who's with you?'

'Paul's got two cars on the way, sir. It won't be an easy search — it's got to be ten, fifteen square miles of woodland.'

Shaw told her to start searching where the lights had been seen and work their way outwards, then he cut the line. He knew the spot — a mile west of the nature reserve, a stretch of pine woods where hardly anybody ever went in winter. There was a road in — a forest track, but part metalled. Voyce's hire car had been dumped two miles away. It wasn't good news, and the stench of roasting turkey flesh didn't make him feel any better.

Jean Walker was back. She washed her hands at a grimy sink, then looked at Shaw. 'You can smoke in here,' she said. 'Nobody gives a damn.'

'Don't smoke,' said Shaw.

'No,' she said, trying to push a fringe of untidy hair back under her waitress's cap. 'You're not really like Jack at all, are you? Just the looks. He broke a few hearts, too.'

She took a Silk Cut Valentine had left on the table for her, holding it as if it was the first cigarette she'd ever seen. She lit it with her eyes closed, and didn't open them until she'd expelled the smoke from between her lips.

'Who were Fletcher's friends?' asked Shaw.

'Will Stokes — he's dead now, but they were

thick as thieves. There was Sam Venn. Like I said, Freddie picked on kids at school and Sam was target number one from the start — but Sam's a survivor: he'd take anything Freddie dished out, then come running back. In the end they were a bit of a double act. Sam could be cruel too. I guess that was the point for him — making sure someone else was the target. Just like Freddie.'

'Venn was in with the skinheads?' asked Shaw, worried at an image that jarred.

'No. No — after school, they weren't so close, and Sam was in with the church and everything, and Freddie hardly fitted in there. But in an odd way Freddie was family for Sam — what passed for it, anyway. They all kept in touch, all of his mates did, from school, and there's some club the boys are still in — they all meet for lunch at the Flask, raise a bit for charity, that kind of thing. Masons without the aprons. They'll be upstairs now, hitting the bottle.' She looked skywards. 'Yeah — family. It was all Sam had, and Freddie. Like I said, Freddie went into care. And Sam's aunt brought him up — the house is in Palmerston Terrace — and she was in the church, one of Nora's cronies.'

Shaw had another question ready but there was something about the way Valentine's sister licked her lips that told him she had something else to say first, but that, being a good woman, she wanted someone to drag it out of her.

'The church . . . ' Shaw shook his head, searching. Then he had it. 'Damn. I meant to ask — that's right, isn't it? Venn's father was in the

Elect, we were told that by Abney, the pastor. So where were his parents? Why was he being brought up by an aunt?'

She ground the cigarette under her black shoe.

'Bit of a local scandal,' she wriggled slightly in her seat. 'Surprised George didn't remember — but he was probably playing cops and robbers with his mates from school.' She laughed bitterly, as if she too had wanted escape.

'Thing is, Arthur Venn — Sam's dad — was a bachelor, in his fifties. Then he discovered sex and along came Sam. Problem was, the woman he discovered sex with was a Venn too — his dead brother's daughter. Uncle and niece, see? So they threw him out of the church — her too. And boy were they smug when they saw young Sammy.' She shook her head, still appalled, at the distance of nearly fifty years, at how cruel the righteous could be. 'It's cerebral palsy, but you know what these people are like. God's judgement — the face, the arm. It did for Arthur — and the niece — they left town. Rumour was they shacked up together in London — because they don't care down there, do they? Anything goes in London. Up here we're still burning witches. So that left Sam and the aunt. And she was a sour-faced cow as well — same pod as Nora.'

They heard plates being set out in the kitchen.

Shaw let this new image of Sam Venn take shape in his head. 'Did you know, back in 1982, that Patrice and Lizzie were having an affair?' he asked.

'Not till the baby came — then we worked it

out pretty damn quick, like everyone else. No, I don't think people knew — not to talk about, anyway. But that's different, isn't it — so maybe they did know. I wasn't really in the in-crowd back then — marrying a copper tends to put the frost on things. And Don thought the place was worth avoiding. He never drank on the manor — just like your dad, Peter. They'd go out of town — or use the Red House, the coppers' pub.'

Shaw was rerunning the cine film of the wake in his head. 'And John Joe Murray — he'd been keen on Lizzie, but she didn't want to know?'

'Everyone loved Lizzie,' she said. 'John Joe tried his luck — sure. But she could pick and choose, could Lizzie, and she chose not.'

'Bad blood?' asked Shaw.

'No — just the opposite, really. Kind of a joke, you know? They'd play up to it with people around — flirting with each other, turning each other down, making out they'd be meeting up later. It's just that she didn't want anyone from here — from the town. She always said she'd marry someone who'd take her away. Knight on a charger — that kind of rubbish.'

The radio, which had been blaring out KL.FM from the kitchen, went silent. The manageress appeared at the door with a mobile open.

'Either of you know first aid?' she asked. 'We need an ambulance — for upstairs. I need them now. Really. People are being sick. Jesus!' She covered her mouth. 'It's like they've been poisoned.'

22

Shaw told Jean to ring 999 and went out into the kitchen. Most of the staff were standing in a huddle, heads together, but two of the men were already cleaning surfaces, sweeping floors, manically scrubbing pots. The oven door stood open, the meat cooling, turkey fat congealing on the metal roasting trays. A woman emerged from the store cupboard and put a large catering bottle of disinfectant on a worktop.

Shaw pushed through a pair of swing doors and found himself at the bottom of a wide wooden staircase, sagging slightly to one side, which led up to the banqueting hall. Here the double serving doors had been hooked back. The hall had a magnificent hammer-beam roof, a complex puzzle of gracefully curving oak beams from which hung six crystal chandeliers festooned with candle bulbs. The room was dominated by a statue in stone of a merchant, larger than life, set in a niche in the end wall, so that he could look towards the great west window which faced the river, as if waiting for one of his ships to come into sight.

The room was in chaos. About twenty circular tables dotted the oak floor, set for the festive charity lunch. But many of the guests were wandering from table to table, or kneeling beside others who were slumped in their seats. A Christmas tree at one end glittered with white fairy lights. The tables were crowded with unpulled crackers. Loudspeakers were still feeding in carols at a discreet if insistent volume, but over that background Shaw could hear a persistent groaning. Several of the guests were either clutching their stomachs or leaning forward, their heads in their hands. Others pressed napkins to their mouths. Several had vomited. One elderly woman was fussing, clearly distressed, telling a waitress she'd clean the mess up herself.

Shaw knelt beside her and took her hand. 'A doctor's on the way,' he said. She must have heard because she tried to smile but then there was a spasm of pain and she doubled up. When she lifted her head again her skin had taken on a green tint and her eyes were bloodshot.

'Soon,' said Shaw, pressing her shoulder.

He surveyed the room, trying to see Valentine. A small crowd had gathered between two of the tables. Shaw pushed his way through, holding up his warrant card.

At the centre of the crowd was a man lying on the floor. He was glistening with sweat and fingering a silver chain around his neck.

'It's the mayor,' said a woman in a hat. She looked around the room. 'What on earth has happened?'

'Give him water — actually, fresh water.' Shaw turned and beckoned to a waitress. 'Get fresh water — don't let them drink this lot . . . ' He picked up a carafe, held it to the light. 'Bring bottled.'

They heard a distant siren and the sound of

someone retching by the Christmas tree. A waiter threw open the window and the sound of the siren swelled.

Shaw jumped as someone put a hand on his shoulder. It was George Valentine. 'I reckon the soup's the culprit. I gave it a miss in the end. Shellfish — always a bad idea.'

'What have you eaten?' asked Shaw.

'Melon. White wine. Bread — that's all fine. Believe me, it's the soup.'

Shaw nodded towards a table in the far corner by the tree, around which sat some of the locals from the Flask, including Freddie Fletcher and Sam Venn. Both were slumped forward. 'Soups all round, by the look of it,' he said. 'So much for 'good local fare'. Check 'em out, George.'

But before he could move they heard a scream, a woman's voice, mangling a word.

Shaw picked his way through the tight-packed tables to get to her. She was young, about twenty, with blonde hair in a neat bob. She held an elderly man's head against her shoulder, heedless of the bib of vomit that covered his shirt, tie and waistcoat.

She looked at Shaw. 'It's my grandad. I think he's dead,' she said, brushing hair back from the man's face. Despite the red blotches on the old man's cheeks, and the tear which welled and then spilt into his mouth from one of his closed eyes, the line of the lips was already lifeless, parted unevenly to show tobacco-stained teeth. Shaw had no doubt she was right: the last seconds of life, he thought, were as ugly as death itself.

23

A catering can of Olde Lynn Fish Soup stood on the long refectory table. In front of the table stood the council's Chief Environmental Health Officer, Guy Poole. The can was unopened, a wraparound label showing a trawler of the Fisher Fleet. Shaw pushed it towards him. 'It's all yours, Guy, but I don't advise cooking it up for the family.'

Poole was not the clichéd pen-pushing bureaucrat of popular legend. Shaw knew him because he'd led a campaign group to save the dunes south of Old Hunstanton from erosion. He lived with his wife and three children in a houseboat at Brancaster Staithe. Like Shaw he never wore a tie, and like Shaw he loved his job. He had a reputation at St James's for using the law flexibly, and avoiding legal proceedings if he could. But if he caught the scent of something genuinely rotten he'd spare no expense to get the culprit in front of a judge.

Poole took a note. 'So — the numbers again?'

Valentine had the details. The DS's skin was still a subtle shade of puce. He might not have had the soup, but the sight of fifty-odd people throwing up in concert had turned his stomach, and the smell was on the air — the sea-spray scent of oyster mixed with Parmesan cheese.

A uniformed PC delivered a tray of coffees from Starbucks and they took them over to one of the round dining tables. 'There were a hundred and three for lunch,' said Valentine. 'Forty-two had the melon, sixty-one the soup — most of whom report nausea, vomiting, or just plain stomach pains. Three with no symptoms. Of those who had the melon, two reported feeling sick — but that was probably the sight of the rest of 'em chucking up. Dead man is a Charles Anthony Clarke — known as Charlie. Aged eighty-two. Granddaughter was with him — says he's had a history of heart trouble.' He paused, removed the lid from his coffee, took a micro-sip and got his breathing back under control. 'Ex-serviceman, was Charlie — the whole table was old soldiers, sponsored by the Co-op, who coughed up for their tickets. As of an hour ago sixteen of the soup drinkers were still in the Queen Victoria — eight in intensive care, and most of those are OAPs.' He flipped the notebook shut. 'Otherwise, it's a happy Christmas to one and all.'

Poole stood and walked away, speaking quickly into a mobile phone.

'Fletcher and Venn?' asked Shaw.

'Fletcher's not good — but we know his guts were shot anyway, it was only being a greedy pig that got him here,' said Valentine. 'Surprised he made it — but then he'd paid for his ticket, and there's no motivation like getting your money's worth. He's one of the worst — but he's not in danger. Venn was sick but went home under his own steam.'

The manageress came to the still-open double doors. She looked a generation older than she had done two hours ago. Jean had left after confirming that she would be paid for a full shift.

'Local paper's got someone on the doorstep, Mr Poole — and the Press Association's on the line in the office.'

Poole pocketed his mobile, slumped back in his seat, then leant forward and picked up the can. 'Right. Well, I think we can safely drop the makers of this stuff in the shite without further ado.' He turned the can. 'West Lynn Foodstuffs: Clockcase Cannery, West Lynn. Hmmm.'

'What?' asked Shaw.

'Nothing — the place is closing down. Planning committee gave change-of-use permission a few months ago. Maybe their health-and-safety rules have gone by the board — who knows? People losing their jobs aren't the best placed to run a tight ship.'

' "Local fare for local people," ' said Shaw, standing. 'What do you think? Definitely the cans?'

'My prime suspect,' said Poole, smiling, turning the can, reading the small print. 'Certainly sufficient grounds to shut them down while we do the tests. It's a stroke of luck, having the unopened can. Manager says they ordered just enough — people were asked to indicate what they wanted when they bought their tickets — but on the day a few changed their minds and asked for melon, so they had this one spare. We can look at the empties, of course — but this way there's no argument: if there's something nasty in the can, there's no wriggle room.

'And seafood's always tricky — packed with dodgy critters — oysters, prawns, scallops, you name it. Then there's the can. We'll get this one back to the lab for a once over. You do get the odd dodgy batch; maybe the seal's rusted, maybe the vacuum's failed.'

Poole stood, bracing himself for the press call.

'Good luck with the reptiles,' said Shaw.

All the windows were open now and they could hear the electronic whirr of cameras. The gloomy fogbound light filtering through the stained-glass windows was boosted by a TV arc lamp.

Poole walked to the door, can of soup under his arm, whistling.

Shaw and Valentine faced each other across the round table, listening to his footsteps fade on the grand staircase. The table had been cleared of cutlery, glasses and crackers but a reservation sign remained on a metal spike: THE FLASK.

Shaw covered his eyes with his hands and tried to refocus. He seemed to spend his life refocusing, and for the first time he thought how tiring that was.

'OK. So Jean's changed the game a bit,' he said. 'We've got suspects. They're not new — but the picture's getting clearer, sharper,' said Shaw, his voice echoing under the hammer-beam roof. 'Maybe,' he added, still worried by all the details that didn't quite fit.

'Fletcher,' said Valentine, helping himself to a glass of white wine from a bottle that had been left on a side table, running a paper napkin round the rim. 'On the night of the wake he's going around asking people where Pat Garrison lives. Maybe nobody knows, or they won't tell him.

254

So he waits, sees the kid leave early, decides to follow him home. Maybe that's all he wanted to do — get the address that way, then plan a little surprise. Something nasty through the letterbox.

'But once he's out in the night anything could happen — the kid sees him, confronts him in the cemetery. Fletcher's beered up — perhaps he's not alone. There was a table full of skinheads in that room, although most were still there for the choir's second session. They give him a kicking, cosh him with the hook, then chuck him in the grave.'

'And where'd the billhook come from?' asked Shaw. 'It's not as though it's a Swiss Army knife that you can slip in your back pocket.' He leant forward and, overcome by a sudden weariness, surprised himself by pouring a glass of wine for himself. They seemed to be circling this case without being able to reach its heart.

'You're right,' said Valentine, refilling his own glass. 'I can't see him doing it on his own. People like that, I've seen 'em on the street: BNP, National Front, British Party — never one-on-one, always in a crowd. That's the way they work. No way he'd have gone after Pat without back-up.'

Shaw told his DS everything his sister had remembered about the night of Nora's wake, and about Freddie Fletcher and Sam Venn. Valentine looked up at the intricate oak roof. 'Venn, then — it's a motive. They're cousins, first cousins, Pat and Lizzie. It's not . . . ' Valentine paused, assembling the right words. 'It's not some biblical debate for him, is it? It's his life

255

— it's what he's like, because of what it did to him.' He took a third refill from the bottle. 'What he *thought* it had done to him. I'm not saying he'd kill for that, but if his mate Fletcher was on a mission, perhaps he joined in. Cowards killed that kid — we know there's more than one of them. Venn and Fletcher fit the bill — nothing on their own, but together they're dangerous. That's where my money is.'

'Don't forget John Joe Murray,' said Shaw. 'He says he didn't know about Pat and Lizzie, but we've seen the film, and I think we can say that's a lie. Why lie? Well, it's a sensible thing to do if you want to avoid being a suspect in a murder inquiry. He doesn't know we've got the film. Perhaps he saw them at the bar that night talking? A bit too close, a bit too knowing. Had he really given up on Lizzie? He admits he thought Lizzie was pregnant, so perhaps he was on the lookout for the father. Perhaps he wanted to scare Pat off, make it crystal clear he wasn't going to get his feet under the table at the Flask. Murray says he stayed until midnight — so get Twine to check that out with our witnesses.'

Shaw stood. 'That's the problem with this crime, George. It's all motive — you can't move for motives. What we haven't got enough of is evidence. Even if we could put all of them in the cemetery that night, at the right time, could we prove which of them struck the fatal blow? I doubt it. Unless one of them breaks down and gives us a nice neat confession I can't see any way forward. One fact hasn't changed right from the start — this is a twenty-eight-year-old crime.

Not many of those get solved.'

Valentine rubbed his stomach under his raincoat. ' 'Cept we know someone was out there trying to dig up the grave this year. Six months ago. That's not a cold case.'

Shaw took a menu off the neighbouring table, turned it over and began to make a list.

'OK — let's concentrate on that. What do we know? Either someone dug the hole and found what they were looking for, or they dug the hole and didn't find what they were looking for. The second scenario seems marginally more likely as we know they were probably spotted and that the police turned up — and went on turning up on a nightly basis, so they couldn't go back. So that implies that what they *were* looking for was still in the grave when we opened it up.'

Shaw completed the note, aware that outside they could still hear the electronic crackle from the mobile TV unit. He turned the napkin round for Valentine to check. On it was a list with three headings:

NORA	PAT	MARY
Brooch	Penknife	Model ship
The Free Church	Billhook	
	Wallet — with scraps of paper:	
	Hangman sketch? Ticket?	
	Coins	
	Two glasses with the Flask motif	
	Missing: watch and keys?)	

'Have I missed anything?' asked Shaw.

The DS studied the list for a full minute, then shook his head.

'One of these items means more than we realize,' said Shaw. 'It means a lot to someone — someone close, someone we know.'

'The glasses?'

'We checked that out. The pub was presented with a set of a dozen etched glasses by the brewery before the war. There's just three left behind the bar — Lizzie uses them. So — they came from the pub, that's all we know.'

Valentine leant back in his chair, his neck bones clicking together like billiard balls.

Shaw thought about the model boat, the tiny shrouded bundle of Mary Tilden. 'Alby Tilden — the father, what's the latest?' asked Shaw, clutching at the one piece of the jigsaw that was still missing from the family picture.

'He's been out for eleven years. Had some psychiatric problems, apparently — agoraphobia. Fear of the outside. They had to drag him out. In 2003 he was on some out-reach network run from Lincoln. Living on benefits. After that he slips off the radar. We know Lizzie Murray writes regularly, and was getting replies until a year ago; her letters to Alby go via Bea Garrison to an address in Retford. That's been checked out, by the way — dead-end. The flat number we've got matches one that's empty. Has been for a year. Tenant died. He was an old lag from Lincoln.

258

And Twine's having a real job getting the pension details as well. Latest promise is sometime today — but who knows?'

Shaw stood, the chair scraping horribly. He was struggling to think straight, haunted by the dead face of Charlie Clarke, who'd survived a world war only to be struck down by a can of rancid soup.

'So that would explain why Alby hasn't written for a year — Lizzie's letters weren't being passed on,' said Shaw.

Valentine continued to stare at his notepad. 'Well, you'd think so, but there's an odd detail,' he said. 'When the Nottingham boys checked out the address in Retford they found that a neighbour's been keeping the post. Twine asked them to check through, and there was nothing there from Lynn.' He straightened his arm so that he could see his counterfeit Rolex. 'I'll get back to Bea Garrison — see what should be there.'

Shaw picked up the list of forensic exhibits from the opened grave.

'Bea. The victim's mother. Perhaps the only person in the world who really knew him. Lizzie had known him for, what, five months? Bea'd seen it all — twenty years of growing up. Get over to the Ark, George; sign out the forensics that were on Pat — the knife, the billhook, the sketch, the lot. Tom's got copies of the sketches. Let's see what she has to say about the contents of her son's pockets.'

'And Warren? We still haven't told him about Jimmy Voyce.'

Shaw closed his eyes. Monocularism put a strain on his good eye, which gave him headaches. He rubbed the temple beside the pain.

'Leave that to me.'

24

On a good day Morston House looked out over the harbour at Wells-next-the-Sea. This wasn't a good day. The mist on land ran hard here into a sea fret, a thick broiling band of fog that tracked the coast. Visibility was fifty yards and falling, light leaching away, ushering in a premature dusk. They'd crawled along the seafront in the Porsche, past a Dutch barge which was always moored at the spot — a floating pub with fairy lights strung up the rigging and along a gangplank peppered with snow. They could just see the chocolate-coloured seawater — a wide channel at full tide choked with ghostly white yachts moored to orange buoys. The quayside was reserved for the little fleet which trawled for scallops, mussels and crabs. Just beyond was the edge of the wide marsh which protected the harbour from the sea, the reeds clogged with ice.

The little kiss-me-quick seafront had lost its daily battle with the bleak winter landscape. From every lamp post hung a gaudy poster for Christmastide, the annual festival in which thousands of children crowded the water's edge to see Santa Claus drift in by boat under a sky full of fireworks. Shaw had taken Fran last year and had promised a return. He noted the date: Saturday, with the evening high tide. The posters were almost the only splash of colour on the street. The two chippies were closed, John's Rock

Shop alone spilling some electric light out on to the snow-swept pavement. There was a thirty-foot Christmas tree on the quay, but its lights were off. Down the channel which led to the open sea an automatic foghorn called to a beat as slow as a dying heart.

Morston House was on the waterfront but two hundred yards east, beyond the old warehouses converted for the Chelsea-on-Sea crowd. A small lane ran to the town's boatyard, and set back was a line of early Victorian villas, playfully painted in pink, blue and yellow, with arched doors, wooden balconies and wide picture windows on the second floors, giving a view, on a fog-free day, to the open sea and the dunes of the north coast. Most, like Morston House itself, had English Tourist Board B&B stickers in their front windows. Bea Garrison's boasted four stars, a pair of wide bay windows in naval style and — alone in the street — a tower room with a 'witch's hat' leaded roof.

Shaw parked outside the Norfolk Arms, a gastropub which, he'd discovered earlier that summer, served up three scallops on a plate at £20 a time. The 4×4s crammed into the car park were all polished, beaded with the mist. It was holiday cottage season, and the town was full of people who didn't know where they were, wandering in search of a coffee shop or book store that would tide them over until it was time to sleep in front of an open fire, or spend a small fortune on dinner. Everyone out had a dog, and most of those were Afghans or spaniels, both they and their owners sporting raincoats. In the public bar of the pub he could just see a group of local fishermen at the window, balefully eyeing the falling snow and the dying light.

The radio in the Porsche was tuned to KL.FM for the news bulletin.

. . . and the condition of six elderly men who fell ill at the dinner is still causing concern, said a hospital spokesman. The dead man's family has been informed. The council's Environmental Health Department earlier served an enforcement notice on the West Lynn company at which the soup was canned. The Clockcase Cannery has been ordered to cease production and is being examined by health experts. Our reporter spoke to the mayor at his home in Gayton, where he was recovering from the illness which had struck at the Shipwrights' Hall lunch . . .

Shaw cut the radio, hauling himself out of the Porsche. Zipping up his jacket, he heard his phone ring and called up a picture message from Lena: Fran, standing on a chair, stringing out paper chains in the cottage.

Valentine stood looking at the façade of the Norfolk Arms, the window frames of which had been painted that precise shade of eggshell blue that wealthy property owners had used on their woodwork all along the north Norfolk coast. The corporate livery of the weekend set. A lunch board advertised samphire, Brancaster mussels, Burnham venison and Sandringham lamb.

Shaw killed the image on his phone. He wasn't in the best of moods after his interview with DCS Warren. He'd been in his office for six minutes and hadn't sat down. Warren had taken the news calmly, his eyes bulging slightly. He said that when there *was* news of Voyce he wanted to be the first to know. If he later discovered that he was the second to know then he'd personally suspend Shaw from duty. Immediately. Shaw thought about DC Lau out on Holkham Sands, overseeing the search of the woods, but said nothing. He'd had no word. There was nothing to say.

They trudged up the sinuous garden path to Morston House past a dripping laurel. There was a sudden breeze from the sea, and Shaw wondered if, after all, the fog might clear in time for sunset. It was a curious magic of the coast that, however bad the day, the sun always seemed to make at least one brief appearance.

Shaw rapped on the door with a knocker cast in the shape of a fox's head.

It was opened by Kath Robinson. Shaw was struck again — as he had been the first time he'd seen her in the upstairs room at the Flask — by her casual beauty, her translucent skin, and by the complete absence of something: Shaw was used to sensing a reaction from women — a spectrum of signals ranging from frank and open sexual interest to a kind of defensive reserve. In Kath Robinson he sensed nothing, as if she was blind to gender, or indifferent to it.

'Bea said to take you up,' she said, standing back to let Shaw and Valentine over the threshold, rubbing a hand on her jeans at the thigh. She had a way of talking which made every sentence sound dead — as if she'd over-rehearsed it before delivery.

Bea Garrison's description of Morston House as a B&B had been disingenuous at best. As they made their way down a wide corridor they glimpsed a dining room and a bar, and at the back of the house an elegant wooden conservatory converted into a breakfast room. On a table in the hallway was a picnic basket, an old-fashioned wicker one with leather straps, the top open, containing several packets wrapped in greaseproof paper and a flask. By the back door Shaw glimpsed three sets of walking boots and a bundle of the curious ski sticks which had recently become an apparent necessity for all serious walkers.

'How many rooms?' asked Shaw.

Kath stopped, considering the question seriously, looking at her thin fingers. 'Four doubles, three singles. And there's a chalet room in the garden — that's popular, and takes four. Full house is fifteen, but we've had eighteen, with cots and stuff.'

'And who else works here?'

She talked as she climbed, following a twisting staircase which Shaw could see would take them up into the tower room. 'I cook when Ian's not here — he does two nights a week. We take non-residents. Two women clean, another one does the beds. There's a couple of handymen — gardeners, odd jobs, that kind of thing. I'm here full time — take the bookings, fuss about, wait at table. Bea used to but, you know, she deserves a rest.'

They reached a landing, then climbed again,

another short curved flight, and then another until they stepped out into the circular room beneath the witch's hat roof. The room was an observatory, with an all round view provided by a series of large windows.

Bea Garrison was standing looking seawards, where the fog seemed lighter. She wore a grey dress, woollen, a silver pin in her short grey hair. 'I thought you'd like to see this,' she said. 'Most people are curious.' She sought the window ledge with one hand, a slightly unsteady action, as if she might fall. 'Thanks, Kath.'

It was like looking out of an aircraft at passing cloud, the mist swirling, dragging past the tower, and then a rip opened up in the fog, a rent through which sunshine poured and which then widened, tearing the sky in half to reveal another day beyond: the intricate channels of the marsh like a cross-section of the brain, the distant blue sea stitched with white breaking waves, and a sky of high snow clouds. It was a stunning transformation which had taken less than thirty seconds to complete.

Bea stood smiling at the view, then she felt behind her for a wicker chair and sat down. Shaw and Valentine sat on the cushioned seats on the curving window ledge. 'This room, and the tower, were derelict until a few years ago — the people before used it for storage because the roof leaked and the windows needed replacing. We put the money in — a master stroke, and Ian's idea, by the way. We put a picture of this view in the magazines — *Birdwatch*, *Birdwatcher's Digest*, that kind of thing;

the Saga magazine, too. We've been full ever since.'

She touched her hair, rearranging it unnecessarily. Shaw thought she looked older than the last time he'd seen her, or perhaps just less sure of herself, less in control, which was odd, considering she was in her own home.

'It's a long way from the Flask,' said Shaw, aware that, like his own life, the life of this family was torn between the urban, claustrophobic seediness of South Lynn and this: the wide skies of the north Norfolk coast.

'Yes,' she said. 'Thank God.'

She smiled again, appearing to forget they were even there. Shaw watched her closely and realized that it wasn't the distant sea that held her attention, but the street below, the quayside, leading back into town.

'Personally,' she said, 'and you'll keep this to yourself, I find birds rather boring. No — *stultifyingly* boring. And that's the problem with twitchers: they have no idea what it's like not to find the sight of two black-backed marsh warblers twice as exciting as one. Ian's better — he can talk to the punters. I just nod and agree, then make a hasty exit, otherwise I'd scream the place down. Still, if it gets really bad I just think of the cheques.' But that wasn't right, and she seemed uncomfortable with the idea that all this was for money. 'And what they'll buy,' she added.

Shaw noted again the lingering lilt of the Midwestern accent, oddly exotic in this quintessentially English setting. He was struck by how

267

open this woman was to the world, how frank, and what a sharp contrast that was with her niece, Lizzie. He saw them as a curious contrast — a woman who'd broken away from her past and one who was still a prisoner of it.

'Pat was your only child?' asked Valentine, nosing the tip of his left shoe into the thick-pile carpet.

She gave him a cool look. 'Yes. So this will all be Ian's one day. My only grandchild. He cooks here sometimes — did Kath say? He's very good. That's the plan, you see.' She intertwined her fingers, which bulged slightly at the joints, and rubbed at one of the silver rings, burnishing it. 'A restaurant. Something really good. Something with one of those Michelin stars.' Her eyes caught the light, excited by the future she could imagine for her grandson.

Out at sea a yacht with a red sail cut in towards Brancaster. On the distant beach they could see horses galloping and a stunt kite twirling, like a hawk on a gyre. The sands were speckled with snow and dotted with people and dogs, circling their owners like satellites. Shaw was always amazed at how quickly a beach filled when the weather turned. He stood and began to place the forensic items they'd checked out of the Ark on the round coffee table that stood near the window, each in a sealed bag.

'We recovered these from around Pat's body on the night we opened Nora's grave. I'm sorry to distress you with this, but we believe that one of these items was very important to his killer. So important that he tried to get it back recently, by digging up the grave. They were disturbed midway through, so we're presuming that whatever they wanted is still here.'

'Someone tried to dig up the grave?'

'In June, we think,' said Shaw.

She let her eyes slide over the objects, then pointed at a cabinet in the corner. 'Sergeant,' she said. 'There's a bottle of whiskey in there — could you pour me one, please — no water. Do help yourself — it's bourbon.' Valentine poured just the one glass. He'd never liked spirits, because he knew what they did to him. Once she had the drink in her hand Bea Garrison moved the wicker chair closer to the table and began to pick up the plastic evidence bags.

She held up the wallet. 'This is Pat's — he was very proud of money, and having his own. He got that characteristic from his father — like so many other things.' She laughed as she picked up the penknife. 'And he literally got this from his father — it's Latrell's knife, from the war. He always said he got it on D-Day plus one, from a German in a ditch by the road.' She looked out at the sunshine which was making the mud in the creeks look silver. 'Oddly, he knew his name — Jasper Hanke. I suppose the German had something else on him, a letter maybe. I think one of the reasons Latrell gave it to Pat was to get rid of it — to break the link.'

And then the small copy of the sketch. She held it lightly in her hands.

'Just this?' she asked, and Shaw noted that her

voice — hard and gritty — had acquired an edge.

'No — there were about a dozen pieces like that, all with ink marks, but we can't make out the pictures. We presumed it was hangman — but it's not a game, because there are no letters . . . '

She held a hand against her lips as if she might cough, and for the first time Shaw thought that — at last — the true significance of these objects had struck home: that her only son had been murdered, and these few things in his pockets were all that remained. But she gathered herself and went on, although Shaw sensed now that she needed the glass in her hand.

'No. It's not a game. That's the last thing it is.' She drank the bourbon in one swig and held it out for a refill without looking at Valentine, without taking her eyes off the little childish scribble. Shaw thought that she was a woman who'd managed to free her life from the support of men.

'It's a warning,' she said. 'A series of them, probably. You can see that, can't you? The first piece just a line on paper. Then two lines, then the gibbet appears, then the hanging man.'

She looked Shaw in his good eye. 'It's a lynching — the coward's way. Pat didn't say what was happening, he just said some of the 'low life' — his words, the 'low life' — at the pub were trying to scare him, trying to get him to go home, back where he came from.' She over-articulated the words, to make it clear they weren't hers. 'I got the cold shoulder too, the

odd remark, but nothing like this.' She held up
the envelope, studying the sketch. 'This is sick.'

'And this . . . hounding — when did it begin?'

'After a few weeks. Early summer. He'd get
them at college — in his pigeon-hole. It went on
for months before he disappeared. In the end he
thought it was amusing, I think. That's the
arrogance, of course — the idea that he didn't
need to fear anyone, or anything. It's what
children think, isn't it? That they're not going to
die. He was still a child in some ways.'

Shaw heard a creak of a wooden stair. He
wondered if Kath Robinson was on the landing
below, just within earshot. Bea Garrison actually
flinched at the noise, then seemed to force
herself to relax, sinking into the wicker chair.
Shaw thought it was as if she was waiting for
something: a visitor?

Finally, she picked up the billhook.

'Yes — well, this is Alby's,' she said, sipping at
the drink now.

'How . . . ' Shaw swapped a glance with
Valentine. 'How can you know that — it's just a
billhook with the maker's name.' As he said it he
knew he was wrong, but the truth was just out of
reach, buried in his memory.

She laughed. 'Yes — that's an easy mistake to
make. They're an American company — Stanley
Tools. Latrell had their stuff always, with the
name in black on yellow.' She held the tool up.
'Not like this. Stanley isn't the maker, Inspector.
It's a ship.'

'A ship?' Shaw repeated, thinking of the tiny
model boat in Mary Tilden's coffin.

'Alby's ship. The *Stanley*. I thought you'd know all about that — he was a hero, Alby. That's why Nora married him I suppose; the reflected glory — that's what my sister wanted. And she got it for a while. But then it faded rather quickly.'

She got up and stood at the picture window. Again the quick glance down at the street, where a necklace of lights had begun to glow orange.

'I remember Alby coming home in 1944,' she said. 'I was still a toddler, the baby sister. You've no idea how exciting war is for children. It's like being at an endless wedding reception — you know, the adults are too busy to notice the children, as if the rules have been suspended. War's like that. Nora was the big sister — nearly seventeen. My mother — our mother — used to say that it didn't matter how plain a girl was, there was always a year when she was beautiful. That was Nora's year. Cruel? That's what sisters are for. There'd been boys about, but Nora was wrapped up in the church so I don't think sex had ever come into it. Prim was the word. A good word. They taught her it was a virtue, that kind of coldness. They tried to teach me too, but I didn't listen.'

She took an inch off the level of the bourbon in the glass. 'Anyway — 1944. I'm really surprised you don't know this,' she said, looking at Valentine. 'This merchant ship — the *Stanley* — was on a convoy to Murmansk. Lendlease, taking food and munitions to the Russians. It was torpedoed off Narvik — at night — and everyone abandoned ship. Alby used to tell us about that — about how he'd spent the night trying not to freeze to death, with the sea calm and the lifeboat surrounded by the cargo — cases of bullets and dried milk. When daylight came they still couldn't see anything because of a fog. They called out but only their lifeboat had survived, they thought. Just six men left.

'Alby said the worst thing was knowing the ship had gone down — they'd all seen the prow sticking up out of the water, then just dropping out of sight. He said they felt so alone. They spent a day in the fog — freezing fog — and two of the men died before nightfall. Alby said he thought he came close to giving up that second night and he was actually surprised to wake up at all. That was when his illness began, of course. Looking back — the fear of the space around him, making him feel so small. It took years to emerge, but that was the seed, that night in the open boat.

'When dawn came the fog had gone. The sea was still calm. And floating fifty yards away was the stern of the *Stanley*. She'd broken her back — snapped in half — but the bulkheads were still watertight, so she could float. He said it looked like a block of council flats, just floating there, with the bridge above, and the funnel.'

She laughed, shaking her head, and Shaw wondered how many times she'd been told the story in her childhood.

'Alby was a leading seaman and the senior man left alive. Which was odd, because he'd been an engineer, and spent all his time below, but technically he was in command. So the four of them got back on board — the rope frogging was still hanging down from when they'd been given the order to abandon ship. The electrics had blown, and there was a small fire smouldering which they never really put out, but otherwise she was OK. They got the engines going that night, then headed south-west. An RAF reconnaissance plane picked them up off the Humber a day later. The day after that they found another life raft with most of the officers on board — including the captain.

'Once the War Ministry got hold of it, the story was everywhere — radio, papers. 'The ship that wouldn't die' — that's what they called it. And it was good for class solidarity as well, how the men below decks had brought the ship back. Or half of it, at least. We went down to the quayside when she came in — large as life. There used to be a picture in the bar at the Flask but Nora had it taken down. They gave Alby the freedom of the city. My dad — Arthur Melville — was running the pub then and he invited the crew to the Flask for a celebration. That's when Nora met Alby. They married in 1947. I think Alby fell in love that first night too — with the pub.'

The sun had set, but its rays still radiated from beyond the horizon, catching high pearlescent clouds.

Shaw picked up the billhook. 'And this?'

'When Alby left for sea again in the fifties, after they lost Mary, he left his kit from the *Stanley* in a chest up in his room. Well, it wasn't just his kit; he'd stolen a fair bit of stuff during the voyage — the ship's bell, the log, anything he thought would be worth a few dollars down the years, anything with the ship's name on it. He told Nora it was like a pension: if times got hard, she could sell it. But she never did. I don't think she wanted to touch anything that had been his because she hated him for leaving. The chest was still there after I came back because I remember opening it with Lizzie to see if there was something in there we could give Ian as a Christening present. Like a keepsake, from his grandfather. There was a tankard — so we gave him that.'

'And that chest had been there since 1944?'

'Yes. In their room — well, it was theirs when they married. Lizzie said that after Alby finally came back they had separate rooms. But it was their room. It's upstairs — the second floor, under the roof.'

Shaw thought Alby Tilden had the quality of being permanently elusive, like a smoke ring, unbroken and perfect until you tried to touch it.

'Alby's still alive, isn't he?' he asked, fishing. 'At least, we think he is. You forward all the mail to some middleman in Retford? Lizzie says she's had nothing back for a year. What about you?'

She shook her head. 'No. Longer than that, even. We keep writing, but nothing. I know it all sounds crazy but Alby really doesn't want to see anyone. We all visited in the early years, but it really did upset him. He asked us to stop, so we did — but he knew we'd never be able to leave him be if we had his address. He told us to write care of a friend — I think it's someone he met in

Lincoln. But there's less and less to say.' She was going to stop there but pressed on. 'Which is selfish, isn't it? He's right, I know, it would be painful. But mainly for him.'

Shaw thought about the report they'd received from the local police. That there was no post waiting to be forwarded from Lynn. He wondered whether Bea was lying to make herself feel better about neglecting a difficult elderly relative, or for another reason. Or perhaps she was telling the truth and someone had taken the letters from Retford.

'The sea chest — it's locked?' asked Valentine.

She shrugged. Out at sea the winter light had gone and the sky had instantly turned to a dark grey. She shivered and from the chair beside her picked up the vivid blue pashmina she'd been wearing at the Flask when they'd first seen her, draping it around her neck. Happy to answer more questions, she said she'd ask Kath to make some tea, but they said they ought to go.

Kath Robinson saw them out. On the step Shaw turned to study her face, the blameless eyes avoiding his.

'So Ian's around a lot?' he asked, zipping up the RNLI jacket.

'Yes.' Again that curious innocence, as if the question could hold no ulterior motive.

'Is he like his father?'

The question was too much for her, so she stepped out from the shadows of the hallway on to the path — to give herself time to frame an answer, Shaw guessed.

'Like Pat? No,' she said, struggling for the

276

right word. 'Ian's good — to Bea, to his mum.'

'But Pat wasn't good to you, was he?' Shaw asked.

She looked out to sea, then stepped back quickly over the threshold. 'Only once,' she said, and tried to close the door but Valentine had his foot in the gap.

'I got the signals wrong,' she said, as if repeating an alibi. 'I had to stop him going any further.'

'Where?' pressed Shaw.

Her face was in darkness. 'In the cemetery, one night. That summer before the wake. I wanted . . . ' She covered her mouth with her hand. 'Him. I shouldn't have gone down there. I couldn't do what he wanted me to do. He got angry. That's all. He said he wouldn't see me again. And he didn't.'

Shaw glanced at Valentine, who slid away his foot, and she closed the door.

For a moment they all stood, the door between them, and Shaw could see the silhouette of her head through the coloured glass. Then the light in the hallway came on and she was gone, leaving just the picture in the glass: a whale again, a harpoon flying towards it across a stormy stained-glass sea.

25

The first flight of the narrow stairs of the Flask took Shaw up to the room in which they'd first interviewed Lizzie Murray and Bea Garrison. Shaw had counted the steps — eighteen — aware that each one had helped to shatter the bones of Nora Tilden. The wood itself was worn and as black and stained as a ship's beam. The first-floor landing was panelled in the same wood, a narrow doorway giving on to a second flight which led up to the attic. There were two attic rooms: to the left, Ian's bedroom, said Lizzie; to the right Alby and Nora's old room — now used largely for storage. The door here was more like a hatch, a hinged flap that you had to step through into the room beyond, which had six dormer windows, three looking over the river, three over the cemetery. Light flooded in from a streetlight by the cemetery gates. Over their heads they could hear seagulls scratching at the tiles. The room held a double bed, some shelves, a wooden cot and an old stainless-steel sink unit, unconnected to any pipes.

'This was their room,' said Lizzie, reluctant to step up from the stairwell. Her voice, usually hard, had a suppressed tension that almost exactly matched her aunt's. She too seemed to be strangely watchful, as if here, in the attic of her own home, something lay waiting, hidden. When they'd asked for her at the bar they'd been told she was resting. When she appeared they could see the sleep in her eyes, and she hadn't added the pearl lipstick, so that her mouth looked dry, compressed, and her eyes were red, as if she'd been crying.

'Staff use it now if they're stuck here late. There's an extra sofa bed over there,' she indicated the far end of the room, which was in shadow. 'Like I said, Ian's across the way, but these days he stays with the girlfriend — she's got her own flat.' She looked down at the uncarpeted boards. 'This place gives me the creeps.'

The bed was modern, and out of scale with the room.

Under one of the windows was a sea chest.

Shaw walked to it, then knelt, as if before an altar. He held out the billhook in its forensic envelope. 'This is what killed Pat that night — the night of Nora's wake. Bea thinks it came out of the chest.'

Lizzie walked over but didn't take it. The colour seemed to drain out of her under the electric light, the sparky eyes reduced to speckled grey and green.

'Can you open it?' asked Shaw.

Valentine stood at one of the other windows, looking down into the cemetery, his hand on the cot, until he remembered that Nora Tilden's baby daughter had died in this room.

Lizzie pulled a key ring from her pocket. The keys and the ivory fob jangled against the wood of the sea chest, but the lock was oiled, Shaw noted, and when the lid flipped back

279

there was no dust.

Lizzie stood back, nodding. 'It's Dad's stuff from the war. Way back — twenty years ago — I had it valued. There's an auction room in Stamford that does military stuff. It's insured for £10,000 — that's because of Dad's story, of course, and the ship. I thought that Ian could decide, when the time comes.'

'What time?' asked Valentine, looking at a framed press cutting on the wall. The paper was yellow, but the picture was clear enough — a crowd on the quayside, the stunted superstructure of the *Stanley* moored, and the headline:

HEROES BRING STRICKEN SHIP HOME

'The time when we leave this place. Ian's got plans — with Bea. He doesn't want the business. So one day we'll sell. Pack it in. Maybe sometime soon.'

Shaw began to pick out items: the *Stanley*'s bell, wrapped in a cloth, the ship's log in an oilskin pouch, a sextant, a radio, and then a wooden box, which he set to one side, feeling along the edges, trying to find a way to lift the lid.

'Sorry,' said Lizzie. 'There's a knack to that.' She worked her fingers around the wood until the lid opened. Inside, set on green baize, was a revolver.

'Ship's purser's,' said Lizzie. 'Dad used to bring it out, wave it about, for the crack. I don't think it's loaded, but you'd better check.'

'It's been polished,' said Valentine.

'Ian,' she said. 'He played up here as a kid and he's proud of his grandfather. Like I said — it's his inheritance. He looks after it.'

Shaw handled the gun, using the cloth from the ship's bell. It wasn't loaded, and the mechanism was rusted, but the leather handgrip was supple with beeswax.

'On the night of your mother's wake, where were the keys?' he asked.

'Where they always were, I imagine. They hang behind the bar. There's keys to the cellar, the spirit store, they need to be where anyone can get them. Anyone who's on the staff.' She looked at Shaw, then at Valentine. 'You think someone took the keys, came up here and found that?' She looked again at the hook, appalled. She took one step back and stumbled, reaching out a hand behind her to find the edge of the bed.

Shaw sat beside her, and he could hear her breathing. 'That night — of the wake — the staff would be you . . . ?' Shaw recalled the cine film they'd watched at the chapel. 'And John Joe — he helped out too, didn't he?'

She nodded, pulling down the skin over her cheekbones. Squaring her shoulders, she seemed to regain control of herself, but instead of answering the question she moved on. 'And the kitchen staff. Jean Walker was in, Kath was helping — Kath Robinson — a whole gaggle of women from the church who did the food. The two Bowles brothers — they worked as barmen. They're all on the list I gave you . . . '

'But John Joe could have taken the key, couldn't he?' pressed Shaw.

Her jaw was set straight, defiant. The idea that she might have spent nearly thirty years living with a killer didn't seem to shock her at all, Shaw sensed. It was only, perhaps, the suggestion that she wouldn't have known, that she'd been hoodwinked, fooled. She clutched at the blanket on the bed, crushing the material. 'John Joe's never really done hatred — plenty of other emotions, but never that. I think he despised Pat — a lot of men did. But he didn't kill him.'

They heard a door creak below and there was a footfall on the stair. Lizzie stood quickly, the clutch of keys falling to the floorboards. A voice Shaw didn't know shouted, 'Lizzie! We're taking a car up the Queen Victoria — I need to leave the bar. It's Freddie Fletcher — he's still poorly. You want to come?'

'Later,' she said.

Shaw had a final question.

The Department of Work and Pensions had finally released details on its pension payments to Lizzie's father — now aged eighty-two. The monthly pension was deposited in an account registered at the post office on the corner of Explorer Street, right here in South Lynn. A special account, with Lizzie Murray listed as an authorized signatory. Paul Twine had checked with the manager: she picked up the cash in person on the first Tuesday of every month. Including this one.

'You lied to us about your father. You do know where he is — you pick up his pension.'

282

Lizzie looked younger, the skin taut on the figurehead face. Shaw thought it was the stress that had peeled back the years and that she was a born fighter.

'No. I said, didn't I, that Dad just wants to be left alone. Yes, I pick up his pension. I give the cash to Bea and she gives it to him. Bea's the one person he'll see — it's always been like that. She's the go-between.'

26

Shaw parked the Porsche on the sandy lane that led down to the sea, a mile south of the beach house and café. He sat in the sudden silence and let the face of his mobile light his face, punching in Paul Twine's number. In the background he could still hear voices in the incident room at the cemetery — and a computer keyboard being tapped. Two things: first, he wanted Twine to arrange a fresh interview, under caution, at St James's for Bea Garrison. She'd lied about not knowing the whereabouts of Alby Tilden. She took him his pension. He was local — how local? Second, he wanted the latest on Freddie Fletcher's condition, and he waited while Twine contacted the uniformed officer they'd left up at the hospital overnight. 'Stable, but still in intensive care.' He felt a creeping anxiety about Freddie Fletcher's illness. If he died he'd lose a prime suspect. And his death would prompt a pertinent question — was there any reason someone would want Fletcher dead, and if there was, could he have been murdered? The answer to the first question was revenge, if he really was Pat Garrison's killer. The answer to the second question was surely no — unless the killer was prepared to risk murdering a hundred innocent people just to get at one man. Even then there appeared no logical reason why Fletcher should die — along with the ailing Charlie Clarke

— while everyone else recovered. No, Fletcher's illness had to be a random event. But still the creeping anxiety remained.

Shaw killed the signal and drank in the dark and the silence. He thought about checking *Flyer*, but decided that was a routine he could do without. Snow lay thick in the dune grass, and along the unlit path which led down to the beach. He got out, threw his jacket on the back seat and started to run, his legs reaching out, eating up the yards. He knew that by the time he got to the edge of the dunes, the point where the beach opened out, the security floodlight on the new lifeboat house would thud on, and then — just a few feet beyond, the view north would be clear and he'd be able to see the light they always left burning on the stoop of the café.

At that precise point he picked up speed, so that when he saw — in the sudden glare of white light — who was waiting for him, the shock made him stumble, one knee taking the strain so that he felt a pain shoot to his back.

Robert Mosse stood on the line of dry weed and flotsam that marked the last high tide. He wore a full-length black overcoat, but his head was bare, and there were snowflakes in the luxuriant black hair, so that Shaw knew he'd been standing there for some time, waiting.

'What is it — a mile?' he asked as Shaw stopped, looking along the beach to the house. 'You must be fit.'

The solicitor's face was almost completely immobile. A snapshot would have shown a handsome man: Action Man looks, lean, with a good bone structure and taut athletic skin. But in real life the effect was oddly modified by the stillness. Only the eye movements — like the eyes on a Victorian doll — showed that he was alive. He'd kept himself fit and well, because he didn't look in his forties at all. The hair was still thick and dark, almost decadent.

'Where's Jimmy Voyce?' asked Shaw, determined not to be kept off balance. He'd checked with Jacky Lau earlier and they'd called off the search at Holkham until daybreak — still no sign.

Mosse wore leather gloves, and he took one off to hold in the other.

'That's why I'm here. I've no real basis for my concerns, but I do have concerns.'

A wind came off the sea and Shaw shivered, the cold cutting through to his skin through the white linen shirt.

'You're cold,' said Mosse, taking a step forward so that they were just six feet apart, pulling a scarf from around his neck and holding it out.

'Voyce?' asked Shaw, not moving.

Mosse sighed, as if with disappointment that they couldn't be friends.

'Yes. He's here, in Lynn — did you know?' Mosse looked at him, and Shaw could see he'd picked his good eye to focus on. 'We met at Hunstanton the other evening. Anyway, to cut to the chase, he tried to extort some money from me. Threatened me, actually, with violence if I didn't give him a cheque for £10,000. I said I would consider my response. I dropped him off at his car and drove to see friends at Snettisham — they can confirm that. He left me his mobile number. I've sent him a text with my response — I told him I'd go to the police.'

Shaw was thinking fast, trying to see what legal status this conversation would carry in a courtroom. It was informal, not under oath, but he'd have to admit it had taken place. He'd made a tactical error, not pulling Mosse into St James's. The warrant had come through that evening, but he'd decided to wait one more night. Now Mosse could claim that he'd stepped forward to alert the police.

'Blackmail?'

Mosse laughed easily. 'No, no. I'm a just man, Inspector. What could . . . ' he looked for the word, 'scum like Jimmy Voyce know about me that would expose me to blackmail?'

Shaw noted the use of 'just', not 'honest', and wondered what that signified. Perhaps Robert Mosse thought he was the judge of good and evil.

'No. I had given some financial assistance to Alex Cosyns over the years. I think Alex must have told Jimmy. But Alex was an old friend, and he was in financial trouble. The money was a gift. Jimmy seemed to think he was entitled to some of the same. He said we 'went back a long way'. Precise words, Inspector. And he got that wrong, because we don't go back. I never go back. The Westmead is where I was brought up. I have moved on, but Jimmy couldn't see that.'

'He went out to see Chris Robins — at the hospital. Just like you did.'

Mosse pursed his lips, checked his watch.

'I thought you should know that Voyce threatened me with violence — as I have said — and that he added that if I didn't pay up he'd go back to New Zealand, but he'd make sure he left us with a reminder that I'd let down an old friend. I wasn't the only old friend he'd looked up, you see. He'd gone to the Tulleys. He seemed to think they owed him something too — a very dangerous misunderstanding.'

Shaw knew the family: three brothers, a Westmead legend, making decent money from a protection racket which had been running for the best part of thirty years. Violence was the currency in which they dealt — calibrated, cynical injury. They'd never faced a court on a charge of murder, but there was a list of missing persons in the file at St James's, each one of whom had last been seen in their company. It was clear they had a reliable and efficient method for removing the unwanted.

'I've not heard from him again,' said Mosse. 'You should know that. Now you do.' He squinted along the beach towards the cottage. 'I have a daughter too,' he said.

Shaw was shivering badly now, his jaw juddering. 'I wonder what it was that Chris Robins knew, or had. Maybe I'll find it.'

Mosse's face was oddly pale, and Shaw wondered where the usual winter tan had gone. He thought about telling him he'd been called to the reading of Chris Robins's will, but held back, reminding himself that knowledge was power and that he didn't need to squander it.

'You've never really considered the possibility that I'm an innocent man, have you?' said Mosse, the voice quite different — wheedling, and weak. 'Have you thought about that? About *your* prejudices? I'm just a kid from the Westmead. Criminal by nature. But you don't actually understand what that's like — you don't understand the loyalty that comes with a life like that. I am a loyal man. Cosyns, Voyce, Robins — they were my friends. They did something I can't forgive. I did what I could to help. But I'm telling you this now — and you should believe it . . . ' He stabbed a finger at his chest. 'I did not do it. I was not there.'

Mosse took half a step forward, raising an arm. 'If you continue to misunderstand this then you will pay as your father paid. That is not a threat. It is a fact.'

There was anger in his eyes, Shaw noticed, but the emotion failed to radiate, as if it was acted out rather than felt.

'I have escaped the Westmead,' he said, and Shaw thought he detected a hint of a sob in the voice. 'I have escaped them. I will not go back.'

The security light on the lifeboat house clicked out. In the sudden darkness Shaw swung an arm to trigger it again, but when the light flooded out Mosse was walking away, down to the sea.

27

At nearly midnight George Valentine walked past the house on the corner of Greenland Street. The sign was in the window, so the game was open, the game was on, but he wanted his bed. He walked on, looking at his shoes and the ice on the pavement. He'd spent the last hour with Freddie Fletcher in a room at the intensive care unit at the Queen Victoria. Visitors had come and gone but he hadn't said a word. The doctors said his body was in shock from the poison he'd ingested, that the dawn would show if he was winning the battle or losing it. Of the other five patients in intensive care brought in from the Shipwrights' Hall four were recovering fast, one was stable — all those five had come from one table, sponsored by Age Concern, and were aged between eighty-five and ninety.

He stopped outside his house. There was a light on, shining through the fanlight.

It had been seventeen years since his wife had died and in those years he'd never come home to a light. He opened the front door and looked down the short corridor into the kitchen. For a second — which he tried to stretch — he thought it was Julie sitting there, her hands on the table top around a mug, the steam from it hanging in the air like smoke from a gunshot.

'Georgie,' said Jean Walker. 'I'm sorry, kid. I didn't know how to get you — did they give you my message at St James's?'

Valentine shook his head, walking towards her, concealing as he did so that the shock had made his knees weak, trying to remember when he'd given his sister a key. He put his mobile on the table. He'd switched it to silent when they'd been in the Flask and forgotten to switch it back. The little message symbol flashed.

He felt the pot. 'What's up?' He turned his back to pour himself a cup.

'Gossip is all it is. But I knew you'd want to know.' She watched him sit down, the cup in two hands, so she looked away in case his hands shook.

Valentine sipped the tea.

'First off, there's a real panic on at the Flask, Georgie, 'cos John Joe's on walkabout. They didn't see him overnight. Not the first time, mind you, but before they've found him pretty quick — down at the Globe or the Sailing Club.' She shook her head. 'Lizzie's always taken him back. Christ knows where he sleeps when he's out overnight. But this time there's no sign of him. Ian was sent out to check the neighbours, round the streets. He said they didn't want a fuss — just asked people to keep an eye out. Then tonight I heard they'd found his boat was gone from the cellar wharf. I've seen him out in it — in the summer he goes up to the coast, but winter's different. They've got a few of the locals together to check the river — moorings, marinas, that kind of thing. But nothing — not yet.'

'Any reason he goes off?' asked Valentine.

'Moods — always has been a difficult bugger.

291

This time it's pretty easy to see why, isn't it? He's always been the hero, the decent man; stepped in to help Lizzie out, brought up the bastard half-caste.' She winced at her own crassness. 'Sorry — but that's what they say. Now it's different. Seems like the kid's real dad didn't desert the ship — that he'd have hung around if someone hadn't stuck a hook though his skull.'

Valentine noticed for the first time in years that there was no shade on the kitchen light, and that the glare was unforgiving.

'And that's the other piece of gossip. Kath Robinson — Bea's housekeeper up on the coast? Well, Kath comes down most days to shop for food and stuff, goes for the fresh fish by the dock gates there? Well, her mum's still alive — I see quite a bit of her, she lives on Gladstone Street — and *she's* been saying that Kath saw Pat Garrison leaving the Flask that night. That'll be right, because she never took her eyes off that boy, I can tell you. But . . . ' She sipped her tea, milking the moment. 'But . . . ahead of him, going out along the path to the cemetery, she'd seen Freddie Fletcher and Sam Venn together — this'd be ten, half ten, before the do was over. And guess who was with them, kidda? John Joe Murray.'

Valentine knew that Shaw had his doubts about casting Fletcher, Venn and Murray as killers. That it was all too easy with twenty-twenty hindsight to put them in the frame. But the picture they were building up was compelling. And unlike Shaw, George Valentine had nothing against an easy life.

'Thanks, Jean,' he said, wondering where John Joe was, and why he was running. But he found it hard to focus on the case. Jean had called him 'kidda' for as long as he could remember. She'd gone on calling him 'kidda' after he started courting Julie. But she'd never played the big sister. She and Julie had got on fine, and they'd ended up close, often, he thought, because they had one thing in common — trying to work out what was going on inside George Valentine's head.

Valentine smoked, but his hand was unsteady as he lit up.

Jean stood, put the mugs on the draining board and kissed him on the hair by holding his face. She looked around the empty kitchen. 'Sorry,' she said. 'I didn't think. I've always had the key. Years.'

She let herself out and then he saw she'd left the key on the table, a dull gold. When she shut the door her hand slipped so that it banged shut, which made the silence that followed overpowering, so he got out his mobile and phoned Shaw. There was no answer, so he left a message, telling him what Kath Robinson said she'd seen that night. That they needed to get her into St James's the next morning for a formal statement. He tried to concentrate on what he was saying, but he'd always found answering machines unnerving, and besides, after all these years alone, he suddenly felt distracted by the empty house around him.

28

John Joe Murray adjusted the oars so that they just brushed the surface, like the legs of a water boatman, skating on the sea. Ahead, in the flooded moonlit marshes, he could see his destination: the old coal barn, brick built, on its island of sand and reeds. He didn't look up, because he knew he'd see the lights of Wells if he did, and that would wreck his night vision which let him see the world in grey, black and silver. There'd be the lights inland too, along the crest of the north Norfolk hills. He'd known this stretch of coast all his life — all his life with Lizzie. They'd helped Bea choose Morston House back in 1983, and they'd come whenever they could to escape from the Flask. And as the years went by he'd come more often on his own, sailing up the river to the sea, then hugging the coast.

So if he looked up he knew what he'd see. The little seafront, Bea's house by the boatyard, the tower, and its single lit room. Bea would be there at the window, waiting for him to signal from the barn when he was safe. Bea had always been there for him and Lizzie, and John Joe knew that was because she'd always wanted Ian to be happy, because the boy was all that was left of the mess she'd made of her life, the one thing she was proud to leave behind. She wasn't proud of John Joe, she was tolerant, but he was thankful, even for that. So Bea hadn't asked questions when he'd tied up after dark. But when he'd told her why he was there, Bea had said he was crazy, confused, because who would want to kill him? He couldn't tell her the truth — she was the last person he could tell. So he'd told her nothing. Just that he had to get away, to vanish. She mustn't tell anyone. Not Ian. Not Lizzie. It wouldn't be for ever, or even for very long, but now — right now — he needed a haven.

But he did know why his life was in danger, even if he couldn't share it.

The night of Nora Tilden's wake he'd gone to Freddie Fletcher's table and they'd talked about Pat Garrison: the black kid who'd *dared* to look at Lizzie like that, with his dark, watery eyes. The black kid who was going to get all this — the Flask, right in the heart of their community — get everything, said Fletcher, their fathers had fought for. And Sam Venn was there too. And he had his own little hateful song to sing: that God was watching, and God would punish them for wanting to mix their blood — the blood of cousins. So they'd drank some more and decided on a plan: they'd wait for the kid in the cemetery, corner him and teach him a lesson. Break a bone. Bruise that unblemished skin. But they needed a weapon. So John Joe slipped back behind the bar and found an optic bottle that needed changing — the malt whisky — lifted the ivory key ring so that he could unlock the cellar. He'd seen Alby the Christmas before with a gun: a grey metal revolver he said he'd salvaged off the *Stanley*. And he knew where he kept it — up in the attic, in a sea chest. So he slipped upstairs and opened it up: but the revolver was useless when he finally got it out of its box, more like a child's toy than the real thing. Then he'd seen the billhook, and he'd stood there in the moonlight by the window, testing the heft of it, and liking what he felt.

When he got back to the bar Sam and Freddie were gone and he thought they'd lost their nerve. He sensed that both were cowards, because they had so much hatred in them, so much belligerent energy. Then he saw Sam through the bay window, out on the deck by the river. Sam whispered in John Joe's ear so that he could smell the whisky on his breath. 'He's getting his coat.' And Fletcher was there, whispering with Kath Robinson. The three of them slipped out to wait for him in the cemetery: Murray, Venn and Fletcher. And Kath had watched them go.

And now they'd found the kid's bones in Nora's grave.

If John Joe hadn't felt so ill, so sick with worry, he'd have gone to the Shipwrights' Hall lunch with Freddie and Sam, because they agreed they had to go on, live their lives as if nothing had changed. When he'd heard that Fletcher was in intensive care up at the Queen Victoria he'd felt not fear, but the ghost of a fear. Did someone know? He'd gone up to the hospital to see him and found him in a small side room off the main ward — and his fear blossomed, because he knew what that might mean, because that was where they put people they thought would die.

He'd looked at Fletcher, sprawled on the bed, his skin like lard, swirled with black hair, and told himself that it wasn't possible. This was chance, an accident. If death came for Freddie Fletcher it would be a random killing. He stilled his panic. To banish it he just needed to see Sam Venn, to check that he was all right. Davey Howe, the friend who'd bought his ticket, had told him that Venn had been sick at the Shipwrights' Hall, but recovered and taken a cab home.

Venn lived in two rooms over the London Road Shelter. Downstairs the kitchen and meeting room were locked up for the night, although the smell persisted in the sticky doorway: cabbage and sweat and damp cigarette butts. He'd thumped his gloved fist on the metal grille. Looking up, there'd been no light, but he knew that if Venn wasn't at the church then he'd be at home, and he'd seen Pastor Abney on Explorer Street, and he'd said the church was closed because only Sam could work the boiler, and he was ill, and it was freezing, wasn't it?

So he had to be home. There was an alley down the back of the building and from there he *could* see a light — not in the bedroom, but dimly in the little window that let on to the stairwell.

The door with the sign that read WARDEN was unlocked. He rested his hand on the brass handle and pushed it open; it flew back, banging on the concrete wall and then rebounding, almost back to closed, so that he'd seen what was inside for only a few seconds, and then the image was gone. Neat, swept wooden steps, and halfway up a jacket, then a scarf above that, and shoes at the bottom, discarded. He pushed the door open again and looked at the shoes. The laces were still done up. He shouted up the stairs. On the fifth step there was a pool of something viscous, a pale fluid which he thought gave off the faint odour of high tide.

He climbed the stairs, stepping over the little puddle, and shouted again. The door slammed at the bottom and that made him jump so badly that he could hear his heart lurching in his chest like a rocking horse.

He found Sam Venn in his bed. He'd died with a bible on his chest, open at Leviticus. Vomit lay in a pool by his neck where it had run from his mouth. John Joe looked at him for only a moment, just long enough to know that he was looking at a dead man, and just long enough to think how odd that was — that as the rigor mortis had taken hold it had equalized the features of his face, so that the lop-sidedness had gone. And the left arm, his good arm, was held as awkwardly as the right, both half-crossed over his chest, resting on the Bible, holding it open. He knew Sam Venn well, and guessed that he'd arranged himself to be found like this, like a martyr. And he thought how pathetic it was that he'd got the Bible upside down, so that he couldn't have been reading it at all.

Standing there, his blood had run cold: ice in

his veins. Because now the impossible was just a bit more possible. If death had come for Sam Venn, and death was waiting for Freddie Fletcher, then perhaps it would come for him. Perhaps someone did know. Perhaps someone wanted revenge. But he asked himself the question again. Who? Kath had seen them go. But there must have been others. And Kath wasn't his enemy. She was family. But he did wonder then, standing at the foot of Sam Venn's deathbed, if that was enough.

The tide was drawing him out from the land, so he stowed the oars and let the boat drift. The salty air and the fear had made him thirsty, and he wondered if there was anything to drink in the picnic basket Bea had given him. And food — he hadn't eaten all day, because there was a coldness in the pit of his stomach. His boat edged seaward, so silently, so effortlessly, that he had the brief illusion he wasn't moving at all, but that the world was slipping under him, sliding past, so that it felt as if the island which held the old coal barn was edging towards him under its own power.

He waited for the inevitable meeting of wood and stone, then edged the boat along the rubble quay, using an oar like a punting pole, around the barn until he was on the north side, hidden from the coast. It was high tide, but the coal barn, all that was left of an old harbour, stood clear of the water. Rising sea levels had inundated the rest since the last boats had brought in coal in the early twentieth century. Now it provided John Joe with all he needed: a place to be, where no one came.

As he tied up his boat snowflakes fell out of a clear night sky. The door, still weatherproof, swung easily on iron hinges, and by torchlight he climbed the stone stairs to the first floor, spread a blanket on a pile of nets and opened the picnic basket. Inside he found food in a supermarket bag, which he hung from a hook in one of the roof beams, and a two-litre bottle of water from which he drank immediately. Then he looked about him: a pile of firewood was stacked along one wall and the fireplace was clean. By the time he'd gathered some dry reed heads from the bank outside and set the fire with shreds of old newspaper it was nearly midnight.

Only when the red light from the flames began to flicker and light the room did the old memories come alive: he saw, strobe-lit, Lizzie's naked back, arched with pleasure, a leg stretched wantonly across a warm blue blanket. He felt guilt then: that he'd just left her without a word. There would be a time for the truth when he was safe, but not now.

He wrapped himself up in the blanket by the fire but couldn't sleep, so he went outside and sat on the stone step looking at the frosty planetarium of stars, and wished he'd had the presence of mind to bring his guitar. But he did have the penny whistle, he always had that, and so he sat and played a tune. He'd played only one verse when he remembered the signal — so he went and got the boat's lantern and set it on the south bank, facing the coast, and sat beside it, feeling better, content that the only person in the world who knew where he was, was Bea. She'd be there, looking north, because she'd promised to wait until she saw the light. And of all the people he trusted, he trusted Bea the most.

29

Friday, 17 December

Freddie Fletcher lay on his hospital bed, his chest bare, the black hair swirled in spirals on his damp skin. The sheet that should have covered him from the waist down was tangled, so that they could see some of his pubic hair, and an old scar like a lipstick kiss on his thigh. His eyes were the only part of him that moved, up to the ceiling, focused on the light fitting, then down, around the bed, and back to the ceiling, as if there was something up there he wanted to hold on to, something that would save him.

There was sunlight in the room, the kind of cheerless sunlight that only hospitals allow. But the most remarkable effect of the light was that Fletcher's skin seemed luminous, so that he appeared to float apart from the drab bed, with its steel frame and stiff sheets. It was a precarious state, Shaw thought, as if he was held there by his own determination not to die, anchored by the image of the light above.

The contaminated food he'd ingested had prompted a series of minor strokes in the early hours of that morning, and the shock had flooded his lungs with fluid, so that pneumonia was now established in the left, and the right was deteriorating too. Freddie Fletcher was suffocating by degrees. But it wouldn't be the lack of air that would kill him, thought Shaw, it would be his inability to maintain the concentration required to stay alive, an effort which patently was growing with each passing minute. His condition had been weak anyway, the doctor had explained, as he'd apparently gone to the Shipwrights' Hall dinner suffering from some kind of gastric illness which had put him in bed for the previous twenty-four hours. While his fellow patients had been able to call on their own internal resources to repel the effects of the poison, he had been at its mercy from the first mouthful of the tainted fish soup.

Fletcher kicked out, revealing a foot, and Shaw looked away, embarrassed by the sight of the pale withered flesh. Valentine stood by the door, trying not to think how much less frightening this would be for Fletcher if he could have held someone he loved by the hand. Shaw was struggling to dispel the idea that because he disliked this man, in several deeply interlocking ways, he would find his death less shocking — viewing it not as a death at all, in fact, but as retribution. He thought about Fletcher lying in wait that night for Pat Garrison, made brave by being in a crowd of three. George Valentine had expanded on the message he'd left after he'd spoken to Jean. They'd dispatched a car to pick up Kath Robinson and Bea Garrison, another to the London Road Shelter to check on Sam Venn, and if he was well enough to bring him in too. They'd got a squad car out to the Flask as well. If they couldn't produce John Joe Murray then he was officially a missing person: TV, radio and the local papers would get a mug shot within hours.

Shaw was troubled again by this complex interlocking jigsaw of a world within a world — the community of South Lynn. The picture depicted was a shifting one. But now, at least, they had a clear snapshot of that fateful night: the three men setting out to teach Pat Garrison a lesson he'd never forget — to teach him he was an outsider, and that he'd always be an outsider.

Shaw looked at Fletcher and tried to imagine that moment when the billhook had swung down against the stars and buried itself in Pat Garrison's skull, slicing down through his brain, so that he would never feel the drop into the open grave. He tried to imagine Fletcher holding the weapon — but again, it wouldn't come. And again, like a tap dripping, his doubts impinged, undermining this all-too-simple solution to the question of who killed Pat Garrison. Three men, each with a motive, setting out on their victim's heels.

Shaw checked his mobile at the sound of an incoming text. It was from Guy Poole: the latest from the Environmental Health laboratory was that the soup had been contaminated by a base metal — a compound of aluminium — which had seeped into the soup, probably from the cans in which it had been delivered. They had a team down at the Clockcase Cannery and they were running tests on the unopened can recovered from the Shipwrights' Hall. Poole's text wasn't just to share the latest news — he wanted advice. Management at the Clockcase refused to believe the fault was with their product. They suspected sabotage by a disgruntled workforce facing redundancies as the factory closed. Poole said it was an incident he couldn't afford to ignore. He needed to seal off the works and get a full team on to the premises. In the circumstances he couldn't trust the company's daytime security — and the resident factory watchman was a pensioner. Could Shaw liaise with St James's and get him a couple of uniformed officers to secure the factory?

Shaw relayed the text to the duty desk at St James's with a recommendation to pull in a squad car off the ring-road traffic patrol.

He killed the phone, then the power, and slipped the dead mobile into the zip pocket on his RNLI jacket. On the bedside table someone had neatly laid out Fletcher's personal possessions: a watch, a wallet and a menu card for the Shipwrights' Hall lunch. Turning the card over, he found a printed seating plan: Fletcher had shared a table with eleven others, including Pastor John Abney, Sam Venn and John Joe Murray — although they knew Lizzie's husband had ducked the meal and given his ticket away before disappearing.

Fletcher's eyes left the ceiling and locked on Shaw. 'Worked it out?' he asked next, trying a smile. His voice was surprisingly clear, but then he gulped in air, as if he'd forgotten how to breathe. His eyes went back to the ceiling. His body stiffened with the effort of reconnecting with that point above his head.

Shaw sat, pulled the chair so close to the bed frame that the wood hit the metal, and spoke into Fletcher's ear. 'We know you were in the cemetery that night, waiting for Garrison. You, Sam Venn and John Joe Murray. We know the billhook you used to kill him was from the sea chest in the loft — Alby's chest. We know you tumbled Garrison's body into the open grave. What more do we need to know?'

'You know fuck-all,' he said. Fletcher clawed at the stiff sheet. 'Sam drew him little pictures,' and the smile came this time, because it was cruel, and just slid into place. 'Just a line on the first one. Two lines on the next one — the start of the gibbet, then the hanging man, because I told him one night, in the dark out by the river. I said we'd lynch him. I said that when they found him swinging they could cut him down with that penknife he always had with him — the one his GI dad left him; the one he was always flashing about to impress the girls.'

He passed out then, a fleeting few seconds of unconsciousness. When he opened his eyes, Shaw knew he'd no idea there'd been a break.

'But that's all Sam was gonna do about it — draw little pictures. At the wake I said that all he believed in was talk. That's why they had their little church — inside it they could hide from the real world the rest of us had to live in. Pathetic. Just because he had a withered arm didn't mean he couldn't act. Do something.'

He took a careful breath this time, sipping the air. 'I said we should teach him a lesson.' His breathing began to dip into the shallows, picking up speed. 'And I'd have done it too, but I was outside, smoking, waiting for the kid to go home when Kath Robinson came up. Bit of gossip for me — she said Lizzie was pregnant. That the black was the father. She thought I'd like to know. Thought that might fire me up . . . '

He licked his lips. The heart monitor by the bed began to buzz and the consultant was beside them. 'I think that's it,' he said. 'Mr Fletcher can't do this — not now.'

Fletcher smiled at the notion of 'now' — suspecting, perhaps, that there might not be a 'later'. He held up a hand, and the doctor shrugged, silently mouthing 'five minutes' to Shaw.

Fletcher tore his eyes from his anchor above and looked Shaw in the face.

'I couldn't do it — not then, not when I knew there was a family. Lizzie's kid deserved a father — even if it was scum like Garrison.'

Fletcher's eyes swam, and Shaw recalled his story. The child who'd seen his mother desert the family, then watched the failure of his father to hold what remained of it together. A childhood in care, separated from his only sister. He remembered the single picture on his mantelpiece, his arm thrown round the woman in the cheap shell suit. Reunited. But he could imagine the damage that had been done to both, struggling through separate childhoods.

'I left them, Sam and John Joe, just inside the cemetery gates. Went home.' His eyes spilt tears. 'I said it wasn't right, told 'em what Kath had said. John Joe said it was rubbish, that she'd made it up because she wanted us to scare Pat off good and proper. Because if she couldn't have him, why should Lizzie? That she might be simple but she wasn't stupid. But John Joe knew Kath was right, deep down he knew, so he was really up for it — he had the billhook under his jacket, and he was high all right, like he'd been doused in the whisky. So I left them.'

He shifted his eyes back to the ceiling.

'Next day I went up with Will Stokes and filled the grave in. We'd covered Nora's coffin the day before, we just had to finish the job. Took us an hour — with a couple of fag breaks. That night I was in the Flask and the rumour was round that Pat had gone. It didn't take long to find out why. Sammy and John Joe always had the same story, that they'd lost their nerve too. Too scared. So I never knew — never guessed. But I was always scared — of what I came close to doing.'

He looked at Shaw again. 'I'm scared now,' he said.

They left him asleep. In the corridor outside Shaw checked his mobile as he watched the patient through a glass porthole. The doctor appeared at his shoulder.

'What are his chances?' asked Shaw.

The doctor was reading a set of medical notes. He didn't look up. 'He hasn't got chances, Inspector. Death's a process — like life. It's started. Miracles happen — but up till now, never on my shift.' He pushed Fletcher's door open and went in to check the bedside monitors.

There was a text on the phone from Paul Twine.

SAM VENN DEAD AT HOME. TOM AT SCENE.

30

The Clockcase Cannery stood against a winter postcard: the black river, the Old Town waterfront beyond, stretching from the needle spire of St Nicholas, past the old Custom House and the mismatched towers of St Margaret's to the Flask on its lonely promontory — gateway to the Flensing Meadow and the low hill of the chapel. It was a panorama in grisaille, viewed through mist, under a grey sky low enough to tear at the single chimney of the old Campbell's soup factory downriver. The only light came from the snow-covered ground.

Shaw drove the Porsche at speed into the empty car park past an unmanned checkpoint and skidded on the gravel, bringing the rear of the car round in an arc. He got out, took a lungful of iced air, an antidote to the smell in Sam Venn's flat: the vomit on the stairs, round the washbasin. And Venn's corpse, decaying already in the overheated room, the features of his face pressed flat, as if he'd lost a fight with gravity which was pushing him down into the mattress.

Shaw took a second lungful of the clean air.

The cannery was a single factory block of three floors, as substantial as an ocean liner, the single stub of a chimney leaking fumes from the boiler. A vast hoarding hanging from the gutter read FOR SALE. Shaw thought that it was a depressing sight — a building, built to work, standing suddenly idle like a man in a dole queue. A short line of HGVs waited silently at the goods-in loading dock, a council Transit van blocking any others from entering the site. A group of cannery workers stood by the gates arguing with a man in a smart green safety jacket who was handing out a printed A4 sheet.

Shaw was struck by just how narrow the river was at this point: he could see the tombstones of the Flensing Meadow clearly. It was one of the aspects of the case which unsettled him, the tight geographical compression of events within this small area of the town. It was as if all their witnesses, all their suspects, were doomed to live and die within sight of each other, as if the buildings themselves — and particularly the Flask — had some kind of magnetic attraction that bound them with an invisible force.

'Let's do it, George,' he said. Valentine considered the dilapidated factory with distaste, and had made no move to get out of the car.

Across the yard Guy Poole was in his 4×4, speaking on his mobile. The health officer cut the line and jumped down.

'Bad news, Peter,' he said.

'You first,' said Shaw.

Valentine lit up, flicking his match into an empty skip.

'Lab's just finished a preliminary sweep through all the food at the lunch: so that's everything from the bread rolls and the butter pats to the tap water in the jugs. Only contaminant was in the soup — that's all the soup, by the way, every bowl we collected, the saucepans and the unopened can. The level of contamination varies very little in the samples taken from the bowls. So that's suspicious for a start. If this was from the cans, from metal fatigue — which, given we're looking for an aluminium compound, would be our prime suspect — then you'd expect some cans to be worse than others. You'd expect variation. There is none. Then there's the actual level of contamination — it's very high, high enough to produce symptoms in almost anyone who took any of this stuff down into their stomachs. High enough to rule out metal fatigue. But not high enough to kill — well, not on its own.'

Valentine felt his guts contort, buckling like a garden hose.

'What are we saying?' said Shaw. 'Off the record.'

'We're saying the management might have a point. This looks like sabotage. These guys are all losing their jobs. So someone with a grudge laced the cans with a metal-based poison. Through either luck or judgement it wasn't enough to be fatal. The death at the scene looks like a result of the victim's underlying condition. Coroner will have the last word, of course, but that's my call.'

'There's been another death,' said Shaw. 'And there's another in the wings.'

Poole's eyes hardened, angry that he'd been allowed to float his theory without all the available information.

Shaw placed his feet squarely apart. 'A man

311

called Venn — he didn't drink and he didn't smoke. And he's as dead as a can of soup, Guy. He was found this morning but he'd been dead all night. In his bed. And another up at the hospital's heading for the morgue. Slowly, but there's no other destination.'

Poole shrugged, fitting the facts to the theory. 'Two out of a possible hundred. It's a random shot. Let's see what the coroner says. Poisoning is a two-part process, Peter. It's all about how your body reacts. I'm sticking with my first guess: I think we've got an industrial saboteur, in the factory. The whole batch was laced, but with no intent to kill. What the culprit didn't know is that any contaminant can be enough to kill in certain circumstances. This other victim — any unusual medical factors?'

Shaw saw Sam Venn's face, up close, skewed. 'Maybe. Cerebral palsy,' he said.

Poole leant back on the 4×4, his arms crossed, more confident now in his theory. 'I've interviewed the caterers — the staff. The soup was made up in three batches. Apart from the mayor's party at the top table, no tables were allocated to any particular sponsor; the caterers just put the reservation cards where they felt like it. And although each table had a suggested seating plan, hardly anybody seems to have followed it. So it looks like these are three random victims. Let's hope it stays that way.'

Valentine coughed, looking at his black slip-ons.

'I don't think they're random victims,' said Shaw.

Poole stared into Shaw's good eye.

Shaw had the grace to look up at the sky. 'OK — this Charlie Clarke, the one who died on the spot, I think his death was an accident. But Venn and the man who's fighting for his life — a man called Fletcher — are two of the three main suspects in our current murder inquiry. The third should have been sitting with them. Was anyone else on the Flask's table affected badly?' He checked his notebook. 'The man who stepped in to take the third suspect's ticket was called Howe.'

Poole retrieved a pile of paperwork from the passenger seat of the 4×4.

'No. Howe went up to the hospital — but symptoms are listed as nausea and vomiting. He wasn't kept in.' He punched in a number on the mobile and turned away.

'How's your maths?' Shaw asked Valentine as they walked away to the riverside. Upriver they could see the ferry crossing, packed with Christmas shoppers.

'Crap,' said Valentine.

'It was one of the rules at school, George: if you got a probability question on the exam paper you didn't touch it — chances are you'd get it wrong.' He smiled at his own weak joke. 'But it's like betting — so . . . ' He let the question hang in the air.

'How's it like betting?' asked Valentine.

'Forget about the hundred guests sitting down for lunch at the Shipwrights' Hall. Think about a roulette wheel with a hundred slots. What are the chances of picking two winning numbers in a row?'

Valentine thought about the fan-tan table. 'It's one in a hundred, times one in a hundred.'

Shaw nodded. 'Yeah. Pretty much. One in ten thousand. So, if this is really random, it's a one in ten thousand shot.'

'But it might happen first time you laid two bets,' said Valentine.

'Sure. But on average it would happen first time once every ten thousand times. I'm not saying it's impossible — I'm saying it's extremely unlikely. And if John Joe Murray had gone to the lunch and paid for the ticket with his life, the odds would be what, George?'

'One in a million,' said Valentine.

'Which would be another way of saying murder. And I think this is murder. But how, George? How do you lace a hundred cans with a poison that doesn't kill but still get the result that your two target victims end up dead?'

'Three men died,' said Valentine.

Shaw shook his head. 'Put that aside; put him aside. If you'd burst a crisp packet behind Charlie Clarke he'd have keeled over. Forget him — someone wanted Venn and Fletcher dead, George. They wanted John Joe Murray as well — but John Joe went walkabout, a decision that looks increasingly smart.'

Poole rejoined them. 'Howe, the man who took the last-minute ticket? He's up and about, feels good, and he's been checked out by his GP. Which doesn't do your theory a lot of good, Shaw. If Howe took your third target's place then he should be dead — or dying. He ain't.'

'If it's murder we can't take any chances,' said Shaw. 'Either we have a random saboteur, or we have a killer who's murdered two specific targets at the Shipwrights' Hall, and inadvertently killed an innocent bystander. We need to take over the site. You all right with that?'

Poole looked relieved — irked, but relieved. 'I'll tell my people. We'll need to keep someone on site — I'll give you a name.' He checked his watch. 'The management's assembled the factory's production-line staff on the shopfloor now. That lot . . . ' he nodded at the crowd by the security gate, 'are drivers — office staff — that kind of thing. None of them have regular access to the product.'

Shaw sent Valentine ahead to organize interviews and get an overview of the production process so that they could pinpoint areas where the cans could have been tampered with. Shaw rang Max Warren and brought him up to date, then made a request to combine the two inquiries. It was a formality. Warren's maths were no better than his golf card demanded — one of the reasons he loathed attending finance committee meetings — but he distrusted coincidence as much as Peter Shaw.

'Autopsies are crucial, Peter,' said Warren. 'Get Justina on it — and if you need fancy stuff we've got the budget. Just don't go fucking mad. All right?' He'd put the phone down before he got an answer.

Shaw rang Paul Twine, whom he'd chosen to head up a unit at Sam Venn's flat. The DC already had a timeline for Venn from the moment the soup had been served at the Shipwrights' Hall at 1.25 p.m. the previous day. Venn had passed out at the table and been attended to in situ by paramedics from the Queen Victoria. He'd recovered well, but had been distressed by the condition of Freddie Fletcher. Offered a seat in one of the ambulances ferrying people to the Queen Vic's A&E, he'd declined, and instead caught a cab on the corner of Norfolk Street. He'd kept the receipt, which was in his wallet. They'd interviewed the cabbie and he said Venn had been silent until he'd asked for the receipt. Then he'd appeared agitated, sweating badly. According to one of the volunteers at London Road Venn had gone to his office and booked the takings from the shelter's 10p lunches: the nominal charge allowed them to monitor numbers and book the clients in by name, each one entitled to a ticket for a twice-yearly food draw.

At four that afternoon he'd declined a cup of tea from the kitchen supervisor. She said he had been on the phone when she'd knocked on his door, but that he'd put down the receiver when she'd opened it. She said he looked pale, distracted, and she had the impression he'd declined the tea because his good hand was shaking. She'd heard about the Shipwrights' Hall lunch on the radio and was concerned for his health. Venn said he was fine now — or he would be, after a good night's sleep. He'd asked her to lock up and said he was going up to his flat.

She offered to fetch the centre's on-call GP but he'd said no. He'd left the office at 4.35 p.m.

316

and walked round to his flat, which he was seen entering by a volunteer cleaning waste bins in the yard. A few minutes after he'd gone inside there was a hailstorm; the volunteer took cover initially, then abandoned work outside altogether.

Forensic evidence suggested that Venn had collapsed on the stairs on the way up to his flat and been sick. There were also traces of vomit in the toilet and wash-basin. A plastic bag of 10p pieces was found by the toilet. He'd died at some point between 8.00 p.m. and 1.00 a.m. in his bed. His mobile phone was under the bed cover. His mobile service provider was tracing any calls he'd made that day. A copy of the Bible was on his chest, upside down, open at Leviticus. Shaw hadn't asked for that detail, and he was quietly impressed Twine had included it in his short summary.

The key forensic evidence at the scene was a set of footprints on the stairs, along the landing and into Venn's bedroom. While the prints — too large to be Venn's — were now dry, a muddy imprint remained of each step, indicating that they had been made by wet boots. Since it had been dry for twenty-four hours before the hailstorm at 4.35 p.m., and given the route the steps took, it appeared that this unknown party had entered the flat, gone to Venn's room and left immediately. The entrance door to the flat hadn't been forced. Cause of death was unknown but there were no exterior wounds. The locum pathologist, Dr John Blacker, had given them a preliminary cause of death as myocardial infarction. The symptoms exhibited matched those for poisoning and a preliminary examination of the vomit revealed traces of an aluminium-based contaminant. There were no bruises, no abrasions of any kind except a slight scuffing of the skin on the knuckles of the right hand consistent with stumbling on the stairs.

Shaw rang off and punched in Tom Hadden's mobile number.

Hadden was back at the Ark with forensic samples taken from Venn's flat and others from Fletcher's — principally a packet of sausages in the fridge, an opened can of tuna fish, some cooked chicken and a piece of salmon wrapped in tinfoil.

'Fletcher first,' said Hadden. Shaw imagined him closing his eyes, concentrating on the detail. 'If we're looking for a cause of his first bout of illness — that's the day before the Shipwrights' Hall lunch — then we need look no further than the fridge. Tuna fish was six weeks past its best-before date and was standing in the tin — not good practice. We've sent that off for analysis at the FSS. The sausages were pretty high too, and uncooked, and were sitting next to the chicken. We'll get the lab to look at everything, including the salmon — although it'll cost. So I'd duck when you see the bill.'

'And Venn?'

'Nothing. I understand Paul's given you a run-down, so you're up to speed. The poison's definitely aluminium based. I'm trying to get something out of the dried prints we lifted from the floor. They're muddy, so there's dirt, a few

318

bits of gravel, but there's other material. It's early days, but I'd say some sort of organic dust — maybe flour, maybe dried milk. Foodstuffs — industrial, maybe. But the amounts are tiny — I mean really minute. And yeast — definitely yeast — and live yeast, too.'

'I'm standing outside a canning works,' said Shaw.

'Maybe,' said Hadden. 'Or a baker's?' he added. 'Venn worked at the homeless shelter and I know there's a kitchen because they had a death last year — heart attack at one of the tables. But the yeast's a bit odd — unless they bake their own bread.'

Shaw rang off and continued to climb the concrete staircase in the cannery to the shopfloor. There were two stationary production lines: serried rows of cans on both.

Valentine joined him, a bundle of papers under one arm. 'The soup was a one-off order — twenty-five cans. It's a tradition — the local soup. Twenty-five catering cans cover the lot.'

'So they did that — canned just twenty-five for the lunch?'

'Manager says that's their market niche,' said Valentine. 'Small runs of canning and bottling orders, speciality foods, organics, health foods, fruit juices — stuff like loganberry, for Christ's sake! Who drinks that?' Shaw thought about the bottle standing in his fridge. 'Then there's local specialities: mussels, scallops, prawns, samphire.' Valentine took a rapid extra breath, the lists draining his lungs. 'That's what the manager calls the 'business model',' he added with

319

obvious disgust, looking around the old factory. 'More like an out-of-business model.'

'So the cans are open like this — then shuffle forward?' asked Shaw.

'Chargehand says the idea of sabotage during production is crazy — no one could do it. Everyone can see — there's half a dozen men on the line at any one time. So he thinks it was done overnight or in the kitchen at the Shipwrights' Hall. Then again, he would say that — he's the shop steward, and one of the men fingered by the management as a troublemaker. The fish-soup order was the first of the day — that's three days ago. So those cans would have been out of sight — under the canopy there . . . ' He pointed at the place where the conveyor belt slid under a metal awning. 'If someone got in, put the stuff in the cans, then that was it. Next time you'd see it would be in your soup bowl.'

Shaw looked around. 'So — at night? Security staff?'

Valentine shook his head. 'Contracted out. Chargehand says the whole site comes under Ouse Security — that's the cannery, the self-storage site, the industrial units, and the sugar factory. We're getting a list of names. One man with a CCTV screen over at the industrial units covers the lot — never gets off his arse. The manager here knows his name, but he's on the phone to the company lawyers. Could be some time. They do still have a night watchman, though — old bloke, lives in the basement. He does his rounds after dark, so maybe he saw something. He's downstairs, if you want a word. Stairwell floods, so they use a lift — it's over there.'

Shaw almost left that for back-up to deal with. He had a profound sense that the answer to this puzzle wasn't here in the cannery, but over the river at the Flask — that it wasn't about cans laced with poison but the intricate cat's cradle of emotions that linked the Tildens and the Garrisons back to the Melvilles. But he remembered what his father had told him — that if he had a chance to see with his own eyes, he should take it. Crime scene, witnesses, forensics: always see them for yourself.

When the lift doors slid apart Shaw saw him: the boiler door open, the red fire within the colour of cherries, his half-naked body on a seat, watching the flames. Shaw was struck immediately by the advanced age of the man — obvious even when seen from behind: the spine slightly buckled, the skin loose, the head — a weight — suspended forward on the neck. But although he stood at the sound of the lift arriving he didn't turn away from the fire, and they could see his sweat-drenched back clearly, the skin tightening, so that they could appreciate fully the tattoos that covered his body, and especially the Nubian courtesan, dancing slightly with the judder and spasm of the old man's muscles.

An illustrated man.

31

'Albert Tilden?' said Shaw, not really needing an answer. The coincidence was overpowering.

'Who wants to know?' asked Tilden. His voice was stronger than his body, and his body was that of a sixty-year-old. But Shaw felt the combative edge was manufactured, as if he was preparing only a token resistance.

Shaw showed his warrant card. Tilden didn't bother to look. 'DI Peter Shaw,' said Shaw. 'DS Valentine.'

Behind Tilden was a tarpaulin over a doorway, and they let him lead the way. Inside was a room. Almost a cell. Two of the walls were concrete, but the other two were made entirely of cans. Set into one wall was a narrow window vent, the view beyond obscured by frosted glass.

Tilden took the only chair, his chin held up as if denying an accusation they'd yet to make.

Shaw looked him in the eyes, which swam slightly but brimmed with intelligence. 'Sam Venn's dead,' he said.

Tilden nodded, but he didn't want to talk about Sam Venn, he wanted to talk about his room, his hidden life. Like many people who spend their lives alone, Tilden spoke more or less constantly — a commentary on almost every movement, a vocalization of every thought. Shaw looked around, aware that he could take his time, that finding Alby Tilden here, with access

322

and opportunity and motive for the murders of Fletcher and Venn, was close to an open-and-shut case: a situation which left him feeling deeply ill at ease. So he listened to the old man talking — telling them how it had come to this.

When he'd left Lincoln he'd come back to Lynn and got the night-watchman's job. The man in charge of security was one of his old cronies from his days at the Flask. He'd been offered a purpose-built flat high in the factory, but it had big Crittall windows, metal-framed, with a view down the Cut to the sea. He'd had enough of the sea. He'd spent the war at sea — on the *Stanley* — oppressed by the circular horizon. It was the beginning of his illness: being surrounded by all that sparkling space. In prison he'd never looked out of his window at all, but if he had, he knew what he'd have seen because he could hear the prisoners walking the 'wheel' in the exercise yard, an endless circuit. Throughout his sentence that had been his only fear, of the inevitable hour spent outside, turning with the others, under the sky.

So he'd asked to live in the basement.

He'd built this room himself. By picking a corner he'd got himself two ready-made concrete walls for his new 'cell', and he'd built the others out of cans he'd ferried down from the defects store — cans without labels, cans past their sell-by date, dented cans. Wheelbarrow loads of them. He'd built two walls six feet high, a foot deep, and although they ended short of the ceiling he didn't care — he still felt boxed in, safe. He'd decorated the walls with posters discarded by the office publicity boys who'd been looking for ideas: a wisp of steam rising from a bowl of chicken soup, another for corned beef: the can tilted to let the fatty meat slide out in a neat cuboid of solid flesh. Shaw noted one detail the old man didn't mention. On the concrete wall hung a mirror. And another — identical, full-length — hung from the tin-can wall opposite. If the old man positioned himself in the centre of the room he could see his own back. He imagined Tilden reviving his painted lady, watching the withered muscles bring her alive.

Because he'd taken on the furnaceman's duties he was the only person who ever saw his world. He was a forgotten man. And that had been perfect too, because they'd just let him stay. If he'd lived upstairs, in the flat, they'd have had to retire him, but down here they could just let him be. They'd cut his money, and his rounds, and left him on part-time. Cheap security. 'Pin money', the man in the office had called it; from the petty-cash box, paid out in a small brown envelope, and anyway, he had his pension. In the day he slept and read his books. Or he wrote letters to the family he never saw, or read their replies, plump with snapshots. He had a TV, rigged up by the man in maintenance. He watched the news, aware the world was changing without him, and so fast that he'd never catch up.

Tilden rose from his chair and sat on the bed, leaning back on a pile of pillows without cases, and his trouser leg rode up to reveal a pale ankle above which had been tattooed a curled serpent. Valentine said he'd need to put some shoes and socks on, and the old man looked genuinely terrified at the thought — because it was the first time he'd thought it through, realized that they could take him away, take him outside.

Shaw caught Valentine's eye and shook his head. Then he sat next to Tilden. 'Tell me about Nora, Alby. She doesn't sound like your kind of woman.'

Tilden looked up at the stained concrete ceiling. 'It's easy to speak ill of her. To be bitter. I try not to do that. I married her for lots of reasons, none of them good enough, so whatever happened is down to me as much as her.' He sat up, put his head in his hands, then laughed to himself, patting his knees. 'Bea's out of a different pod — I loved that kid. She *was* just a child when I met Nora — but you could see she was going to break hearts.' Shaw could see the memory had driven away the reality of the moment, and he sensed Tilden was in control of the illusion, and that was why he was still sane — because he could live in a world in his head.

'Latrell's heart, for one,' said Shaw, leading him on.

'I liked him,' said Tilden, smiling openly now. 'He used to chew gum and leave it under the edge of the bar. Nora used to loathe that. She had that . . . ' he searched for the word, '*ability*. To hate small things.'

'He was black — that bother you?' asked Shaw.

Tilden rubbed a finger into the parchment-like

325

skin on the top of his hand. 'No. It made me like him. Bea used to hold him close, you know — in the bar too. Just so people could see their skins touching, the white and the black — the dash of it. I liked that because it meant they didn't care what people thought. And that makes you strong.'

Suddenly animated, he leant forward. 'I went to see them.' He searched his memory and was delighted to find the right fact. 'In 1961. The ship was in at San Diego — a refit. We had a month, so I got the Greyhound to Hartsville. Three days — you believe that?' He chopped the air with one hand, vertically. 'Like an arrow, the road. I got off in this town. You think Lynn's the end of the line — Jesus! Talk about one horse — they couldn't afford a horse. I walked to the drugstore, kind of a corner shop for the whole town. That moment — when she first saw me, at the counter. You can tell a lot in a moment like that, when you're an unexpected guest.' He nodded to himself. 'She was pleased to see me. That doesn't happen a lot, does it?'

He looked at Shaw and guessed he'd led a different type of life. But Valentine nodded. Tilden leant back, finished.

'But Latrell drank,' he said. 'He drank with me. But he didn't enjoy it and that's a bad sign. If you drink like that, you hate yourself.'

Valentine sipped from a bottle of water he'd bought from the factory canteen.

'Why didn't you go home in 1999, when you came out of Lincoln?' asked Shaw. 'You could have gone back to the Flask.'

Tilden looked at his body, the frail bare feet, and then at the unmade bed, the sheets a dirty-water grey.

'I didn't want Lizzie or Ian to see me. I didn't want that life again. I can write — they send pictures. They don't know, but I see them sometimes, outside, on the riverbank.' He took in a lungful of air. 'And I need this . . . ' He looked around at the artificial cell he'd created.

'You don't go outside?' asked Shaw.

'At night, sometimes.' He nodded, as if that decision was still in his power.

'When did it start? The illness?'

'At sea,' he said. 'When my ship sank. In the raft. I thought I would die. We all did. We were powerless,' he said. 'I thought that at any moment I'd just stop being alive. The cold, perhaps. The cold was dreadful. That's how I see and feel the outside now — as that bitter cold. There was nothing to do in the raft so we just sat in the mist. You could sense . . . ' He held both hands out, then over his head, as if delineating a sphere which surrounded him. 'This space — around us, hundreds of miles of nothing. Thousands.' He looked at his hands. His eyes filled with genuine fear. 'I had nothing to do. Nothing for my hands to do. It makes you realize what you are. Just a piece of things. Then the dawn came, and we saw the ship.'

'The *Stanley?*' asked Valentine, the old man's confessions making him sweat.

'Yes. The *Stan*. And then I was back in charge — of them, of me, inside the ship. On the bridge I could see outside — but not *be* outside. It was perfect, and my hands were busy. But when we got home, I didn't want to get off.' He laughed. 'But they made me. They wanted to give me a medal.'

He looked down at his chest, his chin down, as if the medal was there.

Shaw stood, walked to the wall and picked one of the cans out, like a brick. It was a rusted tin of Olde Lynn Fish Soup. He put it on the table by Tilden.

'Freddie Fletcher's dying too.'

Tilden examined the poster opposite — it was for condensed milk, the product falling in a solid white cascade.

'But John Joe Murray's alive and well,' said Shaw.

That made the old man's eyes flicker, once to Shaw, once to Valentine, and then back to the falling waterfall of sweet milk.

'You put poison in the cans — all of the cans. How did you know it was going to kill only them?' he asked.

'I didn't think it would kill *any* of them,' said Tilden. 'It was a punishment — a childish punishment. They're closing the factory so I don't care. I thought . . . ' He nodded, excited. 'I thought you'd catch me. I can go back to jail.'

He smiled, but then seemed to remember what Shaw had just told him. 'Dead, Sam? Dying, Freddie?'

Shaw nodded.

'It's almost biblical, isn't it? It must be God's will. Then again, I don't believe in God any more.'

'There are two things I don't believe in,' said Shaw. 'God. And coincidence. I think you meant to kill them, and only them. I just don't know how.'

'I want to go back to jail now.' Tilden's voice was aggressive, suddenly belligerent. He looked round the room as if trying to decide what he should pack first.

'Why did you want to punish them?' asked Shaw.

'Because they killed Pat. I loved Pat. He would have made Lizzie happy, and that's all I ever wanted. All I want.' He looked at both of them in turn. 'I don't want to see her now. At all. Or Ian. They've got a picture of me — in the sea, up to my chin; Cape Town, 1971. I want them to remember that — not this.'

'How did you know they killed Pat?'

'I didn't, not until you found Pat's body. We just knew those three went to wait for him that night.'

'We?' asked Shaw.

Alby Tilden lifted a pillow and retrieved a pair of grubby socks.

Valentine stood at the narrow window vent of frosted glass. 'You never go out. How did you know we'd found Pat Garrison's bones?'

'Local rag — one of the late-shift men always leaves a copy by the Ascot in the washroom. Not always, but mostly.' He looked down at his hands. 'It's a kindness.'

'No,' said Shaw. 'The paper ran the story on Tuesday evening — the cans went through on the Tuesday morning. So you couldn't have read

329

it in the paper until after you'd laced the cans.'

'Maybe.' Tilden looked to the side, to the mirror, and seemed to smile.

'You get a pension, Mr Tilden,' said Shaw. 'And letters. Bea Garrison brings them to you. And it was her, wasn't it, who told you we'd found Pat. She told you the day we told her — on Monday.'

He wouldn't meet their eyes. Shaw thought he'd be trying to work out what Bea had told them.

Tilden looked to the tarpaulin door. 'When you take me outside, can it be at night?'

'Does night help?' asked Shaw. 'Did you try to dig up Nora's grave at night?'

Tilden dropped a shoulder so that he could see his back in the mirror, and Shaw guessed that he was comforting himself, that it didn't matter where they took him, he'd always have her for company.

'Why would I do that?'

Shaw changed tack, trying to find a lever, anything with which to prise open Tilden's inner life. 'Why did you leave home — why go back to sea if all that space was so terrifying?'

Shaw squatted down on his haunches so that he could look up into Tilden's face. This close he could smell the sweat on him and his clothes, and he thought he'd never encountered anything so . . . *stale*.

'How did Mary die?' he asked.

For a moment Tilden's face reminded Shaw of Sam Venn's — the right side appearing to slump, one eye filling with water until a tear spilt out.

He shook his head, speechless.

'Mr Tilden — you're asking me to believe that you happily risked the lives of more than a hundred people. You're not a doctor, you didn't know how much to give them. You didn't know the dose you did give them wasn't lethal. If you'd do that, is it really beyond belief that you'd kill your own daughter? Did you hate the child? Did you think you'd never be able to leave while Mary lived — that you'd have to stay?'

Tilden looked through Shaw. 'Nora,' he said. 'She hated the baby. Hated me for giving it to her. These days they'd call it something — a fancy-named depression. I didn't know what to do; she'd look at her sometimes, look at the cot, and I could see the murder in her eyes. I'd hold her.' His elbows sagged slightly, as if taking the weight, accommodating the bundle of bone and flesh. 'But I couldn't be there all the time. The child was sickly. I didn't kill her. I don't know how she died, but that night Nora went to bed and slept well — I think for the first time since the birth. I always thought she'd willed her to death.' He clenched his teeth. 'Sometimes I thought she'd done it — you know, with a pillow. That's why I left, in the end. It took seven years, but I couldn't look at her and not see her standing over the cot with the pillow in her hand. I had nowhere to go but the sea. A nightmare, I know, all that space. I signed on for the engine room. I could live with that for a few years. Then, even that became too much, so I came home. Thank God I came home. Otherwise there'd be no Lizzie.'

'Mr Tilden,' said Shaw. 'I think you decided to kill Fletcher, Venn and Murray. I don't think you did any of this on your own. So we're going to take you upstairs now, and down to St James's, and we're going to have this conversation again. We're going to go on having it until I get the truth.'

As Alby Tilden dressed and packed a single hold-all Shaw and Valentine looked around the room, then the furnace floor, and the single WC beside the lift. In the room they found a line of books on a bare plank shelf, held up on bricks. The titles were maritime — from *Hornblower* to *Master and Commander* — but there were surprises: *Typhoon*, by Conrad, and *Heart of Darkness*. It was as if Tilden had decided to live out the life he'd wanted through books from within his self-made cell.

In the furnace room they found a line of traps; in one a rat lay dead, its teeth as white as pearls. Valentine found the poison bin: a single wooden box with a padlocked lid and a stencilled skull and crossbones.

The key was in the padlock. Inside the box was a jar full of white powder. The label read ALUMINIUM PHOSPHIDE.

'Bingo,' said Valentine.

But even as he said it they heard the scampering in the shadows. Shaw played a torch beam down the long basement floor and saw a chain of rats, nose to tail, emerging as if from the wall itself, dashing twenty yards, then disappearing. Shaw couldn't suppress the image that entered his head like a subliminal advert — the image of a rat that had taken the bait he'd laid under the cottage. He'd heard it shrieking, the poison shredding its nervous system, and when he'd found it with the torch beam he'd seen the blood was vivid, seeping from the nose and mouth. It had shaken itself to death, trying to throw off the pain, as if death was clinging to its back.

'He wants to put more down,' said Valentine.

Then they brought Tilden out through the tarpaulin door, struggling now, the panic gripping. They heard his first scream rise in the lift shaft.

32

The interview rooms at St James's had been built in the fifties and smacked of utility Britain. No two-way mirrors, intercom or dark, non-reflective surfaces here; just tiled walls decorated with a single line of brown paint at knee-height, cheap furniture screwed down and light bulbs encased in miniature iron maidens. This was Shaw's third interview in an hour, and it was difficult to imagine they'd all been in different rooms. First: Kath Robinson. She'd reiterated the story Valentine's sister had heard. She'd seen Fletcher, Murray and Venn leaving the Flask at around ten fifteen on the evening of Nora Tilden's wake. She was sure of the time, because she'd gone back in to listen to the choir begin their second session, and she knew that was set for half past because Lizzie had said they'd keep to the timetable to allow the staff time to clear glasses and circulate sandwiches. But going in she'd bumped into Pat Garrison leaving, coat on and saying he was heading home.

'He didn't say anything else,' she said. No bitterness, no recrimination, just a statement of fact.

Two questions: Did she tell Freddie Fletcher that night the secret she shared with Lizzie Murray — that Lizzie was pregnant?

She'd shrugged, seemingly confused by the straight-forward question. She curled her bottom

334

lip over her teeth. 'I don't even like Freddie. I wouldn't share that with him. Would I?' In Shaw's experience that was a bad sign — answering one question with another.

And if it was true that she'd seen them all heading out towards the cemetery — and she'd just admitted she didn't like Fletcher — why didn't she raise some kind of alarm the next morning, or in the following days, when it became obvious that Pat Garrison had gone? Her answer, this time, was persuasive: yes, she'd suspected the three men were going to waylay Pat Garrison. A beating? Maybe. Worse? She didn't think so. Perhaps they'd run him out of town. But either way he deserved it, she said. She wasn't the only one he'd tried his luck with, and he'd been reluctant to take no for an answer more than once.

Had he forced himself on any of these girls? On her?

'Never,' she said. 'Not really . . . ' she added, realizing perhaps that she'd gone too far. 'He didn't force me to do anything.' For once the pale, translucent skin of her face reddened.

The second interview was with Alby Tilden. He'd made a statement repeating the story he'd told them at the Clockcase Cannery. He'd admitted industrial sabotage, denied he'd had an accomplice. During the later stages of the interview he began to show signs of distress: shallow breathing and chest pains. The on-call GP was with him within twenty minutes and recommended hospitalization. The paperwork was under way, and he'd been sedated and taken to the sick bay. Uniformed branch would provide cover at the Queen Victoria after his transfer. Shaw asked Valentine to have a chat with one of the hospital administrators to see if they could find him a room of his own. One with blinds.

And now the third interview. Bea Garrison didn't look good under a shadeless electric light. She'd chosen a formal suit in charcoal, the skirt to her calves, and it didn't suit her. The silver rings looked gaudy in contrast, and make-up buried her natural colour.

Shaw had already established the basic facts after making it clear they knew she'd lied to them about her relationship with Alby Tilden: she admitted that for the past year she'd been the one contact between the Murray family and Alby. She collected his pension and his post and took them to the Clockcase Cannery once a month. Every first Tuesday Alby would meet her up by the goods-in bay and they'd share a bottle of wine in the strange room he'd built in the basement. But when Alby's former cellmate from Lincoln had been alive she'd sent all the letters to him to pass on to Alby. Even she didn't know Alby was in Lynn. She'd pick up his pension, bank it to his account. That's how he'd always wanted it — distant. He thought about his family every moment of every day, she said. But he didn't want them to see him.

But when he did need a go-between, asked Shaw, why her? Why not Lizzie, or Ian, or John Joe?

'Alby knows I don't find his . . . ' she searched for the appropriate word, 'his *decline*, upsetting.

I'm ageing too, Inspector. But it's more than that. It's the seediness of it — isn't it? The failure. He's always wanted to protect them from that — and perhaps protect himself against the knowledge that he'd know what they thought, even if they pretended otherwise. And I've always thought he deserved our indulgence. And that's why I didn't tell you. I didn't think it was important to your inquiry — but Alby's privacy was important to him.' It was an oddly formal word to use, thought Shaw. 'I wouldn't have wished Nora on anyone,' she said. 'And losing the child turned his mind — on top of the war. I think he's suffered. I wanted to help. We all did.'

But Shaw was still struggling with the notion that this woman was so close to her sister's murderer.

'So — you've forgiven Alby? For what he did?'

'Have I? Yes — I suppose I have. But what did he do? Pushed his wife down the stairs in a violent argument at worst? Or watched her fall down them accidentally after a row on the landing? Living with Nora was a sentence, Inspector. I know — I served my time. She was bitter, cold and calculating. Alby married her for money, so he never had my sympathy, but I liked him because he was everything she wasn't. Warm, open, spontaneous. I was just a girl when I first met him. I was charmed, excited. I was always charmed. And he was colour-blind when it came to people. Again, a stark contrast with my sister.'

It was quite a speech but Shaw didn't miss a beat. 'When did you tell Alby we'd found Pat's bones in Nora's grave?'

They'd given her a sweet tea in a plastic cup and at that her fingers pressed in slightly, Shaw noted, distorting the shape.

'Immediately. I went that night — unannounced. There's a bell at the loading bay and he came and rolled the doors back. I'm sorry. I didn't think he'd do what he did . . . '

'You told him Kath's story?'

She looked from Shaw to Valentine, calculating. 'Yes. Of course — Kath told me that afternoon, as soon as we'd got Lizzie to rest. It was an odd secret to keep all those years.' She shook her head. 'Stupid girl.'

'And Alby's reaction?'

'Anger. I don't think Fletcher and Venn made him angry. He knew them, of course, knew their deficiencies. He could despise them. But John Joe — that's what hurt. Because as far as Alby saw it, you see, it was two crimes. He'd robbed us of Pat — robbed Lizzie, and Ian. And then he'd taken his place. A father's love for his daughter is very intense, isn't it? The thought that she'd spent her life with that man — touching him, letting him share her bed. Alby's not mad — he's ill. But that thought shook him, shook his mind.'

'Did he tell you what he planned to do?'

'No. Never.'

'Kath's a stupid girl,' said Shaw. 'But Alby's not stupid, is he? And yet what he did was stupid . . . We were bound to find him in the end. He'll go to prison. He's unlikely to survive that experience at his age, and with his health. Is that clever?'

She set her hands on the wooden table, the rings striking the Formica.

'Prison holds no horrors for Alby, Inspector. Quite the opposite. And with the Clockcase closing, perhaps he understood that. Perhaps he wanted you to find him. And that night — the night I told him — he asked about Kath, about whether she'd tell her story to you, to everyone. I said she wouldn't. Which is what she'd promised me. I thought the past should be a closed book. But she didn't keep her secret, did she? I don't blame her, really. But there we are. If she had kept it to herself, Alby thought you'd have never known about the three of them lying in wait for Pat that night. So what happened at the Shipwrights' Hall might have ended up being what it started out as — simple food poisoning. So perhaps he isn't that stupid after all. Just unlucky.'

It was a neat summary and Shaw wondered how long she'd had it prepared. Because he didn't believe that was how it had happened.

'This is nonsense,' he said, standing. 'I think Alby wanted to kill the three of them — Fletcher, Venn and Murray. I don't know how — but I think you do, and I think you helped him. Because where's *your* anger? The anger of a mother who discovers that her son has been murdered.'

She reacted physically to the words, rocking back slightly on the chair, but she didn't speak. To buy herself time she tried to smooth out the skirt over her knees.

'My sergeant here will take a statement — but remember, if you are lying, that's an offence in itself, and the law will take no account of your age.' He leant over the table so that he could see her eyes. 'I'd ask you to imagine what it will be like for Lizzie and Ian if they have to visit you in jail. If they have to watch you die there. Ask yourself if they'll survive that. If the family will survive that.'

Shaw waited for Valentine in the CID suite on the top floor.

It took his DS twenty minutes to take the statement which he slid across Shaw's desk. 'She's sticking. No change. We have to let her go.'

'Yes, we do. But here's what we do next,' said Shaw. He asked Valentine to get the incident room to liaise with Interpol, the US Bureau of Immigration and the North Dakota State Police. He wanted everything they had on Bea Garrison's life in Hartsville during the sixties and seventies. It was a big slice of her life, and it was missing. Did her story really add up? Something she'd said about her life back then, when they'd first talked to her at the Flask, still jarred in Shaw's memory. Infuriatingly, he couldn't recall the detail, but it was something about that small town in the Midwest. Something that didn't fit. Something about the little drugstore. He tried to imagine her life with Latrell, the GI returned home, but the picture wouldn't form.

33

The neon lights hanging from the wooden roof beams of the Ark made a sharp contrast with the day outside: stillborn, fading to an early dusk. Tom Hadden was at his desk and Shaw guessed he hadn't slept properly since they'd found Pat Garrison's bones. He was pale, his red hair losing its colour too, the freckled skin as lifeless as masking tape. Shaw reflected that he'd known Hadden for three years and that the sum of his knowledge of this man's life was less than what he knew about their victim.

'I've been working on MOT — the letters on the scrap of paper we found in the victim's wallet?' said Hadden. 'Well, it isn't an MOT certificate. Paper's all wrong. Plus his mother tells us he didn't drive. So, we've done all the usual searches and got nowhere. Ministry of Tourism? MOT is the New York Stock Exchange symbol for Motorola Corporation. I guess that's possible — they're based in Chicago, which in US terms isn't that far from where the kid came from. But why? Other than that, it's a blank — sorry.'

Shaw looked at a sheet of white A4 paper lying on the desk in front of Hadden, in the centre of which he'd written MOT. Shaw couldn't help thinking that if it had just been *any* three letters the puzzle would be simpler — that it was the association of the Ministry of Transport vehicle test which was clouding their thinking. They should be thinking sideways. He picked up Hadden's pencil and wrote MTO, then ACB, HTV, ZCO. That was better. He didn't have the answer, but he felt closer to it. He picked up the paper, made a ball and lobbed it into the basket.

Beyond the plastic swing doors they heard Justina Kazimierz and her assistant preparing for the autopsies following the Shipwrights' Hall poisoning. As Shaw parted the doors he felt his heartbeat quicken, as it always did. Both mortuary tables were covered by sheets. Over them, on the east wall of the original church, the stone angel stood on its niche, both hands pressed to its eyes.

The assistant removed the first sheet as if uncovering a sofa in a dusty summer villa.

Shaw reminded himself of the short conversation he'd just had with Valentine as they'd walked across the yard of St James's towards the Ark. They'd decided to leave the pathologist to come to her initial findings before telling her of the link between the victims. That way they'd get a clear scientific judgement, unclouded by a conspiracy theory. It was what Justina Kazimierz would have done, but that wouldn't make her any happier that they'd done it.

Freddie Fletcher lay naked, the black swirls of his hair covering most of the body, a tattoo revealed on his shoulder: Royal Artillery. He'd died, as they'd known he would, shortly after they'd left the hospital. Shaw recalled he'd talked proudly of his father's military record. He thought it was probably one of the many tragedies of Fletcher's life that he hadn't been able to fight for what he believed in — however misplaced that belief had been.

'Gentlemen?' asked Kazimierz. The assistant set the Stryker saw whirring and handed it to her. Valentine concentrated on the moving hands of the clock on the wall, trying to imagine the mechanism within, the cog wheels interlacing, the steel parts clean, oiled and precise.

Shaw watched the saw slicing through the bloodless flesh, the breast bone severed, the ribs cut, the chest plate lifted clear to allow access to the principal organs. His own work in forensic art had entailed many hours alone in the morgue at Quantico — the FBI's training centre in Virginia. He'd very quickly learned to see a corpse as simply the body in death — the once-living chamber of the soul. He didn't believe in God, but he'd always believed in souls; a contradiction he'd be happy to die with.

Fifteen minutes later the pathologist stood back, picked the bloodstained gloves from her hands and poured a dark black coffee from a Thermos into a small glass.

'This man was a dying man,' she said. 'There's evidence of the initial stages of lung cancer — the left lung. The heart is diseased. The brain shows signs of a recent stroke, but it isn't the first he'd suffered. But none of that killed him. Whatever killed him, however, did so very quickly. According to the witness report . . . ' She snapped a single sheet of A4 upright in her hand. 'The sequence of events was thus: nausea, vomiting, stomach pain, internal bleeding, shock, then a period of nearly twenty-four hours in which his body tried to fight back. His lungs filled with fluid, then death. Even after death the toxin has continued to attack the kidneys — they would have failed if he'd lived long enough.'

'The poison?' asked Shaw.

'Aluminium-based — possibly a phosphide. The chemistry here is very difficult, Shaw. I've sent a blood sample away, but we'll get a better reading from the organs. Tom says there was an industrial rat poison at the Clockcase Cannery, so that could be it. But there's no way at the moment I can be sure. Also, a phosphide is usually delivered as a gas — for fumigation. In powder form, such as our poisoner would have used, I don't know what sort of concentration we're dealing with.'

'But it's lethal?' said Valentine.

'Well, no, clearly it isn't, is it?' She glared at Valentine. 'Because several people ingested large quantities and are still alive. But in this case it is the patient's *reaction* which proved lethal, if I can put it like that. And I don't understand that either, entirely. But as I say, he was already a dying man. So we'll have to wait for the lab report. Clear?'

George Valentine had an answer to that, but he kept it to himself.

They moved to the second mortuary table and the sheet was removed to reveal Sam Venn. An identical autopsy was completed in half the time. Venn turned out to be a much healthier corpse than his one-time schoolfriend Freddie Fletcher.

Justina took them out into Tom Hadden's lab,

to the desk she used when in the building. She sat on the edge of it and drank more of the black coffee.

'Similar — but different,' she said. 'Different because his body has reacted violently to the ingestion of the poison, but over a longer period of time. There may be complications related to his cerebral palsy, or possibly any medication he took to relieve pain in his muscles or bones due to the disease. I'll check. Similar because I suspect the actual cause of death was pulmonary oedema — essentially, a build-up of fluid in the lungs, like our other victim. I think death occurred not long after he got himself to bed — six hours perhaps, maybe ten. So that would make the time of death somewhere between ten last night and two this morning. I did a quick blood test and we have traces of the same poison in Venn's blood as Fletcher's — though at a somewhat lower concentration than many of the diners. But again we need expert toxicology, and for that we need to send away, and for that we need you to sign the forms, Peter.'

Shaw had his head in his hands, elbows on one of the desks, trying to think.

'Why didn't he raise the alarm — call a doctor?'

'Well — we'll never know,' she said. 'My guess would be that he felt ill, went to bed because he thought it was just food poisoning. If he'd slept at all, or even lost consciousness, then the oedema would have accelerated. By the time he knew he was in trouble it was too late.'

'But the way we found the body — the Bible

— it was like he'd laid himself out,' said Shaw.

'Yes. I agree. I can't explain that.'

But Shaw could. He couldn't dislodge the conviction that Sam Venn had accepted death.

'Overall, then — taking the three deaths together — what can we say?' he asked. 'Did you do the other victim?'

She shook her head. 'John Blacker examined Mr Clarke's body — but I've got the file. The first victim was exceptionally frail — any kind of body shock would have killed him. It did.' She took off her hairnet. 'We've got a hundred and three people exposed to the danger of poisoning by an aluminium-based toxin. Sixty-one ingest poison — in varying amounts, but at a constant concentration. It could be a batch of faulty cans — but the coroner's officer tells me there are suspicions of foul play? Sabotage? Well. Maybe. But the three who died did so because they were susceptible to any shock to the system.'

'So, a random poisoning. Three victims die due to physical weaknesses, but each weakness is different,' said Shaw.

The pathologist nodded. 'If you like. But as I say — that's a guess at this stage, and not my finding.'

'There's something we didn't tell you,' said Shaw. He said it quickly, unsettled by the thought that the pathologist was his friend and that he'd led her astray.

He looked away, watching Hadden working on-screen, so that he wouldn't catch her eye. 'Well, several things. First, the cans didn't fail; a toxic substance was added to each before they were sealed. We have the culprit in custody. Second, two of the three victims — the two next door — are suspects in a murder case. A third suspect should have been sitting at the same table for lunch. The chances we have two random victims who are our suspects is one in ten thousand. George worked it out — he's good with numbers. And we know the poison was definitely the powder used to kill rats at the cannery, and that it was aluminium phosphide.'

The pathologist glared at them, then turned her back, refilling her coffee cup. Shaw estimated it would take her twenty seconds to work out they'd done the right thing. Now, armed with all the facts, she could come to a scientific conclusion.

It took her ten seconds. 'Right. Well, my position is clear. It is entirely possible that sixty-one people given a metal-based rat poison would survive. Such a poison is not even completely effective on rats. But if we're saying these men were targeted then there must be a secondary factor. Without the information that the victims were linked I — or any other competent pathologist — would have been happy to rest with the causes of death I've outlined. Clear?'

'Crystal,' said Shaw. 'But what do you mean by 'secondary factor'?'

'Well, it appears, doesn't it, that someone knew these two men would be particularly susceptible to the poison. Someone knew them well — better than they knew themselves. A doctor? Family — friends? Even if they did know their medical history, however, there is no way they could have been sure the dose would be lethal. The human body isn't that predictable.

'Or maybe it was the way in which the poison was ingested. Did someone put poison in their drinks, for example — the same poison? That might mean that while they each took a similar dose it was ingested more quickly. I need to know more about the toxicology — and as I've said, that will take time. Tom needs to be brought up to speed — I hope we've got all the relevant physical evidence from the scene — cups, plates, seating plan?'

Shaw nodded, hoping they had, too.

'And the third man — the intended third victim — what happened to him?' she asked.

'John Joe Murray. He gave someone else his ticket. The man he gave it to was poisoned instead, but has recovered.'

'It would be instructive to medically examine Mr Murray. Is he old, ailing, ill? In other words was he — is he — susceptible to such a poison?'

'About fifty. Drinks and smokes, but otherwise fit,' said Valentine.

'Problem is, he's missing,' said Shaw. 'We're on his trail, but currently there's no sign of him.'

Shaw's phone buzzed, and he heard Valentine's ring tone — a Bakelite-telephone bell. Simultaneous calls — always a bad sign. They had the same text, from DC Jacky Lau: BODY FOUND IN WOODS AT HOLKHAM.

34

Holkham Drive was a grand place to die. Originally it had led from the portico of Holkham Hall down through the woods to the dunes and the beach beyond. Victorian picnic parties would have ridden down in carriages to eat out on tartan rugs. Somewhere in the pine woods it was said the royal family had had a beach hut. Now it led to a car park, a hut which sold refreshments in summer, and the notice boards outlining the birds that could be seen amongst the pines or out at the water's edge, where seals basked. Midweek, in winter, it was a mile of deserted track, a foot deep in snow, the road barred, leading into the pines where the shadows were dark and green.

At the top, by the main road, there was a ticket kiosk, closed up for the winter. Shaw and Valentine drove past, thudding over the sleeping policemen, through the barred gate, heading for the cluster of police and emergency-vehicle lights down by the trees. The snow clouds had gone to reveal a moonless night sky of stars. Most of the light came from the snow on the fields. As Shaw got out of the car he heard deer bolting from the woods. He imagined that the beach beyond the protective barrier of pines would be a landscape of white surf because he could feel, through his feet, the rhythmic thud of the breakers falling.

Valentine got out of the Porsche while Shaw

made a further request for back-up to St James's. Behind them, on the track, they could see Tom Hadden in one of the forensic unit vans, edging through the snow. Valentine stood in the night air, leaning on the car, oddly elated that there was a chance they'd found Voyce, even if they'd found him too late. The skin on his fingers stuck to the Porsche's roof, a sudden ice seal forming between flesh and supercooled metal. He pulled his hand back, as if from a burn, and gave up on the Silk Cut he'd been ready to light since they'd left St James's, slipping it into his pocket.

DC Jacky Lau walked towards them, a silhouette against the crime-scene lights. Without the sunglasses Shaw thought her face betrayed tension, the jawline set hard, the eyes catching the electric light.

'You found him?'

'No, sir. One of the foot units. It's taken a bit of time to sort it out. PC who stumbled on him, on a track, thought it was roadkill — and believe me, it's an easy mistake to make. It's off in the woods, no one goes there in winter, as I said, but this isn't far from where the car freaks saw the lights. There's an estate cottage up by the road and they sometimes see the odd car. Lovers' lane, apparently, if you're desperate.'

She was walking now, leading them into the woods.

'They've seen nothing for weeks. But on Tuesday night, when the lights were spotted, there was a storm blowing. So they wouldn't have heard.' Shaw recalled the sea spray at Hunstanton, washing over the front.

Hadden walked past them with a woman Shaw didn't recognize — both were in SOC suits, and they had a collapsible forensic tent between them. A line of crime tape led deeper into the woods. Then they were there — an open area through which ran a partly metalled track. Two uniformed PCs stood by something in the frozen mud, their boots lit by torches held down.

They waited while Hadden put the tent up: thirty seconds of practised craft. A light went on in the tent, illuminating the neat square, and Shaw thought of the Chinese lantern he'd lit with Fran on the beach that summer when they'd camped out in front of the café. They'd watched it rise to a single point of light, then flicker and die: a vision of freedom. But here in the woods all Shaw could smell was the dampness of the rotting earth.

This moment, when Shaw would have to lift aside the plastic sheeting to enter the tent, was one that always troubled him, because it reminded him that he did have a choice. He could walk away instead. The urge got stronger every time. He fought it.

Roadkill was right. Jimmy Voyce's body had been crushed diagonally across the torso, from the right shoulder to the left hip, leaving the head and legs uninjured. The corpse had been squashed down into the snow, which still dusted the remains. Valentine was struck by the lack of blood. He was always struck by the lack of blood, because his imagination always painted the most lurid crimson scene. The head was looking up, and but for the tent he'd have been

351

staring into the canopy of pines.

Hadden was down on his knees. 'Looks like a hit and run.' He straightened up. 'Looks like. But I don't think it is.'

Valentine studied Hadden's box of tricks — forensic gear in a suitcase, an ordered clinical array of brushes, jars and tapes.

'Here,' said Hadden, indicating Voyce's left leg, just above the ankle. There was a graze, cut deep, with the blood showing in stipples.

'The vehicle's gone over him and the tyres cut down through the ribcage, crushing the vital organs, but the legs are clear of that, so this injury, on the leg, was inflicted before the impact.'

Hadden pushed Valentine to one side and they saw that he'd been standing next to a grid in the forest road, like a gutter drain. When the wind dropped, and the trees stopped whispering, they could hear water gurgling through the iron cover.

Hadden took out a map — Ordnance Survey, in high detail. He checked it against a hand-held GPS. 'I think we're actually on a bridge here,' said Hadden. 'A shallow bridge over the sluice which drains the marsh.' He folded the map under his arm. 'Notice the alignment of the leg with the pre-mortem injury — it points back to the grid. Also . . . ' He lifted the leg and manipulated the knee. They heard a crunch of shattered cartilage. 'Knee's dislocated, well — that's an understatement. It's pretty much severed at the joint. Know what I think?'

He lifted the top drawer of his toolbox clear

and took out a piece of nylon rope about four feet long.

'Justina will give you the official version — but here's a fact.' He closed his eyes tightly, so that the lids vibrated. 'You hit a human body with a vehicle — any vehicle — and it can't inflict an injury like this. One chance in a thousand, perhaps — no more. That's because when the body is hit, it begins to travel with the vehicle, which minimizes the trauma. That won't save your life, but it does mean the injuries are limited. In other words, the *impact* is all over in a split second. After that the body's effectively stuck to the vehicle. That has not happened here. What we have here is a vehicle hitting someone who *couldn't* move. In this case, a glancing blow, otherwise the leg would have been severed.'

He looked down at Voyce's body. Shaw realized that in places he could see through the corpse to the roadway below.

'He was tied in place?' asked Valentine. He didn't mean to whisper, but his throat had constricted because his body was thinking about being sick.

'Well, that's my guess. He was certainly tied . . . here.' He placed a finger in a green forensic glove on the friction burn on the leg. 'And it's possible the other end of the rope was looped round the grating of the drain cover.'

'Why?' asked Shaw. 'Why tie him down — then run him over? If you can tie him down you could hit him, put him out, then finish him off with the car.'

353

'Punishment — like an execution?' offered Hadden.

'Or interrogation,' said Shaw. 'You tie him to the grate. Then ask your questions. Turn the car headlights on, then ask again. Then finish it.'

'Either way it's a cool bit of work,' said Hadden, using the rope from the toolbox to test his theory. 'Professional. A contract killing?'

Shaw shook his head. 'No — that's what he wants us to think,' he said. He thought about Bobby Mosse's calculated part-confession in the dunes the night before. He'd set the scene. Voyce was mixing company with the Tulleys, people who could do something like this. People who did it for a living.

'This kind of impact would buckle the car bumper — do other damage?' asked Shaw.

Hadden was nodding. 'Maybe. Certainly there'd be blood, bone, tissue stuck to the vehicle.'

Shaw thought about Voyce's car, burnt out, down the coast. They needed to double-check for structural damage. It was a hired car, they'd have a record of existing bumps and scrapes.

Then he thought about Bobby Mosse's black BMW. A powerful machine, a lethal weapon. Even a glancing blow would have killed Voyce if he'd been tied to the drain cover. If Mosse had used the BMW he'd have cleaned the vehicle. But Shaw knew just how tenacious trace forensic evidence could be. He jogged to the Porsche and pulled a U-turn, then made a call on his mobile while he waited for Valentine to catch up. On the coast road they hit 90 mph, the marshes a blur

354

on the offside, Jacky Lau's Mégane struggling to keep up, and out at sea, falling across the pin-sharp star fields, a meteor, as if the sky was falling in.

35

Ian Murray saw the same meteor fall. He was a hundred yards from the old coal barn, so he cut the engine and drifted, watching the night sky. It was like an omen, he thought. Here, inside the protective arc of the outer sand dunes, the sea was just choppy, slapping against the fibreglass hull of the *Sandpiper*. The boat had been another one of his ideas — in summer they'd hire one of the fishermen to take out guests from Morston House to see the birds on the marsh. You'd be surprised what you could charge, he'd told Bea. Thirty pounds a head; forty. A minute passed and more meteors fell, this time a dozen, like stardust thrown across the sky. The coal barn was a black silhouette against the churning water. A wavelet caught the *Sandpiper* side-on, the spray soaking Ian, so that he decided to fire the engine back into life.

John Joe Murray was waiting for him on the stone quay. He grabbed the line that his stepson threw. When he got ashore John Joe went to hug him but the young man looked away, letting the awkward moment pass. That should have been the first sign that something wasn't right, but John Joe missed it; or rather he misinterpreted it, thinking it was just a fresh estrangement, another notch on the spectrum of distance as his stepson moved emotionally closer to the father he'd never known. It was a cruel moment, John Joe thought to himself, because in his life he'd done so much that was wrong, even shameful, but he'd never once tried to hurt Ian. He'd never aspired to being a good man, but in his stepson he'd invested all that was good in himself.

'You shouldn't have come,' he said. 'I told Bea.' He helped Ian haul out a fresh bag of provisions. 'But thanks,' he added.

They stood apart, listening to the waves thudding out on the sandbank at sea. The ghost of Pat Garrison seemed to stand between them.

'I made tortilla, the way you like it,' said Ian, handing him a parcel in silver paper. It had been their last holiday together, to Galicia, as a family. Ian, just sixteen, had collected recipes for the restaurant that was his dream. And that was the thing that John Joe was proud of still — the fact that he *had* dreams, as he'd had a dream, and he liked to think that was something he'd given Ian, not something that had come down to him through some arid string of DNA.

Ian lugged the provisions inside the stone barn, looking round the ground floor, clogged with flotsam and old nets.

'Go up,' said John Joe. 'The tide comes in now — tonight, it's a high tide, it'll flood.'

Ian considered that, then climbed the stone steps. He took out more food, a flask, a loaf of fresh bread and a greaseproof-paper parcel. 'Ham — Serrano,' he said, setting it on a stone shelf. He gave a big ugly shiver. 'Christ, it's cold in here.'

John Joe was by the fire, working the logs,

kindling the flames, and he wondered why Ian didn't join him.

'How's your mum?' he asked.

The flames flared, creating a sudden atmosphere of warmth, even if they could still see their breath.

'She's confused. She won't talk — not to me, at least. Bea said not to tell her where you were. Mum thinks you're pissed with us, over Pat. That we've written you out of our story.'

John Joe was pleased with that, because it took them where he wanted to go.

'It's best,' he said. He rubbed his neck, massaging the tattoo of the green guitar.

'Are you going to tell me?' asked Ian. He still hung back from the fire, leaning easily against the rough stone wall, as if he didn't want to be drawn in to that circle of light.

John Joe ignored the question. 'And how's Bea?'

'She says the police came. But she didn't tell them where you were. She says with the spring tides you can stay as long as you like. Even with the water out, you're on an island.'

John Joe ran a hand back over the greying hair. 'Someone wants to kill me,' he said, and laughed as if he didn't believe it either.

'They killed Freddie Fletcher and Sam Venn. I'm next. I should have been there, with them, at our table at the Shipwrights' Hall.'

Ian pushed himself away from the wall with his shoulders. There was something about the languid ease of the movement that John Joe didn't miss, and for the first time he felt a wave of unease, a feeling that he was talking to a stranger.

'Why?' asked Ian, and there was a tone to the voice that turned it from a question into an accusation. 'Why would someone want to kill the three of you? Police said it was food poisoning — some nutter up at the cannery. Who'd want to kill you?'

'It's not important now,' said John Joe. 'Staying alive's important.'

'They were scum — Fletcher and Venn,' said Ian, and in the gloomy light John Joe saw a flash of Ian's white teeth as his upper lip curled back. 'Mum always said that. She said her flesh used to crawl when they came through the door. Sam, self-righteous Sam. Mum said he was just like Grandma: afraid that people would know that he didn't feel anything inside. And Fletcher — do you know what I felt like when Freddie Fletcher used to look at me?'

'How should I know?' asked John Joe, reflecting the angry timbre of his stepson's voice.

Ian spread his hands, the palms lighter than the dark skin on the backs. 'He was a friend of yours.'

John Joe stood. 'They weren't friends of mine,' he said.

'Right. But you were all in the club — the lunch club.' Ian smiled, a smile as insincere as a smile can be, just a rearrangement of facial muscles. 'But there was something else there, between the three of you,' he continued. ''Specially this week — all on the same table in the back room. I saw you. Heads together, at lunch. Then someone tries to kill you — and them. But you're not friends. That's the line, right?'

'I told you, we're not — '

'Your fire's going out,' Ian interrupted, surprising his stepfather with the sudden change of subject.

Ian walked to the wood store, selected a single piece of solid driftwood, then walked, finally, into the firelight. But as he took the final step he lifted the wood and hit his stepfather with the flat side, just above the right ear. John Joe went down on one knee. Ian hit him again — harder this time, at the back of the head. He fell forward into the ashes on the edge of the grate and Ian watched as a thin trickle of blood crossed the green tattoo on his neck.

36

Robert Mosse's black soft-top BMW was parked on the driveway of his house. A sleek black cat crouched before a triple-doored garage. The paintwork on the car was as immaculate as the cat's coat, as pristine as the day it had come off the production line. The tyres looked sticky-black, brand new, not a sign of the gravel or sand from Holkham. The bumper was pristine.

Shaw and Valentine stayed in the Porsche down the street, parked between street lights, and let DCs Campbell and Lau knock on the door. They saw Mosse on the threshold: jeans and a baby-blue sweatshirt, happy to invite them inside. They'd been gone for twenty-five minutes before Campbell came to find them, leaving Lau to finish taking a formal statement. She reported that Mosse's story was clear and confident, once he'd got over his apparent distress at the news that his old friend Jimmy Voyce was dead, murdered in Holkham woods. Yes — he had met him at the pier head at Hunstanton three nights ago. He said he'd explained all this to DI Shaw the previous evening — a statement given freely.

Shaw shifted uneasily in his seat.

But if they wanted the story again, he was happy to repeat it, and it was identical to the one he'd given Shaw. They sent Campbell back to Mosse's house. She was to ask the solicitor for permission for Tom Hadden's forensic unit to

361

check out the BMW — just routine. They were grateful for his cooperation. And they needed his help. Could he identify his friend's body? Either at the city morgue tonight or at St James's in the morning. They could run him there now, get it over with.

While they waited Shaw's mobile vibrated on the dashboard. It was a rare text from DCS Warren: MY OFFICE. EIGHT A.M. BOTH OF YOU.

Shaw was surprised it had taken Warren so long to respond to the news that Voyce's body had been found at Holkham and that he'd been murdered: a man under twenty-four-hour police surveillance, placed directly in danger of his life as part of a plan to entrap Robert Mosse. A plan endorsed by him. Now, after the event, it was clear that Voyce's death had wider implications, because Shaw could see that there were three careers on the line, not two.

'Max'll swing with us,' said Valentine, reading Shaw's mind after he'd been shown the text. His bones ached, and he wanted more than anything else to take them to the Artichoke and let alcohol blur the sharp edges of the day.

'If Mosse says yes to the ID, we'll give it one last try, George. Then it's done. Let's get him down to the Westmead, to the spot itself — where you and Dad found the kid.'

'What makes you think he'll break now?' asked Valentine, studying the façade of Mosse's house, despising him for the carriage lamps and the flounced curtains.

Shaw thought about Peggy Robins and the

reading of Chris Robins's will. He'd filled Valentine in on the development, and both had agreed that they'd be seriously disappointed if they imagined anything that he might have left in his will would crack open the Tessier case after years in cold storage. Even a confession implicating Mosse would fail to get them back into court. Mosse's lawyers, and he'd pay for the best, would attack any postmortem testimony as flawed on the basis of motive. Why speak out now? Robins had had a lifetime to set the record straight. They'd point out the obvious: that the 'confession' had been made in writing, no doubt with copies, to obtain money by extortion while protecting the blackmailer. And Robins was the perfect blackmailer, because even admitting his own guilt while he was alive wouldn't put him away. He'd been detained under the Mental Health Act.

But what if Robins and Voyce, and Cosyns before them, had threatened Mosse with something else? Unspecified, perhaps, but *material*. Something that would put Mosse back in that dock he'd walked free from thirteen years ago?

'I'll use Robins, and the will,' said Shaw. 'Perhaps Mosse doesn't know everything. Maybe Voyce didn't talk before he died. Maybe, for Mosse, there are still unanswered questions. Let's play on that. It's all we've got.'

They watched Mosse's front door open. He stood aside, letting Campbell and Lau go first, then he kissed his wife. A clichéd peck.

'Looks like he's on for it,' said Valentine.

'Model citizen that he is.'

'Radio Fiona,' said Shaw. 'Tell her to follow us.'

Shaw got the Porsche round in time to lead the way, out through the monkey-puzzle streets of the upmarket suburb in which Mosse lived, then onto the ring road.

As they negotiated the turn-off into the Westmead Estate, Shaw smiled into the rear-view mirror, wondering what Mosse would be thinking now, hoping that even his cold blood would have begun to race with the uncertainty, the return to the scene of the crime. Ahead of them the twenty-one-storey block of Vancouver House stood against the night sky, steam leaking from heating systems as if the innards were boiling over. Underneath, in the concrete-pillared car park, Jonathan Tessier's body had been found on a summer's evening nearly fourteen years ago. He wondered what Mosse felt about that, whether he thought of himself as a different person back then. That must be how it worked — or did he survive by protective amnesia? By imagining it was someone else back then, a distant relative who didn't even get a Christmas card any more.

Shaw parked, got out and walked back to the squad car. Mosse's window was down and Shaw was heartened to see — for the first time — a genuine look of fear in the solicitor's eyes as he recognized the DI.

'I thought we'd talked this through, Mr Shaw,' said Mosse, his composure immediately reasserted.

'Just to say I appreciate you offering to do the ID for us,' said Shaw. 'We can get you down there in a few minutes, run you home. I wanted a few words, though — and I thought you'd feel more comfortable away from St James's. Less formal. It's about Chris Robins's will.'

Shaw opened the door. Mosse got out. He was in a full-length cashmere overcoat. His shoes were soft leather. Shaw smelt apple-blossom shampoo.

He walked forward and shook Shaw's hand. It was over before Shaw could stop him. He turned to Valentine, but just nodded. 'OK,' he said. 'But why here?' Shaw thought the expression he'd arranged on his face was perfectly pitched: mild interest, a willingness to help.

'Because this is where it all started.' Shaw looked up at the serried lights in the flats, kitchens mainly, windows obscured by condensation. Shaw could imagine a childhood here, but he couldn't *feel* it.

Mosse used one hand to button the coat at his throat. 'That was a lifetime ago. I don't mind answering any questions you have. But I'd like it recorded that I'm doing this freely.'

'Let's go inside,' said Shaw, and led the way across the snow-covered tarmac, then in through the pillars of the car park. He found the spot immediately, by a lift shaft, a broken fire-exit sign, a puddle on the floor like blood from a head wound. He'd discovered, amongst his father's papers, press cuttings from the first days of the inquiry. There'd been a picture of the crime scene. And he'd been back since with Valentine, as if they were the ghosts that haunted the place, not Jonathan Tessier.

Shaw stamped his foot lightly, marking the spot. 'I wondered — we wondered — why you'd killed Jimmy Voyce like that,' he said. Valentine coughed, taken aback by Shaw's sudden hostile change of tack. 'Tying him down first. There was something, wasn't there, that he wouldn't tell you.'

Mosse's shoulders slumped, as if in disappointment. His hands were in his pockets and he dug them deeper. 'This is going to be a waste of time,' he said to himself, but loud enough for them to hear.

Valentine spat on the ice.

'You can see through his body — right to the ground underneath,' said Shaw. 'The impact nearly cut him in two. I think you wanted information. Because you were being blackmailed, had been blackmailed, subtly, but persistently, And you wanted to be sure it would end when Voyce died. What kind of information was it?'

Mosse looked at his wristwatch and a cufflink caught the light.

'I think it's the same information that Alex Cosyns had,' said Shaw. 'And I think it all goes back to Chris Robins. Something they knew, or something they had; something you were prepared to pay to keep secret. Did they ever tell you what it was — or was it enough to know it was there? That it was sufficient to put you behind bars for the murder of Jonathan Tessier.'

Mosse let a smile form on the otherwise immobile face.

'Of course,' he said, running a hand back through the barbered hair. 'That's what this is about. Your father.' He looked around. 'This was where his career came to an end, wasn't it? Right here. Where he found that glove.'

Valentine was motionless. It was an illusion, Shaw knew, but it seemed as though the cigarette smoke had solidified around him.

'I think Alex Cosyns milked you for years,' said Shaw. 'Low key, nothing in your face. But then he upped the pressure, didn't he? Because Chris Robins got some cash too — although he never got to spend it. And that's why Alex Cosyns died, too — because it was all getting too expensive, and we were getting closer to the truth. You thought it was over then, with Cosyns and Robins dead — although it didn't stop you getting someone to ransack Robins's stuff during his funeral, just in case whatever they had was there. Which implies, doesn't it, that there *was* something. A confession? Maybe. Or something more tangible?'

Mosse tapped the toe of his shoe on the solid ice of the puddle.

'So you must have been pretty upset when you heard Jimmy Voyce on the line — and not long distance, either, but right here in Lynn. What did you give him — a few minutes in the pub, just to make sure he was on the same game as the rest? After your money. But the key question, the one you took him down to the woods to pose, was did *he* have the information. Get an answer?'

Mosse turned to Valentine. 'This is delusional, Sergeant. You really should step in, you know. This is going to look so bad in retrospect. When my complaint goes in to the chief constable's office. You'll both be finished then.' And that's when his neck muscles jerked, just a fleeting spasm, but it made his head lower an inch, like a boxer ducking an imaginary blow. It was the first time the façade had cracked, the stress of the moment short-circuiting his nervous system.

Valentine was watching his face and he saw that Mosse's skin colour was changing, very gradually, the blood draining away so that the tan looked artificial. It was like watching a lizard in the sun.

'But it doesn't have to be the same for you,' said Mosse, licking dry lips, looking at Valentine's tightly knotted tie. 'Know what I think? I think you were loyal. Stood by Jack Shaw. It wasn't your idea to contaminate the glove, was it? But you paid the price.' He smiled. 'And now you're here. Being loyal again. Same mistake. It's a family thing. They're going to take you down with them. Then he'll walk away from the wreckage. There's that nice little business the wife runs down on the beach. What have you got to walk away to?'

Mosse affected a shiver, produced a pair of gloves, fur-lined, and slipped them on.

'Now, I think you wanted me to ID Jimmy Voyce's body?'

'This time next week I'll know what they knew,' said Shaw. He judged the tone perfectly — there was no doubt he was speaking the truth.

'There's been an *invitation*. A family affair. Last will and testament of Chris Robins. I'll know everything — as I said, by this time next week. So, if you were planning on leaving town at all, I'd appreciate notice. Because we'll need to talk again.'

He'd thought about the words to use. He could have told him the stark truth, but Mosse would have seen what a weak threat that was, just as they had. This way Mosse had seven days to imagine the worst.

Mosse's eyes flitted between them. He said he was going, but he didn't move. The uniformed PC stood out of earshot, but they could hear him stamping his boots in the cold. Somewhere, out on the Westmead, a car alarm began to blare.

'You all done?' asked Mosse.

'Not quite,' said Shaw.

'Really?' asked Mosse. 'I think you're all done, because we wouldn't be standing in an underground car park if you could prove any of this, Inspector. We'd be down at St James's. And if this mysterious invitation was so persuasive I think you'd have waited until after the reading. Then we could have talked.'

He ruffled his hair and Shaw thought he caught the scent of it — apple again, or something citrus.

'And, if you don't mind a bit of free legal advice, I'd think twice about a next time. Jack Shaw made a big mistake that night. I don't mean not bagging the glove, or bringing it to the flat — although, frankly, they were disastrous mistakes. No — the big mistake was that he thought I'd killed that child. I didn't. And I find it unforgivable to be accused of that crime — again.'

His voice was angry, but Shaw could tell this was playacting. He wasn't offended at all, he was playing for time, hoping Shaw would tell him more.

'I'm sure your father paid for his mistake. I don't know how, and I don't want to know. But if you make the same mistake, you will pay too.'

'This time next week,' said Shaw.

A Vauxhall Corsa came down the ramp, parked fifty feet away, and a teenager in a baseball cap walked away from it towards the exit.

Shaw could see that Mosse had not only made mistakes in this interview, but that he knew he had. He was recalculating, like a dashboard GPS, but he couldn't do it fast enough.

'And Voyce's car — that's another mistake. Only partly burnt out. You drove it, didn't you? Not a mark on the BMW. So you used his car. There'll be forensics, there are always forensics,' said Shaw.

'That's it,' said Mosse. He turned to Valentine. 'Unless you have any rational questions, Inspector?' He did a little am-dram double-take. 'Sorry — *Sergeant.*'

It was — in retrospect, Shaw thought — his biggest error. He couldn't walk away without that one taunt. It was retaliation, which meant he'd been hurt.

'I'll save my questions,' said Valentine. 'For next time.'

37

Saturday, 18 December

Shaw and Valentine stood on the corner of Explorer Street, the snow falling so thickly that the two lines of terraced houses faded away into a white gloom, as dense as a sauna but so cold that Shaw could feel his skin freezing. A week before Christmas. From almost every window fairy lights shone, and above one door in the mid-distance a single reindeer pranced, flickering tirelessly from front hooves to back. It was just before nine o'clock in the morning and a silhouette trudged past them, a street cleaner in a reflective council jacket on his way to work. Shaw checked his watch, while Valentine listened for the clock to chime at All Saints.

After returning home the previous night Shaw had been trying to get the Christmas lights to work on the pine tree beside the cottage when his mobile had rung. He'd been rerunning in his head their interview with Mosse, admitting to himself that they'd failed to break him, but agreeing with Valentine's verdict that they *had* shaken him. Shaw had taken him to the morgue in the Porsche and he'd identified Jimmy Voyce, but he hadn't said another word. For now it was the best ID they would get. They could hardly expect Voyce's wife to fly all the way from New Zealand only to travel home alone. Voyce's dental records together with Mosse's ID would have to be enough for the coroner. The forensics on Mosse's BMW were still being processed but, as expected, the news from Hadden's team was not encouraging. Unfortunately Voyce's burnt-out hired car was yielding no better results. There was some buckling to the front bumper not recorded on the hire contract, but the flames had charred the plastic, seared the steel, so that their chances of lifting blood or skin were almost nil. It was a blow; a bitter blow.

So, when last night's call had come he'd taken it without enthusiasm, expecting more bad news. It was Chief Inspector Bob Howell, head of St James's uniform branch, who said one of his officers had something for them on the report that a light had been seen in Flensing Meadow cemetery six months earlier. PC Gavin Bright had been serving witness statements on the family of a man arrested for selling drugs outside Whitefriars primary school earlier in the week — an arrest made thanks to a phone-call from DI Shaw himself. The mother of the arrested man lived in a low-rise council block in Gladstone Street — the same block from which the witness had seen the light in the cemetery. PC Bright had something to show them. He'd be on the street corner at nine.

Shaw stamped his feet in the snow, producing a series of muffled thuds, and looked at his watch. He'd come straight to the South End from DCS Warren's office. The interview had been cold, formal, and conducted largely without rancour. Any emotional bond which might have bridged the gap between their ranks had been severed. Max Warren intended his retirement to be long and blameless, and the last thing that was going to throw a shadow over it was the indiscipline of the youngest DI on the force combined with the wilful belligerence of the oldest DS.

Jimmy Voyce had died while under police surveillance. His murder would be the subject of an internal inquiry, Warren said. A coroner's court hearing would be adjourned to allow the investigation to continue. If the press missed the short adjournment — which they often did if they had a full schedule to cover in the magistrates court — then they might be able to keep it quiet. If the press sniffed it out, they'd have no chance. The job of tracking down Voyce's killer would now be the responsibility of DI Raymond 'Chips' McCain of Peterborough CID. His first interview would be with Shaw and Valentine. They were to be completely candid; any suspicion that they were anything less would result in immediate suspension. If either Shaw or Valentine approached Bobby Mosse during McCain's investigation they would be suspended and face disciplinary charges which, Max Warren promised Shaw, would result in their dismissal without pension from the West Norfolk Constabulary.

'That might mean bugger-all to you, Peter, given you've got a nice little business to go home to. But you might consider what having no pension would do to George Valentine's remaining years.'

Which is when the mask finally slipped. 'That is a door,' said Warren, pointing a fat finger at the oak-panelled exit from his office. 'If you break any of these conditions you will walk through it and out of this building. George Valentine will go with you. Either of you transgresses, both will go.'

The good news, Shaw had thought in the lift on the way down, was that Mosse had clearly not made a formal complaint about his unofficial interrogation in the car park at the Westmead. In the three years he had been trying to reopen the case into Jonathan Tessier's death, that was the first time Mosse had displayed any weakness, any inclination to stay on the back foot. But that didn't mean he'd miss the obvious next step — which was to leak the bare details of Voyce's death to the press and sit back while they tore Shaw and Valentine's careers apart.

Shaw felt utterly impotent. Not only were they unable to take the case forward, they frankly didn't know how to. Their only slender hopes now lay with Chris Robins's will and the investigative powers of 'Chips' McCain — a man with a reputation for running steamroller investigations of unmitigated thoroughness. Shaw could sympathize with that, but the problem with thorough was that it was also slow. And they were running out of time.

Valentine stood still, letting the snow accumulate on his thin hair. 'Couldn't this uniform have just told us what he's found?' he asked.

'Apparently not,' said Shaw. 'He needs to show us.'

Shaw tried to lift Valentine's obvious depression. 'Twine had news, by the way. Caught me on the way out from Warren's office,' he said. Twine had received an e-mail from FBI headquarters at Quantico. They'd sent a field officer from Bismarck out to Hartsville to check out Bea Garrison's past history. Shaw summarized: 'The big lie, and the relevant omission, is that it wasn't Latrell Garrison who set up the drugstore. Yes, there had been a programme for GIs to retrain, but Latrell had flunked out of that in six months. The shop was actually a local store called Garrison's — a coffee shop, general grocer's, post office and pharmacy, owned by the family since the twenties. The dispensary had been closed since before the war because they couldn't entice a qualified pharmacist out to Hartsville. When Latrell ducked out, Bea took his place. She qualified in 1971. In 1973 she took a further course in advanced pharmacy. In 1975 Levi's opened a clothing factory on the edge of town — population went from 3,000 to 16,000, and the general store boomed. Latrell drank his share of the profits, that much is true. Bea left in 1982, selling up at public auction for $450,000. Twine worked it out — that's £245,000 at 1982 prices. So she lied to us,' Shaw said to Valentine, as a car crunched past at ten miles an hour, its driver clearing condensation with a waving gloved hand. 'In fact she's lied several times. It turns out she's a qualified pharmacist, and as such she will have — at the very least — a firm grasp of toxicology.'

'But other than telling Alby Tilden how much

rat poison to put in the cans, what could she do with it?' asked Valentine. He'd meant to buy a fresh pack of Silk Cut on the walk from his house. His irritation was growing with each nicotine-free minute. 'Christ, we've checked it out. Justina says the poison in the soup was well short of a lethal dose for most people.' He hauled some air into his lungs. 'So how do we build a murder charge out of that?' He looked up at the falling snowflakes. 'Sir,' he added.

'Justina said that, if anything, Venn had less than the average,' added Shaw, checking his watch. 'Let's put Guy Poole and Tom Hadden together — if they're not talking already. They need to hammer this out — there *has* to be an answer, George. I think Alby and Bea wanted the three men dead. They got two of them — only missed out on Murray because he wasn't there. But how? What about cutlery? The soup bowls? And we know Fletcher was ill the day before the lunch. What about Venn? Check that out, too. And while you're at it, check with the incident room and see what they're doing to track down John Joe Murray. He still hasn't turned up. We need to find him.'

Then, as if he'd beamed down through the snow cloud, PC Bright was with them. He was short, broad, with a formless pale face and strikingly small jet-black eyes. He had that particular pallor which comes with working a night shift.

'Sir.' He stifled a yawn.

He took them down Explorer Street to an alleyway, then cut north and out into the hidden churchyard of All Saints. Here the snow made a blanket for the dead. On one fine civic monument to a long-dead mayor someone had arranged ten cans of Special Brew in bowling-pin formation. The snowfall was so gentle the cans still stood, upright and untouched.

Bright led the way to the church porch. Around them, encircling the churchyard, was a 1960s low-rise block of former council flats.

'That one there, sir — second floor, with the window open in the bathroom? That's the mother of the pusher we arrested outside the school, after your tip-off. The woman who said she saw the light in the cemetery is her next-door neighbour. On the other side the flat has a balcony looking down into Explorer Street. I'd read the witness summaries for your case on the murder incident room website, so when I called round to take her down to St James's to bail her son I took a look. Now, the neighbour said she saw the light in the graveyard over the rooftops. But she couldn't have, sir — the terraced houses are too high. Third floor — maybe. Second floor — never.'

'Name?' Shaw asked.

Valentine beat Bright to it. 'Jade Moore.' The DS looked at his shoes, knowing that was a stupid thing to say, because if he knew the name then he'd read the statement, and he'd lived here, in this neighbourhood, all his life, so he should have known that she couldn't have seen what she said she'd seen.

They let Bright lead the way, into a stairwell then up to the landing.

Jade Moore was in her mid-forties and applying make-up to try to look half that age. She had a job to go to, she was late, she couldn't spend all day talking to them.

Shaw explained why they were there and asked her to open the metal-framed door to the balcony.

'It's snowing,' she complained. But she got the keys, and the door screeched at the hinges as it swung open.

They all stood at the rail, looking across Explorer Street.

Moore had put a cardigan on, which wiped out all the years she'd clawed back with the make-up.

'You didn't see the light in the cemetery at all, did you?' asked Shaw. 'You can't see past the houses from here.'

'Does it matter?' she said, looking at them all in turn. 'There was a light in the cemetery, believe me.' She lost her temper then, throwing an empty packet of cigarettes over the railing and stomping back into the flat.

They heard voices raised, then she reappeared, towing her daughter. She was in her mid-teens, with pancake make-up, clutching a man's blue dressing gown and a copy of *Persuasion*.

'This is Jilly, she saw the light. All right? When she got in she told me what she'd seen so I rang it in to Jamie — Jamie Driver, my brother-in-law. He's on traffic but he wants to get into the CID, so he likes any tips. I didn't want you lot taking Jilly down the nick, that's all.'

They sat the girl down and asked her to describe what she'd seen. She'd been sitting outside the Lattice House with some of the girls from school, drinking cider. She'd gone into the cemetery with a boy. Her mother nodded at that, grim faced, and Shaw guessed that Jilly had already paid the price for that transgression. 'We were just sitting talking,' she said, glaring defiantly at her mother. 'Round by the cedar trees.'

'Time?' said Valentine. 'Incident report said just after three o'clock — that right?'

'Two,' she said. 'Mum rang then — but like I had to get home, see Gav home too.'

Her mother looked skywards.

'There's a gap in the cemetery railings down by the water. Anyone can get in. We heard someone digging — like a spade. And — yeah — a light. But not much 'cos there was a moon.'

'Tell us about the person who was digging,' said Shaw.

'We didn't see anyone, not really. Like I said, we heard them. We just saw the light, down by the riverside. Near that big stone box — the tomb. Then we got out. Went home.'

Shaw and Valentine swapped glances.

'How did you see the light, but not the person?' said Shaw gently, turning to watch the snow fall.

'She was in the hole. But Gav saw her for a second, just her head.'

'*She?*' said Shaw.

'Yeah — I said that.' She looked at her mother. 'I said that. I did.'

Jade Moore passed a hand over her eyes. 'Christ!'

'And where can we find this Gav?' said Valentine, taking out his notebook as she reeled off the details.

'A question,' said Shaw, holding up his hand. 'Did you disturb her, Jilly? The woman in the grave. Did she know you were there?'

'No way. Gav said it was like well creepy, and we should get out. So we slipped back round the trees and away. I didn't get a proper look at her, but he said it was definitely a woman, 'cos she seemed to be really struggling with the spade.'

Outside, they let PC Bright go home to his bed. Valentine placed a call to the boyfriend — who lived up in the North End and was probably still in bed, according to Jilly. After a pause he left a message on an answerphone, telling the teenager to ring St James's as soon as he picked up the call. Shaw stood in the porch of All Saints, trying to think it through. A woman. Which woman? It was a fact that didn't fit his theory in so many different ways.

38

John Joe Murray's body was earthbound, weighted at each limb, so that he lay spreadeagled on the floor of the old coal barn, spatchcocked, but with his head raised on the stone shelf so that he could see through the doorway to the north, and to open water. The cold, which seemed to be concentrated in the stone floor beneath his back, made his bones ache. But it wasn't the cold or the swirling snow which blew in squalls over the grey sea that made him want to scream. It was the tide, edging towards the doorway. The flood boards had been taken away so that the view was clear, right to the cold horizon. Dusk was falling, the sea turning inky black. He looked at the old stone walls of the barn for the thousandth time, running his eye along the mark that clearly delineated the line of the highest tide. It was a foot above his head.

He'd come to after the attack in the hour before dawn, lying on the cold stone stairs, his hands and legs tied in rough fisherman's rope. A light had seeped through the floorboards above. Calling out, he'd felt the blood in his throat, and the stab of pain over his eye where the blow had fallen. Mid-morning his stepson had come down the steps and stood looking out to sea. Then he'd turned and made a decision: 'We'll wait,' he said. 'For tonight.' He'd given him tea to sip, and some tortilla. John Joe asked him why this was happening but Ian wouldn't meet his eyes, let alone answer his questions. After that, time dissolved into patches of consciousness and nightmarish dreams. Mid-afternoon, Ian had given him some more food, then moved him to the floor of the barn and he'd lost consciousness again.

When he saw the first star — Venus, surely, rising with the moon — Ian had come down and removed the flood boards, taking them with him back up the stairs. He tried to raise his head to see the sea more clearly, but when he moved his skull he could hear — through the bone — the slight crunch of something broken in his jaw. The injury, the impact of the blow, had made his right eye swell, so that his vision was murky on that side. But with his left eye he could see the waves sharply. It was a spring tide, and it had already breached the protective arc of dunes, so that the waves he could see were breaking in open water. Not a wild sea, despite the snowstorm, but winterchoppy, flecked, disturbed. When he'd come to, the sand bars were standing out at sea, dusted with snow. But now they'd gone, the grey sea swallowing each one until all he could see through the door was a world of water, the horizon coming and going with the snow squalls.

The first wave that came through the door broke his resolve to stay calm. He screamed, the water white, foaming, laced with ozone, seething over his legs, then flowing out.

When he stopped screaming he heard the

footsteps over his head, and then Ian's narrow slender legs appeared on the ladder-stairs.

His stepson watched him dispassionately, like a fisherman eyeing a float.

John Joe went to speak but the pain made the urge to scream again so insistent he swallowed back the words.

Ian raised a hand, as if asking for time in a polite conversation. It was an oddly civilized mannerism, coldly frightening in its intense self-possession.

'Let me,' he said. 'You must have questions.'

John Joe pulled with his right hand until he felt the skin part at the wrist. He felt his guts turn to water, heavy water, like mercury that wanted to fall through his body and wash out to sea.

'Kath Robinson saw you,' said Ian, momentarily troubled by the congestion of blood in his stepfather's face, the strange mottling, the stress which had tightened his skin and made him look younger, less dissolute.

'The night they buried Grandma. Dad came into the bar to talk to Mum — and Kath didn't want to see that, did she?' He smiled, and despite his terror John Joe was reminded of the boy's father — that same cynicism, almost older than it could be in one so young, as if he'd inherited a distrust of life along with the colour of his skin. The casual use of the word 'Dad' was a calculated cruelty and Ian looked pleased with the effect: John Joe's feet had jerked together, making the rope creak.

'Christ,' he said. 'What do you want?'

'I want — wanted — to see you dead. I tried — we tried — to make sure you died with the others, with Fletcher and Venn. But actually, this is better. Much better, because I get to ask you questions, and you get to answer them. We've got one last chance to find out the one thing we don't know: who struck the killing blow? Mum said we didn't need to know. That you were all guilty, all cowards. And I'd have been happy if you'd died with them. But now we've got this time. And maybe — maybe — I'll let you walk away from this when I know. But I need the truth, and I'll know it when I hear it. And if you lie, you surely won't walk away. They'll find you one day. But it won't be this winter. Or next.'

He sat on the stone steps, the movement of his limbs as fluid and unhurried as always.

'I know you were there when he died, because the billhook was from Grandad's chest. And you'd taken the key from behind the bar. But not alone, right? Kath said the three of you went together. And she'd added fuel to the fire, because she'd told Freddie about the baby coming. About me. Stupid, timid girl. If she'd told us then . . . But we can't change the past.'

'I don't understand,' said John Joe.

Ian's temper snapped and he threw the piece of timber he was holding so that it cartwheeled, hitting the stone wall. Then he walked slowly back up the stairs.

He didn't return for twenty minutes. At first the water only came in once every few minutes, swirling, but no worse, no deeper. But the tide didn't work like that. It surged after falling back,

384

gathering its strength. John Joe had surfed as a teenager, and he'd taught Ian, out on the windswept sands at Holkham. He knew all about the seventh wave. So there was a lull, and then a sudden curtain of white water at the door, and the room was full of the sea: not white this time but a livid green, a foot deep all around him, so that he had to jerk his neck up off the stone step. And cold, just above freezing. The first time he got his breathing just right, but the second time he swallowed a mouthful of seawater and he choked, spewing up over his chin and chest. This time, when the sea sucked out, it left kelp behind, and the white, dirty foam.

Then he heard the question again, although he hadn't heard Ian's footsteps on the stone stairs. Tears welled in his eyes and he shook his head, believing still perhaps that there was a way out, a stratagem that avoided confession. The next wave washed in, and this time when it ebbed there remained a foot of water in the room, a darker green this time, a hint of the pitch blackness of the deeper sea. John Joe could suck in air only if he held his head up, straining the neck muscles so that his body shook with the effort. Darkness was gathering outside the door, as if the bitter cold was extinguishing the light.

Ian came down the steps and with a knife from his back pocket cut the rope at his stepfather's left wrist so that he could roll on to one side, lifting his head slightly.

'There,' he said. 'A reprieve of sorts. For a while. A thank you — if you like, for bringing me up, for the kindnesses; and there's been love

— hasn't there? I can't deny that. But that's all over, gone.' He looked out of the open door at the sea. 'Tell me,' he said.

'It was Fletcher's idea,' said John Joe, and he said it quickly, because he believed now; believed his stepson would do this, leave him twisting here, roped down, so that he'd drown, sucking down mouthfuls of brine.

'He asked one of the waitresses for Pat's address; I heard him. So I knew he was planning something. That night — the night of the wake — we talked, out on the stoop. I loved Lizzie. I could see what was happening; I knew what was going on. I saw her once — when she thought no one was looking. She just reached forward and took something from the corner of his eye. It was a kiss — but with her fingertips. So I said to Fletcher we should teach Pat a lesson — scare him off. That was the plan.'

'And Venn?'

'He'd sent Pat those pictures — the hangman. Fletcher knew that. He said he didn't have the guts to actually *do* something, because the church was all talk — all sermon. It was all very well *reading* Leviticus, but what about living the book — Fletcher had picked that up, see? The phrase. He could play Sam like a fish on a line. So Sam came too.'

The sea washed in, round the room, funnelling out, but each time now leaving enough behind to lift John Joe's body, so that he was beginning to feel his weight seep away with his life.

'We were waiting for Pat in the cemetery — I could see him coming, walking: that walk of his,

386

that swagger.' He looked at Ian, desperate to see if his confession was softening the young man's eyes. 'Then he stopped. He didn't see us — it wasn't that. He'd got to the open grave, Nora's grave. There's a box tomb there, in stone. He sat there like it was a park bench.

'There was moonlight. But we were in shadows, by a cypress tree. The choir was singing and you could hear that, so the night wasn't silent.' He used his free hand to pat down the imaginary earth. 'We got down, on the grass. Fletcher said it was up to me and Sam to start it — to strike the first blow. We'd get him down, kick him. Freddie said he knew how to break a few bones, make him bleed, once he was down.'

Until that moment, Ian thought, John Joe had a life in front of him.

'But Sam said Fletcher should start it, because he knew the words: we'd heard him on the corner with his mates, calling at the blacks. How they should go home, how they weren't like us, how they were scum. So he should start — because it was important that Pat should know why we wanted him to go.'

John Joe heard laughter and realized it was his own, and how inappropriate it was.

'But Freddie wouldn't start it. He said I'd got the billhook — it was down to me. And it wasn't just about Pat's skin, was it? That wasn't why Sam was there. So why should it be him to start it? And the weird thing was, he was crying — Freddie — weeping. He said he'd do time if he got caught. He'd been rounded up the year before with some skinheads, for kicking this

Indian kid down by the docks. He'd got a fine, community service, and if he was caught doing it again there'd be time to do — eighteen months. He didn't fancy that. That's what he said — but I didn't believe it, I still don't. I think he just lost his nerve, and so he was ashamed.

'When he stopped crying he said to me not to hit Pat on the head — to go for an arm or a leg or the shoulder — that was good because the collarbone would snap like a chicken wing. Then he just walked away — through the gravestones, towards the east gate. We couldn't believe it. All that talk. All that hate.'

Ian watched the sea, a big wave buckling up on the grey horizon. 'So that left you and Sam Venn?' he said, edging a step higher, away from the water.

John Joe pulled frantically at the fastened wrist so that blood appeared where the skin was breaking.

'Sam did it. He just walked out in the moonlight, before I could stop him, so Pat could see him. And Pat just smiled — like he was expecting it. He just sat there in his silk shirt, looking at Sam. He'd brought a couple of glasses with him — the green, etched ones, and a hip flask. He'd drink a bit, then kind of wince, then smile.'

'Hip flask?'

Before John Joe could answer the sea washed in, the seventh wave, the one that surges forward up the beach. Two feet, three feet, swirling round the room so that Murray was gone, lost in the water, which wasn't green any more but a dark

388

blue, and black in the shadows. And when it sucked out he was just lying there, swamped, so Ian stepped off the ladder and got him by the shirt at the neck and held him up, so their faces were close. He could smell his stepfather's hair, the natural oils set against the sharp saltiness of the water.

'Quickly,' he said. 'The hip flask.' He put his hand to his back pocket and slipped something out to hold just a few inches from John Joe's drenched face. It was a silver hip flask. The design was unusual — a silver stopper and a silver base, but the main body was of green glass, thick and old, with an etched picture of a whale pursued by a boat, the harpoonist's arm tensed for the lethal shot.

John Joe's eyes didn't understand. 'Yeah, like the glasses — old Melville's green glasses. Lizzie must have given it to Pat.'

Ian unscrewed the top and put it to John Joe's lips. It was another kindness, and it gave him time to think. The flask contained a malt, and John Joe choked, but he drank too. Ian cut the other wrist free, then the ankles, and dragged his stepfather's body to the steps and up, clear of the sea, which had begun to turn in the room now like a whirlpool. He held his stepfather under the arms so that the older man lay on him, and the water seeped down.

It took Ian a minute to work it out, so that the past he'd imagined was transformed, like a landscape through tinted glass. 'Just tell me, John Joe,' he said. 'All of it.' John Joe's chin vibrated with the cold, so Ian left him and came back

389

down with a blanket.

'I stepped out into the open too,' he said, holding the corner of the warm wool to his throat. 'But Pat hardly noticed, because Sam went up to him and he took Pat's hand, like taking a child's, and he put it on his face, so that he could feel the damage that he'd been born with. Sam didn't say anything — I think he was too scared to speak. But I knew what it meant, and I think Pat did somehow, too. That it was evil, cousins together, and this was like God's punishment. I think that got to Pat — which was a victory for Sam, because nothing got to him. Not the taunts, not the way people looked at him. Nothing.'

They sat together for a few minutes without speaking. Outside the tide was moving rocks, so that intermittently the whole building resonated with the boom of stone on stone.

'He slapped Sam with that hand, the hand he'd touched him with,' said John Joe, breaking their silence. 'He slapped him hard. Pat was a big man, powerful, and it took Sam down. And then Pat got Sam's leg and he dragged him through the spoil around Nora's grave to the edge of the pit and he let him slip in. I heard the splash — 'cos by then it was full of water. Sam was screaming, pleading, but when he went in he was silent. I remember that because I heard the choir again — from the pub.

'I saw Sam's hands come up, scrabbling in the wet soil.' John Joe shook his head at the memory. 'Pat stamped on them, kicked soil in. Then he laughed and turned to me, walking away from the grave. Sam got out then, hauled himself out, and ran — along the river . . . so there was just me.'

Ian gave him the hip flask to drink again.

'I ran at Pat and swung the billhook; he swayed back, so I missed him. He just stood there, laughing in my face. I dropped the hook. I left him there, alive. I swear to God I did. I ran. Like we all ran.'

Ian held John Joe's head.

'Later — when Pat disappeared we thought he'd just got tired of Lizzie. Then the baby came and we thought that explained it. He'd run for it too. And the three of us thought we'd helped push him away. Helped him run.'

John Joe looked at his wrists where the blood was beginning to ooze from the wounds made by the rope.

'When they found Pat — Pat's bones — they thought I'd done it: both of them, Fletcher and Venn. I said I hadn't. I said I'd always told the truth, but they didn't believe me.'

Outside the door the snow had suddenly stopped, leaving the air clear, the horizon as sharp as a knife edge. 'I don't know who killed him, Son — I really don't.'

Ian looked at the hip flask in his hand.

'I do,' he said.

39

Shaw waited in the Porsche for Valentine, parked in the shadow of the industrial crane on the Lynn town quayside. Angular, black and towering, it stood out against a field of frosty stars. It seemed to reflect Shaw's mood of gloomy introspection. It had not been a good day: it had taken them until mid-afternoon to track down 'Gav' — aka Gavin Andrew Peck — their one vital witness to the reopening of Nora Tilden's grave. He had been staying at a friend's house after an all-night party and had then gone to the Arndale Centre to hang out with friends in the warmth of the shopping mall. His recollection of the woman he'd seen that night was limited to her gender: he could recall no other detail. They'd taken him back to St James's but his memory had shown no signs of sharpening up. Could he estimate the age of the woman? 'Not really — but it was obvious she'd never used a spade before. She was really struggling.' It was the one cogent observation they'd obtained.

After taking a formal statement from Peck, Shaw and Valentine had been called to separate preparatory interviews with DI 'Chips' McCain — now in charge of the investigation into Bobby Mosse. McCain's approach, at least in Shaw's case, had been clinical, professional, and chilling. He and Valentine had not compared notes.

The bonnet of the Porsche was hot and free of snow, but as Valentine levered himself out of the car, the motion set free a lump of ice which slid down the windscreen. Shaw batted it aside with the wipers, hardly allowing it to displace the image that he'd begun examining in his head: a woman, alone, digging in the shadows of the Flensing Meadow, down into that crowded grave. Not just an image — a noise as well, the slicing of a spade through clay and grit. Which woman? Lizzie Tilden was involved in the search for her missing husband John Joe, so they'd leave her for the morning. Bea Garrison they'd see tonight, at her B&B on the coast at Wells.

Shaw focused on the Christmas lights along the front: sharp pinpoints of festive colour in the sea air which usually lifted his mood. The mobile chip shop had parked in a lay-by, side-on to the water, half a dozen figures crowded by the serving hatch, cradling teas.

Then his mobile rang and he saw it was home, so he picked it up, and knew instantly that it was his daughter, not his wife, because she took a breath before starting to speak.

'Dad? It's OK — Mum said. We'll go next year.' Static blurred the next sentence.

'Sorry — I just can't.' He hated apologies, thinking that they were what they were, valueless in themselves. What he needed to do was make sure that next year he kept his promise, and took her to see Santa floating in on the tide at Wells, and that he wasn't stuck in a car waiting for George Valentine to get him a tray of chips. And he left the real question in the air: would Fran want to see Santa next year, or had they missed the moment, another slice of childhood he'd never revisit?

'We got the results back — from the hospital?' She sounded upbeat, so Shaw feared the worst. Her voice came and went.

'It's some colour I'm allergic to — but they can't say which one . . . '

'OK,' said Shaw. 'Is Mum there?'

She gave him a long drawn out, sing-song 'Bye-eee'.

Lena was sharp, businesslike. 'Where are you?'

'Quayside — signal's dreadful. Must be the storm passing through. I've got to see the team, get up to speed, complete an interview — then I'll ring. Case has just turned itself upside down, again.' She didn't fill the silence up so he pressed on. 'Fran said the allergy clinic had results?'

'Yup. Simple, really — it's something in milk reacting with something in one of the food colourings. Put 'em together and she gets an attack. Houghton — the consultant? He said it would wear off like the milk allergy. Meantime we have to avoid the E-number. I've got a note. But it's part of whatever makes a colour, not the colour itself. So it's not straightforward — but then it never is.'

'Great. She OK?' In the background he could hear the old dog whining, jealous of the attention he was losing.

A further burst of static cut out some of the reply. 'She'd rather be watching Santa float by — but she'll live,' said Lena, her voice floating back with the signal. 'If you'd said earlier, Peter,

394

I could have taken her, but it'll be murder down there now and I can't go out — I've got a shop full of stock and the Speedo rep's due any minute.'

'I know. Sorry. That's where we're headed — Wells. But it's business, not pleasure, I don't think George believes in Santa any more. And you're right, it'll be packed, we're going to give it another half hour, let the crowds get in place at least. I'd better go,' he said, changing his voice, knowing that if he kept the conversation going he'd end up in an argument.

'Me too,' she said. 'Fran's just seen Justina out on the beach, so we're taking the dog out. Bye.'

The line went dead. He thought about the pathologist, the Labrador dogging her steps along the high-tide mark. Valentine pulled the door open and threw himself into the seat, cradling wrapped chips and takeaway tea.

They ate in silence. Then Shaw stopped, because he had that very odd feeling that his brain was working on something, processing detail, trundling towards a synthesis of images, a process sparked by what Lena had told him about Fran's allergy. He thought about the little pillboxes in a line in the bathroom.

He let three specific images float into his conscious mind.

First: Bea Garrison standing behind the dispensary counter of the store in Hartsville, North Dakota. Shaw imagined a white coat, her hair held up with pins, brown paper packets for the drugs. He knew it hadn't been like that, that this image was culled from 1950s black-and-white movies, but it was a vivid snapshot nonetheless.

Second: a soup dish on an abandoned table at the Shipwrights' Hall, some liquid left in the bottom, the outline of a cockle in the thick fishy sauce.

And the third image: Ian Murray, pushing his way backwards through the door marked STAFF into the dining room at the Flask, in his hands three plates loaded with food, heading for a table with three waiting diners.

He scrunched the chip paper and kicked open his door to walk to the bin. He could have stashed it in the car, but he wanted to think in the open air. By the time he got back to the Porsche he'd done thinking, and his body screamed for action. He'd hit 60 mph by the time he got the car to the end of the quay, leaving Valentine to pick chips off his lap.

40

Shaw left Valentine in the Porsche with what was left of the chips and ran to the café along the dark sands. He could have rung Justina but if they were out with the dogs the signal would be weak. And he wanted to get this straight. He needed the medical science, and he needed it now. Because if he was right, then this was the key, the lynch pin. The beach was empty, cleaned by the storm which had blown out, so that the only marks on the pristine moonlit strand were Justina's footsteps. The air was still, the dune grass was frosted, the edge of the sea just trembling on the sand.

He ran up the wooden steps and pushed open the café door.

They were all sitting around a table, Lena and Fran and Justina, and on the polished floor-boards over by the stove, the dogs. Lena had made tea and there was a plate of sliced cake in the middle of the table, but no one had taken any. So he knew something was wrong because the cake was simnel, his daughter's favourite, and her plate was clean.

Before he could sit down Lena shook her head.

'It's Dawid, Peter,' she said. 'He died.'

Justina looked pathetically grateful that some-one else had said it.

Shaw knew that if he didn't touch Justina now

he never would again: that it was one of those moments in a friendship when you have to redraw the boundaries.

He knelt beside her seat and put an arm around her shoulders.

'I'm sorry,' he said. He saw Dawid, sat at this table, and the sudden unanticipated sight of blood on his gum.

'It's not unexpected, Peter,' she said, but her eyes filled as she spoke, one spilling tears. But the shock was real enough, and had changed her face so that it was much more mobile than usual, the emotions running across it like a wind over wheat. She drank her tea, declining Shaw's offer to stiffen it with a whisky shot.

Dawid had been diagnosed eight months earlier, she explained. Polycythaemia vera, PV to a doctor. A rare blood disease in which the body makes too many red blood cells. The extra red blood cells make your blood sticky. The thickened blood flows more slowly through your small blood vessels and forms clots. They cause heart attack and stroke. They knew he wouldn't live — not for long; there isn't a cure, just treatment.

Dawid had always wanted to live by the sea. They'd been saving the move for retirement, but after his diagnosis they'd sold up immediately and moved to the coast. The end had come a few hours ago. A sudden massive stroke as Dawid slept by the picture window. She'd been with him, watching his face change as gravity took control.

They'd taken the body away, leaving Justina a

lonely widow in an empty house.

'So I came here,' she said. She paused then and Shaw sensed that if she didn't go on immediately she'd cry. She took in a breath. 'I had a favour to ask,' she said. Her hand crept towards the tea cup, then pulled back. 'I wondered — if you didn't mind — if I could take Fran out. Not now,' she added, laughing tightly. 'I don't know — once a week? Whenever it's OK with you. Only, there's no family, some cousins in Poland. But no family really. And I'd enjoy that. Only if she wants? We could walk the dogs.'

Fran nodded her head quickly. Justina leant forward, took a slice of simnel and put it on Fran's plate.

Shaw stood. 'I'm sorry. I'd have liked to have known Dawid better.' He zipped up his jacket, looking back along the beach. 'George's waiting. I've got to go. I should be taking Fran to the Christmastide at Wells. But work . . . and Lena has to stay here. Work too.'

Fran studied her simnel cake.

Justina stood. 'I'll take her,' she said, as Shaw had known she would.

'I can drop you both off, but I can't stay.'

'Peter . . . ' said Lena, taking Justina's hand. 'For goodness' sake.'

Justina stood. 'I'd like that. That's a good idea.' She turned to Lena. 'What else am I going to do tonight?'

'There'll be crowds — can you take that?' cautioned Shaw.

'Crowds are best,' said Justina. 'Really.'

Ten minutes later Fran got in the back of the

Porsche, Valentine squeezed in beside her, while Justina took the passenger seat in the front, because Shaw asked her to sit and talk. When they were up on the coast road he was the first to speak.

'This isn't just for Fran,' he said, looking in the rearview. 'It's the case. I need you to tell me something, Justina.' In the back he could hear Fran cross-examining Valentine about what he remembered about her grandfather. She'd always known Valentine had been a friend. When she asked Shaw she got the same anecdotes each time. She thought Valentine might know something new.

Justina's body language was clear. Shaw was pretty certain she was in shock. Her left arm kept rising, the hand seeking a place to rest. But he didn't have time to camouflage the question.

'When I was at Hendon I did a course on poisons. But I've forgotten almost everything. I just need the basics — quickly.' The road was Roman-straight for half a mile, so he took his eyes off the road and looked at her. 'Tell me about toxic synergy.'

41

The Porsche purred in a traffic jam, and Shaw
could see ahead the line of cars snaking down
towards the waterfront at Wells-next-the-Sea.
The car in front lurched, trundled six feet then
braked sharply, the back bumper rising with the
abruptly arrested forward motion. In the
distance he could see the high mast of the Dutch
barge by the quay, decked with fairy lights. On
both sides of the line of cars children and
parents walked past, bundled in winter clothes.
Everyone was late. The snow had stopped,
swelling the crowd, but the temperature had
dropped with the loss of the cloud cover, and
steam rose from the people as if they were cattle
in a winter field.

'Remind me why we're here,' said Valentine,
leaning forward, while Fran looked out at the
crowds. The car crawled past a shopfront where
a man shared a match with a woman, the
resulting halo of cigarette smoke embracing
them both.

'Because if our witness is correct, then a woman
tried to dig up Pat Garrison's impromptu grave,'
said Shaw, answering his question but speaking
to Justina. He tried and failed to hide the excitement in his voice, the surge of adrenaline which
had been triggered in his system by the pathologist's brief description of the principles of toxic
synergy.

He took a deep breath. 'Up until now we had three male suspects for the murder of Pat Garrison: three suspects someone has tried to kill — so I suspect we weren't the only ones who had them lined up for it. But the point is, we now have a woman involved. A woman suspect. Question: which woman?'

The line of traffic juddered forward and Shaw swung the car right, along the road which led to the nearest car park, giving up any chance of getting through the centre of town to Morston House.

Shaw struggled to concentrate, half of his conscious mind recovering from his memory a long-lost lecture on toxic synergy. It had been in the main lecture theatre at Hendon, an old-fashioned 1930s amphitheatre. The science staff at the college had substances in glass jars on the scarred wooden bench at the front. An overhead projector showed atoms and molecules colliding, reforming. And one image of a victim. It was a woman in her fifties, the body lying in a damp cellar, the limbs held in awkward semaphore positions.

'So if we're looking for a woman, then — again — we have three possible suspects,' continued Shaw. 'First, Lizzie Murray. Jealous, maybe — perhaps there was another woman? Sounds like Pat inherited his father's eye for the girls. But it doesn't look likely — first off, *she* wanted to ring the police next morning, long before there was any real need, and long before she could be sure the grave had been filled in completely by Fletcher and his mate. And then

402

there's the child — Pat's child, their child. She'd be unlikely to kill the father. And all the witnesses are clear on her state of mind later that evening: Bea said she was happy, and, more to the point, your sister Jean — our unbelievably valuable objective witness — said Lizzie was positively luminous that night. She didn't shut the pub till after midnight, and we can assume Pat was dead by then, because we've got witness statements from people who walked through the cemetery after closing time and didn't see him. So — we shouldn't forget Lizzie, but it's unlikely she wielded the billhook.

'Then there's Bea. Motive? Maybe she hoped her son wouldn't get involved with Lizzie. She likes Lizzie — no doubt about that — but she hates the Flask and all it stands for. And, of course, the two were cousins. Did she follow him out that night to try to cool him down only to find she was too late, that there was a child on the way? Perhaps tempers were frayed. Pat had come to England unwillingly — we know that. His mum had tried to keep him happy — there was always cash in his pocket. Did he blame her for the mess he was in? It could have happened. And there's something else — I'm certain . . . ' He thought about that. 'Yes, certain, that Bea helped Alby poison Fletcher and Venn, and that she'd have happily poisoned John Joe too. She thought the three of them killed her son because Kath Robinson told her they'd gone ahead to wait for him in the cemetery. Think about that, George. If Bea's behind the killings, which are clearly an act of revenge by someone who thinks

Fletcher, Venn and Murray killed Pat Garrison, then she's pretty much clear of the original murder.'

'Could have been a cover,' said Valentine. 'Perhaps she did both: killed Pat, then helped Alby take revenge on three innocent men — which threw all of us off the scent, didn't it?' Valentine held up both hands. 'And how'd she target the three of them? How did she help Alby?'

'OK — I'll deal with that. But let me finish. Because that leaves the best suspect for Pat Garrison's murder — Kath Robinson.'

The first firework went off in the clear sky over the dunes — a yellow expanding glove of light. Fran screamed in the back. They felt the thud of the explosion and then a long drawn-out cheer, like a wave breaking.

They were still bumper to bumper on the approach road to the car park. Shaw checked his watch: high tide, and 8.45 p.m. His temper finally snapped, because he couldn't sit still with this much adrenaline in his bloodstream. He gently rolled the Porsche up on to the pavement, jumped out and retrieved a magnetic flashing warning light from the boot and put it on the roof, instantly quelling a protest from the driver behind — a father in a people carrier with children packed on the back seats and the head of a red setter sticking out of the passenger-side window.

They abandoned the car, cut down an alleyway between two shops and found themselves on the edge of the dockside. But they couldn't see the black water for the crowd, already ten deep at the iron railings.

Shaw put a hand on Justina's shoulder. 'I'm fine,' she said.

Shaw showed her his mobile. 'We'll give you a lift home. Stay at the cottage tonight. Lena's getting a bed ready. I insist. Fran, you help Justina have a lovely time.'

'I promise,' she said seriously, taking the pathologist by the hand and leading her away.

Valentine stopped, lit up.

'Why Kath Robinson?'

'Come on,' said Shaw, cutting along the back of the crowd, talking over his shoulder, forcing himself to slow down so that Valentine could keep up. 'Lot of reasons, but most of all because she's the wellspring — if she hadn't conveniently recalled what she'd seen that night, Fletcher and Venn would still be alive. It's a vivid picture, right — seeing the three of them set out, planning to teach Pat Garrison a lesson, and then she bumps into the victim leaving the Flask, just at the right time. And who'd she tell? The family — talk about lighting the blue touch paper.'

They heard a firework, like machine-gun fire.

'Then she comes down to Lynn and tells her mum — who's one of Jean's best friends, the widow of a copper, the sister of a copper, someone she could trust to pass the information along. If not straight to us then out into the community, out into the rumour mill. The only person who wasn't going to hear it was John Joe. No one's going to tell him, are they?'

Shaw looked over the heads of the throng towards the waterfront, past the brightly lit fish 'n' chip shops and the pubs towards Morston House. He pressed on through the crowd. Fireworks thudded with a regular beat now, and somewhere down by the harbour office a brass band played 'In the Deep Midwinter'.

'And Kath had a motive, George,' he said, suddenly brought up short by a family of six strung across the pavement, holding hands. 'I don't think Pat raped her, or even touched her. I just think he may have been her first love. Whatever happened changed her life. Rejection is what happened, and she's not exactly well equipped to deal with emotion, any emotion. Perhaps she's telling the truth, perhaps Fletcher and Venn did talk to her that night, telling her what was up. And maybe that was the trigger. That and being told — by Lizzie herself — that there was a baby on the way. Perhaps she didn't want to spend the rest of her life watching Pat and Lizzie play happy families. Maybe that was a prospect she couldn't live with. I don't think she set out to kill him, but she must have been angry. Burning angry. And she could have gone upstairs just as easily as John Joe. She'd have seen Alby wielding the gun. She could have taken the billhook.'

They skirted round a stage which had been set up to welcome Santa Claus when his boat came in on the tide. As they did so, more fireworks broke over the sea and they could see the white yachts along the channel, most of them lit with Chinese lanterns.

Valentine put a hand on Shaw's shoulder from behind, a rare physical contact. 'And Bea — how *did* she target them? How'd she get them and not the rest?'

Shaw was going to tell him then, but he was looking across the road, back up the little high street that led away from the water, a narrow cobbled lane crowded on either side with old-fashioned shops, lit by a zigzag string of white lights.

Looking their way, but past them out to sea, was Kath Robinson. There was a sudden cheer and she smiled, because out along the channel, near the lifeboat station, Santa's ship had come into view, pulled by a pair of inflatable reindeer and surrounded by a flotilla of small boats. Then she turned and began to walk away, pulling a suitcase on wheels.

42

As Shaw ran after Kath Robinson he heard the double echo of his boots hitting cobbles, bouncing off the shopfronts of the narrow high street. The crowd on the quayside was cheering now, a constant ebb and flow of sound like the sea on the sand. A family ran past them down the street, the father with a baby held in a carrier on his shoulders, one of the children crying. The street was so narrow, almost too narrow for a single car, that the shops seemed to reach out to each other, trying to touch — a toy shop unlit, a bakery, a hardware store with empty hooks above a bay window. An ageing Labrador swung its head from side to side, padding down towards the crowd, pursuing the running family.

'Miss Robinson!' Shaw didn't call out until they were almost with her, because even then he thought she might just run, ditch the suitcase, so he was already on his toes.

She turned and Shaw saw the disappointment in her eyes, but nothing else, so that he wondered for the first time if he might be wrong.

'Yes,' she said, setting the suitcase upright.

She looked at her watch. 'I've not much time,' she said. 'My car's up by the church and this crowd will be on its way home soon.'

In the white light she should have looked pale, but her face was flushed, and Shaw thought that for the first time she might have the capacity to be happy. Her blonde hair was pinned back, her head bare despite the cold. She wore a quilted jacket, good quality, but shapeless.

'I thought you lived at Morston House,' said Shaw.

She settled back on her heels, crossing her arms across her breasts. In most people it was a stance that radiated confidence. But, as always with this woman, Shaw thought it looked like an impersonation of confidence rather than the real thing. 'I don't understand,' she said.

Shaw looked up and down the empty street. 'Someone — a woman — was seen digging up Nora Tilden's grave last June. We think she was trying to recover something; something incriminating, perhaps. We think she may have been Pat Garrison's killer.'

Her face was blank, and Shaw wondered what kind of mind worked behind that perfect skin.

'I thought that woman might be you. And that would explain why you were running away.'

'I told you the truth,' she said. She blinked several times and Shaw was certain she hadn't understood the accusation. It was the kind of misunderstanding only the innocent make.

She unzipped a pocket on the suitcase, took out a travel wallet and gave it to Shaw.

As he reached into his jacket for a torch she looked back down the high street to where Santa's boat had just arrived at the quay: a figure clad not in the usual Disney scarlet but in russet, with a crown of winter berries and what looked like a real white beard. Camera flashlights popped and someone out of sight began to address the crowd through a megaphone.

Inside the travel wallet was a return ticket to Tenerife, boat tickets to Gomera and a brochure for a holiday village — whitewashed apartments beside a beach dotted with parasols.

'It's a present from Bea,' she said. 'I've always said she owes me nothing but she's been good — more than that, she's been family, really. Finding Pat, finding his bones, brought it back for both of us. We've both been bad. She was going to come . . . ' She nodded at the tickets. 'But she wants to be near Lizzie — and Lizzie won't leave the Flask.'

Shaw didn't answer. He was looking at the plane ticket. London Heathrow to Tenerife North. LHR to TFN.

Valentine filled in the gap. 'It must have been bitter news — when Lizzie told you she was pregnant, that Pat was the father. Is that why you tried to stir it up with Freddie Fletcher, telling him the black kid had his feet under the table? That he was family now. That one day he'd be running the Flask. Did you follow them out there? Did you take the billhook with you?' He stopped, dragging in a fresh breath. 'Did you finish it when they wouldn't?'

She looked suddenly genuinely exhausted. 'No. Really. I don't — didn't — hate Pat. Freddie was a friend. I knew him from school — he was a couple of years above Lizzie and me. I just wanted to share it — like you do, when you get news.'

Valentine noted that she hadn't said 'good' news.

410

'It was supposed to be a secret, wasn't it?' pressed Valentine. 'Lizzie's secret.'

'She told me fast enough,' said Robinson, unable to keep the bitterness out of her voice. 'I thought she'd tell everyone by last orders.'

'What did you think Fletcher would do — start knitting socks?' said Valentine, concerned that Shaw seemed to have given up on the cross-examination. The DI was still studying Robinson's airline reservation.

Kath Robinson looked at her watch. Shaw handed back the travel wallet. 'You can go,' he said. 'We know where you are. We'll need to speak when you get back.'

'Perhaps I should stay?' Not a statement, a question.

'No. It's OK,' said Shaw.

She looked at Valentine, as if asking his permission as well, then flipped the suitcase back on its wheels. Down by the water's edge the civic party had welcomed Santa Claus aboard a tractor-drawn float. It turned, heading for the church, and behind it the crowd scrambled to squeeze between the narrow shopfronts of the high street.

'You'd better go,' said Shaw. He tried to smile, but an image of Dawid Kazimierz looking out to sea made him give it up half done. They watched her hurry away, one of the wheels on the suitcase trolley squealing. Valentine waited for an explanation — several explanations — but Shaw turned towards the oncoming crowd and plunged in, his mobile already at his ear.

43

Bea Garrison was standing on the balcony of Morston House wrapped in a Barbour, looking out over the now deserted waterfront. Santa's boat lay moored, the inflatable reindeer buckling slightly on the ebbing tide, a light wind exhaling from the streets of the town as if it were preparing for sleep. On a yacht out in the channel a family sat in the cockpit eating, the sound of a champagne cork bouncing back off the façades of the fish 'n' chip shops.

There were three flights of stairs to the balcony and Shaw reached the top well before Valentine.

'Alone?' asked Shaw.

Bea turned her face, the ship's fine figurehead, away from the sea to look at him. Below they heard Valentine's mobile ring, followed by a whispered conversation.

'Always,' she said. 'It's not a problem.' She touched a finger to her face, smoothing the single patch of makeup she wore.

She was standing, leaning easily on the low wall, a glass of white wine on the ledge. Shaw guessed it was a favourite spot; an escape from the people she had to let into her home.

'We don't have time,' said Shaw. 'John Joe's life is in danger — it may even be too late. But you know that. You tried to kill him before, at the Shipwrights' Hall lunch.'

She was prepared for that. Sipping the white wine, she used one hand to fasten the top button at her chin, then tighten a cashmere scarf.

'It's a cliché — but I really do have no idea what you're talking about, Inspector.'

'Toxic synergy,' said Shaw. She was a very still person, but even Shaw sensed an instant immobility, as if those two words had turned her to stone.

Valentine arrived, out of breath, a thin veneer of sweat on his narrow forehead and showing through the thinning hair. He still held the mobile in his hand. 'No sign of John Joe,' he said. 'Lizzie's frightened now. Jacky Lau says she thinks that if he's gone anywhere in the boat it would be here.'

Bea Garrison had spent her life maintaining an impenetrable exterior, but Shaw could see she was struggling now, her eyes drawn back out to sea, to the lights in the channel and beyond, to the darkness of the marshes. Shaw scanned the quayside, the mid-channel moorings, but there was no sign of John Joe's clinker-built sailing boat.

'We don't have time for this, Mrs Garrison. If John Joe Murray dies, you will be responsible. Where is he?'

She set her hard face to the sea. Out along the quayside a council Scarab swirled up the rubbish. Towards the dunes a bonfire flickered. Shaw was struck again by how imperious Bea Garrison was, how she'd carved a life for herself, a woman alone, deserted by men: first a husband she didn't love who drank himself to death, and

413

then — as far as she'd known for the last three decades — by the son she did love. But she'd survived, prospered in a way, and then, provided with the names of the men who'd killed that son, she'd organized a clinical and lethal revenge.

'We know you told Alby that night — at the Clockcase — about what Kath had seen,' said Shaw. 'Did he mention the Shipwrights' Hall lunch then? It's an annual affair. Every year he'd worked at the cannery he'd have seen the order go through. So he knew the Flask would have a table and that all three of your targets would be there. And I think it was you who thought of revenge — an almost instant retaliation. You asked Kath Robinson not to tell us what happened, didn't you? What did you say? That after all those years it was unlikely — nearly impossible — that we'd be able to make a case against them? But she didn't listen. That's the neighbourhood vice around the Flask — gossip.

'But that didn't mean the three of them couldn't be punished. That they couldn't suffer. So you told Alby to lace the cans. You knew they'd have the soup, of course — they eat at the Flask every week, so you knew they were all keen on seafood. And local fare. It's a guess, but I think you didn't tell him how it would work, or that they'd die. He'd have to trust you — trust that only they would really suffer. And anyway, he knew that the dose he was giving them wasn't lethal — it doesn't even work on the rats every time.'

She turned her back on the sea and looked up at the tower of Morston House, and Shaw

414

wondered if she was saying goodbye, trying to imprint a memory that she could take with her.

'Toxic synergy,' he said. 'Occupational hazard if you're a chemist. Which you were, of course. You, Mrs Garrison, not Latrell. That was a lie — and a desperate one. So I think you suggested using the rat poison to make them suffer, then went out to the poison bin to check on its chemical composition. And perhaps that's when you realized you could do it. Kill just those three and nobody else.'

Across the water the sound of a second champagne bottle opening bounded to them.

'The real question,' said Shaw, 'is what did you tell Ian.'

Shaw smiled and took one of the wooden chairs. Out in the channel a water rat surfaced and swam towards the open sea, leaving a perfect V-shaped wake.

'Because that was part two of the plan — the part Alby didn't know about. Before they got to Alby's rat poison at the Shipwrights' Hall you needed to make sure they each had a dose of mercury in their bloodstream. Just a bit — nothing fatal. Again, a non-lethal dose. And they got that, I'd guess, at lunch on Tuesday at the Flask. A lunch Ian cooked. Angry, bitter, Ian. Three daily specials: grilled salmon with bubble and squeak and winter vegetables. And here I'm guessing again. I don't think Ian knew the two halves of the plan, did he? You asked him to trust you, just like you'd asked Alby.

'It's the ultimate toxic synergy: aluminium and mercury. Individually slow acting and non-lethal,

415

but put them together and the result is guaranteed. It's a textbook study: give a hundred rats a dose of aluminium and on average one will die; give a hundred rats a dose of mercury and on average one will die; give a hundred rats a dose of both and they'll all die. Every time.'

Valentine lit a Silk Cut, absorbed by Shaw's account.

Bea turned towards them, a hand finding the wooden shelf on the low balcony wall without looking, an action of familiarity which reminded Shaw of Lizzie Murray reaching for the fruit-machine switch behind the bar of the Flask.

An ice bucket stood in the corner, and she walked to it now and refilled the glass of wine.

'I like it cold,' she said. 'Icy.'

She stared Shaw in his blind eye.

'I'm not sure you have a single item of evidence to support this fanciful scenario,' she said. But her age betrayed her: the wine glass rocking as the tendons in her arm failed to smoothly elevate it to her lips.

'You have three problems,' said Shaw. 'Alby is happy to confess to his side of the plan — although I will concede that he'll never implicate you directly, as he is actually pretty keen to spend the rest of his life in a secure cell at Lincoln. I just wonder how coherent his testimony would be under cross-examination. Especially as his sabotage was carried out *before* the discovery of Pat Garrison's bones was made public, and he admits to seeing you only hours before he laced the cans. Second, I think Freddie Fletcher fell ill during his lunch at the Flask. I

416

think the mercury was in the salmon — he started feeling nauseous before he'd finished, so he used the foil from his sweetcorn cob to wrap up the fish. It's a generation thing: waste not, want not. He wouldn't have suspected the meal he was currently eating. Probably blamed it on a dodgy curry the night before. It's in his fridge, the salmon. Well, it was in his fridge — it's in our forensic lab now. Where we will also be spending some of our budget on a more thorough examination of the stomach contents of Fletcher and Venn. We'll find the mercury, although I suspect the amounts will be truly microscopic. Because that's the dreadful beauty of toxic synergy — the traces of the two poisons can be almost undetectable, especially if you're not looking for them.

'And third, and most importantly, Fletcher, Venn and Murray didn't kill your son.'

She shook her head and tried a laugh, but it died in her throat.

'How do we know this? Well, initially we ignored several pieces of evidence which didn't fit the scenario painted by Kath Robinson — a story, by the way, which I'm sure was genuine in outline.'

'Such as?' She tried to make the question sound casual, but even Valentine detected the edge in her voice, as if she was about to choke.

'The two green glasses we found with Pat's bones, for a start. Why two?'

Bea took a sip of wine.

'But the real breakthrough came just a few minutes ago. Right here. We bumped into Kath

Robinson. She showed us the airline ticket you'd bought her. A kindness you will regret.'

Valentine's mobile rang and he turned away, walking down a few steps.

'Your son died with a piece of paper in his pocket. There's not much left now — shreds. But we could see three letters: bold capitals. MOT — not part of a word, there were no letters missing just those three, so that was it — like a code for something. Something like an airport.'

Valentine came back. 'The Flask — 999 call: ambulance, police, the lot.'

Bea Garrison held the wine glass, poised, but the rim dipped and the liquid began to fall to the ground. Shaw thought she'd be cold now: icy. He couldn't imagine the thoughts she must be struggling with, but he sensed there would be an image in her mind of the home she'd once had on the other side of the world, and perhaps the last time she'd left it, rising through the thin Midwestern clouds above North Dakota.

Shaw showed her his mobile. 'I've just checked MOT is the airport code for Minot, North Dakota. A small municipal airport then, but the one Pat would have used to go home. And that's what he had in his pocket that night. His ticket home. Away from the Flask, and you, and the life you'd tried to make for him. But most of all it was a ticket home away from Lizzie.'

44

A crowd of sixty or seventy stood outside the Flask. The snow fell now as if with relief; a teeming blizzard of wet flakes, the clouds so low that the top floor of the former council flats was lost in the gloom. When he'd dropped Justina and Fran at the lifeboat house on the way into town they'd seen the overburdened clouds banked on the horizon, lit by the moon, edging towards the coast. Most of the spectators had brought their drinks out with them, and as Shaw parked the Porsche he heard laughter, thrilling through the crowd like electricity. The Flask looked as it would have looked when the whalers were still stripping flesh on the fields beyond, the snow masking any hint of the twenty-first century, hanging off the rough brickwork and the timbered frame.

The front door of the pub swung open as Shaw and Valentine made their way through the crowd to a half-hearted chorus of boos.

Fiona Campbell shut the door behind them. 'Sir.'

Shaw looked round. The inside of the pub looked like the *Mary Celeste*. The empty tables dotted with drinks, a tape still playing Christmas favourites, the tree in one corner decked with flickering lights.

'The barman opened up at six,' said Campbell. 'Lizzie Murray was here — but no sign of John Joe or the son, Ian. Mrs Murray went down to change a barrel and found the watergate open . . . '

They heard noises from behind the bar but saw nothing until a paramedic appeared from the cellar. He brushed past them, out to the ambulance, without speaking.

Shaw led the way. The trapdoor was open, the cool dampness of the cellar welling up into the close humidity of the bar. The narrow space between the barrels was full of ambulance gear: a stretcher, a mobile cardiac unit, blankets, a medicine chest. In the gutter lay the thick spillage from the beer. Yeast, thought Shaw. It had been Murray's footprints on Sam Venn's stairs.

The semicircular watergate was still open, framing the dark river on which the snowflakes settled like miniature lilies. On the far side they could see the Clockcase Cannery, just visible, the illusion almost complete now: that it was a liner, edging from the quayside, bound for an Atlantic crossing.

Shaw stepped out on to the stone quay. Below him lay the wooden clinker-built sailing boat they'd seen when they'd first come down to interview John Joe Murray. He was in it, lying on an overcoat, wrapped in blankets. His eyes were open, but studied the falling snow. One ankle was bare, and Shaw winced at the sight of the raw wound where a rope had cut down through the flesh. He pushed aside an image of Jimmy Voyce's shattered leg, his broken, transparent body.

A paramedic was kneeling beside Murray, checking his pulse.

Shaw put a foot in the boat, expertly counterbalancing his weight by putting a hand on the far gunwale. He squatted down, trying to get close to Murray's face. The smell was extraordinary — the smell of the sea, like the crushed ice on a fishmonger's stall. Shaw noted the salt drying on his face.

'Where's Ian?' he asked, close enough now to see that there was still life in those remarkable green eyes.

'The sea chest,' said Murray, and Shaw realized he wasn't watching the snow fall, he was studying the lit attic windows above. 'He's up there now. He knows the truth.' He licked his cracked upper lip. 'Keep Lizzie away.'

Shaw sensed someone at his back and turned to see paramedics, the stretcher between them. He retreated to the cellar, where Valentine was briefing Fiona Campbell. 'Get a description out to St James's,' Valentine told her, then, noting Shaw, added, 'Landlady's missing. Shortly after he turned up,' he said, nodding to the watergate. 'Barman said she'd been hit — bloody lip, and she was crying — pretty much out of control.'

They heard the water slapping against the quay outside.

'Get a unit along the riverside, Fiona,' said Shaw. 'She might do something stupid. George — follow me.'

As they climbed the narrow wooden stairs behind the bar Shaw looked over the banisters and saw John Joe, flat on the stretcher, being carried out through the coffin-shaped door to the bar. Even in the minute since he'd last seen him the colour had returned to his face, the flesh three-dimensional, alive again. A few seconds later the distant sound of the crowd, joyful, festive, died instantly.

At the first landing Shaw halted, unable to suppress the image of Nora Tilden falling, her bones breaking, until she lay in a jagged heap on the floorboards below. The last flight, a corkscrew, climbed into the roof of the old building to the door like a man-sized cat-flap, hinged at the top. Shaw pushed his way through, stooping, his hand on the smooth surface of the old oak floor.

Ian was kneeling in front of his grandfather's sea chest. His hands, palms up, were pale in the light that poured in through one of the dormer windows from the street lamp outside, casting deep shadows in the otherwise unlighted attic. The heavy, silently falling snow produced an odd effect, dappling the orange light as if reflected off moving water.

With a sudden burst of sound the ambulance pulled away from the front of the pub, the siren ringing out briefly.

'What happened to John Joe?' asked Shaw.

'He told the truth,' he said. 'At last. It's only taken twenty-eight years.'

Ian looked at his hand and Shaw saw a dark stain. 'You hit your mother?'

'Yes,' he said. 'That's all. Just once.' He looked about him as if only now aware of where he was. His body turned at the hips, and Shaw noticed

422

for the first time that on his lap was a silver flask: oddly designed, the body in thick glass, the stopper and base metallic.

Ian picked it up. 'Strange where you find the truth,' he said. 'Even John Joe didn't know, because he didn't know what this meant . . .' He put the flask on top of the sea chest.

'I come up here a lot,' he said, settling back on his heels. 'It's like a link — to family. I've always had Mum — but I felt she was always holding back, as if any display of emotion would let something out, something she wanted to keep inside.' He nodded, seeing how true that was. 'So I'd come up here, see if I could feel the past. Last night I came up again. The ship's log is my favourite because Grandad filled it in, after they found the ship again. They saw an iceberg — did you know that? Just, like, *there*, one morning, a few hundred yards from the ship. He says they could feel it — the cold — on their faces.' He shook his head in wonder. 'I understand why he doesn't want to see me — but I think it's unfair. Selfish.'

Shaw didn't answer. Valentine was wondering how hard he'd hit his mother.

'Because it's like Grandad has run away, too, just like I thought Dad did. But it's worse, because I know he's been near, watching, and there's been so many times I wanted to speak to him but I couldn't. So . . . ' He looked around, seeing his fixation as pathetic. 'I used to come up here, though not for a while. But last night I came up for a lantern — a storm lantern. I knew where John Joe was — out at the old coal barn at

Wells, on the marshes. Aunt Bea rang. I needed the light. And there was something right about taking Grandad's lantern. It was like it made it official — a ceremony. Because it was going to be a trial, of sorts. And then an execution.

'I found the lantern, but I also found something new — this.' He held up the flask. 'See? It's got that picture on it, like the one on the glasses — the whalers. It must have been part of the set.' He unscrewed the top of the flask and drank, coughing, not bothering to put the cap back on. 'And it hadn't been there before. And no one comes here now except me or Mum, so I thought she'd put it away, because she's fond of the glasses but they get broke, and perhaps she wanted to make sure she'd always have the flask. But I thought — I could do with a drink if I was going to finish it, finish what we'd started. So I took it. I took it — and the lantern. I'd always promised Mum I wouldn't take anything. They gave me something when I was a kid — a tankard — but she said I had to leave everything else, because one day they'd sell it all, and I could have the money, help set up the restaurant, maybe.'

He laughed as if that was a fantasy.

'Then, tonight, John Joe told the truth. It saved his life. He said that the three of them were waiting for Dad that night — him, Fletcher and Venn. But Fletcher lost his nerve, and Dad humiliated Venn — threw him in the open grave. Then Venn ran for it too. And John Joe couldn't do it — not on his own — and I doubt he ever wanted to do anything . . . ' he searched for the word, 'permanent.'

He drank some more, and on the still air Valentine caught the scent of malt whisky.

'But he did say he'd seen Dad waiting by that big old stone box tomb — and that on the stone he could see two of the green glasses, and the flask. This flask. But when John Joe left Dad that night, he'd been drinking from it. His head thrown back. So how did it get back to the sea chest?' It wasn't really a question, because he had an answer.

He put both his hands on the sea chest, like a priest at an altar. 'I asked Mum why she did it. Why she killed him. Tonight — after I hit her. She wouldn't say. She said it would be better if I didn't know.' He shook his head and looked at Shaw and the shimmering orange light showed that his eyes were full of tears. 'How can she think that, after all that's happened to us? How could it be better not to know?'

He stood, lifting his jeans at the knees so that they were straight. 'I don't know where she is. In the river? She said she might — if she had the courage. Wherever she is it's because of the lies. Her lies. I can forgive her — I can forgive everyone. I just want someone to stay. Not run away or hide. I wanted her to stay. I don't think she heard me ask.'

They heard the single pulse of a police siren outside.

'Can I see him?' asked Ian, standing. 'I'd like to see Grandad.' He touched the sea chest. 'I never have.' What was astonishing then, thought

425

Shaw, was that for the first time he could see Alby's genetic input in Ian's face: because he had his grandfather's precise air of almost childlike curiosity.

45

They found Lizzie Murray on the Flensing
Meadow — Jacky Lau, checking the footpath,
saw her sitting on the box tomb through the
trees, so still that the snow had collected on the
shoulders of the overcoat she wore, and on her
knees, so that for a second she confused her with
the stone angel that stood nearby, its hands
cupped to catch water, a single small finger
broken. Visibility was just a few feet, so she'd
retreated, sent a text to Twine and waited by the
railings on the riverbank.

Valentine had appeared first, a narrow figure,
sloping shoulders, the collar of his raincoat
turned up, one hand at his neck, holding the
lapels together. When he reached DC Lau he
didn't speak, but pointed towards the spot where
he knew Nora Tilden's grave lay, still open,
covered in boards, ringed with scene-of-crime
tape.

She nodded.

Shaw appeared almost supernaturally, as if
he'd just risen straight up out of the ground, at
the DS's shoulder.

'Well done,' he said to Lau, then checked his
mobile, the screen lit with a blue light.

'Get close,' he said to Valentine. 'But don't
spook her.'

Shaw stepped off the path into the under-
growth around a line of Victorian headstones

427

which had so far escaped the council's exhumations. His boots sank down in nearly a foot of snow. The gentle sound, the compression of snow, flooded his mind with an image from childhood. The beach again, on Christmas Day. They'd always gone down to the slipway, to the café which opened even on that day. His father would buy teas and they'd take them down to the sand, and Shaw would play with whatever had been under the tree that morning — there'd always be something for the beach: a kite, a model aeroplane, a cricket bat. But that day the snow had lain right down to the water's edge and they'd built a snowman, just in time before a fresh blizzard had swept in off the North Sea. He'd been dragged away crying, because he could see the grey figure of the snowman disappearing in the storm, the waves beginning to break around it.

And now he saw another figure. He stopped, and for a second he heard twigs breaking as Valentine circled the spot. It was the angel. He walked towards it and put a hand on the pitted stone of the face. Turning slightly, he saw Lizzie Murray, sitting on the tomb. It was startling in this black-and-white world how much the blood on her face stood out, a line from the corner of her mouth down her neck, as if her skull was cracking to reveal the flesh and blood beneath. The light caught the diamond stud in her ear.

He walked forward, aware that the wind that had brought the blizzard along the coast had gone. The air was absolutely still, the snow propelled by gravity alone, wandering down, as if each flake had to find its own way.

'You're hurt,' he said.

She tightened the belt at the waist of the overcoat, but that didn't stop her shivering.

'Ian — he had every right.'

Shaw could see the wooden planking over the open grave. He stepped forward and pulled it clear so that the sudden black square of the pit was before them, widened by Tom Hadden's team so that they could take their pictures of the soil profile.

'It was a stupid place to meet,' she said.

'What did he really say when you told him at the bar that night — that there was going to be a child?'

'I told the truth,' she said. And something about that statement made her cover her mouth. Taking her fingers away she examined a trace of cold pearl lipstick.

'He said he was happy for us. But we should talk — not later, now. I said I couldn't — just couldn't. The choir had something for me. I couldn't just not be there. So I said we'd meet later — at eleven, here, while they collected glasses and cleared the pub. I gave him the two glasses and filled the hip flask for him to take. I thought he'd hang around, then wait after closing — but he went then. He hated the bar. He said it was like being in a zoo, being the one in the cage. But he never really gave anyone a chance to like him.'

'So you met here.'

429

'Yes. We fought. I'm not going to tell you why,' she said.

'We found something in Pat's pocket,' said Shaw. 'We didn't know what it was — just shreds of paper. I know now. There were just three letters visible — MOT. It's the airport code for his trip back to Hartsville.'

In the white gloom he saw Valentine's silhouette move between a Celtic cross and a figure of the Virgin Mary in grey stone.

'He was going home, wasn't he? A one-way ticket. Bea was always going to stay and she thought Pat would too. But he wasn't. He'd booked his flight. And it didn't change anything, did it? That the child was coming?'

She stood at the grave's edge and looked at the blood on her hand.

'He was bleeding that night,' she said. 'Here,' she added, touching her left cheekbone. 'When he said he was going home I thought it was because of those three, and what they'd wanted to do. That he'd decided to leave behind all that hatred, not just those three, everyone — almost everyone. The way they looked at him. Everyone except Alby.

'But it wasn't. He'd decided weeks before because he showed me the ticket. Taunted me with it. Said the baby was my fault — that I hadn't taken precautions and that I'd tried to trap him. He said babies were a kind of death. Those are the words I've always remembered.

'He said there was a baby in this grave. I think Bea must have told him — about Mary, who

430

would have been my sister. He said Mary had ruined Mother's life, and Dad's. Then he said it again, that babies were death, and he got up and stood by the grave and spat in it.'

She still hadn't cried, and Shaw felt certain now that she never would.

'So I just took the hook — it was lying here ... ' She drew a circle in the snow on the stone tomb. 'And I swung it. It was luck, really — catching his skull. I didn't hit him hard.' She looked at Shaw, still astonished by the ease of murder. 'The point just sliced in.'

She was looking at a point in front of her now, the precise spot, Shaw thought, where Pat Garrison's life had ended.

'They'll say he died instantly, won't they? They always say that. But he didn't. I don't think he knew what had happened — just that something *had* happened. He was holding the flask and it fell from his hand to the grass. He turned to look at me, but I don't think he could see at all, because the cruelty had gone from his eyes, and I thought perhaps he was dead then, dead standing. But he put his hand behind him and tried to reach the handle of the hook. He knelt, reached again, then fell sideways onto the grass.

'I dragged him to the grave, took his keys out of his pocket, threw the glasses in after his body, then covered him with earth. Then I realized I'd missed the flask. That went in last, so it was nearer the surface. I found it almost straight away that night I tried to get his bones out.' She shook her head.

She stood stiffly. 'But before I dragged him to the grave,' she said clearly, as if confessing, 'I watched him die. He was curled up — on the grass, like a child himself. So maybe he was right — perhaps babies are death.'

46

Friday, 24 December

Christmas Eve: 10.00 a.m. sharp, the offices of Masters & Masters, solicitors, reached by Shaw and Valentine via a staircase through a door marked only with a brass plaque between W. H. Smith and Waterstone's in the Vancouver Shopping Centre. The view from the one window in the office of Mr Jerrold Masters would, on most occasions, have been suicide-bleak — across the flat roofs dotted with air filters and flues, a copse of satellite dishes and a ramshackle night-watchman's hut. But the snow had continued to fall overnight so that the cityscape was transformed into an Arctic scene — completed in the far distance by the three masts of a naval training ship on the quay. The cranes on the far bank of the Cut were decked out with fairy lights, immobile, like giant Meccano sets opened early for Christmas.

In the outside office Shaw had left his daughter with DC Fiona Campbell. He'd promised her a tour of St James's, a look in the cells — an area she seemed particularly obsessed with — and breakfast in the canteen. Campbell had volunteered to be her guide, as Fran — no doubt prompted by his wife — seemed determined to see how women fitted into the West Norfolk Constabulary. After breakfast there'd be Christmas shopping for Lena's presents, and for the dog a new winter jacket, then they'd all meet for lunch out on the coast. He had a week off. The thought of it made his blood buzz, as if he'd started to run.

'Is Mrs Robins coming?' asked Shaw.

'A minute,' Masters said, checking his watch, then setting a large envelope on his blotter beside a letter-knife in the shape of an eel.

Shaw considered Chris Robins's last will and testament. For what could he hope? At best, a confession — a confession implicating Robert Mosse? Admissible in court? Hardly. If they had a new case to present to the CPS on Mosse a confession from Robins would be powerful corroborating testimony. But what they needed was evidence to get a new case in front of a judge and jury. Shaw looked around the shabby room and thought the chances of that were negligible, close to vanishing point, like the ghost-grey masts of the ship on the Cut. All they had was an envelope on a blotter.

'Busy?' said Masters, suddenly overcome with embarrassment at the silence. He held up the previous Tuesday's edition of the *Lynn News*.

Lizzie Murray had been charged with the murder of Pat Garrison. She had insisted, despite counsel's advice, on making a statement in which she confessed to the crime. Shaw had taken little pleasure from the moment, frustrated rather by the continuing silence of Alby Tilden and Ian Murray. They might face charges for what they'd done, but unless they confessed to the crucial intermediary role of Bea Garrison, all three would escape a charge of murder. Neither had administered a lethal poison, and Bea Garrison's silence was impenetrable.

Shaw tore himself away from his own thoughts to answer the solicitor's question.

'Sure. But then it's Christmas. We can all enjoy that,' he said. He thought Valentine said something then, under his breath, but he couldn't be sure.

There was a carpet in the corridor outside so they didn't hear footsteps approaching the door. When it opened Robert Mosse walked in, carrying a long metal safe-deposit box and a slim briefcase. Shaw's heartbeat raced, and something about the moment made him smile, despite the surprise and all the questions that crowded into his mind.

Mosse froze, but his face didn't respond, as if each micro-muscle was under direct control from the brain — an impossibility, Shaw knew, but Mosse appeared to have the skill. Only the eyes revealed a life within the skull, taking in Shaw, Valentine and the envelope on the blotter.

Shaw was pleased to see that he looked once back at the door, twice at the window — a classic fear response, checking out the means of escape.

'Bob,' said Masters, standing, holding out a hand.

'Jerry,' said Mosse. The voice was as perfectly judged as the slate-grey suit, the swept-back lustrous black hair.

'This is unusual,' he continued, looking at Shaw and holding out his hand.

Shaw shook it, noting the sandpaper dryness.

'All will become clear,' said Masters, smiling. Shaw knew then that Masters was one of those people who manage to get through life without ever realizing they have no ability whatever to sense the emotional temperature of those around them. There was so much tension in the air Shaw expected to see a spark suddenly leap from the eel-shaped letter opener.

Mosse sat, but Shaw noticed his eyes again flicking twice to the door by which he'd entered. He'd have seen Fiona Campbell in reception with Fran and presumed it was a child-protection case. Mosse's jawline hardened perceptibly — the first time his body had betrayed him.

Masters pressed a buzzer on his desk. A minute later the door opened and Peggy Robins was shown in by the secretary. Shaw hadn't seen her in reception and guessed she'd been put in a side room with a cup of tea to wait until the last moment. It was thoughtful, and Masters fussed like a family doctor. She sat quickly, didn't look at anyone, and Shaw was reminded of his first impression: that she was a strong woman, but always braced for a blow. She gathered herself in her seat and then looked at Mosse's polished black leather shoes, then his face. She knew him instantly, and her mouth fell open.

'Mrs Robins,' said Masters. 'Peggy. Right — all present and correct.' Again, the beaming inappropriate smile. He slit the envelope open. Valentine massaged his scalp with one hand, aware that the headache stealing from the base of his skull over the cranium was self-inflicted.

Mosse quickly opened the briefcase and checked a note, his head down so that none of them could see his face.

'Client MM 45/65/82?' he asked.

'Yes, indeed,' said Masters. 'Sorry — you'd no name until now. That's it — Christopher Alan Robins.'

Masters began to read the will, Mosse's eyes fixed on some point in the snowy roofscape outside. The estate had been valued at £13,700. It all went to his mother. It took his solicitor less than a minute to read in full.

'Now,' he said, setting the document aside. 'One other duty. Mr Robins — it seems odd to call him that. I knew his father, you see — John,' said Masters. 'He had a shop down on the quay — shoe repair. I always used to call him John . . . ' He trailed off, looking at each of them in turn, unable to work out why everyone was so silent, so studiedly impatient.

'Well. Anyway. Christopher had two unusual requests. He asked me in . . . ' he checked a note on the blotter, 'in 2002 to take receipt of some items, and to lodge them in our offices for safe keeping until he requested their release. Or, in the event of his death, they would form part of his estate. Two years ago he asked that these same items be transferred to Mr Mosse's firm but under a client number only — no name. You'll remember that, Bob?'

Mosse's chin moved a centimetre in answer.

'Yes, I'm sure you do,' Masters continued. 'He specifically asked me to make sure the signatory should be Mr Mosse himself. And that was undertaken — at an annual fee of thirty-five pounds and seventy pence, I see from my records.' Again, the mindless smile.

'And one further alteration — that, upon the reading of the will, these items were to be released into the custody of DI Peter Shaw of the West Norfolk Constabulary.'

Mosse was looking at the metal deposit box, his legs crossed casually at the ankles.

'Did he say why?' asked Shaw.

'He said that would become clear on the day. Yes — those exact words.'

The door opened and the secretary came in with coffee cups, a pot, Nice biscuits. The tension in the room was almost intolerable. Shaw imagined the crockery shattering. She left the tray, retreated.

'And the other unusual requirement was a statement, lodged with us, to be read on this occasion.' He leant across the desk and gave Shaw a second envelope. 'By you, Inspector.'

'I don't have to listen to this,' said Mosse.

Masters missed the intonation, but was quick to respond to the legal niceties.

'Mr Robins stipulated that the statement was to be read before the contents of the deposit box were transferred. I'm sure it will only take a minute.'

Mosse looked into the middle distance. Shaw tried to imagine just how fast Mosse's brain must be calculating.

If he walked out now he wouldn't know what he was facing. And why leave, why run, when all the life he'd built was here, in Lynn? Job, money, reputation, family, children, not to mention a shiny black BMW.

'You might as well stay. You're going to hear it one way or another,' said Shaw. Valentine was standing now, staring at Mosse.

Shaw opened the envelope and extracted a single sheet of A4, typed, single spaced.

'I typed it,' said Peggy Robins. 'And signed it.'

Shaw nodded, noting the scrawl at the foot, the two signatures almost merged.

He read.

' 'I know this statement is worthless — that I'm as guilty as Bob, and the rest, of these crimes. But it seems to me — to all of us — that we've suffered, paid the price, and he hasn't. Ever.' '

'Oh,' said Masters. 'Goodness.' He held up a hand, as if suddenly deciding it shouldn't be read.

'It's all right. Carry on,' said Mosse. He took out a yellow legal pad from the briefcase and started making a note.

' 'The night those people died in the car, it was Robert Mosse what drove. He was down from Sheffield and he wanted a bit of action. His idea. We went out to Hunstanton and he got the Mini over the ton. We drank — all of us. Bob was taking us home by the back roads, trying to keep the car over eighty — even on the lanes. He didn't see the T-junction until it was way late. It wasn't until afterwards that we realized he'd stayed in the car — let us get out, wander round. So those first few days was a nightmare. I didn't tell you, Mum, did I? I'm sorry for that. And I stayed out — with the others, down at Alex Cosyns's lock-up. We got the car in there and me and Voycy got a drum of paint from work to respray it — yellow, tractor yellow they called it. Alex was soft on that dog he'd taken from the car. Night of the crash he cried about it — 'bout the old people in the back. He'd taken the dog because he said he wanted something to live. Like I said — soft. Then that evening — the evening the Tessier boy died — Alex took the dog for a walk. When he came back the kid was with him. Alex had tried to tell him that it wasn't the same dog. But the kid could get it to do stuff — beg, roll over. Odd kid. He wasn't going anywhere. We let him play with it and decided on a plan: we'd let him go, let him take the dog, sit tight — that would work in our favour when the police came. We'd say it was the driver who was drunk at the crash, but we wouldn't say who it was. We'd admit the rest. Bob needed to lie low — and we'd fix up an alibi for him on the Westmead.

' 'Bob said it wasn't going to work. That one of us would crack and tell the truth. He told the Tessier kid to stop crying and cuffed him on the back of the head. And then he put those gloves on, his driving gloves — the leather ones with the fur on the inside, and he had a bit of nylon rope.' '

Peggy Robins took out a tissue and pressed it to her mouth, looking out of the window.

' 'Then he kind of hugged the kid, turned his back on us. And he held on. It was Alex who realized what he was doing first. He told him to stop. But we all kind of froze. I've never forgiven myself — and I know I could have stopped it, but I didn't. And Bob pulled the kid around, behind him, like I said, so we couldn't see their faces. There wasn't any noise at first. I heard a snap, like a plastic snap, a bone giving. And then the kid made a noise, just once, and it was over. He dropped the kid to the floor. He had one of Bob's gloves in his mouth, stuffed in. Bob took the other one off and just dropped it on the floor, like he'd finished a job. He didn't smoke, but he took one of mine.' '

Shaw realized his breathing was shallow, so he too took a lungful of air.

' 'So we made another plan. Bob thought it all through. He said they'd be looking for the kid, that they'd go on looking until they found him, so the trick was to give them the kid. Dump him — under the big tower. That's where you get the gangs, the crime, and they'd think the kid had got caught up in something nasty. I was to clean up the garage. Bob went to get his car, Alex went to check out where the kid lived, see how long we had, see if they was searching already. We put Voycy on look-out up by the community centre. When Bob got back with his car we waited until after dark and then rolled the kid up in a bit of old carpet, put him in the boot. The light was bad by then — and we dared not use the mechanics' lights we had for working on the car, 'cos we thought the police would be out on the estate by then looking for the kid. I took all the things I could find in the garage that might be linked to us — bagged it, took it to the bins under our flat. Later, when we knew they was searching for the kid, I took it out on the roughlots and burnt it. Then we all met at the pub on the estate — the Painted Lady. Bob said he'd been seen dumping the kid, and he had to get rid of the car. So he reported it missing and we fixed him up with an alibi — at the cinema, 'cos his mum had been and all we needed was a ticket. I'm sorry for what I did. We tried to make Bob pay but we never had the courage to face up to what we'd done. He knew that. But I am sorry. Tell the kid's mother I'm sorry. And tell her that what I've left is for her. I didn't burn everything.' '

Shaw leant forward, put the sheet of A4 on the desk. Valentine beckoned for Mosse to hand him the box, then passed it to Shaw. Masters opened his desk, took out a pair of identical small gold padlock keys and handed them to the detective. Shaw worked one into the lock on the box. As he lifted the lid a look of disappointment crossed his face: the box appeared to be empty. Then he saw a plastic bag tucked into one corner, knotted, with an unbroken paper seal signed by Chris Robins and Jerrold Masters. He held the bag up: inside was a single fur-lined leather glove. In the leather was imprinted the marks of a child's teeth, pressing down, a faint ghost of the last bite, drawing blood at last.

LYNN SOLICITOR TO SERVE LIFE FOR 'COLD-BLOODED' CHILD MURDER

By Our Crime Correspondent

Lynn solicitor Robert Mosse was yesterday given a life sentence after being convicted of the murder of a nine-year-old boy in 1997 on the town's notorious Westmead Estate.

The trial judge recommended that Mosse, 34, should spend the rest of his life in custody. Leave to appeal was denied.

'In over twenty years on this bench I have never encountered a more cold-blooded crime,' said Mr Justice Lamfrey. 'Robert Mosse is a calculating killer who poses a continuing threat to society.'

Mosse, through his solicitor, said after the verdict, 'It is clear the police have fabricated the evidence upon which my conviction is based — as they did at my original trial. I am innocent of this crime.'

Mosse, who was due to be called to the Bar later this year, is a founding partner in Mosse, Turnbull & Smith. His wife and three children live in a million-pound house on the exclusive Clearwater Estate.

The Crown Prosecution Service said in a statement after the trial that the files on two subsequent murders, which the police claim Mosse committed to cover up his original crime, would now be closed.

Mosse denied killing nine-year-old Jonathan Tessier on the night of 25 July 1997 at a lock-up garage on the Westmead Estate in Lynn's North End. The prosecution's case was that Mosse had strangled the child to prevent his implication in another crime.

Mosse was charged with the killing at the time, but the original trial was unable to proceed owing to a legal technicality. Recently, however, the police obtained new forensic evidence linking him to Tessier's murder.

A fur-lined leather glove, the partner to one recovered at the murder scene, was found to contain skin shed by Mosse and was heavily impregnated with dried saliva, later matched by DNA analysis to the Tessier family, and exhibiting bite marks that matched the victim's dental records.

Mosse's first trial in 1997 was stopped because the investigating officers had taken the glove discovered at the underground car park where Tessier's body was found to Mosse's home — a flat in the tower block above — potentially contaminating it.

The original trial judge implied that this might have been done deliberately in an attempt to secure a conviction.

'I would like to say at this point,' said Mr Justice Lamfrey after passing sentence, 'that today's conviction in large part clears those original officers of any improper or criminal behaviour.

'Furthermore, I would like to commend publicly the work of DI Peter Shaw and DS George Valentine of the West Norfolk Constabulary, for their tireless determination to bring Robert Mosse to justice.'

DI Shaw, the lead investigating officer in the case, is

444

the son of DCI Jack Shaw, who led the original murder inquiry. DCI Shaw took early retirement on the grounds of ill-health shortly after Mosse's acquittal. He died in 1998.

The prosecution alleged that Mosse and three other associates, all now dead, were involved in a road accident three days before Tessier's murder, in which two elderly women were killed.

Mosse was driving when the four, in a Mini, struck another vehicle at a T-junction near Castle Rising. They fled the scene. When the emergency services arrived 45 minutes later the two passengers were found to be dead. The driver survived.

One of the fatalities was Jonathan Tessier's grandmother. She had been travelling with her pet dog — a puppy — which was taken by one of the joyriders from the rear of the car, according to CCTV footage of the crash.

Three days later the four teenagers were in the lock-up garage on the Westmead respraying the damaged car. Jonathan recognized the puppy when one of the gang took it for a walk on the estate, and followed it back to the garage.

Mosse's defence argued that the killing of the child had been an accident. One of the other members of the gang, Chris Robins, had hit the child to stop him crying, Mosse claimed.

But the court heard a statement left by Robins as part of his last will and testament. It outlined a different version of events in which Mosse — at the time a law student — decided to kill the child to save his career.

The defence argued that Robins's version of events was designed to divert the guilt on to an innocent

445

man. But the forensic evidence corroborated Robins's version of events.

The jury retired for sixteen hours before returning a majority guilty verdict.

Police believe that Mosse also killed two members of the gang — Alex Cosyns and Jimmy Voyce — because they had threatened to go to the authorities with the truth.

DCS Max Warren of the West Norfolk Constabulary released the following statement after sentencing.

'The verdict in this case restores the high reputation of the officers of the West Norfolk Constabulary. It illustrates that we were always determined to give Jonathan Tessier and his family the justice they were denied in the months after his brutal and callous murder.'

A spokesman for the Law Society confirmed that Mosse's conviction would result in his name being permanently removed from the Society's register. His partners at Mosse, Turnbull & Smith declined to comment.

In depth: The Case of the Missing Glove — page 21.

Acknowledgements

I would like to thank my agent, Faith Evans, in equal measure for both her criticism, which is always subtle and constructive, and for her friendship, which is valued. My team at Penguin — editors Kate Burke and Stefanie Bierwerth — have completed yet another thoroughly professional job. I would also like to thank Francesca Russell for her enthusiasm in promoting the book.

Now to specific debts owed. (I should warn the reader that the following reveals some plot.)

I have often relied on Paul Richards's excellent book *King's Lynn* for historical background. Martin Peters has again been invaluable as a general consultant on all things medical. I also consulted the comprehensive and definitive *Book of Poisons* by Serita Stevens and Anne Bannon. Professor Paul Cullis of the University of Leicester found time for some invaluable guidance on poisons and their properties.

A note on poisons. The general principles upon which the plot relies are real. The specific poisons used in the text have been selected to fit the plot, and therefore any attempt to replicate the perfect murder will be doomed to failure.

Lastly, I must thank my loyal copy editor Trevor Horwood, for his tireless attention to detail and helpful suggestions. Jenny Burgoyne has again provided us all with the reassurance of reading the final manuscript. And I must thank my wife Midge Gillies, who, despite facing her own deadlines, has always been on hand with helpful advice about character and plot, and who found time to read the text and provide both encouragement and criticism.